DOMÁNI

Carolyn Gross

1

Lulu knew why they lived in darkness. The knowledge existed in her bones. She knew that the darkness was what the people of Dalia deserved. She could feel it as surely as she knew the flames were coming to end their existence. This very thought plagued her even as she carefully made her way through the crowd gathering before the steps of the Sanctuary.

Why did she even bother?

"You know it's dangerous to listen to him, Lu," her father had admonished her while she had been lacing her boots in the doorway that morning.

He sat in his favorite chair with the back against the wall. Lulu knew, no matter what her father said, he only liked that chair because he could see the front door as well as the back of the small apartment they shared.

"I know," she had said quietly, standing and brushing off her knees. The dust was everywhere lately.

"So then why are you going?" he asked.

Lulu didn't have an answer for him then. Trotting past dark alleys to reach her destination, she realized she didn't even have an answer for herself. Distracted by her own thoughts as she weaved through the gathering mass of people, she nearly collided with a crawler. She pivoted gracelessly to fall hard on her left hip, covering her pants in dust again. The crawler glanced down and seemed to smirk at her before dutifully turning his head back to face the Sanctuary.

Lulu averted her eyes quickly but knew that he had seen the disdain on her face. Crawlers were the self-appointed guards who watched over the doyen of Dalia. They were secretive, exclusionary, and terrifying to most Dalians. Disturbing one was like taking your life into your own hands. Lulu cursed herself for the face she had made but knew she could never keep her emotions hidden. Her father always said that was her biggest weakness.

She stood slowly and felt dwarfed standing next to the statuesque crawler. Lulu was considered short by most, but she was like a child next to this monster. She looked up at the stairs before them. Seemingly endless, they led to the black stone monolith that was known as the Sanctuary. It housed the council of Dalia and the doyen. The doyen was the living prophet and face of the Sanctuary. When the fire appeared overhead, he would descend the steps and speak to the commoners, as he always had.

Lulu looked up at the giant planet spinning slowly above their heads. The planet Laima had always shielded Dalia from the fire behind it. Its black face with swirling orange gas clouds kept Dalia in permanent darkness. They lived in Laima's shadow, held captive to its rotating landmarks. The edge of the enormous fire cyclone peaking over the top of the planet meant the doyen would soon be descending to make his speech in its fleeting light. Lulu watched, still fascinated by the fire that spun around Laima but never went out.

"Must be boring staring at a bunch of steps all the time," Lulu remarked to the stoic crawler beside her.

The crawler didn't look down, and his face didn't change. He stood, with broad shoulders shrouded in a thick black cloak. Lulu knew that there was steel hidden underneath that cloak. She had only seen it used once, and it had been terrifying. Still, she couldn't help herself.

"If I had to wait for a doyen to appear to justify my life, I would want to throw myself down these steps," she said, watching him carefully for a reaction.

The crawler's jaw clenched, and she smiled. Her father would have smacked the back of her head for that. She couldn't help herself. Maybe it was the flames that were coming to destroy them, but she no longer feared for her own safety. She was about to open her mouth to say something even more reckless when the crowd around them silenced, and the crawler stiffened.

She looked up at the stairs once more and realized that today she was standing in the front row. The people pressed behind her but didn't dare move past the crawler beside her at the base of the stairway. Lulu stumbled forward as one man inadvertently kicked the back of her boot.

"Watch it!" she exclaimed, pinwheeling her arms to stay balanced.

She dared not set foot on the bottom step.

Finding her balance, she cursed her own clumsiness even as she glared at the man behind her. He acted like he didn't even see her, and she watched as his face became tinged in the yellow firelight of Laima's fire cyclone reaching its zenith. She looked back up at the steps bathed in its soft yellow glow and saw the motes of dust in the air highlighted before her. The light picked up the dry particles like tiny crystals. Seeing the dust, Lulu covered her mouth and nose with the top of her shirt. She knew she had been breathing it in before, but the action made her feel better.

The doyen descended the steps, his back lit by the fire's glow with his black hair ringed like a halo. Lulu took a step back, feeling exposed in the front of the line. The doyen looked down at her, and for a moment he met her eyes. His face looked tired and resigned.

Lulu had been present for every speech he had ever made, and she had grown used to the message of peace and hope that he delivered. They would trust in Laima and ignore the speculations of stargazers. The tenor of fear grew as Laima continued to shift above their heads and the flames moved closer. The doyen assuaged these fears. He told them this was a cycle of the planet that had been ordained by the gods themselves. The planet Laima would never fully abandon them.

Today, he seemed different. Something wasn't right.

He stopped at the tenth step as he always did, flanked by two crawlers. He cast a worried glance back at the Sanctuary before turning to face the crowd once more. The hair on Lulu's neck stood on end, and she felt her breath catch in her throat.

"Fellow Dalians," he said. "May the shadow protect you."

This characteristic greeting was no different from what it had always been.

"And you," the crowd murmured dutifully. Lulu mouthed the words along with everyone else.

"But the shadow is not going to protect us anymore," the doyen said, almost to himself.

Lulu felt the energy of the crowd behind her shift as whispering started to build. She looked up at the crawler beside her and saw him casually reach under his cloak. The dust in the air seemed to freeze with time. She saw the doyen glance over his shoulder once more, back toward the Sanctuary.

"Laima is shifting," he said with finality, turning back. "Dalia is going to burn."

His words hung in the air like electricity. The crowd grew still behind Lulu. Nobody moved, except the crawler next to her. His forearm was now completely hidden in his cloak, and he took a step forward, bracing one foot on the bottom step. Lulu felt her heart thrum against her rib cage as her body moved.

On Dalia, one thing was certain. You did not touch a crawler. It was the same as assaulting the doyen himself. As Lulu dived for the enormous man's cloak in front of her, her last thought was of how stupid she was for dying this way.

The crawler's hand emerged, and the wide curved blade reflected Laima's cyclone, making it look like it was on fire. With no regard for her own life, Lulu collided with the crawler just as his hand was about to release the blade. Instead of flying into the doyen standing a mere ten steps above them, the blade flew wide, clattering back down the steps. The sound was loud in Lulu's ears as the blade finally came to rest just three steps away from her head.

For one horrific moment, Lulu looked up and watched as the doyen was dragged back up the steps by the crawlers beside him. His steel-gray eyes met hers again. She had seen that look before in her life. It was the look of acceptance and resignation that only comes in the moment before death. The doyen had expected to die in that moment.

Her own dire situation was suddenly brought into focus as she was lifted off the stairs by her right ankle. She faced the crowd before her and was disoriented to see them suspended upside down. Her head felt heavy as blood pounded down her neck, and she twisted to see the crawler who casually held her by one leg in front of him.

"You made a mistake today, little one," the crawler said in a voice so deep and raspy that Lulu felt it resonate in her bones.

Lulu turned her head and tried to make out the faces of the crowd through vision suddenly blurred with tears. She wanted to call out for her father but knew he wasn't there. He was in danger now and would hopefully go into hiding once he found out her fate. With little else to do, she called out a last message for him.

"Tell Mikal Destin that I'm sorry!" she yelled to the faceless blobs in the crowd.

The crawler squeezed her ankle painfully and swung her back to face him. His closed fist met her face without warning, and she felt her nose crunch beneath the blow. Hot blood trickled down her forehead to mingle with her hair as he draped her over his massive shoulder. She helplessly watched as the stairs passed beneath her. With dawning horror, Lulu realized the crawler wasn't going to kill her right away.

He was taking her to the Sanctuary.

2

"The Sanctuary?" Mikal asked quietly.

"Yes," the boy answered meekly.

The boy looked to be at least two rotations younger than Lu, but he stood at least as tall as her. They were standing in the main room of the metal hole he and his daughter had called a home. It boasted two additional rooms. Each was large enough to fit a bed and storage chest. On Dalia, this was more than most families could afford, and they had been fortunate to have this space to call their own. His eyes traveled unwillingly to the dark hallway by the front door where he had last seen Lu lacing up her boots before leaving to see the doyen speak.

"Sir," the boy continued respectfully, "I saw it myself; she saved the doyen. She's a hero."

"She's a stupid girl," Mikal murmured before turning back to his room.

He left the boy standing awkwardly in the main room while his fingers found the compartment in the front of his storage chest. In the darkness, he easily found the latch that he was seeking and pressed on it, revealing a hidden drawer. He reached in and grabbed a coin with three depressions in the center. He walked out and tossed the coin to the boy with a dismissive wave, hardly noticing the expression of disbelief on his face. The tri coin was at least a year's worth of food for that boy's family.

For Mikal, it was worthless.

Rotations ago, after he lost Lu's mother, Mikal had almost lost control. Lu had been his anchor. She was the only thing that kept him standing on a black planet abandoned by the gods and anyone who should have cared. Now, like her mother, she had been taken from him.

He stood with his jaw clenched for a quiet moment after the boy left him. Out of habit, he slowed his breathing, and his heart rate followed. Mikal relaxed and clenched his fists in time with his respirations until his thoughts became coherent again. Once back in control, he strode back into his bedroom, ignoring the empty room next to it. He never went into Lu's space; it had been hers to occupy as she saw fit.

He lifted the secret compartment that was still open and blindly felt until he found a heavy metal case. Grabbing the corner with his fingertips, he dragged it out of the narrow slot in the custom-made chest. Holo-pictures of Lu as a baby in the arms of her mother briefly lit the room with their light as they were dislodged from the drawer he had shoved them into.

The case hit the stone floor with a sharp clink, and he wasted no time pressing his thumbs into the tiny scanner that would unlock it. Mikal waited until he heard the characteristic beep and the case unlocked. He opened it without ceremony or thought to the gravity of what he was about to do. This was the first time in five rotations that the contents of that case had seen open air.

Still, even though it had seemed like a lifetime ago, his hands needed no light to know exactly where everything was. His movements were cold and calculated as he loaded and strapped on each priceless weapon. On Dalia, such items were not only forbidden: each one was worth a man's life. Mikal never told his daughter how he had amassed their hidden wealth. She had never asked.

He stood and grabbed a long black coat that had been carefully folded behind his normal clothes. Adjusting it over the blades and energy weapons he now carried was second nature. It was like he had never put them away. He walked over to the front door without grabbing anything else. He glanced back at the home he and his daughter had shared and cleared it from his mind. Mikal knew he would not be coming back.

He laced his boots, crouching in the same place he had last seen Lu that morning. He opened the door and shut it casually behind him, walking out onto a dark and dust-laden street. Laima hung above his head like it was held only by a string. He ignored the so-called protector planet and kept his eyes on the people passing by him. No one could possibly know what his intentions were or the potential for death he carried on his body, but they parted before him as if they did.

A man who was preoccupied with his own feet nearly collided with Mikal but immediately averted his gaze when he looked up and saw Mikal's face. The people of Dalia were repressed, but if they maintained one instinct, it was the ability to sense death and fear. Mikal Destin knew this because in a past life it had been his job to deliver it. He had been an assassin for the Sanctuary.

3

Lulu concentrated on her breathing and heart rate like her father had taught her. She felt panic and fear bubbling at the surface of her consciousness like a mythical beast living under the desert sand. She focused on the present and tried to keep herself grounded, but it was difficult with no sense of time. She had no idea how long she had been in her dark prison.

When the crawler had first dropped her on the floor and closed the door behind him, he had not said a word. There was no light. She had frantically paced the room and felt along the cold walls, seeking any defect or opening. It was only six paces in all directions, about half the size of her room at home. She slid with her back against the rough stone wall opposite the door and tried to avoid imagining the walls moving closer together. No one else had come for her since then.

Lulu brought her hand to her face and gingerly touched her nose where the crawler had broken it. She wiped away the last remnants of cracking dried blood, feeling a dull throb in her head with even the slightest pressure. The pain was helpful. It allowed her to focus.

She thought about the doyen's face. He had known what was going to happen. His life was forfeit the moment the truth about Laima and the flames behind it left his lips. Yet he had done it anyway. Lulu had been raised on a planet that worshiped the doyen, even when he was a baby. For all her twenty-four rotations of life, she had grown up with him and believed that he had been chosen for a reason. He had been born in the exact moment that the doyen before him had died, exactly one rotation before Lulu herself was born into this world.

Her thoughts were interrupted by a loud click reverberating through her tiny prison. The door had been unlocked. She sprang to her feet and kept her back to the wall behind her, bending her knees slightly so that she could run. Lulu stared at the door in front of her for what seemed like an eternity, her eyes straining to see even a sliver of light.

Nothing happened.

Lulu felt her fingers shaking even as they touched the door and tested it. A small push caused it to swing outward, and the dim torchlight from the hallway flooded her prison cell. Lulu leaped back against the far wall, expecting a crawler to barge in at any moment. None appeared and she tentatively stepped forward, peering around the corner.

The hallway was empty and silent except for the occasional crackle from the regularly interspersed torches along the walls. The streets and homes on Laima had artificial light, but such luxuries were forbidden in the Sanctuary. Only the pure light of fire was allowed in here. When she looked at the flames dotting otherwise stark stone walls, Lulu felt like she had been transported into one of her storybooks. Glancing over her shoulder once to make sure no one was following her, she padded silently into the hall.

Her fingertips trailed along the stones as she approached the first intersection. The feeling in the pit of her belly grew with the knowledge that this was surely a sadistic trap laid out for her by the Sanctuary. Even knowing this, she knew she had no other choice but to keep moving. Her father had always said that movement was life. His voice was in her ears, telling her not to lie down but to keep moving.

Lulu held her breath as she peered first left, then right at the end of the hall. The corridor was empty. She gripped the cornerstones like they were holding her upright before making the split decision to run left. She bolted down the hallway, trying to put distance between herself and the cell behind her. She quickly came to the end of the next hall and took a right turn, trying desperately to keep a mental map of the stone maze that she had traveled so far.

She heard voices around the next corridor and stopped dead in her tracks. Lulu's eyes fell on an ornate wooden door ahead and to the right. Making a quick decision, she darted to push on the heavy wood even as her fingers, numb with fear, fumbled with the latch. The voices sounded closer, but the door gave way before anyone could see her and she fell inside. She shut the door behind her and turned with her back against the heavy wood to look in the room.

Lulu's breath caught in her throat even as her eyes registered the woman calmly sitting on the bed in front of her. The woman stared back at her, seemingly unfazed by the sudden intrusion. She was the most beautiful woman Lulu had ever seen. Her golden locks made Lulu's own jet-black hair seem like an affront to nature. Those curls framed a porcelain heart-shaped face that had never seen the sheen of dust that seemed to cover everyone else on Dalia. She watched Lulu with intent green eyes that belied intelligence and power. Lulu stood still and silent against the door.

The voices from the hallway passed behind her, unaware of the quiet drama between the two women. Lulu glanced at the room around them and noted how well kept it was. The furniture was not ostentatious, but sturdy. The rug in the center of the room looked worn but clean. There was no window, but on the dark planet Dalia, windows were rare. The room was not something that Lulu had pictured would be in the monolithic Sanctuary. For that matter, she would not have expected to encounter a woman occupying it. Women were never seen entering or leaving the building—only the crawlers and the doyen.

The woman stood gracefully and took two steps toward her.

Lulu pressed her back against the door firmly, her fingers blindly finding the latch to her right. She would take her chances in the stone maze hallways if necessary. The woman saw the motion and stopped.

"I don't mean any harm," she said.

Her voice was fluid and cultured. It was nothing like Lulu had known, growing up in the streets of the city below. She felt herself wanting to trust this woman.

"How did you get here, little one?" she asked.

Little one. That was what the crawler had called her. Lulu felt herself stiffen, and her fingers clicked the latch with a soft snick.

"You shouldn't go back out there," the woman cooed.

It was a threat.

Lulu never responded well to threats. With one arm, she pushed the door open behind her back and whirled back into the hallway. She pivoted to run and immediately felt pain explode behind her eyes.

The crawler's large palm met her broken nose, and Lulu saw pinpoints of light float before her vision. She found herself lying on her back and focused on the upside-down flame of a torch on the wall next to her. The flames appeared to be laughing at her.

"Bring her," the beautiful singsong voice demanded sweetly.

4

Mikal focused on the sounds of his own footfalls echoing on the stone as he walked the main street leading to the Sanctuary. Lu must have run this route a thousand times to see the doyen. Thinking about her, his fists clenched beside him. His eyes flitted to a scene ahead at the entrance to the steps leading up to the black tower known as the Sanctuary.

A group of boys, half as old as his daughter, were gathered in a circle around a pair that were fighting. Mikal could see over the heads of the tallest and noted the tattered clothing and dust-caked faces of the boys inside the circle. These were homeless beggars—orphans. They lived on the outskirts of the Sanctuary, protected by the presence of the vile crawlers at the base of its steps. Mikal looked around and noted that for once, there were no crawlers to be seen.

Mikal didn't slow his gait as he approached the group. The larger of the two fighting boys held the smaller one by the front of his ragged shirt front. The fabric was twisting in the boy's hand so that it pinched the skin of the smaller one tightly. The smaller boy looked up at his tormentor with a look of defiance that reminded Mikal of Lu.

"Take it back, liar!" the taller boy shouted. Spittle flew from his mouth, and his voice cracked with emotion.

"It's the truth," the smaller one calmly proclaimed.

"It's not!" the taller boy spat back, and just as his other arm wound back to strike the boy in the face, Mikal reached the group.

Mikal grabbed the wrist of the taller boy and pinched the nerves with the tips of his fingers until he let the smaller boy go.

"Hey! Back off, old man!" the boy turned and shouted at Mikal even as he struggled against his grip. The boy's fingers dug at Mikal's hand ineffectively, and his efforts quickly became frantic.

"What is the meaning of this?" Mikal asked. "There is no violence within sight of the Sanctuary."

Mikal said the words, knowing that he himself had taken lives while the black stone image of the Sanctuary stood tall in the periphery.

"The Sanctuary's meaningless," the smaller boy whispered. Tears fell through the dust on his cheeks, creating streams on the boy's skin.

"Take it back!" the boy in Mikal's grip shouted again.

"I won't!" the smaller boy shouted. "The doyen is dead, and a crawler tried to kill him. I saw it with my own eyes."

"You saw the doyen killed?" Mikal asked.

The boy shook his head. "The crawlers took him though!"

Mikal sighed in exasperation and released the boy in his grip. He looked at the group gathered, and the boy whom he had held rubbed his wrist petulantly.

"You should hide from this place," Mikal said. "There is danger here."

When none of them moved, he flipped his cloak open enough so that they could see steel underneath. Their eyes widened, and they all scattered in different directions aside from one. The shorter boy stood still and looked intently at Mikal.

"You heard me," Mikal said. "Hide."

The boy looked up at him and said, "There's no hiding from the flames."

Mikal had no response. He left the boy standing in the square, knowing that he was watching his back. He ascended the stairs deliberately, expecting at any moment to be overtaken by a crawler from above. He didn't look back at the dust-covered boy. He looked up toward the planet above his head. Laima rotated in the silence of black space, shielding them from the fire of the sun behind it. In his gut, he knew that the boy had been right. Dalia would come to an end—but not before Mikal brought the Sanctuary to its knees.

The stairs to the Sanctuary felt endless as they always had. It had been many rotations since his feet touched the polished stone, and the air seemed to echo around him. Mikal watched carefully and climbed ever higher, even as he saw the giant shapes appear from the tower above him. The crawlers advanced down the steps with inhuman speed, and Mikal held his back straight, never taking his eyes off them even as he calmly reached under his cloak.

There were three.

The fastest one took point, barreling down the stairs, and Mikal brought the energy weapon up with his left hand. He held it and aimed with both eyes open, feeling his breath slow down as his finger found the trigger. Before the bolt of electricity left his gun, his right hand had already found the handle of the blade strapped to his leg. The forbidden steel flew from his hand, and Mikal didn't wait to watch it hit the target before he dropped the energy weapon in his left hand to clatter on the stairs and grabbed the second gun from his waistband. He used to curse the energy weapon's need for precious seconds of reloading time, but he had learned to not rely on it.

Mikal extended the second gun in front of him with a straight arm and watched this time as the projectile landed firmly within the chest of the third crawler, detonating in a small blast as it connected with flesh. He picked up the energy gun from the step in front of him and walked up to the crawler on his back with Mikal's blade sticking out of his chest.

Mikal pulled on the handle, dislodging it un-ceremoniously. The unnaturally thick muscle of the man tensed and relaxed as he took his last breaths. The crawler's already wide pupils seemed to dilate further as his eyes settled on his assassin.

"You won't live long," the dying crawler croaked behind Mikal as he resumed his ascent toward the Sanctuary.

"Yes, I know," Mikal replied calmly.

He didn't look back to see the boy standing still in the square. He knew he was there, watching death itself move toward the revered Sanctuary above.

5

Lulu kept track of the twisting and turning corridors. Her father had always taught her to pay attention to her surroundings. Counting and taking a mental map was like a reflex for her, but her head ached with every movement. Every corridor looked the same with stark stone walls and evenly spaced torches. Suddenly, her feet fell on a softer surface, and Lulu focused her vision again. The enormous crawler in front of her blocked the way, but she could still see the thick red tapestries hanging from the walls and the matching cloth beneath her feet.

The two crawlers beside her had seemed unfazed by Lulu's initial efforts to escape. Her arms were like twigs held inside their meaty hands. They looked straight forward, not even glancing in her direction. Lulu gave up fighting and started to focus on the number of left and right turns, the number of footfalls before each turn, and the changing smell of the corridors. She was initially immersed in the damp odor of the prisons and enclosed stone, but now a new smell was taking over. It was the clean scent of soap.

Lulu recognized it from the few times her father brought home a bag of it. She had cherished each tiny grain and used it to rub clean the dust that coated her hands, arms, and face. She would never forget such a smell. Now it permeated everything they walked by. Lulu unconsciously reached out to touch a tapestry, and her fingers grazed the soft edge of it before the crawler holding her arm snapped her hand back forcefully.

Lulu rubbed her fingers together, imaging that a remnant of the soft tapestry still coated her fingertips. They rounded another corner, and the ceiling was suddenly three times as high as it had been before. The sound of their footfalls on the cloth managed to find purchase on the walls and traveled to echo back from the space above.

A door as high as the ceiling loomed before them, and Lulu was abruptly stopped by the squeezing of a crawler's hands on her arms. The heavy stone door in front of them creaked open, and the beautiful blond woman who had been leading their procession stepped delicately into the room beyond. The crawler in front of Lulu moved to follow her, and the space before Lulu opened wide.

Lulu knew her feet were moving, but she hardly paid attention to her own steps. She gaped at the opulence before her, and her eyes drank in the scene above. The ceiling disappeared, and only the sight of Laima, slowly spinning and closer than Lulu had ever seen, hung above them. If she reached up, she felt like she could almost touch the dark gas planet with it spinning fiery embers. She was so engrossed in the sight of their protector planet that Lulu hardly noticed the others in the room until one of them spoke up.

"What have you brought us, Mel?" A soft voice carried through the chamber.

Lulu's eyes finally settled on the scene around her, and she saw the room was lined with a high balcony, so close to Laima that it was lit from behind. Twelve women lined the edge of the balcony and looked down on the center of the chamber like beautiful statues. They wore white dresses that flowed with every tiny movement they made. They looked down to the center of the wide chamber that was empty aside from Lulu, her blond captor, and three crawlers.

The crawlers stepped away from them now to line the shadows of the walls, and Lulu felt naked in front of these clean women.

"She found her way into my prayer room," the woman Lulu now knew as Mel replied.

The center woman who had spoken smiled, and Lulu noted that it did not reach her eyes. A shiver ran down her spine, and she had to force herself to hold the other's gaze.

"This is the one who had interfered with the fate of our doyen on the steps today," another woman on the balcony stated matter-of-factly.

Our doyen.

"The doyen is everyone's," Lulu said louder than she had intended.

At seeing the backs of the women above straighten menacingly, she immediately regretted her words.

"Is that so?" the woman in the center asked. Her smooth red hair fell across her shoulder as she lifted a delicate hand to point past Lulu's head. "Well, let's ask him ourselves then."

Lulu spun around to look behind her. He was there, flanked by crawlers as she had been. The doyen stood defiant on the threshold of the door, and even though he had obviously been coerced, he looked for all the world like it was his idea to be there. Lulu had stood in the city square every day to watch the doyen speak. She had grown up with him and had learned to have faith in an unforgiving environment through him. Now he stood mere feet away from her.

His black hair was disheveled, and he had a cut above his eye. His usually pristine white robes were covered in the city's dust, and his normally kind gray eyes were hard. There was hatred and resentment buried behind them, and they stared, not at Lulu but at the beautiful redheaded woman above her.

"This girl is here because of your disobedience," the red-haired woman said to the doyen.

He glanced at Lulu's face, and she saw his hard jawline soften and a brief look of profound sadness cross his face. In the instant she had seen it, it was gone. He looked back at the woman on the balcony with renewed anger.

"She is here because she interfered in your vile attempt to martyr me," he said softly.

Lulu looked back at the picturesque woman on the balcony. Her fine features reminded her of the blond woman who had brought her to this room. As she was watching her, Lulu's hair stood on end, and Lulu heard a humming vibration that seemed to originate from Laima itself.

Lulu looked at the doyen, and the same look of acceptance that she had seen on the steps outside took over his face. He closed his eyes and spread his arms wide. The crawlers beside him stepped away as though he was on fire. Lulu felt the humming sound gather to a high pitch, and she looked back at the redheaded woman on the balcony just in time to see the air crackle with sparks around her.

Without thinking, Lulu dove for the doyen. Her shoulder collided with his chest, and they flew through the doorway to slide against a stone wall on the other side. Lulu's face was buried in his robes, and she disentangled herself to look back at the open chamber. Black scorch marks marred the red cloth of the entryway, and the smell of soap was replaced with the smell of burned fabric.

In her life, Lulu had heard stories of magic and sorcery. These were just fairy tales. They were distractions from a hard existence on a dark planet filled with dust and the fear of being scorched by an unforgiving sun. They weren't real. This couldn't be real.

The doyen grabbed her face in his hands and forced her to look at him. His eyes met hers, and she saw confused bewilderment. His mouth was moving, but Lulu found her ears were still ringing with the high-pitched thrumming from behind her. It was getting louder.

Her shoulders tensed as his words broke through.

"We have to run!" he shouted.

Lulu rolled to the side and whirled to start running down the hall. She felt the doyen running beside her, and the thrumming in her ears broke just in time for her to register the pounding feet of crawlers pursuing them.

6

Mikal walked through the main entrance to the Sanctuary like he had done so many times before. There was no need for subterfuge. With the dead crawlers on the stairway, the Wards had to know he was coming. Mikal had killed only one crawler before this. For all their genetic and hormone-induced strength, they died just as easily as ordinary men. One thing he had not forgotten though was their connection to the Wards. Those abhorrent women were connected to the crawlers like mothers in a crowded market with an uncanny knowledge of how far their children wandered.

Like everything else the Wards knew and did, Mikal could never figure out how. As a young man entering the Sanctuary for the first time, he had been awed by their mysticism and power. Now he wanted nothing more than to put an end to it.

He stood on the threshold of the tallest structure on Dalia and noted the emptiness and echoes around him.

"The Wards must be convening," he noted to himself.

Mikal checked his weapons and straightened his cloak on his shoulders. He walked inside, looked straight ahead, and listened past the sounds of his own footsteps ringing off the walls. It was unprecedented that there were no crawlers guarding the entryway. With a sinking and cold certainty, Mikal knew that they were preoccupied with something else. With an effort, he kept his footsteps even and measured as he turned down the unassuming narrow stairwell that led to the bowels of the Sanctuary.

Mikal walked past the prison cells and empty maze of corridors; he knew that the back of the Sanctuary opened to the sky. Beyond that room was the back of the cliff that held the stone monolith like a cancerous tumor in its wall. Looking off the edge of the cliff, one could see the unoccupied part of Dalia. The scorched ground and bright sunlight was just over the horizon, and on a clear day, the dust that was baked from the ground could be seen rising like a blanket off the skin of the planet. It was a sight that no one in the city below had ever beheld.

Mikal walked through the stone torch-lined corridors, taking the right turns at every intersection with hardly a second thought. As a boy, when he had first been invited into this place, he had been intimidated by the maze. Now, even after having been away from it for rotations, he could walk it in his sleep.

His balance was suddenly rocked to the left as reverberations made their way through his feet and into his shin bones. He caught himself on the stone wall with his left hand and unconsciously grabbed the energy gun on his right hip with his other hand. Without hesitation, he picked up his pace and ran toward the source of the aftershock. When his feet hit cloth, he slowed his gait and turned the corner to nearly collide with none other than his daughter and the doyen himself.

His daughter skidded to a stop from a full run and looked up at him briefly before crashing into Mikal's arms.

"Dad, we have to run!" she said with her face buried in his cloak.

She tugged at him, and Mikal looked past her to see the crawlers collecting themselves and building up speed down the hall. They were coming for his daughter and the doyen. He pushed her back with his hands on her shoulders to look at her face.

A wave of anger rushed over him at the sight of Lu's bruised nose, but her eyes still shone bright. A look of understanding passed over them.

"Go," he said. She was about to protest when he said, "I love you, Lu." He looked at the doyen, who was looking at Mikal as though he had seen a ghost. "Take her," Mikal said.

His words had barely left his mouth before the doyen wrapped his arms around her shoulders and took her past him, down the hall. Mikal closed his eyes against the look of anxiety and pain on her face and reached for his weapons. His fingers found the trigger of the gun in his hand at the same time his eyes opened to see a crawler at arm's length away from him.

The crawler collided with Mikal at the same time he took his last breath and the energy pulse penetrated his chest. Mikal was thrown backward with his momentum and landed painfully on his back. He ignored the tight feeling in his chest that came with the impact and rolled to his feet in time to face the next one.

The crawler viciously flew at Mikal with a force he was unprepared for. The beast's giant hand found its way around Mikal's neck, and he was pinned against the stone wall.

"Your insolence will not be tolerated," the crawler spat.

Mikal knew the words were not the crawler's but the Wards' behind him. He brought up the edge of his blade to slice open the side of the open mouth of the crawler in front of him. The crawler released him, and Mikal dropped to the floor and buried the point of his blade in the back of the beast's neck.

As the crawler fell to the ground, Mikal whirled around to see three more filling the corridor behind him. He shot one and dropped the gun so it could reload and moved to grab another weapon, but the other two were faster. One brought his fist down on Mikal's shoulder, and the assassin dropped the blade he had been holding from now limp fingers on the floor. Mikal fell to his knees, and his other hand moved to block the next blow from landing on his face.

Out of his peripheral vision, Mikal saw the other crawler move to run past him and toward where Lu and the doyen had escaped. In desperation, he dove for that one's legs and pulled a blade from the sleeve of his cloak to slice across the tendon in the back of the crawler's leg. The animal fell with a satisfying thud against the wall, and Mikal rolled back in time to see the other one bring a club toward his head.

His last thoughts as blackness overtook him were of Lu. With any luck, she had gotten away. Mikal's life would have been worth that.

7

"Your father is Mikal Destin?" the doyen blurted out in a harsh whisper.

Lulu blinked back tears of frustration and tried to focus on the religious figurehead in front of her. She had the distinct feeling that her body was not present and the ground would fall away from under her at any moment. She leaned against the wall and slumped to the dirt, bringing her knees up to her chest and wrapping her arms tightly around them.

After their escape, the doyen had led Lulu through the winding corridors to the dungeons. One hall beyond Lulu's own prison chamber, he ducked into a stairwell hidden by a defect in the wall. Without knowing that it was there, a casual observer's eye would likely have slid right over it. If she had not been running for her life, Lulu would have been consumed by hysteric laughter at how close she had been to escaping when she first left her prison cell. If only she had turned the other way.

They ran up narrow winding stairs with walls that brushed both of Lulu's slight shoulders at times. The doyen in front of her slipped through by turning sideways. It was obvious he had traversed this path many times. When they burst into a beautiful marble-lined entryway leading to the familiar and formidable stairs to the city, Lulu had seen why. He had come this way every day for rotations to deliver his sermons.

Running down those stairs in the open with their backs exposed to the Sanctuary felt even more dangerous than running from the crawlers they could see inside. As if he could sense her discomfort, the doyen had moved to run behind Lulu, shielding her. No one pursued them though. They slipped into the slums lining the Sanctuary, past the confused looks of the parentless children who occupied that territory.

Now, the doyen looked at her in the darkness of their hiding place behind a shanty, and his face softened. "Look," he said in a gentler tone, "it's my fault you're here."

"The choices I make are my own," Lulu shot back. "You can't take responsibility for what I did." She felt tears spring to her eyes and silently cursed her own emotions as she swiped her sleeve across her cheeks. It was not sadness that made her cry. It was anger. Lulu was angry with herself. "It's my fault he's in there."

The sound of laughter made her look up, and even in the darkness she could see the doyen's bemused expression as he studied her.

"It's not funny," she said a little more petulantly than she intended.

He took a breath and said, "You're right. It's just that you criticized me for the same thoughts mere seconds before you had them about your father."

Lulu blinked and realized he was right.

"I know you're worried," he continued in a soothing tone. "If anyone could survive in there, it's Mikal Destin."

"How do you know my father?" Lulu asked.

The doyen looked acutely uncomfortable and ducked his head. "That is a story I would feel wrong in telling if Mikal hasn't told you himself."

Lulu had always known there was a great deal her father had never told her about himself. With a painful thought, she realized that he may never get the chance to. She brushed aside those thoughts and studied the doyen in front of her. Born only one rotation before her, the lines on his face made him look far older than that. In the darkness, where everything looked gray, his irises still managed to stand out. Their light color was in stark contrast to his black hair. He saw her studying him, and Lulu looked away like she had been caught doing something wrong.

"Your name is Lu?" he asked.

"That's what my father calls me," she said quietly.

"Then I won't call you that," he said.

"No," she said, not knowing why. "Lu is fine."

After a moment, he said, "Lu, then."

"What should I call you?" she asked, realizing she didn't know if he even had a name. He was only known simply as the doyen.

He seemed to consider her for a moment before answering. "Sen."

"What now, Sen?" Lulu asked. "Why were those women trying to kill you?"

He laughed darkly. "Those women, as you call them, are the Wards. For generations, they have raised and controlled the doyen. Behind those walls, the Wards rule Dalia through fear and spiritual co-ercion. I am nothing but a false prophet, and Laima has never given its power to me."

Lulu took a moment to think about every time she had ever heard the doyen speak. It had always seemed like his words were what everyone needed to hear every time. When there had been a shortage of water from the deep mines and wells outside the city, he had spoken to them of Laima's wrath and equal forgiveness. The following day, water seemed to flood the wells from nowhere. Of course, it had been divine intervention.

When a riot broke out in the market over palia, the cracked bread that was so coveted on Dalia, the doyen had spoken of vengeance against such violence, and those people disappeared that night. It was like they had been struck down from the planet above them itself. No one had looked for them or spoken of them again.

If the doyen was controlled by a group of mysterious women who ruled from behind the stone artifice of the Sanctuary, then maybe he never communicated with Laima at all.

Lulu stared at the doyen in incredulous horror, knowing she couldn't keep her feelings off her face. There was a shame and regret in his eyes, but he did not look away. He held her gaze in the shadows, waiting for her to speak.

"I believed in you," she whispered.

He looked hurt before his eyes turned to steel against her. "You choose to believe in what and who you want to. Don't make me responsible for your beliefs."

Lulu's back straightened in anger, and she was about to retort when his hand quickly covered her mouth; he pushed her against the wall of the shanty, bringing his face next to her ear.

"Quiet," he whispered.

Lulu held her breath and waited. The doyen was surprisingly strong considering his life of supposed piousness above. Just when she decided she had had enough of this game and was about to try to wriggle free from his grasp, she heard the sound. They were the unmistakable heavy footfalls of a crawler.

Sen was like steel, still against her, and Lulu felt her heart beat so hard against her rib cage that she was sure they must be able to hear it. The crawler approached their shanty and rapped loudly on the side of the small mud-built structure. Dust fell from the roof of the building they were up against to land softy in their hair.

Shuffling was heard from inside, and a boy's voice could be heard at the doorway.

"Yes?" he asked with only a small tremor to his voice.

"We seek the location of the doyen," the enormous crawler rasped in a deep voice.

"He's not in the Sanctuary?" the boy asked. Lulu thought his voice changed with the question, and it almost had a hopeful ring to it. The crawler must have shaken his head because the boy spoke again after that. "Why would the doyen wanna be in our slums?"

The crawler didn't answer the boy's question but walked away as purposefully as he had come. The rapping sounded on the next shanty over, and it was the same question asked that was greeted with a fearful response from the younger occupants inside. Lulu and Sen remained frozen until the crawler moved on and could no longer be heard before they finally relaxed.

"We have to move," Sen whispered.

Lulu nodded, knowing he felt her assent in the darkness, and they both wordlessly stood, leaning against the shanty to look around the corner. Standing behind Sen, Lulu startled and almost knocked him over when she saw the boy standing behind her watching them.

"Hasn't anyone ever told you not to sneak up on people?" Lulu admonished the boy harshly.

"You're the doyen," the boy said, ignoring her and looking at Sen.

Lulu snorted derisively, and Sen glanced at her before turning back to the boy.

"Thank you for not giving us away just now," Sen said smoothly.

"Bale's never gonna believe this," the boy said breathlessly.

"He needs to hide," Lulu said, trying to break the boy's gaze on the doyen. "Can you help him?"

The boy nodded and darted back, deeper into the shanties ringing the Sanctuary. He was running further toward the stone cliffs at the edge of the city. They watched for a moment before Sen looked at her and shrugged his shoulders. He trotted off after the boy, and Lulu hesitated before following. She looked up at the Sanctuary where her father was, under the slow rotation of Laima above. Reaching a decision, she followed the false prophet and the boy through the mud shanties sitting in the Sanctuary's shadow.

8

The crawlers held Mikal by his arms so that he dangled with bent knees between them. His thoughts were disoriented, and he tried to force himself to struggle. They held him effortlessly before the Wards, and Mikal found his eyes focused on the only one that mattered to him. Her black hair stood out beside the ethereal blond-and-red locks overlying pure white dresses. Mikal swallowed back the bile that threatened to rise in his throat at the sight of her.

"You would have made a fine crawler," the one with red hair said.

"Why didn't you make me one then, Lana?" he spat.

"Oh, I wanted to, but your talents seemed to lie elsewhere," she said, glancing at the black-haired woman to her right. "They have ceased to be needed for quite some time though."

"Of course," he said with a smile. "What would you need with a quiet assassin when you keep harvesting orphaned boys to surround yourself with these perversions of humans?" he asked, trying to shake off the thick hands gripping his arms.

Lana's face hardened, and the air seemed to crackle around Mikal. The black-haired woman put her hand on the other's arm, and the atmosphere cooled. When he was a boy, Mikal had feared the Wards' retribution. Even held by crawlers as he was, he found that he was no longer afraid.

"You know why Laima has granted us the power to rule here. You know why the guards are necessary," Lana said coolly, regaining her composure.

"The reasons no longer matter, Lana," he said. "Can't you see that we've been abandoned? The flames won't spare you in your high tower."

"Mikal, please." A voice long buried in his past pleaded from the ledge above him.

Mikal refused to look at her. His eyes kept contact with Lana's, and she looked back at him with an intensity that threatened to burrow into his skull. Lana was a formidable woman. As the hidden ruler of a hostile planet, she would have to be.

"Why did you try end the doyen's life?" he asked between clenched teeth.

Lana's eyes softened slightly. "We gave him one chance to prevent mass hysteria, and he chose a different direction. His usefulness is at an end, just as yours was."

Refusing to rise to the bait, Mikal tried a different tactic. "I see your crawlers weren't very effective at killing one young man."

Lana tensed and Mikal resisted the urge to flinch, held as he was by the crawlers next to him. Their hormonally and genetically manipulated bodies seemed to prevent a certain amount of independent intelligence. Still, Mikal could never tell how much they understood behind those black eyes.

"You think you could have done better in front of a crowd of innocents that included your own daughter?" the black-haired woman asked.

Mikal looked at her then. Tess. Her dark eyes studied his as if she was trying to speak into his mind. His pulse quickened, and he averted his gaze. After so much time had passed, he couldn't know if Tess would try to help him or not. He had abandoned her there for the sake of his daughter. No, he amended his thoughts, she had chosen to stay.

He decided to go along with her now and spoke to the ground in front of him. "He would have been dead before the words left his mouth. Lu would never have had a chance to save him."

"And yet she remains with him now, in harm's way," Tess said coolly.

Mikal looked up and saw Lana intently studying the woman he had once loved above everything else in his life.

"That girl is his weakness," Tess said, turning to Lana.

Lana seemed to consider her for a moment before turning to Mikal. "I have ordered her dead alongside the doyen."

Mikal didn't think. He twisted his arm painfully in the grip of the crawler until he felt the bones in his shoulder start to slide apart. Light exploded in his vision as his arm popped out of its socket, and he spun to bring his knee into the belly of the crawler on his right. The crawler stumbled back in surprise and released his right arm.

Mikal paid no heed to the advancing blow of the crawler on his left. He drew the hidden energy gun strapped to his thigh and brought it forward. The whining ping that signified it was ready to fire reverberated off the walls of the chamber, and he held it steady, aimed for Lana's pretty face.

The crawlers froze beside him. Mikal felt his fingers start to depress the trigger. He knew it was going to be his last action, and he chose to watch Tess's face instead of his final target.

"Stop!" Tess yelled.

Mikal's finger held on the trigger. The pleading in her eyes held him still.

Tess turned to Lana in desperation. "Maybe there is one more use for him. We need the doyen silenced, and he's right—the guards are not getting the job done."

Lana's wide eyes, which had been staring at the end of Mikal's gun, seemed to soften with calculated thought. The room remained silent and still for several moments longer.

"Perhaps," Lana said with only a slight tremor to her voice, "you are right. I propose a compromise."

Mikal straightened, his right arm held like a statue in front of him. Lana may have been shaken, but his resolve had never been stronger. "Continue," he said, noting the crawlers step to the side further away from him.

"Her life for his," Lana said.

"I kill the doyen. Then Lu and I are free to go?" Mikal replied.

"Free as one can be on Dalia," Lana said.

"Call off the crawlers," he said.

Lana seemed to hesitate before she replied. "You have two cycles."

Mikal glanced up at Laima. The fire cyclone had just passed beyond the rim of the planet.

"Agreed," he said gruffly. He turned to walk out of the chamber, his footsteps ringing off the stone walls loudly. He stopped at the doorway and turned his head, refusing to look at Tess. "When this is finished, you will never see me or my daughter again."

"We can only hope that is Laima's will," Lana replied.

"For your sake," Mikal said honestly before walking out of the vipers' nest.

9

Bale, as it turned out, was the unofficial leader of the boys who scrounged for food at the base of the Sanctuary. Lulu stood in silence and listened as the doyen spoke with him. She glanced around at the other boys and noted the respectful distance that they kept from Bale and his guests. They varied in ages from three rotations to slightly younger than her. Their dress ranged from scraps of expensive cloth strung together to strings of the phosphorescent plants that grew on the city's edge. It gave them the appearance of an eclectic horde.

The boys numbered close to fifty, and Lulu thought she saw more gathering on the periphery. They stood beyond the maze of shanties beside the stone wall that had been erected on the edge of the cliff that held the Sanctuary. The building's shadow still loomed over them, but from here they could see the backside of the monolith—a sight Lulu had never seen.

The rock of the cliff blended with the bottom of the building, and in a way, that made it look as though Dalia's stone was eating the man-made structure. The wall beside them grew seamlessly from the Sanctuary and stood three times as tall as Lulu herself. She stared up at the top, noting the cracks that spanned down its length. The wind had eroded it like so many skeleton fingers branching through the rock.

Sen's voice broke her thoughts. "We desire nothing more than a place to hide, but we do not want to endanger anybody."

The self-appointed leader of orphan boys seemed to consider his words. Bale was stocky, but he carried himself as though he was a tall man. His sandy hair kept falling onto his face, but he ignored it as he studied the two of them. "We know of a place where you can disappear for a time. It comes with a price."

Sen's back stiffened, and his jaw clenched expectantly. He glanced at Lulu briefly before turning back to Bale.

"Name it," he said.

"You leave her with us," Bale said, gesturing at Lulu.

Lulu opened her mouth to stay something, but Sen put his hand up to stall her. "For what purpose?"

The normally peaceful doyen had a hard tone to his voice that reminded Lulu of her father.

"We have young ones," Bale said. "We need someone to care for them after some of us older ones are recruited by the Sanctuary. Not every day we have a girl among us."

"No," Sen said. "She goes where I go."

"Well, you both can't stay here. You can leave to be taken back by the crawlers together." Bale shrugged.

"That is your doyen," Lulu interjected, unable to keep her mouth shut any longer.

"No," Bale said. "We have always been taken care of by the crawlers. They give us food and allow us to live here." He glanced at Sen and continued, "He's *your* doyen. He caters to the weak-minded and tells them everything is going to be all right. We know better though."

Lulu looked around and saw that some of the boys looked angry and nodded their heads. Still others looked hopefully at Sen. She had seen them crowd around the shadows of the staircase and listen to the doyen speak, just as she had once done in what already seemed a lifetime ago.

"You don't know anything," Lulu said. "I don't think you could help us anyway."

Bale laughed without humor. "I don't think anyone could help you. From what Stap tells me, you are marked by the crawlers, girl."

The smaller boy who had brought them looked at his feet and shuffled slightly.

Sen looked up at the wall next to him before glancing at Lulu. "Come on, Lu," he said. "These boys can't help us."

"No one can help anyone," the one called Stap murmured next to Lulu.

Lulu looked at the boy's face, and he met her gaze unflinchingly. "I'll take 'em out," he said to Bale, never taking his eyes off Lulu.

"Makes no difference to me," Bale said. "We have no use for false prophets here."

Stap nodded and grabbed Lulu's hand, leading her through the throng of boys who had been listening in. Sen followed her closely. Lulu heard the boys whispering and caught snippets of words as they passed through.

"Bad omen," one said.

"Laima will not be happy we aren't helping the doyen," another responded.

"He's got no real power," an older one said reassuringly.

Lulu had grown up in the city, surrounded by the faithful. They had been cared for by the Sanctuary, and the doyen was the chosen voice of Laima. These boys had only known what it was like to eat the scraps from the crawlers. Something told her that they had been conditioned to lose respect for the doyen as they grew older.

Stap led them along the stone wall, avoiding sleeping pallets and the occasional pile of ratted clothing. Lulu allowed him to hold her hand while they made their way. She glanced back at Sen, who seemed focused on the dark nooks of their surroundings. He held himself like a fighter, and Lulu was struck, not for the first time, by how he moved with a natural athletic grace.

Stap suddenly stopped, his small hand releasing Lulu's. He was standing with his arms at his sides staring at a section of the wall in front of his feet. He kicked an oval-shaped rock with his toe, and a large crack was revealed.

"What are you doing?" Lulu asked. They had moved far enough away from the shanties, and no one was within earshot.

"I wanna show you," Stap said in a determined tone.

He knelt and his fingers searched the inside of the crack in the stone until he seemed to find what he was looking for. Stap bent his knees and started pulling on the rock until it slid free from the rest of the wall. Sen didn't ask any questions; he bent down next to the boy and helped him move the rock, pushing it until it rested in front of the wall. Stap glanced at the doyen in awe before lowering his head to dust his hands on his pants.

Lulu knelt in front of the hole in the wall and was blasted in the face by a gust of wind and needlepoint sand.

Stap moved her out of the way by squeezing through the small gap in the rock. "It helps if you hold your shirt up like this," he called back, pulling his shirt over his face.

Lulu looked up at Sen, who obediently did as Stap had done. Lulu shrugged and did the same, squeezing through to follow Stap, with Sen close on her heels.

The hole through the wall was small, but she could easily fit. Sen seemed to have trouble behind her but managed to twist through. Lulu saw that there was a small ledge on the other side, and beyond that, the ground dropped away to disappear into an abyss. She stood straight and gasped, pinned against the wall by the wind and fear of falling.

She looked down and found that she couldn't see the ground below. They were too far up, and the desert ground was being churned into thick, swirling dust clouds. Lulu felt her knees go weak, but she was bolstered by the hand that suddenly pinned her abdomen back against the wall. She had not realized she was falling until Sen had shoved her back.

"Don't look down," he said into her ear.

Lulu nodded and looked straight ahead. What she saw was almost as frightening and mesmerizing. The light over the horizon was blinding, and the ground beneath it burned, releasing smoke up into the atmosphere, almost touching Laima itself.

Lulu stared, etching the vision of it into her brain until she was pulled away by the small hand to her left. She looked down to see Stap grabbing her by the forearm to follow him along the ledge. She forced herself to slide her feet to the side, following him. Sen held her shoulder, steadying her against the wall. Stap walked like he had lived on that narrow ledge. His feet were sure, and he didn't hesitate, even when the ledge angled down.

The dust had blanketed the stone that they walked on so that Lulu was sure it would slide and slip out from under her feet. She concentrated on following Stap's footsteps as the ledge led them down further toward the abyss below. They traveled slowly, not saying a word, until Stap finally ducked into a depression into the wall.

Lulu gratefully followed him in the safety of the shadow and saw that what she thought was a depression was actually a large cavern. She fell to her knees inside, not caring what anyone thought of her, and placed her hands flat on the ground. Sen followed her, and she looked up at him watching her with a bemused expression on his face.

"Did you see that?" Lulu asked, knowing the question was stupid even as it left her mouth.

"I have been seeing that for the past rotation," he said quietly. "It grows brighter and closer every cycle."

Lulu shook with fear and emotion. She had heard of the fire and breathed in the dust. She had watched as a crawler tried to destroy the voice of warning on the stairwell. Nothing could have prepared her for seeing it though. Laima was moving away from them. The ground she walked on and the air she breathed were catching fire. She looked at Stap, who watched her with a serious expression on his young face.

"We should go before Bale realizes I brought ya here," Stap said.

He lifted a torch from the wall of the cavern and lit it with a spark from metal rods in his pocket. He didn't wait to see if Lulu and Sen were following him before taking the torch deeper into the black depths of the cavern. In a city, lit by the soft fluorescence of artificial light, it was the second time in as many cycles that Lulu had been guided by firelight. She couldn't help but feel a heavy sense of foreboding settle in her chest.

10

Mikal kicked aside an empty tin canister. It bounced off the side of a shanty with a satisfying clink that echoed through the narrow alleyway ahead of him. He knew he was being followed by crawlers but had no desire to be quiet. His prey was most certainly in hiding, and he needed to flush it out. The doyen had stupidly risked his own life in order to bring panic to a planet that was helpless to stop its own demise. In doing so, he had risked the life of Mikal's daughter. Mikal would not hesitate to fulfill his end of his agreement with the Wards when he found him.

A small scuffing sound in the trash heap behind him signaled the presence of someone or something in the otherwise quiet alleyway. Mikal kept walking as though he hadn't heard it. He started to let out a soft whistle between his teeth. It was a song from another life—a lullaby he used to sing to Lu when she was small. He had learned it from Tess.

When Tess sang, even crawlers could be brought to their knees. Her voice was haunting, and the thought of it forced his mind to conjure images of her face beside him in the bed they had once shared. Her black hair cascaded across his arm, and the sound of her voice filled his chest with warmth. It seemed fitting that he whistled her lullaby while on his way to taking the doyen's life.

His whistles echoed down the empty alley and had the desired effect. His follower was growing careless. Mikal walked on, looking straight ahead. He turned a corner, stopped, and knelt on the dusty ground with one knee. His shoulder still hurt from where he had dislocated it, and he ignored the dull throb of pain that came with each movement. He had slammed it back in place using the corner of the entryway to the Sanctuary. Several crawlers had stoically looked on while he fumbled the first few attempts. They had no doubt communicated with each other, in their creepy way, how he had torn it out of its socket in the first place.

Poised now on the ground, he made as if to check his boot heel for something. His fingers lightly grazed a blade hidden along his calf beneath his pant leg. He used his thumb to release it from the strap that held it beneath the fabric. The blade handle fell silently into his waiting palm, and he continued to whistle softly.

His follower was close enough now.

He spun around on his heel and released the blade. Its point stuck satisfyingly in the dried mud wall of the shanty behind him, mere inches in front of the bare feet of the orphan boy who had been pursuing him. Mikal straightened. The orphan was only a few rotations younger then Lu. His face was caked in dust, and his hair hung in oily strands past his shoulders.

"Surely you're old enough to be a crawler by now, boy?" he asked as he casually strode forward to retrieve his blade.

The boy was frozen in fear, and he flinched as the blade made a scraping sound while it was being extracted. Mikal stood in front of his follower, idly rolling the knife handle between his fingers. He leaned against the wall, inches from where the boy still stood with his eyes closed shut.

"Maybe you're a mute," Mikal speculated aloud.

Mutes were just a small subset of the increasing number of deformities affecting the children of Dalia. The fire's radiation bounced off the planet and rolled through the atmosphere like a wild animal. Mikal shuddered inwardly, thinking of the last baby that had been abandoned on the steps of the Sanctuary. His features had not been human. It was the same radiation that caused nine out of ten babies born on Dalia to be boys. Girls like his daughter were becoming increasingly rare.

The boy next to him adjusted his feet uncomfortably. He still did not open his eyes.

"You know," Mikal said, casually pulling a piece of palia wrapped in foil from his inside jacket pocket, "I'm looking for someone."

He pulled a flake of the soft bread out of the foil and passed it next to the boy's face. He hid his satisfaction at seeing the boy's eyes open involuntarily at the smell. Mikal popped the piece into his mouth. It was two cycles old and only slightly stale, but still satisfying. The boy shifted his feet again and Mikal acted like he had forgotten he was there.

"Oh, would you like some?" he asked innocently.

The boy nodded imperceptibly.

"Then answer one question," Mikal said.

The boy shrugged his shoulders uncomfortably but couldn't take his eyes off the palia in Mikal's hands.

"Have you seen the doyen?" Mikal asked quietly, studying the boy's face.

The boy shook his head.

"Pity," Mikal said and carefully wrapped the rest of the palia in the crumpled foil before stuffing it back in his jacket.

Mikal turned and started to walk away when a shaky voice behind him stopped his feet.

"Bale says we're not s'posed to talk about the doyen," the orphan said. "But there was a girl with a face like yours. I would never forget her."

Mikal calmly walked back to the boy and grabbed him by the front of his shirt, twisting the fabric tight in his fist. The lanky boy, almost as tall as Mikal, shrunk back against the wall of the shanty but had nowhere to escape.

"You're safer talking about the doyen than her," Mikal said dangerously. "Where did you last see her?"

"She was with Bale!" he said, starting to panic under Mikal's grip.

It was the second time he had mentioned this Bale. Mikal sighed, relaxing his hand slightly. "Are they still together?" he asked.

"Bale kicked em out," the boy said. At seeing Mikal's face, he stuttered, "Bu…but I bet he knows where they are now. Bale knows everything that goes on out here."

"Take me to him," Mikal said roughly, releasing the boy to land awkwardly on the dirty stones of the alley.

Looking at his hollow cheeks, Mikal took pity on him and grabbed the foil wrapped palia. He tossed the food that was no doubt priceless to the boy and turned on his heel, not waiting to see him eat it. He busied himself kneeling to replace the blade strapped to his calf, and by the time he stood, the boy was already finished and licking the foil before carefully folding it and sliding it into his pocket. Mikal buried the feeling of sympathy and reminded himself that the boy would be a crawler one day.

"I don't have time to waste here, you understand?" Mikal said gruffly.

The boy nodded and trotted ahead of him down the alleyway. Mikal considered the shadows behind him before taking off to follow. He knew the crawlers were there, watching him. Their oversized pupils, making their eyes seem like black marbles, allowed them to navigate in the darkness of Dalia better than anyone. He shook off the feeling of being followed and focused on the twists and turns ahead.

The boy kept a ground-eating pace through the dust-coated alleys ahead, finally slowing down when the shanties poured them into an open patch of dirt next to the wall. Mikal had once been an orphan of the Sanctuary. He had once lived as these boys did. He had never seen so many gathered in one place. They emerged from the shanties nearby and leaked out of the alleys to stand around the clearing before him. The boy who led him there stood in the center and yelled for Bale frantically.

Mikal had not meant to draw so much attention to his presence there and cursed himself for telling this boy that he has in a hurry. Too late now. He straightened his shoulders and turned to the face the self-appointed leader of the orphans, who had finally emerged to walk into the clearing in front of him.

Where the other orphan boy was tall and lanky, this one was a walking barrel. Mikal had a tough time assigning him an age, but he was suspicious that he was too old to still be living in the shanties. Bale was studying him with the practiced eye of persons who had survived when they should not have. Mikal was familiar with that type of suspicion and stood with a nonchalant expression on his face. He involuntarily glanced up at Laima to see if the cyclone was reappearing over the planet's horizon yet and noted that Bale saw his impatience. The boy smiled.

"You look like a girl we met earlier today," he said. "Or should I say, she looked like you?"

"Where is she?" Mikal asked quietly.

The boys surrounding them leaned in and shuffled closer to hear the conversation in the clearing. Mikal saw that they still afforded Bale a respectful distance. They seemed to fear their leader more than the assassin that he spoke to.

Bale kept the smile on his face, but his eyes were serious.

"I don't know," he said.

"Yes, you do," Mikal countered.

This boy knew the whereabouts of everyone in his small kingdom.

Bale shrugged. "Stap took her and the doyen out of the shanties."

Mikal stifled a sigh, tiring of the game. "Where's this Stap?" he asked, still playing along.

"What's it worth to you?" Bale asked finally.

Mikal casually tossed a tri coin into the center of the clearing. It spun on its edge for several ticks before landing on its side. The three depressions glinted in the dim light around them. Mikal watched Bale's greed flash across his eyes for a brief instant before forced indifference returned to his face. The coin sat in the dust even as the boys on the edge of the clearing clamored over each other to get a closer look. A tri coin was a fortune that none of them were ever likely to see again.

Mikal held Bale's gaze and waited.

"I'll take you to where Stap likes to hide," the orphan leader finally said.

11

Lulu watched Stap's back, outlined by the light of the torch he held in front of him. They had been walking in the darkness for what seemed like half a cycle. The cave system below the city was more extensive than Lulu could have imagined, and they had passed countless offshoots, branching off the main corridor like so many black appendages. Her father's training had subconsciously kicked in, and she had counted the steps between each turn. Her mind split between the mindless task and thoughts of the flames threatening to engulf Dalia behind her.

Seven hundred and twenty-three steps—left, two hundred, five hundred, and ten steps—right. Lulu's foot caught on a ledge, and she slapped the wall beside her, steadying herself against the cold, damp stone. She had hardly noticed Sen moving beside her until she felt his strong hand wrap around her other arm. He squeezed and she caught his worried expression in the darkness.

"I think it's time we stopped," he said while looking at her, but his voice carried to Stap ahead of them.

"It's not far now," the boy called back, full of energy.

"I'm fine," Lulu said with a little too much force.

She shook Sen's hand off and trotted ahead, cursing herself for forgetting to count her last steps. Obviously, the doyen was used to getting his way, and he stood for a moment before the echoes of his footsteps resumed behind her. Lulu was too tired to figure out why she resented him trying to take care of her. She resumed her counting and focused on the resolute boy in front of her.

Stap hadn't lied, and it was only 209 steps before he turned right into an enormous cavern. Lulu stopped and stared at the entrance, not trusting her eyes. The ceiling was as tall as ten men stacked on top of each other, and the walls spread so far before her that she could not see the opposite side. Each wall was lit by the artificial fluorescent lighting that the Sanctuary provided the homes on Dalia. Each light was precious on the dark planet, but there were at least a thousand of them dotting the cavern ceiling, and Lulu had to squint while her eyes adjusted.

"It must be as bright as the cyclone in here," she whispered to herself, referencing the flame that circled Laima above.

"You get used to it," Stap said ahead of her.

The boy was putting his torch away in a hole in the wall to her left. He stood on the tips of his toes to reach, and the flame dipped perilously close to his hair. Sen moved silently behind Lulu and grabbed the torch out Stap's hands to place it carefully in the wall. Stap saluted the doyen comically before trotting back to grab Lulu's hand.

She allowed the boy to lead her further into the cavern and almost felt the light bathe her skin as she was more immersed in it. Her free hand anxiously ran up and down her other arm that Stap held out in front of her. She glanced back at Sen, who remained behind them. The doyen seemed as awed as Lulu as he slowly surveyed the empty cavern around them. He had stayed at her back the whole time they had been down there.

"What is this place?" he asked.

Lulu looked at Stap, and he smiled. "Well, if you ask me, it's where the Sanctuary gets its power," the boy said and winked at Lulu.

She looked ahead, and in the vast empty corridor, she could finally see the opposite wall. Her eyes focused on the chaotic lines carved into the enormous stone. Jagged and in straight lines, the carvings ran across the wall in rows from floor to ceiling. Her hand reached out in front of her as they came closer, but Stap held her back.

"Who could have possibly carved these?" she asked with Sen coming up beside her.

They stood with their necks craned within arm's reach of the wall.

"No one knows," Stap said. "Not even Bale."

"Bale knows about this place?" Lulu asked without looking away from the carvings.

"'Course," Stap answered, and she felt him shrug beside her. "All boys destined to join as soldiers in the service of the Wards know about this place." He shuffled his feet uncomfortably and continued, "We're not s'posed to come down here without a soldier."

"Without a crawler you mean?" Lulu asked.

"Whatever you want to call them," Stap said a little defensively.

"Why did you bring us here?" Sen asked.

The boy's face turned red in the fluorescent lighting, and he looked down at his feet. Lulu squeezed his hand, and he looked up at her.

"Well, it's stupid really," he said. "All the older boys say that anybody can touch this wall, but the doyen."

"Why can't the doyen touch it?" Sen asked, looking at Stap intently.

"Well, I never believed it, but the other boys say that if the doyen touches the wall, then the Sanctuary will be destroyed." Stap's voice trailed off, and Sen met Lulu's eyes. "They dared me I wouldn't bring you to it!" he wailed, juvenile anguish echoing off the walls around them.

"Why would you want him to do it?" Lulu asked.

"I want the Sanctuary dead," the boy said quietly, speaking to the ground in front of him. "They lied to us."

"It's just a silly story they made up," Sen said, and without hesitating, he strode forward with his hand held out in front of him.

Lulu jerked involuntarily in his direction, but he laid his palm flat against the black runes before she could do anything. Nothing happened, and she laughed nervously. Story or no, for a moment, she had been fearful of what would happen.

Stap sniffled next to them, and after a moment he said, "I told them it was stupid."

"The doyen has no power here or anywhere," Sen said thoughtfully.

Lulu thought she heard a touch of sadness to his voice, but he turned away from her to trace the runes with his fingertips. Lulu stepped away from them and the wall. She didn't know why, but being that close to it made her nervous. While Sen busied himself studying the wall, she started to walk around the cavern, all the while looking up at the lights above. She turned her face so that when she closed her eyes the light still penetrated through her eyelids. It made the white light orange and easier to face.

She heard a trickling sound off to the side of the cavern, and she followed it to a small clear pool of water collecting from moisture wicking from the stones above. Lulu sat in front of it and cupped her hands in the freezing water to bring some to her face. She hadn't realized the mild throb of her bruised nose was still there until the shock of icy cold water on her face, and she busied herself gingerly scrubbing at the dried blood.

She ran her wet fingers through her long knotted black hair until they ran smooth and twisted it back to itself at the nape of her neck. Feeling better, she glanced around and saw Sen sitting not far from her with his back against the wall. He kept a respectful distance but still watched her.

"We should leave this place," he said when he saw her looking at him.

"What's the point in surviving?" she asked. "Only to be killed by the flames tomorrow."

"We were built to try to live," he said seriously.

Stap watched them intently, and Lulu closed her mouth against the defeatist retort she had for him.

"I want to stay in this light a little longer," she said knowing her request sounded petulant, but not caring.

Sen nodded and leaned his head back against the wall, closing his eyes. Lulu curled into a ball beside the pool, resting her head on her arm. She hadn't slept since being in a prison cell inside the Sanctuary. Her overwhelmed mind quickly took the opportunity, and she instantly fell asleep to dreams of crawlers chasing her, their black eyes invisible against the darkness around them.

12

Mikal bridled at the delay, but Bale had insisted on going along with him to find Stap. When they emerged on the ledge outside of the wall, Mikal paused to watch the flames lick Dalia like a serpent eating a prey larger than its own body. As an assassin for the Sanctuary, many rotations ago, he had seen the first signs of flames along the edge of the desert's horizon. Now, seeing it move closer and watching the smoke and dust cloud billow in front of him, he felt his own mortality blossom in his stomach.

Bale, obviously used to the sight, tugged at Mikal's sleeve to follow him. Several larger boys were on his other side, keeping an eye on them. The stocky leader of the orphans had built himself quite an organized following around the base of the Sanctuary. Mikal suspected that if Bale jumped off the ledge, the other boys would follow suit. His thoughts were distracted as they turned into a cavern leading underneath the city above.

Mikal carefully kept his face expressionless in the shadows, but inside he was sick at the thought that Stap had led Lu here. This place was dangerous. Not even the Wards came here. Bale grabbed a torch off the wall and looked at Mikal with an overconfident expression.

"Didn't you know this place existed?" he asked, knowing that most of the residents on Dalia had no clue.

"No," Mikal lied.

He allowed himself to be led down the dark path but counted the steps before each turn he knew they would take. He remembered what it had been like as a boy, first following the crawlers to this place. He had been awed by the secrecy and beauty of it. He had envied their knowledge of such wonders. It wasn't until much later that he would learn that the crawlers had no idea what the runes meant or where the lights had come from. They didn't even know who carved the tunnels around the cavern.

The Wards had gathered lights from the ceiling of the cavern and doled them out as they saw fit to the people living in darkness. Then, when the fire first appeared, the Wards decided that taking the lights was forbidden and angered Laima. Since then, only crawlers used the tunnels, and no one had been allowed to step foot in the lighted chamber.

One boy walked with Bale ahead of Mikal, while two larger ones walked behind him. They arranged themselves without speaking to one another and fell into formation as easily as any crawler retinue Mikal had ever seen. It was just as well that they were used to militant thinking, Mikal thought. After all, they would all be crawlers eventually.

Hearing something in the distance ahead, Mikal stopped walking causing the boys behind him to nearly collide with his back. Bale stopped and turned to him in the darkness, swinging the flame torch around to face him.

"What?" he asked, annoyance lacing his voice.

"Quiet!" Mikal whispered the command.

He listened intently, not caring for the impatience of those around him. The quiet sound of wind being sucked through the tunnel system filled his ear canals. Just as he was about to relax, he heard it again. It was the unmistakable heavy clank of shifting armor. Bale heard it too, and his mouth closed against the words he had been about to say.

"We need to turn back," he whispered to the boys around them.

"Good," Mikal said. "I know my way."

He strode forward, but Bale pulled on his sleeve to stop him. Mikal stared down at the hand that grabbed the fabric of his shirt, knowing the other could see the menace behind his expression.

"Stap has her in the chamber of lights, waiting for us," Bale said. When Mikal didn't speak he continued, "We were going to keep her for ourselves."

Mikal almost smiled. "You are an orphan of the Sanctuary, destined to become a monster. You own nothing to keep, not even your mind."

Bale looked at him shrewdly. Mikal was overcome with a feeling of sadness that someone who had been born to lead was going to be so wasted. He pulled his arm free and strode forward in the darkness. He didn't need the light of the torch and left them standing in the ring of its light. Mikal had counted the steps behind him and knew how many were left.

13

Lulu opened her eyes.

She had always had a talent for waking up quickly, and she stood quietly. She had dreamt of crawlers chasing her through dark tunnels that led into a pit of flames. Even though she knew it was a dream, the sick feeling of despair stuck to her bones, and she found it difficult to shake it. Standing now, she looked around in the bright artificial light.

Sen slept with his back against the wall behind her, but Stap was not with them. Lulu studied the doyen for a moment. This was a man whom she had grown up admiring. He had simply been a puppet, but looking at him now she realized she had never believed in any divine power granted from Laima through birth. She had always derived strength from listening to his words. He was still someone she would follow.

Quietly, she knelt beside him and laid her hand on his shoulder. He tensed and his eyes shot open. He stood quickly with his back still against the wall, grabbing her hand and pulling her instinctively beside him.

"Where's Stap?" he asked.

Once again, Lulu was reminded of her father. There was definitely more to the doyen's story than she had been led to believe.

"I don't know," she answered.

The chamber was vast and wide open, but the floor seemed to curve unnaturally up toward the center of the vast space so that they had to walk to see the opposite sides. Sen kept her close behind him, and they walked toward the center, looking, but not calling for Stap. They stopped in the center, and Lulu felt exposed in so much light and open space. She shivered and focused her eyes on the walls around her.

Then she found him. Stap was crouched against the wall next to the entrance into the chamber. He had not seen them and seemed focused on the black tunnel beside him. Lulu squeezed Sen's wrist, and he looked where she was staring.

"What he is waiting for?" Sen asked.

"Or who." Lulu amended for him. It was clear their guide had brought them here for a reason.

That was when a crawler emerged from the darkness, stepping into the light. His black eyes squinted, and he looked down at Stap crouched against the wall. Lulu watched in horror as the crawler knelt and grabbed the boy by his arm, lifting him bodily off the ground. She was frozen where she stood, but Sen wasted no time. He wrapped his arm around her waist and pulled her back toward the runes and away from Stap.

Her voice caught in her throat, and it took her several backward steps before she collected herself enough to run beside the doyen. They reached the wall, and the doyen dragged her down to crouch low. Lulu could no longer see the entrance to the cavern, and Sen held his arm over her back as they scrambled for the far corner. Once there, they stopped and listened.

Lulu expected to hear Stap's screams, but she heard nothing except for her own blood pounding into her ears. Her panicked breath came in spurts, and she swallowed it down with effort. Sen was like a statue beside her, and Lulu forced herself to focus her thoughts and calm down. Seeing the crawler emerge from the darkness had been like watching her dream manifest itself in the light.

"Easy," Sen murmured in her ear. "Their vision is terrible in the light. We only need to be patient and double back behind it."

Lulu nodded and listened. What she heard was not the footsteps of a crawler though. She heard the footsteps of several. Their heavy footfalls echoed off the walls, and still she waited beside Sen for them to find them. They emerged, four crawlers, into the center of the chamber. One of them held an upside down Stap in his hand, dangling the limp boy by an ankle. The crawler extended Stap out in front of him like an offering and yelled in a raspy voice.

"His life for the doyen!" The sickening parley reverberated off the walls around them.

Beside Lulu, Sen stood. He held his hand out beside him, his eyes pleading with her to stay where she was. She watched helplessly as the doyen walked slowly yet fearlessly to the center of the chamber. The crawlers turned to face him, and the one holding Stap smiled. The expression unnaturally contorted his broad face, and Lulu felt her stomach clench with dread.

Without thinking she stood and took a step toward Sen.

A hand on her shoulder and a familiar voice pulled her back and down. "He's made his own choice, Lu," her father said into her ear.

Not caring how he found her or how he had approached her without being seen, Lulu buried her face in her father's shoulder and embraced him.

"We have to leave," he said, resting his chin in her hair, and he started to pull her away from the crawlers and Sen.

Lulu followed numbly. A soft thud caused her to turn back, and she saw that Stap had been dropped to the floor to land in a heap at the crawler's feet. Sen stood with his back straight facing the four crawlers with no weapon in his hand. Lulu felt like she was standing outside of herself watching her own hand reach for the energy gun her father had holstered at his hip.

As a child, she had seen the weapons he brought home, but she had never touched one. The weight of the gun surprised her, and her slender fingers barely fit around the thick handle. Her father had quick reflexes, but there was one person he would never strike. Lulu knew as soon as her fingers found the trigger that she had one shot before he could wrestle the energy gun away from her.

The whirring ping and metallic scent filled the air around her and light erupted from her fingers.

Sen turned at the last possible second and ducked as the shot went above their heads to bounce off the wall behind them. It was just a momentary distraction, but it was enough for Sen to pull Stap upright and run. The two darted down the slight decline toward the runes behind the crawlers. Lulu dropped the gun, and her father, cursing behind her, swept up the weapon and grabbed her arm, dragging her in the opposite direction.

Lulu had never acted against Mikal in her life. She had listened to and heeded his instructions like her life had depended on it. Every instinct in her railed against him, and she started to struggle against his grasp.

"I have to go back!" she protested.

"You are not what they came for," he said against gritted teeth.

"Yes, I am." She said the words knowing them to be true, but not knowing why.

Her father stared at her, and behind him, in the entrance to the cavern, Lulu saw Bale emerge into the light with several boys beside him.

"They have Stap!" she called to them.

Bale stared at her as if she had gone mad, but she didn't care.

"Father, we have to save the doyen," she said to Mikal, not bothering to wipe the tears that had begun to stream down her cheeks.

"I came here to kill him," Mikal replied, and Lulu's breath caught in her throat.

14

Mikal looked at his daughter and registered the hurt behind her eyes. It was the same that he had felt when Tess had chosen the Wards over a life with him and Lu. He had broken her heart. He thought back to the last conversation she had with him. Lu had not known why she went to see the doyen speak every cycle, but Mikal knew.

He clenched his jaw and tightened the grip on her arm. "You are leaving this place alive," he said with no little force.

"Only to die in the fire outside," she said.

"If that is Laima's will," Mikal said sarcastically.

This was ridiculous. Crawlers had cornered the doyen, and there was no hope he was still alive as weaponless as he was. Mikal had completed his end of the bargain by seeing that Sen's life ended. He should be fleeing with his daughter to escape the Sanctuary's influence over her. Instead, he was standing in the middle of a forbidden cavern under annoyingly bright artificial lights, arguing with her. He thought seriously about knocking her unconscious and carrying her out quietly.

As if she could read his mind, Lu whirled around and twisted her wrist out of his grip and scrambled away from him back toward the crawlers. Mikal reached her after ten steps and grabbed her calf, causing her to fall on her face. He winced at the pain that must have caused her nose, but he didn't care. She was leaving with him, voluntarily or otherwise.

Mikal had been so distracted dealing with Lu that he hadn't noticed Bale and his minions approaching until it was too late. He turned just in time to see the edge of the pipe that was brought down on top of his head. Blackness overtook his vision for a moment, and he fell to his knees. Mikal, assassin to the Sanctuary, killer of crawlers, had been taken down by his daughter and a few orphan boys.

By sheer force of will, he staggered to his feet. He focused his vision in time to see the retreating forms of his daughter and the orphans. Mikal stumbled after them, gaining ground with every passing second as the pain behind his eyes started to recede.

When he caught up with them and saw the scene that unfolded before him, he froze.

The doyen stood with his palm flat behind him, mere inches from the runes scrawled on the wall. The crawlers stood indecisively before him, weapons drawn. Mikal's daughter stood defiantly in front of those weapons beside Sen. Mikal recognized the look of frustration on Sen's face at his daughter's presence. Lu was not easy to control. The orphan boys had gathered Stap and were backing away from the scene cautiously. Mikal didn't have time to address them, so he let them go.

One of the crawlers lifted his arm with a blade in hand, and Sen inched closer to the wall.

"Make one more move and the entire Sanctuary will be destroyed," Sen yelled.

The superstition about the wall was well known among those in the Sanctuary and apparently held the simple-minded crawlers at bay. Mikal watched as the one closest to him stepped back, and his eyes glazed over. He knew they were asking the Wards what to do. It wouldn't be long now.

Mikal released the blade under his left sleeve and let it fall into his palm. He held it and crouched low behind the crawlers, distracted for the moment by the impending doom before them and the communication they were receiving from the Wards. Lu watched him carefully, and he held his finger over his mouth to keep her still.

Just as he was about to slice the throat of the nearest crawler, his eyes met Lu's, and something in them made him pause. His daughter looked entranced. He straightened and watched her even as she took her own palm and stared at it. Mikal stiffened and shook his head, hoping she would register his message. She saw him and seemed to look right through him.

With one smooth motion, she turned and laid her hand flat against the runes behind her. Mikal's breath caught in his throat, and he found himself shoving in between two armed crawlers, knowing he couldn't reach her in time. Light had blossomed from her fingertips to fill the black grooves of the runes embedded in the stone. It expanded out from her like a river dividing into so many tiny streams. The green hue lit up the wall and climbed ever upward toward the Sanctuary and the city above it.

Mikal reached his daughter, and she collapsed in his arms, releasing the wall behind her, but it was too late.

He looked up and saw the artificial lights flickering until they finally went dim. The lights that had no known origin and were distributed throughout the city, the lights that had never darkened in Dalia's history, winked out of existence.

Mikal gathered Lu in his arms and backed away from the wall, staring up at the lit runes in horror. He glanced at Sen beside him. The former doyen wasn't looking at the mysterious and magnificent runes that heralded the end of the Sanctuary. He was looking at Lu with an expression that was impossible to read.

Sen glanced up at Mikal in the eerie quiet of the cavern and asked, "What now, assassin?"

Mikal looked at the crawlers, who seemed to be coming out of a trance, and said to Sen, "You take her and run."

He handed his daughter off to Sen, who grimly nodded. Mikal didn't watch the former doyen retreat with Lu in his arms. He turned back to the crawlers, releasing an energy gun from his belt.

15

Lulu saw green rivers behind her eyelids. It was quiet and sounds were muffled, but they were becoming clearer. Her head felt like it weighed seven hundred stone, and she found that she couldn't move it. The heavy pain above her eyes was almost unbearable, and she felt hot tears run down her cheeks. She was moving and being held at the same time and started to blindly struggle. The more she struggled, the tighter she felt strong arms close on her, and she forced herself to focus and find her breathing.

Lulu waited for the pain to ebb and for her captor's grip to relax. She tried to listen to the sounds around her and registered the echoes of footsteps bouncing around a hollow corridor. The tunnel. Images came rushing back, and she remembered facing the crawlers next to Sen while her father tried to save her. Lulu opened her eyes in panic against the pain and looked up.

Sen's chin was lit in the torchlight, and he looked forward. His jaw was clenched, and he held Lulu against his chest with her feet dangling over his arm. They were alive, but he was moving fast and something was wrong.

Lulu tried to yell, but she only managed to croak, "Stop."

His gait slowed, and he looked down at her with worry etched in his face.

"I'm fine," Lulu grumbled, not sure if her words were true. "Put me down."

Sen glanced back in the direction they were running from and slowed to a stop. He gingerly put Lulu on her feet and held his arms out like she might fall any second. Lulu gave him a withering glare she thought he should be able to see in the torchlight. Truthfully, she felt like her knees would buckle at any moment, but she wasn't about to let him see that.

"How did you do that?" a familiar voice asked next to her.

Lulu looked down to see Stap standing to her left, looking at her with an expression of reverence that made her feel slightly uncomfortable.

"Do what?" she asked.

"You took the light away," Bale said angrily.

"I did what?" Lulu asked.

"It doesn't matter right now," Sen said, glaring at Bale. "Our orders are to run and get her to safety."

"I take orders from no man, and you're not the doyen," Bale responded.

Lulu looked at Sen questioningly, but he ignored her. How could he not be the doyen?

"You will take orders from Mikal Destin if you value your life," Sen said dangerously.

"He's as good as dead back there; one man against four crawlers," Bale scoffed, waving the torch in his hand. "Besides, we took the last torchlight."

Lulu rested her hand on Sen's wrist to stop him from attacking the self-proclaimed orphan leader. She wasn't about to question her father's orders.

"Let's go," she said before turning to run.

She had only taken five steps before Sen and the others joined her. Her legs grew stronger with each stride, but she knew the boys beside her had slowed their pace to accommodate her. Thoughts of green light running in rivers dominated her thoughts. Her father was somewhere behind them fighting off crawlers in the dark. This was her fault.

She tripped over her own feet and would have landed on her face if not for Sen's sudden grip on her arm. His face was a mask she couldn't read. The doyen, whom she had watched every cycle in her lifetime as he spoke to the masses of Dalia, had always been out of reach, and now he seemed even further away from her.

It wasn't long until Bale led them into the cavern mouth, lit by the fire on the horizon outside. The dark planet seemed so bright when compared to the tunnels behind them, and Lulu squinted, standing at the hollow's mouth.

"We wait here for Mikal," Sen said to the others.

"He isn't coming," Bale said under his breath.

Lulu looked back in time to see Sen move toward Bale with a menacing stance. She was about to yell at them when a low rumble started to build beneath her feet. The vibrations moved up the walls of the cavern causing cracks and fissures to form, racing each other to the top of the cave. Sen moved first, quickly grabbing her by the hand and pulling her out of the cavern to walk along the precarious ledge outside. The sand and rocks vibrated underneath her to fall into the dust abyss below, and Lulu almost went with them more than once.

She glanced back before ducking into the defect in the wall that led back to the shanties. The boys followed closely behind her, and she saw Bale grab Stap's arm, pulling him back from certain death below. Her eyes lingered on the cave entrance for a moment longer, hoping to see her father emerge. He never appeared though, and Sen pulled her through to the other side of the wall.

They stood, waiting for the others and stared up at the monolithic Sanctuary. A torrent of green light left the top of the building and climbed ever upward to leave the atmosphere and bathe the planet above them. Lulu was entranced as she watched Laima's fires take on the green light like an infection. It washed over the planet, and the fire cyclone that had heralded a cycle's beginning for as long as Lulu could remember burned green, casting a new bright light for all to see.

"What did you do?" Bale asked, emerging beside her.

Lulu had no idea what he was talking about, but a sick feeling had been creeping through her stomach. Without knowing why, she knew he was right. This was her doing.

"We have to go," Sen said, watching the Sanctuary warily. He looked at Bale and said, "You have to get the rest of the boys away from here."

Bale didn't argue and led the way through the shanties, back to the central meeting place where they had first met him. Lulu looked at her feet and watched as they were lit up by the increasingly bright green light from above. She noticed the contrast between the dust-encrusted laces and the grooves in the material of her boots. Every imperfection that had been hidden before was highlighted. It was as if she was seeing her own feet for the first time.

Lulu had always known that Dalia deserved to live in darkness. The light could only destroy them.

16

Mikal counted. He focused on the steps ahead of him and tried to ignore the rumbling of the walls around him. The darkness surrounded him like a smothering blanket, and all he had were the numbers of his steps to guide him. The crawlers had been easy to dispatch, coming out of their trance and distracted by the runes on the walls, but Mikal had chafed at the delay.

After incapacitating all four, he knelt to clean his blades on one of their shirts. He stood before the runes and watched as the light started to leak into the stone of the ceiling above him. Unlike the others, Mikal had known where he was standing. That chamber was directly beneath the Sanctuary. He watched with an uneasy feeling as the light started to disappear from the runes, and he knew with the first rumble that the legends had been true. The Sanctuary was doomed.

Tess and the Wards were condemned with it by the hand of his own daughter.

Now, running through the black corridors, he tried to focus on the numbers. Thoughts of Tess clouded his brain, but he shook her away. A light breeze from the left made him take a sharp turn, and he cursed himself for almost missing it. When he finally emerged into the light, the line of fire in the distance seemed to dim in comparison to the ambient light flooding the planet from above.

"Lu," he said to himself, "I should have never let you get near that wall."

Mikal noted the cracks in the cavern wall and the pebbles falling around him and moved quickly along the ledge outside to get back into the city the way he had come with Bale. On the other side, he stopped briefly to stare at Laima and its magnificent green rivers of fire—like veins along the surface. The light fed the planet from the Sanctuary like an umbilical cord, and Mikal saw that it was growing dimmer.

He turned and ran through the shanties in a line as straight as he could make it for the bottom of the stairs that led into the building. Mikal spared one thought for the irony of returning to the Sanctuary so soon after vowing to not come back. He didn't encounter a soul on his journey and wondered if the boys living in the shanties were cowering inside their huts or if they had fled. He couldn't have spared time to find out even if he had wanted to.

Mikal reached the Sanctuary steps just as the light feeding Laima ran out. The planet above cast everything around him in bright, sharp relief, and he squinted his eyes to run up the stairs. On his way, crawlers and servants passed him fleeing down the steps, but Mikal pushed through them. He scanned faces briefly, but only saw panicked strangers. No Tess.

A mere ten steps from the top, a rumble shook the foundation, and he was thrown to land hard with his shin against the edge of the stair in front of him. Likewise, others were tossed down the stairs to land awkwardly beside him. Mikal ignored them and pushed forward through the pain radiating in his shin bone. He ran through the familiar, massive doorway to find the small stairwell that led down into the maze of the building. Behind him, the frame of the door collapsed, trapping those who were still fleeing inside with him. Confused screams started to build and echo into the halls around him, but Mikal focused on his own feet.

As he neared the main chamber where the Wards resided, he saw that the halls were empty. The ceiling above him cracked, and he ran into the safety of the open-aired chamber of the Wards before it fell and crushed him. Mikal spun on his heel and looked around frantically. The once-marvel of architecture was in ruins. The balcony that lined the interior had crumbled to collect in heaps of heavy stone. It looked like a giant's hand had squeezed the room.

Laima spun green above and lit the chamber like a searchlight, and Mikal started to desperately dig through the rubble. It wasn't long before he found the delicate forearm of a Ward, crushed beneath the stone. He felt for a pulse and found none. He inspected the long fingers and skin, knowing it wasn't the one he was searching for. A noise from the corner caused him to turn, and he saw the fire-red hair of Lana emerge from the wreckage. She was disheveled, but intact. The two met each other's eyes before Lana turned to leave, crawling over the shards of stone that led back to the stairs. Mikal let her go without a word.

He continued to doggedly search the debris until he found the person he had been looking for. Her black hair, normally shiny, was now muted with dust and entangled among the stone pieces. He moved the heaviest to reveal her face and chest. Mikal fell to his knees beside her and watched the pulse beating too quickly in her neck. She opened her eyes to look up at him, and he forgave her everything in that moment.

"I freed her from that prison cell," Tess said before coughing painfully.

Mikal noted the tiny splatter of blood on her chin and ran his fingers through her hair.

"She's beautiful," Tess continued after catching her breath.

Mikal nodded, not trusting himself to speak. Tess looked up at Laima with wide eyes, and a tear ran from her eye to land on the dust-covered stone beneath her cheek.

"Our beautiful daughter lit the beacon," she said.

"The beacon?" Mikal asked quietly.

"This place," Tess said, shaking her head. "This place is a prison. We are descended from the lowest and worst of a beautiful society full of light. We were sent here to be punished until the fire consumed us."

She coughed again, and Mikal rested his hand lightly on her chest and leaned in to whisper in her ear. He had so many words for the beautiful woman who had given birth to his daughter. He had so many things left unsaid to the Ward who had kept her post within a religious stronghold only to lie dying in it now. He couldn't say any of those words. Instead, he sang a lullaby—a lullaby he used to sing to Lu when she was small. He had learned it from Tess.

When he finished, he didn't need to look at Tess to know she had died. Her chest had stopped rising and falling beneath his hand before the last verse, but Mikal finished the song anyway.

17

Lulu studied the organized chaos in front of her. Bale had prepared nearly fifty orphaned boys to gather in the central meeting place amid the shanties in the event of the flames. This wasn't the same thing; conditioning kicked in, and the boys milled about in front of Bale, each with sacks on their backs containing their precious few belongings. They looked at Bale and Sen and waited for instruction.

"We have to leave the shadow of the Sanctuary now," Bale yelled so that he could be heard by the smallest in the back of the crowd. Even as he spoke, rumbles sounded ominously from the enormous black building behind them. "Pair up and stay close. We are going to the edge like we planned."

"The edge?" Lulu asked him.

"The edge of the city, opposite the flames." Bale nodded his head in the direction of the wall beside them.

The city's enormous, Lulu thought. It contained the entire population of Dalia. She had never ventured as far as the edge, and her father had never brought her there. The only things beyond it were canyons and fields of palia grain. She tried to think of a better plan though and could not. Bale jumped down from the rock they were standing on, and he extended his hand up to Lulu for her to take.

She let him steady her as she hopped down and waited for Sen to land lightly beside her. Something in his face made Bale release her, and Lulu felt her neck flush. She and Sen walked in front of the large group of boys who obediently followed in pairs, leading them out of the shanties to emerge into the chaos of a city suddenly exposed to the bright light of Laima above.

Once in the square, they were passed by people running in terror from the Sanctuary. Lulu looked up and watched as the entire back portion of the building crumbled to fall into the waiting maw of the desert below. It took part of the wall with it, and an enormous dust cloud rose above the city. As the dust settled, Lulu heard whispers build around her, and people walked unconsciously toward the newly exposed desert to see, for the first time, the line of flames that rose from the horizon.

Sen wrapped his arm around her and moved her away from the crowd and the collapsing Sanctuary. They kept their heads down, weaving through the streets like a funeral procession, followed by paired and somber orphans. Lulu glanced back at Bale, who had Stap under his arm. The two were walking directly behind them, and she wondered how they must feel, seeing the building that once sheltered them crumble into dust. She herself pushed aside the rising panic that threatened to engulf her when she thought about her father.

"Don't worry," Sen whispered as if he could hear her thoughts. "If anybody could survive those tunnels, it's Mikal Destin."

"How do you know?" she asked, trying not to sound like she was on the verge of tears.

"I grew up with him," Sen answered reluctantly.

Lulu stopped walking, causing the boys behind her to nearly collide with her back.

"Watch it!" Bale snapped at her.

"Sorry," Lulu murmured even as she started walking next to Sen again.

She was quiet for a while as they sidestepped another group of people huddled on the street, staring at Laima above. Everyone else on Dalia seemed to be slowly making their way for the ruins of the Sanctuary. Lulu felt exposed. They were walking in the wrong direction. No one else seemed to notice their group though. They were too busy watching the bright green light signaling the end of Dalia and spinning ominously above them.

"You couldn't have grown up with him," Lulu finally said. "He was with me."

"Not always," Sen said. "When you were young, he worked for the Sanctuary. He raised me just as much as he raised you, Lu. When the Wards weren't looking, he even taught me how to fight."

Lulu couldn't say why this bothered her. She knew her father kept secrets from her. She knew that he had a life before her and that she shouldn't be surprised by what Sen was telling her. She couldn't figure out where the feelings of hurt and betrayal were coming from.

"That makes sense" was all she could say.

"What makes sense?" Sen asked.

"That's why you move the way you do," she said.

"How do I move?" Sen asked.

"Like him," she said.

Sen didn't respond. He kept his head down, and they both walked in silence with their backs to the Sanctuary for nearly a cycle.

Finally, nearing exhaustion, Lulu felt a tug on her shirt. She turned to look at Bale, who indicated an empty house beside them. This far from the Sanctuary, houses were mostly abandoned. The population of Dalia was dwindling, or so her father had told her. Lulu blinked up at the house and saw that it was one of the rare homes that had more than one floor.

"Seems as good a place as any," Bale said as if he was convincing himself. "May even fit all of us."

Lulu looked back at the tired line of boys and nodded. Her feet felt swollen in her boots. Bale watched her as if waiting for her approval before they went inside. Sen was studying her, and she shrugged her shoulders uncomfortably before following the orphan leader inside. She didn't wait to see if Sen followed her.

Once inside, Lulu stopped on the threshold. The boys behind her cautiously shoved their way past her, but she hardly noticed them. The house was one of the oldest she had ever been in, with decorative details that seemed ostentatious to her practical eye. The stairs were near the entryway and wound up in a spiral. She stepped forward and placed her hand on the cool, delicate, metal bannister. She lifted her fingers and was surprised when she didn't see the thick coating of dust that she had become accustomed to.

"Somebody still takes care with this place," Sen said next to her.

She nodded and said, "We shouldn't stay here long. They'll be back soon."

"Are you serious?" one boy said as he walked by her, stuffing his face greedily with a slice of palia pilfered from the kitchen. "You're gonna have to drag me out of here!"

"Yeah, we can take 'em," another chimed in, "whoever they are!"

"There's prolly more of us than them!" the first boy yelled back from the next room.

Sen gave Lulu a comically resigned look before retreating to the kitchen. She looked up at the ceiling and noticed the painting above her. Mesmerized by the swirling design on the ceiling, she walked slowly up the stairs, hardly looking at her own feet. All the lights that had been inside the house had gone dark, but Laima's light that came in through the lookouts on the second floor illuminated the details above her. It wasn't until Sen joined her at the top of the stairs that she realized her neck was starting to hurt.

"You need to eat," he said.

She absent-mindedly took the palia he was holding out in his hand and popped a piece in her mouth. The starchiness hit her tongue, and she soon found herself stuffing the rest down quickly.

"What is it?" Sen asked, looking up.

"I think they're stars," Lulu said swallowing roughly. "It doesn't make any sense though; they can't be real."

Stars were only seen during certain cycles of a rotation on the edge of Laima. In the history of Dalia, they had only mapped and named close to a hundred. Now, painted in exquisite detail above her, Lulu stared at a green backlit ceiling covered in thousands of swirling stars.

"I've seen paintings like this in the Sanctuary," Sen said. "They're kept hidden in rooms that I was never allowed to enter." After a moment he amended, "Or at least they used to be."

Lulu suppressed a shudder at the thought that the Sanctuary no longer stood to protect them. She looked at Sen, and he smiled awkwardly back at her. It occurred to her then that this was likely the first time that the former doyen had stepped foot outside of the Sanctuary. She had lived modestly with her father out in the city but had always been free to venture on her own. As disoriented as she felt, Sen must have been feeling even more thrown.

She was about to say something to that effect when her thoughts were interrupted by Stap joining them at the top of the stairs.

"Whoa," the boy exclaimed. "Look at this!"

"Yeah, could you imagine somebody wasting their time on something as useless as this?" Bale asked not far behind.

Sen gave the orphan leader a look that was hard to read, and the other shrugged. Lulu suddenly felt exhausted and left to find some privacy. She found the waste room and found that there was no light to see by. She awkwardly left the door ajar, but the boys in the house respected her enough to leave her alone. When she had finished, she washed herself as best she could in the darkness.

Lulu walked out to find that almost every boy had crowded in the open space at the top of the stairs on the second floor. They were arranging themselves in neat rows with blankets and cloth pulled from their packs. Many of them were already asleep where they lay. Sen stood waiting for her, and Lulu sat down in the empty space next to his feet. He lowered himself gracefully with his legs folded under him, next to her.

"Tell us a story about Laima," she asked him, needing to hear a familiar sermon.

"I am no longer the doyen," he said. "You are."

The boys around them who were still awake watched and listened to them shamelessly. Lulu felt like she was on display in a stranger's house.

"How do you know?" she asked, fearing the answer.

"You sent all of Dalia's light to Laima," he said quietly. "You did it when you touched the wall."

"You destroyed the Sanctuary," Stap said on the other side of her.

She looked around with tears welling in her eyes, feeling the truth behind their words. Bale was watching her critically, and she met his judgment head on.

"You hate me for that," she said to the leader of the orphans.

He shrugged and said, "I never saw myself as a crawler anyway. I suppose this is a more interesting way to die than by fire."

Stap nodded next to him, and many of the boys looked to agree with him.

Lulu took a shaky breath and started to speak. She delivered a sermon that was a perfect replica of Sen's words. She spoke the words like a song that she had listened to every cycle of her life. She had watched Sen speak so many times that the words had been ingrained in her memory, and she found that once she started, speaking them came easy. Her words rose and fell with a beautiful and familiar cadence.

"Laima is our protector from the fire. She watches over us and will one day bring salvation from the darkness even as we live in her shadow."

The boys around her fell asleep to her voice, and she spoke until exhaustion took over. Only Sen stayed awake to keep vigil beside her.

18

Mikal felt the rumbling beneath him and knew he had to leave Tess. Still, he had waited too long to leave her side and found himself navigating through unstable rubble while half the Sanctuary fractured to fall to the desert below. Mikal closed his eyes briefly against the pain after he watched it carry Tess down in a cloud of dust. With a line of fire behind him, he emerged at the top of the steps that now led up to nowhere.

The people of Dalia gathered at the base of the stairs, murmuring and staring at the desert and the fire that was now exposed. As he descended the stairs, Mikal saw the panic in their faces. He searched the crowd for the one person whom on all of Dalia he cared anything for but didn't see his daughter. When he reached the bottom stair, an old woman grabbed his wrist and forced him to look at her.

"Is this the end?" she asked.

"I can't say it's not," he said, hearing the resignation in his own voice.

Mikal registered the fear in her eyes, buried under wrinkled and dust-burned skin. He couldn't bring himself to care.

"He went into the Sanctuary just before it collapsed!" someone yelled from the crowd.

"He came out without a scratch on him," someone closer to him said.

Mikal felt the fear in the crowd find this new current of anger, and he clenched his fists, bringing them behind his back. He did not wish to fight these people.

"It's his fault," the old woman yelled, tears now spilling down her cheeks.

"You know not what you speak of, beautiful mother," Mikal said quietly.

"Don't talk to my mother," a man stepped in front of the old woman, and Mikal stiffened in response.

The man positioned himself in front of Mikal, preventing him from walking any further. The crowd started to gather around them, but they maintained a steady distance from the two men, like magnets turned the wrong way and driven back by the energy in the center.

Mikal looked up at the man who was much taller than himself and gauged his bulky arms and shoulders. Only harvesters looked like that, toiling on the edge of the city to harvest palia grass.

"Move, harvester," Mikal said dangerously.

The man's eyes opened wider, confirming that Mikal's assumption about his profession had been correct. The green light beating down on them from Laima was causing a pain to build behind Mikal's eyes, and he found that the insolent body language of the harvester in front of him was almost too much to tolerate. Mikal rolled his shoulder back and casually peeled back his cloak to reveal some of the shiny weaponry held at his belt. His hands relaxed, and he smiled at the man in front of him.

The harvester took a step back and held his hands out in front of him. "Look, I didn't mean anything."

Mikal nodded and stepped past him to leave the crowd. People moved out of his way all the way to the street corner at the edge of the square. Murmurs built behind him like the buzzing of wind in his ear. The former assassin found he didn't care about the scared and beaten people of Dalia. They were doomed anyway. He only had one goal left in this life and that was to protect the one piece of Tess that he had left for as long as he could—their daughter, the doyen.

She had left the tunnels under the city in the company of Sen and the orphans. Given the dramatic collapse of the Sanctuary, Lu would have been unlikely to stay nearby. The citizens of the city had all migrated toward the danger, but he had taught his daughter better than that. For that matter, he had also instructed Sen better than that.

Thinking about his daughter and Sen together, Mikal shook his head at the irony. He trotted down the street he and Lu had lived on for the past five rotations and found it to be mostly abandoned. The stragglers that stayed behind had shut themselves inside their homes to wait out the apocalyptic green light of Laima, and Mikal glimpsed silhouettes of their scared faces shuttered inside.

He stopped at his own doorstep and examined the edges of the doorframe for a brief moment to ensure no one else had gone inside. Lulu knew about the loose edge and made sure to put it back in place every time she entered or left. She had been so well trained that she did it unconsciously. Mikal entered the home they had shared to find it empty though. It had been too much to hope that they would go there.

Mikal took the opportunity to change his clothes and recharge his energy weapons while methodically checking and replacing the blades he carried. Once everything had been checked to his satisfaction, he lay down to sleep for the first time in cycles. He had always had an internal clock that wouldn't let him drift for longer than absolutely necessary. While Mikal chafed at the delay, he knew his daughter was safe with Sen—for the moment.

He dreamt of a boy who thought he was the doyen, caged in a Sanctuary to serve a planet with abilities he would never possess. It was Mikal's fault.

He awoke a quarter cycle later and lay still, allowing his eyes to adjust to the light filtering in from outside. Mikal had imagined Tess lying next to him on waking every cycle since he had known her, but this time she was nowhere to be found, not even in his brain. He was empty. Fully dressed, he sat up on the edge of the bed and walked to the door. He didn't know where to start looking for his daughter, but he knew he had to keep moving.

Closing the door, his fingers moved to replace the loose piece on the edge, but they froze to find it had already been moved.

Mikal froze for a moment, considering his next move, keeping his face carefully impassive in the green light outside of his door. Someone had tried to come inside while he had been sleeping. It was not his daughter. He casually adjusted his belt and closed the door behind him, taking off at a leisurely trot toward the edge of the city. He made himself seem distracted, but his eyes searched everywhere.

The light exposed everything in his path, and the dust that had coated everything in a grimy layer was visible even from a distance. It was as if the city itself had been bathed in corruption that was now made obvious in Laima's light. It was disgusting.

Mikal saw the movement behind him in his peripheral vision and heard the heavy footfall of the crawler. He slowed his gait, allowing his follower to catch up. He turned into the center of a wide street and slid to an abrupt stop, pulling an energy gun from his jacket and spinning on his heel to point it at the street corner. The whining charge of the weapon sounded too loud in the empty street, pinging off the stone and abandoned buildings lining the sides. There was no help for it.

"Show yourself!" Mikal called to the empty air.

After a moment, a crawler appeared on the corner. He did not hold his hands up in surrender, and he did not show fear or reluctance.

Mikal relaxed his hand slightly, but he held it on the unarmed beast in front of him. Like all crawlers, the man who appeared too large for his own frame gazed at him with black eyes that had been adapted to the darkness. This one was squinting painfully in the green light.

"I don't hear them," he said in a gravelly voice through shredded vocal cords.

Mikal lowered his weapon. They hardly ever talked, and when they did, it was mostly the words of the Wards that spoke through their mouths. This was not a Ward speaking. If Mikal didn't know any better, this one sounded afraid.

"Crawlers can't feel fear," he said quietly to himself.

The crawler tilted his head and blinked.

"Is that what this is?" he asked. "I had forgotten."

"You don't hear the Wards?" Mikal asked.

The crawler shook his head and swallowed painfully as though his voice hurt from speaking so much.

"They are not all dead," Mikal said, thinking of Lana leaving the ruins of the Sanctuary.

"Why can't I hear them?" the crawler asked.

"I don't know, but you should go find them and ask yourself," Mikal said.

"I don't want to," the crawler said lamely.

Mikal blinked at it. In the all the rotations he had worked for the Sanctuary, he had never seen a crawler want anything for itself. It had always seemed that they were incapable of self-awareness. Tools of the Wards and soldiers of the Sanctuary, they were not alive anymore.

"Then do what you want?" Mikal asked callously.

He turned and continued to make his way through the city, looking for any sign of his daughter or Sen. He had barely reached the end of the street when he heard the footfalls of the crawler behind him. He turned to see him slow down as he did. He stopped and waited for Mikal to move again, squinting at him with no expression on his face.

Mikal shook his head. He did not have time to babysit a lost crawler.

"Go back to the Sanctuary!" he yelled harshly.

"That is not what I want," the crawler said.

Mikal did not have a response. He stared at the crawler for a moment before reaching a decision. He turned and continued his search through the city— the heavy and even footfalls of a misplaced crawler not far behind him.

19

Lulu woke to the sound of snoring and the harsh green light of Laima's fire cyclone pouring in through the lookouts. For a moment, she was disoriented and didn't know where she was. She sat up quickly and looked down to see that she had been resting her head in Sen's lap. He was still asleep, leaning against the wall behind him. Around them lay the source of the snoring. Orphan boys had strewn themselves about the room, making themselves comfortable on the floor around her. She was surrounded.

Lulu studied Sen's face in the light. He looked the same as he did when he was an untouchable doyen, speaking to the masses on the steps of the infallible Sanctuary. That was only cycles ago, but Lulu felt like she had aged a lifetime since then. She had been certain that Sen would never have looked twice at her in the crowd. She had been no one. Looking at the bright light outside, she couldn't help but think it would have been better for Dalia had she remained that way.

Lulu carefully lifted herself off the floor and navigated through the room of sleeping boys to the stairs. Once or twice she almost stepped on someone's hair or fingers, but her toes managed to find balance, and she made it out without disturbing any of them. She looked back at Sen one last time and made a decision. She crept silently down the spiral stairs to the door of the house. She didn't know where she was going, but she knew she couldn't stay there.

The street outside was quiet and still. The lack of sound wrapped around her like a blanket. Lulu looked up and squinted in horrified fascination at Laima. The fire cyclone that had marked the passage of time since the beginning of Dalia was now lit green. The details of the fiery current were in stark relief against the planet rotating above her, and Lulu found herself mesmerized by it. She stood in the street staring at it until she felt a hand smaller than her own slip into hers.

She looked down and saw Stap standing next to her. He was not looking at the magnificent display above them but was watching her expectantly.

"You would leave us?" he asked.

"You do not need me," she said. "I only bring danger with me." As soon as she said the words, she knew them to be true. "Besides, you have Sen and Bale," she finished lamely.

"Bale ain't nothing special," Stap said. "I would know; he's been there my whole life."

"He's kept you alive this long," Lulu said, not knowing why she was even having this discussion.

"He has to," Stap said. "He's my brother."

"Oh," Lulu said, wondering what it must be like to have a brother.

Children were so rare on Dalia that it seemed odd for a couple to have more than one and then abandon them to the shadow of the Sanctuary. She kept her thoughts to herself though. A noise at the house caused her to look up to see Sen standing in the doorway watching them. Bale was not far behind him.

"Get back in here," Bale said to his little brother. "We don't need no doyen with us anyhow."

Stap shook his head at Bale, and the older boy took a step down toward the street menacingly. Stap let go of Lulu's hand at the implied threat and ran off to stand behind Bale. Some of the other boys started to spill from the doorway, rubbing sleep from their eyes.

"Look at the cyclone," one said, and the others looked up, just as awestruck as Lulu had been.

Sen was watching her, not saying a word. It was like he was patiently waiting for her next move. Lulu looked away and down to the street in the direction of the Sanctuary. She had been about to go back there she realized. She needed to find her father.

That's when she heard it. The quiet of the street was broken by the sound of marching. Lulu watched the empty street in front of her, standing still while the sound of footfalls grew louder in the distance. Sen was suddenly beside her; his hand had found its way around her arm, and he was starting to urge her back into the house. Lulu stood her ground.

"We need to get back inside," he said.

She shook her head. She felt something clicking in her head, like pieces of her brain that had been lost to her were falling into place. She wanted them to come to her, whoever they were. The footsteps filled the street to their left, and she kept her eye on the entrance to her own street from that direction. It sounded like an entire planet marching toward her.

Sen stood next to her, but the orphans scurried back into the house. Bale stayed on the doorstep, mere inches from the door, watching them. Lulu and Sen were exposed in the center of the stone street, but she was not afraid.

Then she saw them.

A man she would have recognized in a thousand lifetimes led the way wearing a black cloak she had grown to trust and love. Behind him, followed the crawlers.

Sen stiffened beside her, and Lulu put her hands over her ears to block out the sudden noise. There were at least thirty of them, and their eagerness to find her washed over her in a cacophony of sound.

"They're so loud!" she exclaimed to Sen.

Sen looked at her like she had gone mad. Lulu realized then that he couldn't hear them. It was all in her head. The sound of them was almost too much to bear, and she crouched to put her head under her arms. The crawlers stopped moving toward her, and they stayed back. She could barely hear her father's footsteps running on the stone to get to her over the roaring noise.

Mikal lifted her in his arms and squeezed her so tight, Lulu thought she would pass out from not being able to find her breath.

"They led me to you," he said into her hair.

"They're so loud," she said.

Mikal put her feet down and held her at arm's length, carefully examining her face. Lulu tried to bring her hands to her ears again, but he held her arms at her sides. He looked back at the crawlers who stood as still as statues behind him.

"What do you hear?" Mikal asked.

"Them," she croaked. "They're in my head."

Lulu felt tears welling in her eyes, and her father grimly nodded. His face showed a brief flash of despair as he looked at his daughter. He turned back to the crawlers and talked to the one who had been standing closest to him. Lulu couldn't hear what they said, but the noise lessened. She stood next to Sen on shaky feet and watched as her father turned to walk back to her.

"Better?" he asked.

Lulu nodded dumbly and allowed Sen and her father to lead her back inside the house. They left the contingent of crawlers standing on the doorstep. Lulu glanced back before the door closed, and she saw them watching her before turning back to guard the house outside. The stunned orphan boys around her seemed to recognize her father, and even Bale had a look of awed astonishment. Mikal had brought an army of deadly crawlers to their doorstep.

"Where did they come from?" Sen asked once they were inside and Lulu was sitting perched on a chair in the center of the main room.

"I don't know," Mikal answered, annoyed. "They found me, one by one, following me until we got close to this place. Then they started to insist on which direction to take."

He looked at Lulu like she was doing something wrong, and she felt sick to her stomach. Her father hadn't looked at her like that since she was a child caught stealing trinkets from street vendors.

"I'm sorry," she began in earnest, but he waved her off.

"This is not your fault," he said. "It's mine."

"How?" she asked.

Mikal looked around the room, and his eyes stopped on Sen. He looked at the former doyen while he spoke as though he was atoning for his sins. Even though his words were directed at Lulu, the apology was for Sen.

"Your mother was a Ward, Lu," he started. "You were born in the exact moment that the doyen before you had died. We knew as soon as it happened that you were different. Your mother was terrified of the life you would lead. You were the first female doyen who had ever been born on Dalia."

"You knew," Lulu whispered.

"How could I not?" he asked, looking at her for the first time.

Then, looking at Sen, he continued, "No one else did though. Not even Lana. At your mother's behest, I went out into the night to hide you in the city. I meant to have you raised by someone else, but I couldn't leave you." He looked at the ground. "That's when I found him."

"Who?" Lulu asked, knowing the answer already.

"He found me," Sen answered for her.

Sen's jaw was clenched, and he was watching Mikal carefully.

"He had been left on the stairs to the Sanctuary, destined to be an orphan and eventually a crawler." Mikal continued, "I took him back to Tess, and we presented him to the Wards as our son."

"Tess!" Lulu said the name of her mother, testing it on her tongue.

Then she looked at Sen, realizing he had no idea that Mikal wasn't his father—until now. Sen had been raised as a doyen, watched over by the assassin who claimed to be his father. He looked like he wanted to say something, but he kept silent, letting Mikal finish.

"I should have known that you would manifest yourself as the doyen eventually. It was naïve of me to think otherwise. I should have never let you out of my sight. If I hadn't, then Tess would still be alive," Mikal finished.

It was almost as if he had been talking to himself at the end, but the meaning had been clear to Lulu.

"I killed her when I released that light," she said quietly.

"No," her father said forcefully at the same time as Sen.

She looked up at Sen, as if seeing him and his actions for the first time. "You thought you were my brother," she said.

He looked down sheepishly. Lulu was suddenly overcome with anger. She felt betrayed by her father for the secret he had kept from her for her entire life. She would never meet her mother now, and she searched her memory for the faceless Wards who had stood above her in that room in the Sanctuary.

Surely one of them was her mother, and now she would never know her.

"You're right. This is your fault," she said to her father.

"Lulu, he didn't mean to—" Sen started, but the look she gave him stopped the words from leaving his mouth.

Sen had thought she was his sister, and now his sudden friendship toward her made sense. That was the only reason he had cared anything for her life. No one thought that she was strong enough to know the awful truth about herself, and she allowed the anger that had been building in her stomach to climb into her throat.

Just as words were about to manifest themselves, the front door flew open. Orphans scattered frantically to get away from six crawlers that burst into the house to surround Lulu. She soon found herself encircled by them, protecting her from the sources of her own emotions. She could barely see past their shoulders and found herself absurdly calmer with them around.

Then, like a gentle knock on the door of her mind, one of them asked a question, clear as day.

"Would you like us to kill them?"

20

It took all of Mikal's willpower not to slice the throat of the crawler closest to him as they blocked him from his daughter. He rolled his shoulders and tried to center his emotions, but it was useless. They had formed a protective ring around Lu, and it was clear who they thought they were protecting her from.

"Lu?" Sen asked tentatively.

For having just discovered the truth of his own identity, or lack thereof, Sen was outwardly calm. Mikal watched him, waiting to see if this attempt at diplomacy with his crawler-wielding daughter would work.

"Lu, are you all right in there?" he asked, peering in between the massive shoulders of the crawlers.

On the outside they looked like statues, but Mikal knew by looking at their eyes that they were talking to each other. He watched Sen try to talk to his daughter and sat back on a chair against the wall. The ring of crawlers took up half the room and the orphan boys were peering at the spectacle from around every piece of furniture and corner they could hide behind. Finally, Sen took a step back and scratched his head. Mikal had had enough.

"Look, you half-brained science experiment," Mikal said to the one closest to him, standing while he spoke. "If you don't move away from her in three clicks, I'm going to drive a blade through your throat."

Mikal knew that even if the crawler believed the threat was real, it didn't matter. In all the rotations he had spent in the Sanctuary, he had never been able to make a crawler do something it didn't want to—not for lack of trying. It still felt good to threaten them though. Mikal needed to try a different tactic.

"Look Lu, I don't know what you're doing in there, but Sen is really worried about you," he said. Sen gave him an exasperated look, and Mikal smiled at him. "He's really upset about everything, just like you. Maybe you two could talk to each other...without the assistance of your large friends here."

"I don't know how to make them go away," the muffled voice of Mikal's daughter called.

"Oh, I'll help with that," Mikal said, releasing a blade from his sleeve.

"Hold on," Sen said, fearlessly gripping Mikal's forearm.

Mikal looked at the former doyen as if seeing him for the first time. It had been several rotations since he had spent time with the boy, and something no-ticeable had changed. When Mikal had first started training him, it had been a welcome diversion. He had been able to stay close to Tess while his daugh-ter stayed hidden safely in the city outside of the Sanctuary. He had left her with a friend who would later die from a coughing illness that plagued many in Dalia. While he eventually had to abandon Sen for good, Mikal had been happy to spend time with the boy while he was young.

Training the doyen had also carried the added bonus of annoying the other Wards. They would nev-er say why they didn't want Sen to learn how to fight, only that they thought it was against Laima's wishes. Sen had been all too eager to learn, though he would never grow into the broad-shouldered, forceful fight-ing style that Mikal employed. The boy had never been one to embrace violence either. Looking at Sen now, Mikal reevaluated his time spent with him.

Nothing had been wasted on that one.

"Lu, listen to me," Sen said calmly into the circle of crawlers. "I've spent my entire life around these guys. I know when they're waiting for a command." There was a moment of silence, and then Sen said, "Try thinking at them."

"Think at them?" Lu asked.

Even muffled as she was, Mikal could still hear the heavy skepticism coming from his daughter.

"I don't know," Sen said. "Maybe envision what you want them to do?"

"You don't sound like you know what you're talking about," Lu said.

Mikal tried not to smile. He made an encouraging signal to Sen to keep going.

"No, I think that's what the Wards did," Sen continued, looking frustrated. "Just try it, Lu. Imagine one of them leaving and sitting in the chair on the other side of the room."

"That chair is too small for one of them," Lu responded.

Sen sighed loud enough to be heard across the room, and he was about to say something in response when one of the crawlers next to Lu moved. Mikal, who had only ever seen them do the Wards' bidding, tried to keep the astonishment off his face as the crawler walked over to the opposite side of the room. He picked up the heavy chair that had been sitting there and placed it on top of his head.

Mikal didn't wait long. He saw the opening and grabbed his daughter's arm, pulling her out of the circle she had been standing in. He held her behind him and faced the remainder of the crawlers, expecting a fight. They didn't move though, and the one across the room stood still with a chair on his head.

Mikal looked down at his daughter, who had a slightly mischievous look on her face.

"The crawler is too big for the chair, but the chair's not too big for the crawler," she said.

"This isn't a joke, Lu," Mikal snapped, still holding her behind him protectively with one arm. "These things are dangerous."

"They're not things," she retorted. "At least, I don't think they are."

Mikal shook his head. He had lived with them in the Sanctuary. Crawlers were machines created by the Wards. They had chosen to lose their humanity in exchange for a life of brutal servitude, all in the name of Laima. He looked at Sen for support. The boy had grown up with crawlers after all.

If Mikal thought he was going to get backup from Sen though, he was mistaken. The former doyen had his hand over his mouth, but the mirth was evident in his eyes.

"For Laima's sake, Lu, have it take that chair off his head." Mikal sighed.

Several clicks later, the crawler lifted the chair off his head and joined his fellows on the other side of the room. The six who had burst inside the house formed a line near the stairs and obediently stood with their massive arms folded over their chests. Mikal relaxed and Lu moved to stand in front of them. She looked at the one who had held the chair over his head and stood facing him for a while, as if they were having a conversation.

"Well, we know one thing is different now," Sen whispered to Mikal.

"What's that?" Mikal asked.

"We can't do anything to make Lu angry."

21

They spent the next two cycles in the house near the city's edge. Lulu hadn't spoken more than two words to her father during that time, and she found herself focusing on the crawlers that now lived inside her head. They were respectful at first, only intruding in her thoughts when she initiated an exchange. She quickly learned that they had different personalities and followed a hierarchy within their own kind. The leader had been the first to find Mikal and the very same that had tried to kill Sen on the steps of the Sanctuary.

Learning that little fact had shaken Lulu to her core, but she kept her feelings to herself. The way the crawlers spoke to her was so natural that she barely needed to form sentences in her head. They understood her meaning before she even finished a thought. They, in turn, rarely communicated back to her unless it was important.

"*Why did you try to kill Sen?*" she had asked the leader, whom she had dubbed First in her head.

"*Lana,*" First had replied simply.

"*Don't you follow and protect the doyen above all others?*" she asked, remembering what her father had taught her.

"*He wasn't the doyen.*"

This, apparently, had been common knowledge among the crawlers. Lulu had no idea why they would have kept this key piece of information from the Wards. Based on the feeling Lana inspired from First, the crawlers had hated their former employers and creators.

Sitting on the steps outside of the house, Lulu now found herself watching the crawlers spar with each other in the empty street. Their enormous forearms, covered in serrated steel, clashed loudly with each contact. Their normally expressionless faces lit up with the joy in fighting each other. Lulu watched them closely, trying to find differences in their features that would distinguish them from one another. Try as she might, she could not tell them apart just by looking. When she searched her mind though, the differences became clear. They were ranked among each other as plainly as if they wore badges on their sleeves.

When they looked at her, it was as if she could see their black eyes soften. The rough pale skin that looked too thin to hold the muscle underneath didn't seem as ugly or terrifying. Lulu could almost see the men they once were.

Sen sat down next to her on the stairs and watched them in silence. After spending time among the crawlers, Lulu found it disconcerting that she had no idea what Sen was thinking. The sound of laughter caused them both to look left down the street three houses down. One of the crawlers was standing still while two orphan boys dared each other to climb on him to reach the top of his head.

The smaller boy tried to scramble up the crawler's back and grabbed on to his tunic, stretching it out for leverage. Sen stiffened beside Lulu, but he relaxed when she started laughing.

"*What do I do about this?*" the crawler asked her, worry lacing his voice.

Lulu didn't have time to answer before the boy made his way to crouch with one foot on each of the crawler's shoulders. The boy lifted his arms victoriously and lost his footing, falling backward. Before anyone else could react, the crawler spun to catch the boy in his arms and gently placed him on the ground. Both children ran off, squealing with laughter.

"That is something I never thought I would see," Sen said, astonished. "What did you do to them?"

"What did I do to the crawlers?" Lulu asked. Sen nodded, and she shrugged. "Nothing. I just told them to do what they want."

"They truly were slaves to the Wards," Sen said almost to himself.

Looking at the crawlers, Lulu realized he was right. The giants were clumsily trying to figure out what to do with themselves. She wouldn't give them their marching orders though, much to First's frustration. Maybe she wasn't the right person to lead them.

First stopped sparring and looked at her then, in silence. His black eyes pierced through her and erased any doubt. The crawlers knew they were in the right place, even if she didn't.

Lulu and Sen sat in silence while Laima shifted overhead. The green light around them highlighted the caked dust and dirt in the city, and the footprints of the crawlers could be seen, clearly outlined. It was beautiful and disturbing to see their shadows dance on the dust-caked stone.

"I'm sorry, Lu," Sen said quietly.

Lulu nodded, not trusting herself to speak. They were stuck in limbo, waiting for something to happen on the edge of an abandoned section of the city. Every other living soul on Dalia was staying close to the Sanctuary. The light coming from Laima heralded change, and that was deeply frightening. It made no sense to hold a grudge toward the people who were stuck with her.

Lulu's hand was on the stone step between them, and Sen's hand cautiously engulfed her slender fingers. He had grabbed her hand before, but this was different somehow. She didn't pull away but sat with him in comfortable silence, watching the crawlers.

It wasn't long until they were interrupted by Bale. The self-appointed leader of the orphans cleared his throat obnoxiously behind them, and Lulu pulled her hand away. Seeing the annoyance flash across Sen's face as he regarded Bale, she regretted the action.

"We're running low on food," Bale said.

Lulu nodded and stood. "We should gather some volunteers from the older boys and go look for more."

"Why can't you get your giants to go foraging for us?" Bale said, indicating the crawlers.

They had stopped sparring and were looking at Lulu expectantly.

"They want to stay near me," she said.

"Who cares what they want," Bale retorted derisively. "They chose to be soldiers. They're made to follow orders."

"I care," Lulu said, realizing it was true.

"I'll go," Sen interjected before Bale could respond.

"I'll go with you," Lulu said.

"No," they both said at the same time.

Lulu straightened her back and placed her hand on her hip without thinking about it. She had been a free citizen until very recently. Her father had placed very few restrictions on her, and she knew how to take care of herself.

"There are still Wards out there who survived the fall of the Sanctuary," Mikal said behind them. "They won't be happy with your existence now, Lu."

Lulu bristled at being ganged up on by the three of them and stalked out into the street. First obediently trotted to her side, and Lulu gave the three men on the porch a look that dared them to argue her safety while standing next to the giant crawler.

"We all go then," Mikal said with a defeated smile. "We shouldn't stay in one place for long anyhow."

22

Foraging for food and supplies on the mostly abandoned edge of the city that had a dwindling population clinging to a broken Sanctuary was predictably frustrating. Mikal was scouting ahead with several young orphan boys flanking him. His daughter was behind him, surrounded by her contingent of crawlers and Sen. The former doyen had good instincts, and his upbringing under Mikal had left him with reasonable fighting skills. Still, he had looked at Mikal askance when he handed him a blade to carry.

"I'm leaving you with Lu," Mikal had said matter-of-factly.

That had settled the matter, and Sen had taken the blade and hidden it in his belt. Mikal had been grateful to see he held it properly; not all his training as a boy had been lost. Bale and Stap emerged from a house in front of him. The boys were never apart, and Bale's serious nature was in sharp contrast to his younger brother's lightheartedness.

"Anything?" Mikal asked, trotting up to them.

"Not much," Stap said, swallowing a mouthful of candies he had pilfered.

"I see," Mikal said sternly.

Stap finished swallowing. "Well, not much for anyone else."

The boy grinned and ran off, followed by Bale, who shook his head, resigned to his brother's antics. They had been forced to travel further toward the inner city and the ruins of the Sanctuary. Most of the outer houses had been picked clean by scavengers. With every step, Mikal felt his nerves fraying with the inevitability of facing the Wards and the life they had left behind.

Not for the first time, he considered stealing away with Lu in the night. It would be much easier to conceal themselves if they didn't have so many others with them. He knew his daughter wouldn't leave them though. In the short time since the fall of the Sanctuary, Lu had certainly acquired a loyal following. Even Bale, for all his blustering, regarded Lu with awe and respect when he thought she wasn't looking. Mikal was damned to stay tethered to a bunch of orphans and crawlers.

The houses that lined the once-busy streets of Dalia had their doors flung and left open carelessly. Belongings and clothes had been rummaged through and left to spill out onto the streets like so many guts. The people of Dalia had obviously left in a hurry. Mikal looked up and noted the angle of Laima. They should surely have seen someone by now. They were merely half a cycle's walk from the Sanctuary now.

Mikal slowed and turned back abruptly, leaving Stap and Bale inside the house ahead of him. He realized that he had grown used to the quiet edge of the city and hadn't noticed when they should have started seeing people again. Instead of the busy streets circling the Sanctuary, there was no one. The feeling that had been growing inside his stomach was now demanding attention, and he quickly trotted back to find his daughter.

He came upon Lu standing in the middle of the street with Sen by her side. She was ringed by six crawlers while the rest were searching surrounding houses. Mikal had a sneaking suspicion that the six who stayed with her now were the same six who had surrounded her inside the house. He would have no way of telling them apart though. He was still getting used to seeing them so close to his daughter.

"Have you seen anyone?" Sen asked as Mikal approached them.

Apparently, he was feeling the same uneasiness that Mikal was. He shook his head, and Lu gave him a worried look.

"I'm going to send the orphans back to you," Mikal said. "Stay here until I return."

"Where are you going?" Lu asked.

"The Sanctuary," he said, ignoring the flash of protest in her eyes. "I'll be fine. I do know how to take care of myself."

Lu hugged him then, and he smoothed back her long black hair, looking over her head to meet Sen's eyes. The former doyen clearly understood the directive; protect his daughter at all costs. He pushed her back and held her at arm's length. Against all odds, she had become an adult.

Mikal turned from her without another word and trotted back to the street where he had left the orphans. Bale quickly understood the situation and released a short series of whistles between his teeth. Orphans started appearing from alleys and houses up and down the street to join him. Mikal kept the smirk off his face. Bale already had a big ego, and it wouldn't help to let him know that Mikal was impressed with his little operation.

He took off at an easy stride by himself, heading down the now familiar street toward the ruins of the Sanctuary. It was only three streets down that Mikal heard the characteristic footfalls of a crawler following him. He turned to see the crawler maintaining a respectful distance but keeping pace with him.

"Lu." Mikal sighed.

His daughter would have the last word, and now he was stuck with a crawler for backup. Stealth was no longer an option. He slowed to allow the giant to catch up to him.

"She's keeping tabs on me, eh?" he asked, not expecting an answer.

The crawler shrugged slightly in answer, and they both turned toward the Sanctuary. As they drew nearer, the feeling of uneasiness spread down the back of Mikal's neck, and he found himself loosening an energy gun in his belt. They were two streets away from the square in front of the Sanctuary when the crawler suddenly grabbed Mikal's arm and pulled him into the shadows between two houses.

Mikal was so on edge that he nearly pulled a gun on the crawler. The giant had him crouched in the dust-and-dirt-layered alleyway, and Mikal felt his enormous hand enveloping his shoulder, keeping his trigger arm still. They waited in silence for several clicks before Mikal turned on the crawler.

"Is this your idea of fun?" he whispered.

The crawler squeezed his shoulder but otherwise ignored him. The alleyway was a tight fit for Mikal, and the giant bearing down on him was almost too much to bear. He reached down to pull the crawler's foot out from under him when a noise stayed his hand. It came from the street in the direction of the Sanctuary. As the noise grew louder, Mikal closed his eyes to listen. It was two men talking to each other. Their conversation was broken by intermittent laughter that was in stark contrast to their desolate surroundings.

"I don't know why he's making us search the city anyway," one of the men exclaimed in frustration.

"It's stupid; we already have the Wards...or what's left of them." The other commiserated.

"Can you believe that some of them actually thought Laima would save them?" the first one asked.

The other man guffawed.

Mikal listened to their footsteps drawing closer, and he crouched further into the grime, hunching his black cloak over his shoulders. He could hide himself, but the giant crawler behind him was another story. The two men walked noisily toward their alcove, and Mikal drew a deep breath.

"Tek was right," one of the men said more seriously. "These people have been isolated for too long."

They were almost on top of them at that point.

"We should have just ignored the beacon," the other replied. "Could you imagine the Capitol's reaction if we had just kept going?"

Mikal tensed when he saw them saunter past the alley. Their clean red boots were an affront to the dust of the cobblestone they walked on. The remainder of their matching uniforms was black except for one stripe down the left sleeve. It wasn't their unusual dress that made him almost start though. It was their skin. These men were not the pale white of Dalia.

Their skin had a slightly golden hue that made them look like aliens. Even as they spoke Laima's tongue in front of him, Mikal was convinced these people were not from the planet Dalia.

The crawler behind him tensed at the sight of the men, and Mikal felt his own pulse quicken with adrenaline. His foot shifted beneath him, and the two men on the street suddenly stopped. One brought his hand forward with a small metallic triangle in hand. He looked right into the alley and fired a quick pulse shot into the wall next to Mikal's head. He glanced up and saw a black scorch mark that was three times the size of anything his weapons could have produced.

"Step forward, citizens!" the other one called with a calm voice of authority.

Mikal made a quick decision and released his belt to fall quietly in the dust underneath him. He stood in one fluid motion, dropping the blade in his left sleeve to fall softly next to the belt. He walked forward and kept a hand out behind him, urging the crawler to cooperate with him.

"I'm just a harvester from the edge," he said. "I came this way to seek answers from the Sanctuary about why Laima's lit up green. I don't want any trouble."

He emerged into the light and drew back his hood, trying to convey fear and respect on his face. The two men seemed preoccupied with the monster behind him, and as the crawler emerged into the light, they both took a concerted step back.

Mikal looked up at the crawler and said, "Don't mind him; he's my mute helper in the fields. Couldn't hurt a chitling." He was referring to the small rodents that plagued harvesters.

"He's been tampered," one of the men whispered.

The other nodded, clearly disturbed by the crawler. Mikal tried hard to keep a dumb expression on his face. He had never heard the word "tampered" and searched his memories in the Sanctuary of the Wards talking about their genetically manipulated giants.

"We have to bring them to Tek," one of the men said.

The other sighed and said, "I know." He looked at Mikal and asked, "Will that one follow you?"

He gestured at the crawler with his small energy gun, and Mikal nodded. "This one follows me everywhere, even when I don't want him to!"

"Fine then, follow my comrade here," he said, purposefully placing himself behind the crawler as they started walking back toward the Sanctuary and away from Mikal's daughter.

23

"This is where you lived?" Sen asked.

"I know it's not much to look at, but it was home for us," Lulu said defensively.

They were standing in the middle of the small living room she and her father had occupied for the past several rotations. The orphans had unashamedly emptied out her closets of all their food, and the place looked slightly ransacked. Lulu had changed her clothes and had grabbed a small bag, stuffing it full of more.

She also slipped on a bracelet her father had given her when she small. The simple band had scrollwork etched into it, reminding Lulu of the fire cyclone on Laima. It was too precious to wear every day, but she would not leave it behind now. Now she absentmindedly toyed with it while Sen inspected what had once been her life.

"I didn't mean anything bad, Lu," he said, noticing her discomfort. "It's just that the assassin of the Sanctuary lived differently than I had imagined."

"Well, what did you imagine then?" she asked roughly. Mikal was her father, not the assassin of the Sanctuary.

"I just thought he would have all kinds of secret passageways with weapons stored in alcoves and stuff like that." He shrugged uncomfortably.

"He has a chest for his weapons," she said, realizing how unimpressive that sounded.

Sen awkwardly took her hand to stop it from fidgeting with her bracelet, and Lulu blushed.

"Are we going to stay here until cyclone?" Bale asked from behind Lulu, and she startled.

The leader of the orphans looked at her casually, as if everybody was waiting for her.

"Mikal said we should wait," Sen snapped.

"Mikal's not the doyen," Bale said calmly. "She is."

Lulu was about to reply when First burst in through the small doorway from the street. The crawler looked distressed, and Lulu released Sen's hand to focus on what was going on with him. The crawler she had sent to keep an eye on her father was still with him, but they weren't alone anymore. The images were forced and hazy in her brain. This was the first time they tried to show her what they saw, and she almost fell with the double vision that hit her.

Bale caught her, but Sen's voice steadied her. "Close your eyes, Lu. That's what I always saw the Wards do at first."

She closed her eyes, and the street her father was walking on opened before her. He was okay, but he walked with his hands up in the air behind a golden-skinned man with bright red boots. The crawler's emotions dripped concern for their situation, and he practically itched to kill the man in front of them. Lulu felt a sharp stab in her side that caused the crawler to look back at the man behind them. He had prodded him with a thin rod that lit with power in his hand. Lulu suspected it had released no small amount of energy at the resilient crawler.

The crawler released her then, and she felt the pressure behind her eyes bloom back into her head painfully. Lulu looked at First and asked, "Why did he force me away?"

"*You felt pain, little sister,*" he replied simply in her mind.

She looked at Sen, who was looking at her with a mix of curiosity and concern. "We have to go now," she said, trying to swallow past the headache.

"Where?" Bale asked.

"They have Mikal and Five," she said, gathering her bag and cloak in her arms.

"Five?" Bale asked with a scoff. "Is that what you call them? Numbers?"

"In my head," Lulu answered, waving him off. "I don't care what you do. I'm going after them."

She stood at the door of the home her father and she had shared and looked at it one last time before turning out into the street. First and Sen both flanked her on either side, and she started off at a trot toward the Sanctuary, ringed by the other crawlers. It wasn't long before she heard Bale's whistle, and she knew the orphans weren't far behind them.

As they drew close to where she had last seen her father through Five's eyes, Sen pulled ahead and put his hand in front of her to slow them down.

"We should go around to the other side of the square," he said. "There are too many of us to approach unseen from this direction."

"He's right," Bale said, joining them. "Follow us, we know the way."

Bale and Stap took off right, and the other orphans scattered ahead. Lulu caught her breath for a moment before following them at a ground-eating pace. As they led her through the seedy narrow streets that ringed the shanties, she looked up briefly to see the cyclone of Laima appearing overhead. Its green light that had seemed so bright the previous cycle now shone sickly overhead. Lulu slowed when she saw Stap step out into the middle of the street with his arms out. He was waving for them to be silent.

Lulu looked back to see the crawlers practically melt into the shadows with their black eyes giving no reflection. She walked ahead with Sen, feeling her throat burn from the dust they had breathed in while running. Stap led them to a small shanty, and they climbed over the back of it to find Bale already on the unstable roof. He was lying on his belly, watching the square that opened up in front of the Sanctuary before them.

The ruins of the once-impervious Sanctuary pierced the green backlit sky like broken black claws, but Lulu's eyes barely registered the sight. She only saw the square in front of her.

"What in Laima's name?" Sen whispered next to her.

Lulu felt her stomach clench even as she lay down on her belly next to Bale. Hundreds of Dalians had been herded into the square to stand in front of an enormous metallic structure that perched on the broken wall next to the Sanctuary. It was in the shape of an insect with thin arms and legs, grabbing the wall with talons. It reflected the light around it to blend with the stone in front of it and the desert behind it. If Lulu shifted her gaze on it, her eyes slipped off the top to the horizon and the dust cloud beyond. It was at least the size of the Sanctuary itself.

"That didn't come from Dalia," Bale said, his shaking voice betraying his fear.

The people who stood were walking in circles, pacing the perimeter of the square. Others huddled together in the middle for comfort while still others sat alone, watching the metallic structure in front of them. The Dalians were strangely quiet, with only a nondistinctive murmur emanating from the crowd.

"Why don't they leave?" Stap asked.

"They can't," Sen said, pointing to the golden-skinned men lining the perimeter of the square.

Their complexions set them apart so starkly from the porcelain Dalians that they almost looked like a different species. They held the black rods across their chests menacingly, and even from her vantage point, Lulu could see the light of energy envelope the hands that held them. The people who paced the edge of the square kept their distance from the red-boots. Lulu felt bile rising in her throat at the sight of so many Dalians kept prisoner.

"There he is," Stap whispered and pointed.

Lulu followed the boy's finger toward the metallic monstrosity and saw the crowd peeling away from four figures heading for the structure. Two were red-boots, one was her crawler, and the fourth was a black-cloaked assassin calmly walking through the crowd for all the world as if it was his idea to be there.

She watched in horror as her father was led into the waiting black maw underneath the structure. Once the red-boots behind him disappeared into the darkness, she slid backward, scraping her belly on the edge of the roof to land lightly on her feet. Sen was not far behind her, and he put his hand tentatively on her shoulder to still her. She hadn't even realized she was pacing in the tight alleyway.

"Lu," he said, "you're building power."

Lulu could feel her fingertips vibrating and tried to focus on Sen.

"You look like a Ward," he continued cautiously.

"I do?" she asked, pulling her shoulder away from his touch.

She tried to focus on her breathing like her father had taught her to and quickly found a calm center. She turned back to Sen and noticed the agitated crawlers who had crowded into the alleyway behind the shanty. The orphans backed away, nervously giving them space. Sen stood still, watching her like she was a cornered animal.

"I'm fine," she said, more to herself than anyone else. "We have to figure out how to get them out of there."

"You want to get them out of that thing?" Bale asked, still crouched on the roof of the shanty.

Lulu looked up at him with a look that she thought might make a Ward proud.

He flinched slightly and put his hands up placatingly. "We're with you," he said. "I just wanted to confirm."

Stap snickered next to him, and his brother cuffed him over the head.

"Can you see what it's like in there?" Sen asked.

Lulu looked at First before closing her eyes to focus. She found Five quickly and saw the mild-green hue of the lights inside the structure. They were being led down a long hallway, intersected at right angles every ten steps. Her father looked calm and didn't fidget or struggle. Lulu felt like the noise around her was muffled and off. The crawler looked down, and she saw that they walked on a soft padded floor. Having grown up with the constant echo of stone and rock under her feet, this change alone was disorienting. The walls were not the stone or dirt-caked stucco that was so common on Dalia. They were smooth and clean. They absorbed the sound around them, making it feel like her ears were under water.

Lulu watched and waited, following them through the claustrophobic silence.

24

Mikal counted his steps. He nonchalantly watched the back of his daughter's crawler in front of him. He knew his face was a calm mask, but his insides were roiling. The Dalians, herded like animals outside, had watched him pass by with fear etched on their pale faces. The Wards, for all their machinations, had never confined ordinary citizens against their will. Dalia had been invaded.

Mikal walked into the belly of the strange quiet beast perched on the city's edge and followed his captors into its center. The muffled hallway opened before him into a large central room domed in translucent material so that the swirling green fires of Laima were visible overhead. No dust settled on top of it though, and the air inside felt clean in Mikal's throat. The room was lined with screens scrawled in a language he couldn't read, though the symbols were familiar. It was the same language that had covered the cursed wall in the cavern below the Sanctuary.

In front of the screens sat golden-skinned men wearing red boots. Many glanced in his direction when they entered. Their narrow eyes seemed to slide over him to settle on his large crawler companion. Whispers and murmurs filled the room as the giant stepped completely out of the hall to stop before the center.

The former assassin drank in the details in one glance before his own eyes focused on the man sitting in a raised chair at the center of the room. The man seemed content to study the subjects brought before him with frank appraisal. He was in poor condition, and the golden folds of his skin piled below his chin like a pillow. His unnaturally narrow eyes were almost swallowed by heavy eyelids, and a light sheen of sweat could be seen over his thick arms protruding from the billowing sleeves of a thick gray robe. Mikal had seen enough and decided not to wait on the pleasure of this man.

"You must be Tek," he said, taking a chance and recalling the name used by the soldiers outside.

A sharp jab in his side made him drop down hard on his knees. The soft floor was small comfort, and Mikal used his hand to stand up again, glancing disdainfully at the guard who casually held the offending energy wand.

"It's interesting," Tek said in front of them in a smooth and heavy voice that filled the room around them. "You are only removed from myself by five or six generations, and yet, you have diverted from grace so much as to be made almost unrecognizable."

Mikal stood still, focusing on his breathing. He wouldn't rise to the bait.

The creature presumed to be Tek gave him a predatory smile and crooked his head slightly to the side as he studied Mikal. "It was all too easy to subdue you people, gathered before our building like sycophants. There were so many of you here once, and now you are diminished to a mere fraction of your former numbers. You didn't even bother to explore the rest of the rock, did you?" When Mikal didn't answer right away, he continued as if he had, "Well, no bother, the rest of it is burning as we speak, isn't it?"

"What would you want with a burning planet then?" Mikal asked, keeping his voice flat.

"It's not your tiny black rock that interests me," Tek said. "We've known its eventual fate long before the first fires started." He paused as if deciding whether Mikal was worthy of his next words. "It's not the real estate or even the guard in your possession, though I would like to know how you made one of those."

Mikal waited in silence, refusing to ask the question.

"Very well, then," Tek said suddenly.

He lumbered out of his chair, settling his weight on feet that looked too small to support him. His black slippers hushed across the soft floor with surprising grace, and he stopped barely a foot from Mikal's face. His nose was in line with Mikal's chin, and he was forced to look up at the former assassin. The expression in his eyes was searching, and he calmly studied Mikal in silence.

"I seek the one who lit the planet above you," he said quietly.

Years of withstanding the manipulation of Wards had trained Mikal to withstand scrutiny. Mikal's face was a careful mask that didn't change even as the one in front of him grabbed his forearm with his meaty fingertips digging in between the tendons of his wrist. He was distracted by the pain so that he didn't notice the probe in his mind at first. It wound its way into his thoughts and spun them from the present back to the moment when the doyen lit the wall in the cavern. Mikal sucked in a ragged breath and closed his mind before his daughter's face was conjured in his mind's eye.

"You will not touch the doyen!" A voice ragged from disuse spoke to his side.

Trapped in Tek's grip, Mikal had almost forgotten about the stoic crawler. Now he looked at him and shook his head sharply, hoping to avoid a fight they couldn't possibly win. The men ringing the room had risen to their feet as Tek had stood, and they now closed around them like a noose.

The crawler ignored Mikal's signal and grabbed the wand held at his side by the energy spark. His fingers gripped the weapon, and the smell of burnt flesh permeated the room even as the crawler tightened his grip to wrestle the weapon free from its shocked owner. Mikal glanced at Tek in front of him and was momentarily rewarded with fear in the other's eyes. It was quickly replaced with cold calculation, and Tek brought a small energy gun out of the folds of his robe and pointed the tip of the weapon at the front of Mikal's throat.

Mikal swallowed involuntarily and felt the cold metal move up and down with the motion against his skin.

The crawler, who had been incensed in a growing rage, stilled. His eyes clouded over slightly, and Mikal recognized the command behind them. His daughter was trying to diffuse the situation from afar, and the crawler visibly wrestled against the unseen control. Tek's narrow cunning eyes shifted from Mikal to the crawler, and he moved to let the soldiers around them pull Mikal to the ground. Mikal hissed as the edge of the wand grazed his back; he relaxed with two of them holding his shoulders down.

Tek walked to the crawler with his hands held casually at his sides. He moved like a snake, studying the other's clouded eyes.

"The doyen is listening, is he not?" Tek asked.

It took effort not to sag with relief at the pronoun. Tek had not seen his daughter's face in Mikal's mind.

"I don't know what you're saying," Mikal replied with a casual shrug of his shoulders against the hands that held him.

Tek glanced down at him and spit at the ground in front of him. Mikal didn't flinch as moisture droplets sprayed his face.

"You are no harvester," Tek said almost to himself. "You walk like a soldier of the Domain. This tampered one is not alone. There is someone in his head," he said, again turning to study the crawler. "Speak to me, doyen."

"Release those inside and the Dalians outside," the ragged voice of the crawler spoke with demand.

"In exchange for what?" Tek asked softly, a small smile forming at the corners of his mouth.

"I will make myself known to the soldiers outside," the crawler said.

"Done," Tek said with finality. "They will all burn in mere cycles anyway."

Mikal felt his chest tighten with panic. Lu was like her mother. She would sacrifice herself to save an innocent life without hesitation. He would not lose her to this bargain. The soldiers at his sides lifted their hands to release him even as Tek made his way back to the chair in the room's center.

Mikal fingers slid into his boot and found purchase on the tiny blade hidden there. These people clearly didn't employ the use of primitive weapons, and the surprise on the first soldier's face was unmistakable as the metal slid easily across his abdomen. Mikal whirled on the other soldier with his forearm colliding with the other's mouth. Mikal forced the soldier to back against the wall and felt his weight give with unconsciousness when the back of his head snapped back.

Holding his blade out in front of him, he spun back to face others, but they held still, surrounding Tek at the center. He looked to his side and saw that the crawler still held the energy wand and had taken out three men at the same time that Mikal had. He waited precious moments for the others to attack him, but they didn't move.

"Attack me!" the former assassin yelled hoarsely.

Tek smiled infuriatingly.

"You are free to go," he said, licking his lips as he studied Mikal.

Mikal looked at the crawler next to him and saw that the cloudiness behind the other's eyes was gone. His daughter was no longer watching. Without another word, he turned and ran back through the soft-padded corridor to get to Lu before she did anything stupid. The hulking crawler was not far behind on his heels.

25

Lulu scrabbled for purchase on the rough cobblestone. She didn't know how she ended up on the ground, but the square in front of her was now in sight between the shanties. Panic had forced her out of Five's head, and she knew what she had to do.

"They want the doyen! Let me go!" she yelled as loud as she could under the weight of the crawler now sitting on her back. "Don't you have to do what I say?" she asked futilely.

"We can do what we want now." The crawler's words rang in her head with no little amount of amusement.

Tears of frustration sprang unbidden down her cheeks, and she closed her eyes. Lulu felt her fingertips start to vibrate with power building. She imagined the light from Laima pouring into her veins, and she started to feel light-headed. Then, warm fingers held her face, and she opened eyes to see Sen crouched in front of her. His touch was so light, and he smiled at her calmly.

"I'll take care of you, Lu," he said with finality.

Confused, Lulu searched his eyes and saw the pain of good-bye behind them. Her breath hitched, and his mouth found hers before she could ask him what he was doing. The kiss was brief, but Lulu felt the power she had been building diffuse into it, drawing it out over a lifetime. Her frantic energy calmed under his touch like a torch put out in the sand. His hands tensed on her face, and he released her.

Lulu watched helplessly as the man who once held the most powerful title on the planet strode purposefully into the square. His straight back was resolute as he lifted his arms before speaking. The weight on Lulu's own back lessened, and she sat up on the ground between the shanties, enclosed in protective shadow to watch Sen give himself over to the those malevolently holding Dalia captive.

"Fellow Dalians," he called over the crowd calmly. He spoke as he did during every cyclone on the stairs of the Sanctuary.

People in the crowd turned, hope lighting their faces as they slowly walked toward the familiar source of Laima's salvation.

"May the shadow protect you," he said quietly. His voice was laced with regret, and Lulu felt her throat close as a desperate sob tried to escape.

"And you," the crowd dutifully murmured back, rotations of repetition ingrained on them taking over the panic of being held captive.

"We have been set upon by messengers sent from Laima herself," Sen continued resolutely. "Through your doyen, Laima has granted us brief salvation from the shadow and freedom from the yoke of the Sanctuary that once held us."

The Dalians in the crowd murmured among themselves, confusion falling over them like a dust cloud. Lulu absently let Bale help her stand. His hand was steady on her arm as though she might still run yet, but it was too late. She looked in horror at the faces of the red-booted soldiers surrounding the Dalians. They watched Sen with predatory satisfaction. Their quarry had been found.

"Now I command those who hold you captive to release you back to your homes," he said. "Find solace in each other, for Dalia's final cycles are here."

The last was said so quietly that Lulu was sure those in the crowd couldn't have heard it. The soldiers dutifully stepped back and made their way over to Sen through the now scattering crowd of people. The red-boots were still given a wide berth so that Dalians parted before them, heading in an opposite tide. Lulu stood still, holding her breath as the first soldier roughly gripped Sen's arm.

"I go willingly," he said over the noise in the crowd.

Lulu turned and scrabbled up the edge of the shanty, lifting herself with her arms to crouch and then stand on the roof. There was no reason to hide, and she wanted to watch Sen until he disappeared. He was easy to spot in the crowd, surrounded by red-boots and moving in the opposite direction from everyone else. On his way, he passed Five and Lulu's father.

Mikal held his shoulder briefly in passing and said something in Sen's ear. The former doyen nodded gravely and kept moving past them to disappear into the darkness below the metal. He didn't turn back to look in Lulu's direction once.

She stared off to her right and out over the desert that was now exposed and the line of fire that drew closer to where she stood. She watched her father approach with Five in tow. Mikal looked up at her, his face set in grim lines.

"You let him sacrifice himself," she said when he stopped before the shanty to look up at her.

The orphans gathered at the edges of her vision, finally convinced it was safe to be near her.

"To save you," he said. "I would expect no less from the boy."

Lulu recognized the tight lines around her father's eyes and knew it hurt him to let Sen walk into the hands of the invaders.

"What is inside that thing?" The question was called out from a large man in the thinning crowd.

He towered over other Dalians around him, and when he spoke, several others stopped to listen.

Mikal slowly turned to the voice and said, "That is none of your concern, harvester."

"Must be a friend of his," Bale whispered next to Lulu.

"He doesn't have friends," Lulu said.

"You're wrong about that," the harvester continued, staring at Mikal fearlessly. "For Laima's sake, our doyen walked into that place just as you walked out. It seems to me that wherever you go, disaster follows you."

A crowd of people were now gathering around them, heedless of the danger in Mikal's stance. Lulu knew the Dalians were looking for someone to blame. In the past few cycles, their Sanctuary had been destroyed and golden-skinned invaders had held them hostage before its ruins. Little did they know that there was a culprit, but it was not the man standing before them. It was his daughter watching from the roof of the shanty behind him.

"Your anger is misguided," Lulu said loudly, causing both men to look up at her.

Once again she felt the light of Laima building in her like a caged animal. Mikal's eyes widened, and her father vaulted onto the roof of the shanty and made to hide her behind his cloak. Bale was right there with him, and the two coaxed her off the ledge to land back in the dark alley. Tears that she had held in check while Sen was taken away sprang unwillingly to her eyes, and Lulu let her father hold her while she sobbed.

When her breath finally felt easier in her chest, she wiped her face on her sleeve and lifted her head off her father's arm to look at the orphans around them. They were close by and clearly concerned, but they were all carefully looking anywhere but at her. She almost laughed at them but held still when her eyes lighted on the harvester and several of his friends patiently waiting at the end of the alley.

Just as she was about to say something to them, a group of crawlers materialized out of nowhere and casually surrounded them. The big men suddenly looked nervous, and they fidgeted closer to each other. Mikal followed his daughter's gaze to the men at the end of the alley and sighed.

He started to walk toward the group, and to Lulu's amazement, Five joined him. The crawler looked at her and conveyed a conspiratorial smile inside her head, and she blinked. The crawler loosely held an energy wand in the hand that had not been burned. He crowded her father in the alley. Mikal looked up at the crawler and gave him a brief smile.

Lulu felt the presence of First behind her, and she watched the harvesters. The lead one looked up at the crawler next to Mikal, shock warring with confusion plain on his face.

"How do you command the crawlers?" he asked Mikal.

"I work for the doyen," Mikal said simply.

The harvester seemed to consider his next words carefully. "When are you going back in there to get him?" he asked.

Without missing a beat, Lulu's father said, "Before the next cycle. We will need to get control of that." He pointed to the camouflaging metal hulk at the edge of the now mostly empty square.

The harvester looked around him, assessing the orphan boys—many only a rotation from having become crawlers themselves. He looked at the crawlers again, counting the number crammed between the shanties. Finally his eyes fell on Lulu, and he said, "She's the one who saved the doyen on the stairs." It was not a question.

Lulu unconsciously touched the still healing cartilage of her nose and nodded.

The harvester seemed to come to a decision then. "We will help."

26

Mikal smiled at his daughter, trying to convey a calm and confidence he did not feel. They gathered next to the crumbling wall beside the remains of the Sanctuary. The clearing in the shanties had been used as a base of operations for the past two cycles. Bale and the orphans had been instrumental in gathering supplies and weapons. The boys had been surprisingly organized. When young Bale spoke, they jumped to comply.

For the past half cycle, Mikal had found himself in charge of a growing supply of contraband that had been cached across the Sanctuary's city. He tried to hide his amusement as blades and makeshift stone shivs clanked into the pile at his feet. In a society where weapons had been forbidden to everyone but the crawlers, it was amazing how many these orphan boys had accumulated.

The crawlers themselves had been quietly (as much as a crawler could be quiet) rummaging through the Sanctuary's ruins for any remaining energy weapons that had been left behind. Five, as his daughter had referred to the beast, led the scavengers under Mikal's orders. The four crawlers above Five never left Lulu's side. They stayed always in sight of her like an honor guard, which was all well and good as far as Mikal was concerned.

Kelvin, the harvester who had confronted Mikal, had turned out to be a useful yet reluctant ally. The large blond man had rallied many of the able-bodied men left on Dalia. They brought supplies for makeshift weapons out of the harvesting machinery used on the arid ground at the city's edge. The sharp blades in the handheld machinery wielded by the harvesters would come in handy. With the addition of the harvesters to the orphans and crawlers, they numbered nearly two hundred. It would be a desperate attempt. Mikal glanced at the line of fire moving inexorably closer to where he stood. Their fate was sealed no matter the outcome.

He stood on the roof of a shanty looking at the amalgam of Dalians gathered before him. Mikal's daughter crouched on her heels beside him, using her fingertips to balance on the smooth metal roof. Her jaw was set in grim determination as she surveyed the players in their makeshift insurgence gathering before them. Something flashed in her eyes, and she glanced at First. The crawler made brief eye contact with her before looking back at the crowd. Mikal shivered involuntarily. He didn't think he would ever grow used to his Lu talking to crawlers.

She looked at him then and smiled. He could see so much of Tess in her smile that it pained him.

"What do you think our chances are?" she asked, her smile vanishing as quickly as it had appeared.

"What do they think?" Mikal answered her with a question of his own, nodding toward First.

The crawler acted like he hadn't heard them and stood with bulky arms crossed over the front of his chest. Mikal knew better. They were far more intelligent than he had ever given them credit for as an assassin.

"First says that it will be an honor to die this way," Lu said. "I told him that wasn't the plan."

Mikal nodded at his daughter, giving her a wry smile. He was grateful she would be staying behind, hidden in the shadows of the Sanctuary ruins while they fought. She had argued with him for what seemed like half a cycle before finally relenting. In a desperate attempt at reason he had told her that he might die if he was distracted by her presence. Lu had gaped at him, words caught in her throat. There was no good counterargument for that. His daughter had practically stamped her foot as she turned to leave the small shanty that had been their base of operations.

Now thankfully, she seemed resigned to watch.

Mikal looked out over the men silently shifting and watching him. Crawlers ringed the square in leather armor, metal glinting green from the now muted light of Laima at their sides. Harvesters stood in crude lines with arms and broad shoulders built from a lifetime of hard labor. They casually held scythes and improvised weapons made from machinery that had once been used to mow down palia grain. Those instruments that had been used to feed a small planet would now be used in violence to defend it.

Orphans stood in the front now, their silent, thin faces were upturned in grave expectation. Their short lives had already been burdened with harsh reality, and now they would help fight for Dalians who had never shown them love. Bale, bitter and protective of his kin, stood at the end of their line. He now looked at Mikal and his daughter with resentment. Lulu had gotten the orphans involved, and now the boys would do anything for the girl doyen and her crawlers. It had been no small accomplishment keeping that little fact from the harvesters, but they all had agreed it was best if the crawlers appeared to follow Mikal, not Lu.

Mikal steadied his breathing and said, "Now is the time to take back what was stolen from us." His voice rang clear over their heads and was carried by the metal walls of the cheaply built shanties around them. "Since our earliest record, Dalia has lived in darkness. It has been sheltered by the planet that now gives us light from above. To live in Laima's shadow has been our destiny. To fall under the yolk of the Sanctuary was our birthright."

Mikal surveyed the faces below and saw rapt attention in their eyes. "Now," he continued, allowing anger to suffuse his voice, "an enemy seeks to take that from us." He was rewarded with nods from below and shifting of weapons. "They have arrived on Dalia like scavengers preying on wounded chitling." He saw many harvesters wince at the reference to the small, harmless vermin plaguing their fields. "I have seen the face of the enemy inside," he continued quietly so that those in the back of the horde had to lean in to hear him better. "I have seen it, and it is gluttonous. It is lazy and callous greed that was drawn to Laima's new light."

He glanced at his daughter before lifting his hands for effect.

"It may be a new light," Mikal yelled, "but it is a light we Dalians have always been able to see!"

The mass of men, boys, and crawlers surged forward with weapons, both sophisticated and basic, held in arms outstretched above their heads. The shanty he and his daughter stood on shook with the force of their battle cries. The time for silence and subterfuge was over. It didn't matter that the invaders heard them now. They would hear them clearly soon enough.

27

Lulu stood next to her father, and he reached for her hand. His fingers easily enveloped hers, and he squeezed once before letting go. Mikal dropped down to land lightly on his feet. Each man below knew where they were supposed to go next. They had hammered out every detail until Lulu had fallen asleep, curled in a ball on the packed dirt in the corner of the one-room shanty that served as their base of operations. When she woke, she had a sick feeling settle in her stomach that weighed her down and now rooted her to where she stood. Everyone had a role to play to distract them from the death they faced—everyone except her.

First stood just below the edge of the roof and looked up at her. His expressionless face was a careful mask, identical to his fellow crawler, but Lulu could practically feel his concern in that piercing black gaze. She leaned down and allowed him to lift her to the ground with enormous hands beneath her arms. He released her, and she stood on shaky feet, watching the men trot away in all different directions. Her father had already left to lead the attack.

"Well, we better get good seats while we still can," she said to First.

The crawler tilted his head slightly, and she laughed nervously at his inquisitiveness. Lulu turned to walk out of the line of shanties with four crawlers flanking her. She may not have been allowed to join in the fight, but she wasn't going to stay hidden in shadow like her father had expected her to. She led her crawlers to the side of the massive black stairs that once led to the Sanctuary. Now they climbed to a sharp drop-off toward the vast empty burning wasteland beyond.

She rounded the corner and started the long walk up the stairs until they nearly reached the top. The last and only other time she had been up those steps was when she was half-conscious and bleeding on the shoulder of a crawler. Now she sat down on the fifth stair from the top, four crawlers sitting around her like points on a diamond.

Even though First sat four steps below her, his head and shoulders still blocked part of her view of the square below. She craned her head to drink in all of the details of the now empty and silent space that had once held crowded Dalians worshiping the doyen for countless cycles. She glanced up at Laima, so close now above her head, and saw the edge of the green fire cyclone peaking around the edge of the planet. Its fading light still shone down like a beacon from above, and she felt her skin drink in the affects, exposed as she was at the top of the stairs.

As the fire's light rose to light up Dalia, the light reflected metal weapons held in the hands of men. They were still lining the shadows, everyone taking their place. Lulu knew where to look for them, and her practiced eye still had difficulty making out details. Her father's words had filled her veins with anticipation and caused the tiny hair on her arms to stand on end. Looking down now, she felt no glory in what was about to take place, only the heavy feeling weighing on her like a crawler sitting on her chest.

Then she heard the whistle.

Her father walked into the center of the empty square as though he was taking a casual stroll. His crawler, Five, walked two steps behind him like an enormous shadow. Lulu closed her eyes briefly, letting the melody of his whistle fill her with its top notes. It was a melody from a childhood spent in the safety of the darkness with her father. It was a lullaby he sang when he thought she was asleep, but she knew every cadence.

Now it brought death.

Mikal stopped and stood in the center of the square. His whistling was lower now and quieter in anticipation. Then they emerged from the belly of the hulking ship perched on the edge of the square. Their red boots contrasted sharply with the blackened dirt of the square. They held energy wands before them menacingly, and Lulu held her breath as they approached. She quickly counted fourteen of them and smiled grimly. It would seem her father had made an impression on them.

They started speaking, and Lulu sought out Five to hear what they were saying. The double vision came easier now, and she no longer felt dizzy as she focused her attention on the crawler.

"I would like to deliver a message to Tek," Mikal said.

"You should choose your next words carefully, exiled," the soldier in the front said. "A threat against Tek is a threat against the Domain. You wouldn't want your time left here to be cut short, would you?"

Mikal's smile did not reach his eyes as he studied the face of the man in front of him.

"You should be careful dealing with men who have nothing to lose," he said, his low voice almost a growl.

The soldier took an involuntary step back, and Lulu felt the crawler inside of her smile in satisfaction. Her heart rate was increasing, and she could sense the drive to destroy those who stood in front of her. It took all of her will not to snap them in half. Then a hand on her shoulder made her open her eyes, and she was back on the steps, watching. First gripped her small shoulder in his enormous hand gently as if she were an insect he might accidentally crush.

"I'm fine," she said, hearing the lie in her voice.

Her eyes had been so fixated on the conversation below that she almost missed the movement at the edge of the square. Small shapes skittered to take their places, and the head that had his back to her turned to face her on the stairs. Bale shot Lulu a brief savage smile before raising his arm and lowering it.

Like chitlings on silent feet the boys crept along the shadows, surrounding the fourteen soldiers in the square until they were almost upon them. The red-boots were so preoccupied with her insolent father that they never noticed the orphans until it was too late.

Mikal drew a blade, and the soldiers started to advance on him.

Then, like a hive mind, the boys struck from the ground. Their crude weapons that they had kept hidden from the Sanctuary now sliced and punctured calves and the soft hollows behind their knees. At least seven soldiers crumpled in that first strike. They swung wildly around them, searching for enemies that had already retreated to the edge of the square.

Confusion seemed to dominate as those in the front stopped at the sounds of fallen comrades around them. That's when Mikal struck.

Lulu watched in fascinated horror as her father and Five laid waste to those still standing. Five took a direct blow with an energy wand to his midsection, which only seemed to make the crawler stronger. His anger released itself in animalistic screams as he tossed soldiers above his head to slide unconscious across the square. Streaks from their fight in the caked dirt could be seen from the stairs like brush strokes on a painting.

Mikal's moves were deliberate. He moved as if in slow motion while the others' frenetic motions were met with unhurried responses. It was the first time Lulu had ever seen her father dance.

Then the others poured out of the ship.

28

Mikal reveled in the fight. Frustration and anger that had been burgeoning since Tess's death found release in every blow. It was cathartic. The skirmish was over almost as soon as it had started, and he almost attacked Five before realizing that all of the soldiers that he had been fighting were on the ground. He and the crawler stood for a brief moment alone in the square before the sound of boots caused him to turn toward the ship.

During all of their planning, he had hoped that this initial scuffle would draw out most of their reserves. They had no way of knowing how many they faced, and the more they drew out into the open, the better. While he had thought they would lure a large number outside to play, Mikal could never have hoped for what he saw. Soldiers spilled out from under the beast to fill nearly half of the square in front of him.

"It would seem Tek is a fearful man!" he yelled out to the men organizing against him.

Then, he raised his hand as if to throw a blade, but at the last minute, he pivoted away like they had planned. Running had gone against every fiber of his nature, but Mikal would not deviate. He and Five ran at breakneck speed toward the other end of the square. His blood pounding in his ears muffled the sound of pursuit at first, and his stomach clenched at the thought that their plan had failed.

Then he felt the vibrations of the red-boots shaping to follow in an organized fashion. The lead soldier of this group barked out orders to fan out across the square, and they trotted forward in unison. Mikal had grown on a planet where assassins fought causes and kept peace in the darkness. He had never witnessed organized fighting. These men moved with a purpose following strong leadership. It was terrifying.

He and Five reached their goal with the hum of energy wands at their backs. Mikal separated from Five, and they split in two directions, racing through the twisting alleyways of the shanties. There was no rhyme or reason to the orphan slum. Poorly constructed squares were haphazardly placed throughout like a child's hand had put them there. An invader would have difficulty finding a pattern.

Once most of them had spilled into the alleys like water through cracks, the harvesters and remainder of the orphans struck. They had been lying on their bellies on the rooftops, making themselves as flat as possible. Mikal ran by one such occupied shanty, and a long arm reached down after he had passed, viciously slicing the soldier pursing him across the throat with a scythe. Mikal glanced up and Kelvin smiled grimly at him before turning back to surprise others.

For the soldiers pursuing Mikal and Five, the shanties were deadly. Boys who had navigated the twisting alleys struck like serpents in their nest. When they lost sight of each other, the hive mind collapsed. All you could hear was the sound of grunting as soldiers fell to their deadly attack. Once he was in the middle of the shanties, Mikal turned to fight two soldiers who had stayed on his heels. In the close quarters, they were easy prey, and he picked them off one at a time, easily avoiding the painful energy wands that they wielded.

Once alone, he ducked behind a shanty and listened intently for the voice he sought. Over to his left, he heard him.

"Soldiers of the Domain to me!" the voice cried desperately, echoing off the tin buildings surrounding him.

Mikal had recognized the leader and had hoped he would follow him. Mikal's team knew what to do if he died. He hoped that these soldiers had no such contingency plan. He listened to the orders that were being barked but had a hard time pinpointing his location. He met up with Five—his bloodied crawler—in one of the wider alleys, and they both wordlessly crept toward the noise. Five stayed at his back.

Then the leader did a monumentally stupid thing. In his frustration at not being able to rally his soldiers, the leader vaulted himself up to the roof of a shanty and now boldly stood on top of it, his red boots like a homing beacon.

"Soldiers of the Domain!" he called. "Rally back to the square!"

Mikal lifted a blade and was about to release it at the soldier, only five alleys over, when the man fell by someone else's hand. Bale, the leader of the orphans had hit him over the head with a club. The sickening thud of cracked skull could be heard from where Mikal was standing. Bale stood tall on the roof of the shanty, looking down at his conquest with his hands on his hips.

Mikal felt an icy cold dread creep down his neck, but that was the only warning he had. If the leader of the soldiers had put himself at risk in the open, so had the leader of the orphans. Mikal heard the spike of energy even as he was weaving his way in between lean-tos to reach him. He was too late.

Bale fell from the roof with a confused look in his eyes and was dead before he even hit the ground. Mikal reached the alley behind the shanty in time to see the soldier standing over Bale with an energy gun that he had stolen from one of the harvesters. The soldier had discarded his own energy wand for something much more crude and deadly. Mikal swallowed bile at the thought that Bale was killed by one of their own weapons.

He drank in the macabre scene and felt Five pushing behind him with menace toward the soldier. Sounds seemed muffled in his ears for that moment in time until the primal scream of a child broke through. Stap struck from behind the soldier, cutting his legs out like he had been taught, tears streaming down his red face. The soldier, whose attention had been on Mikal, fell backward, dropping the gun. Stap moved like a crazed animal to stand over him, one foot on either side. He raised the blade he carried over his head with both arms, meaning to drive it down into the defenseless man's chest.

Without thinking, Mikal caught the boy's wrist from behind. In that moment, he was reminded of the defiant boy denouncing the Sanctuary in front of the steps the cycle Mikal had come to rescue Lu. The same rebellious eyes flashed up at him accusingly. He pulled the boy off and nodded to Five. The crawler made fast and painless work of the soldier.

"You could have saved him!" Stap yelled as Mikal hauled him off to the nearest empty shanty.

He shoved him inside and twisted the thin metal frame so that it bent at an awkward angle. He slammed it shut that way, securing the warped frame against it. Stap slammed himself into it from inside, and Mikal ignored him.

"Let me fight!" the boy cried through sobs.

"You fight for the wrong reason, and you will regret it," Mikal said.

"Bale was all I had!" Stap cried, slowing down his attempts to open the door.

"Not anymore," Mikal said and walked away with Five in tow.

He glanced back to see that the Five had placed Bale's body in the shadow of the shanty. His head was resting on his arm like he was sleeping. The crawler cleaned his blade on his tunic, like Mikal had done so many times, and they continued the ugly work of fighting their way back out of the shanties. The soldiers had unfortunately heard the command to retreat to the square before their leader had died. It was now a race to see who could reach the ship first.

29

Lulu felt Five's anger as she watched Bale die. She could no longer tell if the rage behind his eyes was the crawler's or her own. She stayed with him long enough to feel the satisfaction of killing the soldier responsible, but then she felt a queasiness start to spread from her belly to her limbs.

"Easy, little sister," First said in her head.

She left Five and looked up at the crawler by her side. His black eyes seemed to penetrate her soul as he studied her.

"I'm fine," she said and took a deep, steadying breath.

Her gaze looked past the crawler and at the square below to see red-boots staggering back out into the square. Many were bleeding, and their number had been cut down to a mere fraction of what they were. Those in the front made it back to the ship, but those who couldn't move fast enough were cut down from behind by harvesters. They cleared the square in a methodical and deadly manner, like the soldiers were so much palia grain.

Her father stood out with the crawler in tow. Lulu could feel the ripple effect of the command coming from Five to all her other crawlers, who had been waiting for this moment. Mikal refused to have the boys involved past the shanties, and they obediently stayed back, though many were old enough to dwarf Lulu's father in height.

"I will not have them trapped in the narrow halls of that padded cell," he had said, waving in the direction of the ship. "A crawler is best suited to the task. Their bulk will block any escape."

Lulu shivered remembering his words. Mikal meant to annihilate these invaders. It would not be enough to just let them leave. As if her thoughts were made into reality, a rumble started in her feet and the entire ship started to vibrate, sending small rocks and pebbles cascading down to cliff and into the square where they bounced. It made the floor of the square look as though it was moving and crawling with the motion.

Mikal and Five started running toward the ship, meaning to board before it left. The other crawlers, besides the four surrounding Lulu, materialized out of the shadows and joined him in a heavy vanguard, mowing down any soldiers who still stood in their path. They reached the wide door before it could shut, and just like that, the ship was invaded by over twenty crawlers led by a methodical assassin.

Frustrated at not being able to see what was going on, Lulu made to look through Five's eyes. She could feel disapproval from the crawler standing in front of her, but much like she had often done with her father, she pretended not to notice. She pushed back the pain building in her head.

Five was once again in the soft, muffled space inside; he strode just behind Mikal, who ordered the crawlers to break away at each intersection they passed. It wasn't long before they reached the main corridor that led to Tek.

Reaching the entrance, Mikal strode forward purposefully, ignoring the soldiers who had stayed behind with Tek as they stood in front of their stations around the room. Lulu tried not to smile at the surprise etched on the portly invader's face as he took in the crawlers fanning out behind Mikal.

"So many tampered men," Tek whispered. "How did you get the power on such a small planet?"

The question had been rhetorical, but Mikal answered anyway.

"The Wards," he said easily.

Tek appraised him frankly. There was no need to hold anything back.

"Your Wards are impotent, and your doyen here is powerless," Tek said, indicating the prone figure on the floor next to him. "It's a pity." He made a sucking sound with his teeth. "He must have used every last drop of power he had for the light show up there. The Domain would have had boundless opportunity for another gifted one."

Tek's words washed over Lulu like sand and smoke blowing from the burning desert behind her. She searched the man lying on the floor next to him for any sign of movement, any sign of life. A pool of blood had sprayed the soft padding around him, and her eyes searched frantically for the source. Almost against his will, Five stepped forward to get a closer inspection.

She ignored the energy wands held up at the movement from the soldiers around them and saw the scorch marks on Sen's back where the fabric of his robe had been ripped. They had tortured him with one of those nasty wands until he lost consciousness. He couldn't produce the result they wanted. Sen wasn't the doyen. She was.

Five glanced at Mikal, and her father shook his head imperceptibly, but Lulu ignored the warning. Back on the stairs, she felt her fingers go numb with gathered light and power. She drained it from the planet above like so many Wards before her—like her mother must have. Only, she allowed it to wash over her so that it stole every last ounce of breath in her lungs and filled it instead with heady power. She stopped herself only when she was sure she would lose consciousness. Stars danced in her vision, and she barely noticed the darkness starting to leach back into her surroundings.

Dragging in a harsh breath, she looked at First. The normally stoic and implacable crawler looked at her warily. Lulu almost barked a laugh. How ridiculous must she look to change the expression on a crawler's face!

"Little sister?" First asked in her head.

"It's time we join the fight," Lulu said in his head, knowing that every crawler left on Dalia could hear her.

As they descended the stairs, Lulu found she could still watch what was happening in the ship even while she focused on her footing outside. A laugh started to echo through the chamber inside, and Five found the source quickly enough. Lana's red hair, which had once cascaded brightly down her shoulders, was now sheared to her scalp. She was bound with her hands behind her back, but she carried herself regally all the same. She was sitting on the ground against the wall behind the center dais with several other similarly bald Wards.

Lulu studied them callously and thought she recognized Mel, the blond Ward whose beauty had once surpassed any of those around her. Now her face was covered in bruises, and the light behind her green eyes had faded. The women who had stood on a balcony bathed in the firelight of Laima now cowered on the floor at the will of the bloated specimen standing in front of them. All looked beaten except one—Lana.

Lana's laughter pealed over the men in the room prettily. If Lulu had not known what she looked like before, she would say that the bound and shaved woman who stood there was regal.

"What is funny, you powerless charlatan?" Tek spat.

"Don't you feel it?" she asked. A sadistic smile spread across her face to reveal perfect teeth. "She draws power."

"Who?" Mikal asked the question he already knew the answer to.

He looked at Five and saw the dull confirmation behind the crawler's eyes.

He grabbed the crawler by the tunic and yelled in his face, "Stay away!"

Lulu saw and heard her father's command. She forced the raspy, barely used voice of the crawler to answer.

"He is planning to leave without paying for the crimes he has committed against us," she said, and Five pointed at Tek for emphasis.

Her father released Five and paced away. As if in answer, Tek smiled.

"We are the only ones who can operate this ship," he said to Mikal, honeyed reasoning dripping off his tongue. "Let us take the Wards and you can have this man you called the doyen and we will leave you to burn peacefully with your planet. No more bloodshed."

Lulu listened with half an ear as she reached the bottom of the steps. Her pace quickened across the square, and she saw the harvesters and the orphans gathering outside the ship. They moved aside for First, and she entered the ship with her crawler vanguard surrounding her. Whispers of those assembled outside followed her, but she ignored them.

30

Mikal pretended to consider the offer put before him. He had to admit, it was tempting. He could leave with Sen and be free of the Wards and these invaders in one fell swoop. What little time they had left on Dalia would be peaceful. All consideration of peace had left when he saw Sen. His only son, for all that Mikal had raised him, lay tortured and beaten on the ground. No, there would be no quarter given to Tek.

Mikal had the upper hand; the crawlers were taking control of every corner of the ship as they spoke. He glanced over at Five and saw that the crawler's eyes were back to normal. Lulu was no longer watching, and that was either a good thing or a very bad thing as far as his daughter was concerned. Mikal had to distract Tek long enough to keep the ship grounded while the crawlers did their work.

"Why torture him?" he asked, waving at Sen.

"The power of some of the gifted ones can sometimes only manifest under great stress," Tek said as if he was talking about the weather. "This one is empty, and my interest in this place has lost its palatability. I should have never responded to the beacon."

"You're right." Lana laughed. "You shouldn't have. We bred so many Wards to make one with so much potential. Who could have ever guessed that that she would do this? Now she is going to be the death of you."

"She?" Tek asked, confusion plain on his face.

"How did you know?" Mikal asked, ignoring Tek.

Lana looked at him with eyes that bordered on sympathy. It was the first time in memory that Mikal witnessed any soft emotion from the Ward.

"Tess told me before she died," Lana said softly. "I still can't believe she had the strength to keep it secret all these rotations."

"She was stronger than you knew," Mikal said.

Before Lana could respond, Tek stumbled backward. His ungainly weight landed in the chair behind him, and his mouth hung slightly open with eyes widened in disbelief. Mikal turned away from him to see his daughter, flanked by four crawlers, enter the room. It was not the crawlers who had Tek shaken though. It was Lu.

Mikal's hair stood on end like she had poured static energy into the room. Her face was a mask of focus and determination, and she directed every ounce of it to the man now cowering in the chair. Mikal couldn't see the energy she harnessed directly, but he could feel it swirling around her like a cyclone. If he turned his head away, it was there in the periphery, surrounding her like a green cloak.

"So much power," Tek whispered. "Wait until the Domani see you."

Mikal's daughter cocked her head to the side, and she studied Tek like she was looking at an insect.

"You need me," Tek started to blather at her. "I can bring you to them, away from the husk of this planet and into the bounty of the Domain. They will welcome you with open arms, and you will never want for anything!" Sweat was glistening on his brow while Tek spoke, and his eyes took on a feverish light. "They will of course reward me for bringing you into their fold, but it will be a minor thing compared to the riches that await you."

Lu glanced at the prone form of Sen and smiled at Tek. It did not reach her eyes, and Mikal felt a cold chill of certain dread sink in his belly.

"I do not want your riches," Lu said. Her voice had a dangerous lilt that Mikal had never heard before.

"Lu," he started but stopped when she put her hand up.

Five moved to stand in front of Mikal, as though to shield him from what was coming next. Mikal grabbed the huge crawler's arm and stopped him from blocking him completely.

Tek looked at her as if she was truly an alien standing before him. "How can you not want the Domain's riches?" he asked. "You have grown up on this filthy moon with no hope of anything better. Now I offer you a life of luxury. What a stupid girl you would be not to take it," he said. "Now I know why most of the gifted are men."

"Moon?" Lana asked behind him, her voice cutting through the silence that followed his tirade.

"Yes," Tek answered with a dismissive wave at the intrusion. "You really think we would use a viable planet for the likes of you?" he scoffed.

"Enough," Lulu said and walked forward to place her hand on Tek's chest.

Mikal moved to stop her, but Five held him back with one arm like he was a mere child.

She looked at Sen on the floor one more time before leaning forward so that her face was only inches away from the blubbering Tek.

"There will be no reward for finding me," she said. "I don't care why you think Dalia exists or whether or not it's even a planet. It is my home, and you have invaded it."

Absurdly, Tek smiled at her. "It's a moon that sticks to a planet fried by an unforgiving sun. You will find that the Domain is equally unforgiving.

You have clearly not evolved far from your ancestors, the common thieves that were left on this rock. The Domain will not quarter with murderers. Killing me will seal your fate with the Domani."

For an instant, it felt like all the air was sucked out of the room they were standing in. The static energy that made Mikal's hair stand on end was blanketed in the sudden quiet. He heard his ears pop just before Lu released blinding energy at the source of her anger. He closed his eyes against it and only opened them when sound rushed back into the room in the form of a deafening crack.

The smell of burnt flesh permeated everything, and all that was left in the center of the room was a melted stalagmite of charred plastic that had once been a chair. The crawler, First, held the unconscious form of Mikal's daughter in his arms.

"She's unharmed," Five rasped before Mikal could even move.

Mikal took a ragged breath and tried not to choke on the smell surrounding him. He looked at the remaining soldiers in the room, their golden-skinned faces now almost as pale as his own as they looked at the center of the room in horror. Nothing remained of Tek.

"Take the rest prisoner," he said to Five. "Find out who is next in the line of command."

31

"We only have enough reserves to reach the outer ring if we carry that many people," Caden said.

The Domain guard nervously glanced at Lulu sitting on the other side of the table, before turning his attention back to Mikal. She tried not to sigh at his obvious fear and kept her face as impassive as possible while she listened to his protests. Over the past several cycles they had been working with Caden, the newly elevated first-in-command, to plan an exodus of Dalia.

Lulu tried to empathize with the young soldier. He was supposed to be fifth in the chain of command and had never anticipated his current position. He was only slightly older than Lulu herself, and his young face already looked like it had aged considerably since he found himself in charge of what was left of the decimated crew. He had a square jawline and wavy brown hair, held back in a knot with a black cord. Lulu had seen most of the soldiers wear their hair similarly and wondered at the style.

"Then our destination will be the outer ring." Mikal smiled viciously at the hapless Caden from across the table.

Sitting in between Lulu and her father, Sen shifted uncomfortably. She had not spoken to the former doyen much since she recovered, but she could tell he was still in a considerable amount of pain from his ordeal. Despite that, his was the first face she saw when she first opened her eyes in the strange room on board the ship they now knew as the *Raider*. She didn't know how long he had held vigil at her bedside. As soon as she was awake, he left before she could say anything. Now he seemed to avoid her at every turn.

"We have been through this more than once," Sen said with a forced calm. "Why do you hesitate to go to the outer ring?"

Caden looked down at his hands, hidden under the table. He seemed less nervous around the Dalians, except for Lulu of course, but he still fidgeted at the mere mention of the outer ring. It was unclear why the shell of planets that made the boundary of the Domain was to be avoided. The soldiers were so far unwilling to talk about it.

"The Domain exists by the grace of the gifted ones that reside in its center," Caden said quietly, trying not to look at Lulu. "The gifted ones talk to the gods. The further from the center you live, the more godless you become."

Lulu laughed quietly, and everyone in the room looked at her.

"I don't see what's so funny about that," Kelvin said.

Lulu looked at the former harvester and smiled. "I have never talked to a god."

"That melted hunk of metal and plastic in the other room might have something to say about that," Kelvin muttered.

First stood behind her, and Lulu could feel the crawler's agitation. Before she could respond, Mikal slammed his hand on the table.

"Godless or no," he said looking at Caden, "you and your crew will take us there."

It was not a question. Looking chastised, the Domain soldier nodded. Mikal smiled grimly.

"Whatever lies in the outer ring cannot be as bad as the inferno that awaits this planet," Sen said.

Looking at Caden's sick pallor at the mere thought of the outer ring, Lulu wondered if that was true.

"We will leave in two cycles," Mikal said with a note of finality. "Caden, ready the crew. We will instruct every Dalian to take only what they can carry in their arms."

Lulu swirled the delicate bracelet her father had given her around her wrist. It was still the only object she wanted to take off the planet—or moon she amended. Sen looked thoughtful before standing to leave with everyone else. Mikal and Five followed Caden to speak with the rest of the crew. The soldiers were terrified, but once Tek was gone, they obeyed orders from Caden without question. If there was one thing the Domain had bred in them, it was obedience.

Lulu had been uncertain of her role since she regained consciousness. Everyone she knew treated her with kid gloves. Those she didn't know treated her like a monster to be feared. The only ones that were still comfortable around her were the orphans and crawlers. Like her, they were uncertain in their own new roles.

Lulu walked through the maze of corridors that was now becoming more familiar to her. It had initially been surprising to find so many vacant rooms inside the ship. There was far more space than could be accounted for by the deaths of the soldiers in the shanties and square outside. Caden had told her that the Domain ships always traveled this way, in case they had to pick up new passengers. Still, they could not have been prepared for all that was left of Dalia to board.

At each room she passed, the orphans and harvesters that had helped fight were now being recruited to help clean out rooms and build makeshift bunks so people could be packed on top of each other. Even the cargo bay above her was being rear-ranged to make room for even more supplies and people.

Lulu quickly sidestepped one of the orphans who was carrying a box of blankets bigger than his torso. The box was top-heavy so that the boy's weight shifted from one side of the other with each step. First reached down and took the box from him, tucking it under one arm.

"I had it!" the boy yelled in protest.

"I know." Lulu tried not to laugh. "First likes to feel like he's helping is all."

She winked at the crawler, and he squinted back in confusion.

"*He was going to fall,*" he said in her head defensively.

Lulu made a mental note to teach him what a wink meant later. They walked up the stairs to the cargo bay and stood at the entrance to the enormous bay. Lulu watched the flurry of activity as boys crawled over towers made of Dalian boxes and Domain supplies fit together like an awkward puzzle. They were directed by a large harvester who stood in the middle of the room, waving his arms like a dance.

She walked up to the man, searching her head for his name but coming up empty.

"*Finn.*" First supplied helpfully.

"*I would have gotten it,*" she shot back at him.

The unflappable crawler shrugged. The boy they had interrupted in the corridor snatched the box back from First to join the others.

"You've done a wonderful job here, Finn," she said, coming up behind him.

The harvester subtly flinched when he looked down and saw who had been speaking. He smiled nervously to cover it up and wiped his hands on his pants.

"These boys are so easy to teach," he said, wonder plain in his words.

Lulu nodded and said, "It is a wonder they had all been abandoned to the Sanctuary."

Finn looked a little defensive and said, "Well, resources out there were scarce; too many mouths to feed." He looked back up at the ceiling of the room they were standing in; it was plated in a shiny metal that reflected the activity below in a bent and distorted image. "The Domain must be bountiful."

Lulu nodded, uncertain after their conversation earlier. She didn't want to influence the harvester and smiled encouragingly. Feeling sick at the enormity of the change they were going to embark on, she left the cargo bay with her crawler in tow. As she and First got closer to the massive door leading out to the muted light of Laima, she saw thousands of black-dust-coated footprints painting the carpet. They grew more pronounced the closer she got to the exit, almost as if the dirt was trying to claw its way inside.

She breathed in deep, allowing the small dust particles that permeated the air on Dalia to fill her lungs. It felt like she was trying to allow it inside her so it could stow away that way. Her vision was slightly blurry with the thought of leaving, but movement on the stairs to the Sanctuary caught her eye. A familiar form was making his way to the top with some difficulty.

She made to follow Sen up the stairs, glancing back at First.

"Please stay here," she entreated.

The stoic crawler looked like he wanted to object, but he obediently stood at the bottom of the steps with his arms folded across his chest. Lulu scurried up the steps just in time to see Sen's limping form disappear among the rubble.

She followed on silent feet, navigating between the unstable chunks of debris. As a child, she had always tried to follow her father when he left her behind. He had always known she was there.

"I know you're there, Lu," he would say before turning to find the stubborn girl sneaking behind him.

Since then, she had grown considerably more practiced in her skills at staying silent and undetected. She found she was much better at it when she wasn't skirted by crawlers. Sen made no effort to be quiet, and he stumbled over the rocks, still favoring his right side after being beaten by Tek. Lulu's father wouldn't tell her how bad his injuries were, but she worried it was only the first taste of what the Domain was capable of.

She ducked behind a rock when Sen abruptly stopped at a small alcove in what was once the main hallway. The charred remains of the doorway leaned to one side and looked like they would fall at the slightest touch. He carefully walked through without touching anything. Lulu followed and watched closely as he knelt in a patch of dirt and dusted a square object with the sleeve of his black robe. He lifted it and held it to his chest irreverently.

Still facing away from her, he said, "I know you're there, Lu."

Lulu's breath caught in her throat. How had he known she was there? Feeling like she was intruding on a private moment, her face flushed.

"I'm sorry," she croaked.

"No need," he said, turning to face her. "I came here for you."

He looked once more at the object in his hands before extending it out toward her. Lulu walked into the burnt alcove that was once a room and reached out a tentative hand to take it. It was lighter and thinner than she had thought, like it would disintegrate in a strong wind. She reached up with both hands to cradle and examine it safely.

It was a singed etching to a beautiful woman with wavy red-shaded hair and piercing eyes. Lulu stared at the face, finding the familiar lines she had seen so often in a mirror.

"It's Tess," Sen said.

"I know," Lulu whispered, running her fingers reverently over the image in her hands. She realized she knew her without ever having seen or recognizing her. "Thank you for this," she said, looking back up at Sen.

He ducked his head, seeming uncomfortable. The silence between them was no longer awkward as they made their way back down the steps of the Sanctuary for the last time.

32

Mikal found him in one of the shanties. They were due to leave in half a cycle, and no one had seen Stap since they had released the door from where Mikal had locked him inside. They had buried Bale along with the soldiers of the Domain in the black dirt in the shadow of the Sanctuary, but Stap had remained hidden, even then. Now, he was crouched in the back corner of a well-kept shanty with no intention of moving.

"We have to leave now." Mikal coaxed him gently.

He had searched for him alone, leaving the task of leadership to Sen in his absence. Stap deserved his full attention. Now, he felt ill-equipped to reason with the grief-stricken boy. He should have brought Lu; she would have known what to say.

"Look," he reasoned, crouching down to be on the same level as the boy but keeping his distance. "I know what it's like to lose someone, but Bale wouldn't want you to stay here and burn."

Stap looked up from where his face had been buried between his knees, and he looked at Mikal with haunted eyes. "He was all I had."

"No he wasn't," Mikal said. "You have us." He was never good at this emotional stuff, but Mikal swallowed his pride. "We need you up there."

"Why would you ever need me?" Stap asked. "You wouldn't even let me kill Bale's murderer!"

There it was. Mikal knew Stap would hold resentment toward that moment. Now he looked at him, and hatred flashed through Stap's eyes when he looked at Mikal. He had taken that opportunity away from the boy.

"I'm sorry," he said. "I thought it was what Bale would have done."

"You didn't know him like I did," Stap said, burying his face again.

"I know," Mikal said. "No one ever will. His memory will live only with you."

Stap looked up at him with tears streaming down his face. Mikal saw that he had him.

"To die here on Dalia will be like killing Bale all over again."

Stap grimaced and gritted his teeth in frustration. Mikal tried not to smile as the boy reluctantly stood. Stap waved off any help as he gathered the few belongings that he shared with Bale in their shanty and wrapped them in a blanket and tied it with a knot on the end. Mikal walked solemnly next to Stap as they made their way toward the ship. The boy held his head high, and the orphans who had been loading foodstuffs from the square all stopped and watched him walk onto the ship. Stap didn't even glance back at Dalia or the shanties that he had grown up in.

Just before entering the ship, a disturbance caught Mikal's ear. He glanced at Five, who seemed to understand immediately. The crawler swiftly took his place to walk Stap inside and ensure the boy made it to his room safely. Mikal smiled gratefully at the gentle giant as he trotted off toward the commotion at the edge of the square. His hackles were raised, but he wasn't prepared for the scene he encountered.

"You will listen to me!" Kelvin roared above the heads of the gathering crowd.

Mikal pushed his way through to see the old woman who had once accused him of destroying the Sanctuary. Her leathery expression held firm and proud as she stood with arms folded across her chest. Her belongings were strewn about her feet, and she stood on top of a blanket, refusing to budge.

"This is my home," she said calmly. "If it burns, I will burn with it." Her white hair stood out on all ends, giving her a feral look.

"No you will not," Kelvin said. "Your sister can do what she likes, but you are not staying behind."

She looked up at her son. His size dwarfed her own. "I only have a few rotations left, Kelvin," she said softly. "You want me to spend it gallivanting into the stars with you, but I know my home is here."

"Please!" The big harvester practically begged, his voice thick with emotion.

"I have nothing to offer on this journey," she said. "I will only be a burden to you on that metal monstrosity. Here," she said, sweeping her arms toward Laima, "I can be a final witness to the death of Dalia. This is the planet that has given us life, Son. I don't care that those heathens call it a moon. It is our home. Your father died here. His bones are a part of this place. Don't make me spend my final cycles away from it."

Mikal watched in silence and felt the restless agitation around him grow still. The woman drew herself up as straight as she could with a spine bent from countless cycles of hard labor. Her withered countenance was proud as she faced her son. He looked at Kelvin and saw the anguish written on his face. Truthfully, he didn't know what he would do if the roles had been reversed. Talking a sullen grieving boy into leaving had been easy. This was not as straightforward.

Kelvin's broad shoulders seemed to slump under the weight of his mother's words.

"Take me home one last time," she said.

The request held a note of finality to it. Kelvin gathered her scattered belongings in his arms. He held out his elbow, and his mother grabbed it with gnarled, shaking fingers. The harvester kept his eyes straight forward as he walked her back into the city. Mikal stood in silence and watched until they disappeared behind the first row of houses.

Walking back to the ship, he looked beyond the ruins of the Sanctuary and stared at the rising cloud of black dust kicked up from the fires. It drew closer every cycle they stayed. As he turned to board the ship for the last time, he wondered how many had chosen to stay behind and burn in the shadow of Laima.

33

The doors had shut. The air they breathed inside the ship was filtered free of dust. It was so clean that Lulu feared she would choke from the lightness of it. She watched Caden, now standing next to the melted metal that had once been a chair in the center of the room. It had been left in that room, which—Lulu now knew—was called the "bridge," like a scar in an otherwise perfect face. Her eyes slid away from it, and she watched the spinning Laima through the clear ceiling above them.

Kelvin, morose since he had boarded the ship, now stood behind her against the wall. The others, including Sen and Stap, stood beside her and stared, lost in their own mixture of grief and excitement, at the spinning gas planet that had once protected them. It would be the last time they would ever see it from this angle. She and her father were surrounded by five crawlers, who also watched with passive regard for the gravity of what was about to happen. It was the last time they would stand in Laima's shadow.

With a certain amount of dread and resignation, Caden said, "On my mark, take off for OR-32562."

Lulu now knew that OR was the designation for outer ring, and she keenly understood the trepidation in Caden's voice. There was no turning back now, she thought, staring up at the soft-green swirling light of the fire cyclone on Laima.

Suddenly, it was as though the planet shifted away from them. In the blink of an eye Laima was gone.

Lulu thought she would feel the movement, even though Caden had told them the gravity of the ship adjusted to the velocity of their movement. It was disorienting to feel like everything else was moving even though they were surely standing still. She looked down as a hand gripped her own to see Stap standing next to her.

"Bale would have loved this," he said in wonder.

Lulu nodded at him and looked back up to see the endless swirling patterns open before them. New stars that had once hidden behind Laima now appeared in endless multitudes. She closed her eyes and saw the painting in the house at the edge of the city. Her ancestors had traveled past these stars, and now she was seeing them for the first time. They washed over the ship, and she stood watching in silence for endless moments until the movement of those around her distracted her back into the bridge of the ship.

Her father had left and was no doubt orchestrating the management of so many Dalians crammed into so little space. Lulu now stood with four crawlers and the crew members of the *Raider* casually going about the enormous task of flying the ship. She felt acutely small.

Caden noticed her and moved to stand next to her, eyeing the crawlers warily as though he was afraid to get too close to her.

"They don't bite," Lulu said. "Well, not too hard anyway." She amended at the look on his face.

"We only landed on Dalia because of you," Caden said, ignoring her jab.

Lulu studied his profile while he watched what was left of his decimated crew. No one spoke as they moved about their jobs. It was because of her that so many had died and were now prisoners of her people. That was the meaning behind his words.

"You should blame Tek for bringing you to Dalia. Not me," she bit back.

He looked at her askance. "You really have no idea what you are, do you?"

Lulu had enough of the cryptic language and turned to face him. "Why don't you just tell me?"

"You're one of them," he said. "You're a Domani, forced through the genetic filter of a harsh environment to evolve past everyone else. Why do you suppose they follow you?" he asked, waving dismissively at First.

The crawler, sensing Lulu's agitation had now moved to stand menacingly next to her, his arms folded across his chest. Caden took an unconscious step back, but his voice was now rising and the others on the bridge were staring at them.

"You lit the beacon, and now you're sending us into damnation itself with no regard for anyone else!" he said.

Lulu had never been able to keep her mouth shut and now was no different. She felt the acid rising in her throat and her fingers tingling with pent-up anger. Her head had been aching since her encounter with Tek, and the pain was getting worse by the minute.

"You don't know what it's like to live in isolation and darkness," she said, looking at the golden-hued skin on his arms. Her own skin looked porcelain standing next to him. His body condition wasn't excessive like Tek's, but he was by no means as lean or wiry as a Dalian. She glanced at everyone else on the bridge and spoke louder. "You people of the Domain are weak and soft. I don't know what the outer ring is like, but maybe it's where you deserve to go."

"No one knows what it's like except those who live there," Caden said quietly.

"If there are people there," she said, "then it can't be that bad."

"You don't know anything about the Domain," he said and turned on his heel to walk away from her.

Seething, Lulu left the bridge and walked into the crowded corridor to find the room she had been staying in. Dalians who had been hastily crammed onto the ship lined the halls, sitting on the soft, padded floor and leaning against the walls. Many had their eyes closed, and some were trying to sleep, huddled in fetal positions. She walked carefully, avoiding their fingers and toes. By the time she arrived at her room, her headache was a persistent aching throb. It was different from the one she had experienced when she looked through a crawler's eyes, but it was becoming more painful by the second.

The door to her room opened, and she found that she now shared it with no less than five other Dalians. They were women, all older than her. Their ages were not surprising, given that there had been practically no female births on Dalia since Lulu was born. She scanned the room to look for a dark corner to lie in, but one bald head drew her eyes away from everything else. Lana turned and looked at her with an ironic smile.

"I mean no harm to you, Domani," the Ward said.

The word was spoken like a curse.

"Do not call me that," Lulu groaned.

Lulu didn't even know how Lana knew that word and decided that she didn't care at the moment.

"As you wish," Lana said smoothly.

The woman's polite bearing was far worse than if she had screamed at her. Lulu spun, ignoring the shifting of pain in her head and left the room that had once been hers alone. The crowded hallway seemed even smaller as she made her way toward the open cargo area, needing some escape. She nearly collided with Sen as she entered the cavernous bay.

"Whoa, Lu," he said, reaching out to steady her. "Everything okay?" he asked, concern in his eyes.

"My head," she said. "I just need a place to lie down."

"That's odd," he said, leading her to the back corner of the cargo bay where blankets had been piled up. "My head's been killing me too."

Lulu looked around the room and saw that every Dalian was lying down or sitting with squinted eyes.

"Of course," she murmured. "It's not just me then."

Years of living in darkness hadn't prepared them for the white artificial light on the ship. She left Sen standing in the cargo bay to find the nearest crew member. She found him organizing large hollow bins against the opposite wall. He looked up as she approached and flinched at the sight of her.

She looked back and belatedly realized that First was still following, at a discreet distance. She waved the crawler back, but the crew member's nervous demeanor didn't lessen at all.

"How can I help you, Domani?" he asked, his voice rising to an unnaturally high pitch.

That word again.

"How can we turn off these lights?" she asked.

"The lights?" He blinked at her, dumbfounded.

"Yes," she said slowly.

"There's a switch on the bridge, but why would you want it dark in here? We keep the switch close to the captain so we can hide in the darkness of space if we have to, but there's no one following us now," he said.

Groaning in unconcealed frustration, Lulu turned to make her way back to the bridge. The last thing she wanted to do was to see Caden again, but there was nothing she could do for it. She smiled briefly as Sen joined her on her way back, and chatter went silent when they both stepped onto the bridge. Her eyes scanned the crew members along the walls until she found Caden's blond hair tied back at the nape of his neck. He turned as she approached, and his face fell. He clearly didn't want to see her again either.

"We need to turn off the lights on the ship," she said, feeling the pain grow sharper behind her eyes as she focused on his angular face.

"Why?" he asked, shrewd eyes studying her.

"Because we need the darkness," she said in frustration.

Caden's eyes flicked imperceptibly toward a metal box against the wall, and Sen walked over to it without another word. He flipped the box open and revealed hundreds of metal switches. One by one, he started flipping them over, and darkness swept across the ship like a wave. Lulu had not realized that there had been a humming in her ears until it was gone, and silent darkness swept over her. A knot that had been about to crush her started to loosen, and she smiled despite herself.

For one disorienting moment, she couldn't see in the darkness. Then, as if she had called them, green lights from behind the glass screen above them coalesced around the ship, shining into the bridge. The crew members around them stared in stunned confusion as the soft-green light lit their workstations. It was the same light that had been given to Dalians, distributed by the Sanctuary.

"Well, now where did they come from?" Sen asked, referring to the soft lights.

"I don't know," Lulu said honestly.

"Domani," Caden whispered.

Lulu heard the note of fear in his voice and ignored it.

"The lights stay off," she said firmly, not even knowing if she had the authority to deliver such a command.

Lulu left the dumbstruck Caden and his crew and made her way back toward the cargo bay. She was happy to see that while the halls were almost pitch black, most of the rooms had small circular windows to the stars, and the soft light permeated through to spill into the corridors at varying intervals. Sen and First followed her back to the cargo bay until she found a corner to lie down. They left her there to sleep in peace, but she could still hear the murmuring of Dalians and crew members who seemed to follow her through the ship. When she closed her eyes, she saw the sardonic smile of Lana and shuddered.

34

Mikal felt something release behind his shoulders when the harsh artificial light turned off. At first, those around him in the kitchens gasped in worry.

"Is the ship crashing?" Stap asked beside him.

Mikal listened and waited. Nothing else had changed. Then, as if called by the darkness, a green light slowly filled the small window that had previously only held darkness and pinpoints of distant stars. The soft glow looked very much like the lights that the Sanctuary had hoarded.

"No," Mikal finally answered Stap. "It's just the light of Laima following us."

Many of the Dalians in the kitchens with him smiled at that and seemed to work on the meal prep with renewed vigor. Mikal knew it wasn't Laima though; his daughter definitely had something to do with this.

Finn, one of the harvesters who had fought beside him on Dalia, had eagerly volunteered to take over the kitchen and oversee food distribution. Mikal had practically dragged Stap to help him and was making sure the two had everything they needed. One of the crew members was sulking in the corner and making intermittent sneers at their handling of the Domain's food stores.

"That doesn't even go with salmee," the crewman muttered derisively.

Mikal walked up to the man who had been casually leaning against a metal counter. He looked down at his badge and read the name before bringing his nose inches away from the man's face. His eyes were set narrow in his face, and he had a nose that was slightly too long. In the green light, his golden skin looked almost as pale as Mikal's.

"Gordo, is it?" Mikal asked.

The man nodded nervously, now standing straight.

"Perhaps you can enlighten us as to what 'goes with' salmee then?" he asked nicely. "We are only familiar with plants and things that grow in the darkness."

"Well, salmee is an animal, not a plant," Gordo answered reflexively and then swallowed and snapped his mouth shut.

Mikal had no idea what that was, but he wasn't about to ask. He merely stepped back and allowed enough room for the crewman to escape. Gordo scurried to stand next to Finn, and the harvester nodded to Mikal, a large grin spreading across his face.

Mikal saw that the sullen Stap had started to helpfully chop the thick brown material into evenly sized portions under Finn's watchful eye. Gordo continued to eye him anxiously even as he started rotating the meat in his hands, explaining how to prepare it. A crowd of Dalians were gathering behind, listening intently.

"The meat has to be heated all the way through to be safe. It'll change color when it's ready, but a true connoisseur knows it's the feel of the meat that tells you when it's perfect," Gordo explained.

"Connossar?" Stap asked, his street slang butchering the inflection of the word.

"Yes," Gordo answered absent-mindedly, "someone with taste and class."

Stap nodded at that, but Mikal knew the boy still had no idea what that meant.

"No, I can't have you Dalian moles ruining everything in this kitchen," Gordo continued matter-of-factly. "If I must teach you, I will."

"How gracious," Finn murmured, and Mikal smiled.

"What's a mole?" Stap asked and Gordo sighed loudly.

"It's you," he said.

"Oh," the boy responded.

Satisfied that they wouldn't starve under Gordo's watchful eye, Mikal left to find Lulu. As he walked through the welcome darkness of the ship, he saw that the tension behind the movements of the Dalians crowded in the halls had been released. Now they slept peacefully or huddled together and spoke in soft tones. He made his way to Lulu's room and knocked expectantly.

The door opened, and he was greeted by a familiar face.

"She's not here," Lana said before Mikal could ask.

The Ward held her head proudly as though losing her hair had been her decision. She was still beautiful, but Mikal knew there was venom behind her sapphire eyes.

"Sorry to disturb," he said with a slight bow.

He turned to leave but stopped when he felt Lana's light touch on his arm.

"I'm sorry for your loss, assassin," she said. "Tess was the best of all of us."

Mikal forced himself to meet Lana's eyes and found only sorrow and regret.

"I know," he said.

"I should have seen it sooner," Lana continued. "That daughter of yours carries a copy of Tess's spirit."

Mikal rotated his arm away from her touch, finding that his shoulder still ached from being dislocated. He smiled at the welcome painful distraction.

"You'll find that Lulu's spirit is less easily manipulated," he said and walked away.

His back itched as he turned on the once-powerful Ward. It was an action he would have never survived to talk about on Dalia.

"Stubborn like her father," Lana called behind him, causing the audience of Dalians in the hallway to murmur.

"Thankfully, I gave her something good," he whispered to himself as he rounded the corner.

It had taken a considerable amount of effort to maintain a leisurely pace with Lana piercing holes in his back with her eyes. He couldn't help but exhale loudly once he was out of sight. Five joined him just as he approached the cargo bay, and Mikal saw that the rest of the crawlers had congregated in the hall. They lined themselves up like statues outside of the stairs, and the Dalians had given them a wide berth.

"Well, I think I found my daughter," Mikal said to himself.

If he hadn't known any better, he would have thought that Five smiled down at him. The giant's teeth flashed in the green light with more humor than menace.

"I'm glad you guys are on our side now," Mikal said before turning to take the steps two at a time into the cargo bay.

It was easy to find Lulu curled in a ball against the back wall. Sen and First sat at a respectful distance.

The former doyen had his legs crossed, and he was leaning against a stack of boxes with his eyes closed. Mikal had taught the boy how to meditate, and he knew, despite Sen's serene expression, he was listening to his surroundings carefully. Mikal folded himself to sit next to Sen, and he focused on each muscle group, allowing himself to relax after methodically tensing each one.

After a moment of silence, Sen opened his eyes and turned toward him. Mikal felt his scrutiny and opened one eye to acknowledge him.

"She turn off the lights?" Mikal asked.

"Just as she called new ones to replace them," Sen answered.

"Intentionally?" Mikal asked.

Sen shook his head. "I can only imagine what this ship looks like from the outside," he mused. "We're like an insect covered in glowing parasitic lights."

"Well, we knew we couldn't just sneak into the outer ring anyway," Mikal said.

Comfortable silence settled between them for a moment before Sen spoke again.

"How much of this do you think the Wards knew?" he asked.

"I think Lana would like us to think she knew about all of it," Mikal answered. "I think that is a lie though. They worshiped that planet as a source of power, and I believe they knew it could be a beacon, which is why they tried to control the births on

Dalia." He studied Sen's face as he spoke. "It's why they cared so much about the doyen. You were supposed to light the damn thing for them."

Sen barked a laugh that echoed off the ceiling of the cargo bay. Subdued Dalians shifted, but Lulu continued to sleep like the dead.

"You really messed it up for them," Sen said.

Mikal smiled, thinking about Lana's bald head. Instead of presenting the Domani to their rescuers like dutiful heroes, the Wards were interrogated and punished for not being able to produce Lulu. Tess would have loved to see the Dalians directing their own fate and taking over the ship.

"Now we just have to stay alive," Mikal said, looking at Lu's sleeping form.

35

Lulu shifted uncomfortably after taking her seat at the table. The food that Stap had proudly placed before her looked like a congealed blob of brown excrement.

"It's salmee," Stap whispered excitedly before moving on to her father's dish.

The stuff plopped onto Mikal's plate with a sickening slap, and her father smiled at her expression. They sat at a long table in a surprisingly large room hidden off to the side of the bridge. The table sat at least a hundred diners, and Caden had insisted they have dinner together. Lulu's father agreed that it was a good idea, and they sat purposefully alternating with Domain soldiers. Lana and the other bald-headed Wards sat a mere five seats away from her, but Sen and Mikal sat between her and them as a buffer. No one sat at the head of the table, but Lulu still felt the eyes of everyone there on her as she picked up her fork.

Stap stood off to the side, his face beaming as he watched her take a small morsel on the end of a prong. Lulu felt the bile rise in her throat and closed her eyes. She envisioned glowing palia grain, the blue phosphorescent tips blowing the breeze with dust settling around them, providing nutrients from the ash. She had never eaten anything else that was alive.

The salmee hit her tongue, and her mouth filled with saliva. It wasn't just a new flavor for the girl who had been raised on a desolate moon. It hit her hard palate with a satisfying sensation. She swallowed and couldn't help the smile that spread across her face.

"Yes!" Stap exclaimed, unable to contain his excitement any longer.

The others at the table laughed, and Stap turned red in embarrassment.

"This is delicious," Lulu said in relief.

Then the table erupted in conversation as Domain soldiers asked the Dalians questions about their boring fare; their disbelief was plain on their faces. For one moment, two universes collided over food. Lulu watched as her people, pale and lean, shared her experience of tasting salmee for the first time.

"Not bad for a mole," Lulu heard Stap say to the portly man who stood next to him.

"You have a gift, young one," the man said grudgingly.

"What's a mole?" Lulu asked Sen.

He shrugged and a smooth voice cut above the din to answer her. "Moles are vermin that crawl in the darkness," Caden said loud enough for everyone around him to hear.

The silence that followed was thick with tension.

"Vermin have the capability to destroy even the healthiest field of palia," Sen answered. "Their intelligence should never be underestimated."

Lulu was relieved the see Stap nod seriously, and her father smiled next to her as he lowered his head back to his plate. Those at the table rejoined their previous conversations, and Lulu winked at Caden from across the table. The handsome soldier of the Domain showed her a brief flash of ugliness as his face contorted in growing resentment. Lulu felt a cold pit in her stomach at the look, but before she could say anything, Caden's expression returned to stoic indifference.

Lulu tried to shake off the sick feeling, and found Sen's calm face studying her. She smiled and dug into the salmee in front of her. Sen smiled back, but Lulu could see that he knew something had transpired. She focused on the delicious invention on her plate and pushed Caden's hatred for her to the back of her brain.

"Not all of us blame you," a woman next to her mumbled between mouthfuls.

Lulu looked at her and said, "I don't know what you mean."

The woman was one of the few soldiers of the Domain who was female, and this was the first time Lulu had ever heard her speak. She wore the same uniform as the men, but hers was impeccably pressed and her mousy brown hair was pulled back in a perfect imitation of Caden's. She gave off the appearance of trying too hard without actually saying or doing anything to indicate that.

"Well, it's just that there is some tension," she whispered between delicate mouthfuls of salmee. "I wanted you to know that not everyone believes in the Domani mission."

"The Domani mission?" Lulu asked, trying not to let her overwhelming curiosity show.

"Well, yes," she said. "Don't you even know what this ship is for?"

Lulu shook her head slightly and tried to study her food with forced indifference.

"It's for you," the woman whispered. "We patrol the outer ring in search of newly fledged Domani."

Lulu turned to stare at the woman, silently willing her to keep talking. Those closest to them were now listening, and the woman seemed to realize they were the object of scrutiny. She glanced nervously at Caden, and her face flushed.

"Maybe later," the woman said in answer to Lulu's unspoken questions.

"What's your name?" Lulu asked, trying to force casual conversation.

"Charli," she said, flashing Lulu a smile.

Her plain face practically transformed with that smile, and Lulu couldn't help but smile back. Despite her uptight appearance, there was something about Charli that was endearing. They spent the rest of the dinner in easy conversation, with Charli talking about the ship and Lulu telling her about life on Dalia. All the while, they were conscious of the stares from both Caden and Lana from across the table, though neither one addressed it out loud.

Once the plates were cleared, Charli asked, "Would you be able to come with me to the observatory?"

"What's that?" Lulu asked.

"Oh, you'll see!" Charli exclaimed, practically bouncing out of her seat.

The observatory, as it turned out, was just that. It was a room hidden behind a small door off the bridge that was enclosed by crystal-clear walls, ceiling, and floor. It was so seamless that it felt like they were standing in a floating bubble. It was bright inside, lit by Laima's green lights.

Charli looked slightly chagrined when they entered the room. "Well, normally you can see all of the stars as they pass by, but you get the idea."

Lulu could feel the other girl's disappointment, and she tried to imagine what it would look like without the light. She allowed herself to want darkness, and after a moment, she could feel a pull in her arms, like the straining of muscles even though she wasn't lifting anything. Then, like a curtain, the lights stripped away from the bubble they were standing in to reveal endless swirling stars surrounded by infinite space.

Lulu dared not move for fear of falling into it, but she couldn't look away. She knew her mouth was hanging open, but she couldn't help it. She didn't even want to breathe for fear of shattering the quiet beauty that surrounded her. She looked over at Charli, who was surely sharing in her delight, and her face fell.

"How did you do that?" Charli asked warily, fear tinging her voice.

Lulu wasn't bothered by the Domain soldiers fearing her, or even her own people who now moved out of her way when she walked by them with her retinue of crawlers. For some reason though, this girl's new reticence felt heavy on her shoulders. Maybe it was because she had never had a girl her age to relate to.

"I don't know," Lulu said.

"Even the strongest Domani can only move objects, never energy or light. At least not without the help of the runes anyway," she murmured. "Did you really melt the captain?"

Lulu nodded, unable to say it out loud. She didn't have the heart to tell her about the Wards on Dalia. From what Lulu could tell, they were pretty powerful too. Charli pursed her lips thoughtfully as if coming to a decision, and her face relaxed.

"Well," she said, "I would never speak ill of my superiors, but he made me want to."

Recognizing that Charli was trying to make her feel better, Lulu forced a smile. "What were you trying to tell me at dinner?"

As if just remembering where she was, Charli started to talk animatedly. "You see," she began, "I was born on the Capitol. That's the planet where the Domani live. My mother—she was a servant to my father, who is one of the Lessers."

"Lessers?" Lulu interjected.

"Yeah." The girl waved her hand as if it was no importance. "The Lessers are the less-gifted Domani. Not like you." She qualified before continuing, "He sat on the councils, but he never made waves. He and my mother had me in the hopes that I would be gifted, but I disappointed them. So did my brother." She paused as if deciding to say something but shook her head before continuing, "No Domani has been born on the Capitol in anyone's memory though."

"Why not?" Lulu asked.

"My father says it's because if you want steel, you have to use fire," Charli said, studying her.

Lulu looked out into the vast empty expanse around them and below her feet. She thought of the fire on Dalia and the feeling of hard despair that came with the rising cloud of smoke on the horizon.

She looked at Charli. Like everyone else from the Domain, she was golden and soft. Her hands, held in front of her, were delicate and smooth. Lulu looked down at her own hands, hardened with calluses and years of dust caked under her fingernails. She made fists to hide them.

"This ship is meant to patrol the outer ring and find gifted people born from fires." Lulu surmised.

Charli nodded solemnly.

"What if I hadn't lit that beacon?" Lulu asked, feeling anger start to ignite in her bones. "Would you have let us burn?"

"The Domain had expected Dalia to be nothing but a black husk, rotations ago, in Laima time," Charli said, now wringing her pretty hands. "We were surprised to see it was still supporting life, never mind that someone had actually lit the planet above it."

Lulu ignored the awe and respect in the other's voice. The expanse around her that had once seemed wondrous now seemed cold and unforgiving. Without thinking, she drew the lights back around them and turned to walk back out on the bridge. Before she left, she had one question that had been bothering her since she had discovered that her life had been a lie.

"How did we get to that moon in the first place?" she asked with her back to Charli.

"No one told you?" she asked.

Lulu shook her head.

"Your ancestors were selected to live there, based on screening procedures," she said.

"Selected by who?" she asked, already knowing the answer.

"The Domani of course," Charli answered.

36

They watched OR-32562 grow larger through the clear ceiling above them. Without being asked, Mikal's daughter had moved the green lights aside so they could have a window to view their approach. Those lights seemed to follow her along the windows, growing brighter as she walked by over the past several cycles. Mikal knew enough to know that she was angry, but he knew it wasn't with him or any of the Dalians on board. The refugees of the now dead moon seemed to follow Lu like a baby follows its mother. For her part, Lu seemed not to notice the growing admiration.

She had spent most of her time on the ship talking quietly with her new friend, Charli. The girl was sweet, and Mikal felt relief that his daughter had someone besides a crawler to confide in. He looked over at her now and noticed that Charli was wearing her hair in a twist—a clear imitation of Lu's hairstyle.

Sen had also noticed, and he smiled at Mikal from behind Lu.

The former doyen also seemed happy for Lu to have a friend, and he had said as much after their sparring match the previous cycle. After briefing with Caden and his deck crew, Mikal wanted to work off nervous energy, and Sen was more than up to the challenge.

They cleared a space in the cargo bay, and the Dalians, along with some of the Domain crew, passively gathered to watch the two fight. They found long metal poles and wrapped cloth around the center to allow for gripping. It was a fair imitation of the sparring sticks they had practiced with in the Sanctuary when Sen was young.

"I don't know if you can defeat me as easily as you used to," Sen said with a cocky air as they lined up on opposite sides of the makeshift circle. "After you left I was forced to work with crawlers!"

"Your first mistake is assuming that crawlers are tougher to fight than me." Mikal laughed.

They met in the center with a clash of sparks. The sound of hollow metal reverberated off the walls of enormous cargo bay, and Mikal found a measure of peace in the rhythm of their blows. He allowed his muscles to loosen between each parry and found the meditative trance that he had been missing. He sensed Sen doing the same thing, and he quickly changed the tempo, catching Sen on the forearm with the end of his pole. The strike must have hurt tremendously as it bruised the bone, but Sen smiled in response, matching Mikal's new rhythm.

Mikal was unable to connect with Sen for the rest of the match, and he had to admit to himself that he was impressed, not that he would ever tell Sen that. They sat afterward, watching the crowd disperse and spoke quietly to each other.

"I'm worried about her," Sen said.

There was no need to clarify who he was talking about.

"She seems angry," Sen continued. "The crawlers are agitated."

"She won't hurt anyone," Mikal said, quick to come to Lu's defense.

"I don't care about anyone else," Sen said, and Mikal heard the conviction in his words. He glanced at Sen then, and the former doyen flushed, slightly embarrassed. "You know what I mean."

Mikal nodded. He understood exactly what Sen had meant.

Now they stood on the bridge of a ship traveling at light speed and watched a deadly planet on the outer ring grow in size as they hurtled closer. The planet was backlit by a blue star behind it, and as they approached, Mikal could see that it was covered in green.

At Caden's direction, the ship slowed to orbit the planet. They looked up at it while it spun above them, and the Dalians on the bridge, aside from the seemingly indifferent crawlers, were mesmerized by the rich verdant green covering the planet like a piece of clothing. It was beautiful and peaceful.

Mikal looked down and noted the Domain soldiers shaking; their backs were straight, and sweat was beading on the back of the neck of the man sitting closest to him. As awestruck as the Dalians were, the Domain soldiers were just as afraid. He looked over and saw that Sen was studying them too. Lu was speaking quietly with Charli, and he walked over to them.

"What is it?" Lu asked the other girl.

"What is what?" she asked in return.

"The green," Lu asked.

"Trees," she said as if that explained it. When Lu stared at her, silently demanding more information, the girl continued, "They're plants like palia, but their stalks are firm and tall, allowing them to grow into the sky. They use the light of the star for energy. We have some on the Capitol. They grow flowers and fruit, but none grow as big as the ones on OR-32562."

"How big are they?" Lu asked.

"As big as your Sanctuary was," Charli answered quietly.

The girl's face was serious when she spoke of the trees, and Mikal felt uncertain when he looked back up at the vast expanse of green now filling the ceiling above them. They watched and waited while the planet spun, and Mikal walked over to Caden.

"Why are we waiting?" he asked.

"We need a clearing," Caden said, absently watching the ceiling above them. "The ship can grab on to the trees, but we don't want to do that here. Initial reports on OR-32562 showed a safe place to land on the southern pole. From there, we can relay a rescue beacon and wait for the next patrol ship."

"How long will that take?" Mikal asked.

"Cycles," Caden said. "We should be fine as long as we stay in the ship."

"What about the people here?" Lu asked, joining them.

"What about them?" Caden asked with irritation. "No one has lit a beacon. They stay where they are, and we won't bother them."

Lu looked like she was about to say something when Charli put a light restraining hand on her arm. She didn't say anything more, but Mikal knew that wasn't the last they would hear from his daughter on the matter. He looked at Five, who was watching the exchange patiently. He would have to enlist the crawlers to keep an eye on Lu.

The green blanket covering the planet above them suddenly gave way to show an oval brown patch of dirt. It reminded Mikal of the deserts on Dalia. Caden gave the signal, and the ship smoothly shifted toward the outer planet. As they descended closer, what once appeared as a modest patch of dirt grew large, and the enormous ship seemed small by comparison. Air pushed by the disturbance of their arrival rose to form swirling motes above them. When the dust settled, they could see the blue-gray light. Lu's green light had disappeared, and Mikal looked at his daughter.

She shrugged as if reading his unspoken question in the glance. No need to announce their arrival like a giant green bonfire. As the air around them settled, everyone on the bridge stayed quiet and tense as though they were expecting an attack. When none came, Caden walked over to a console and turned a switch built into the station. A blinking red light appeared on the screen. Even though it was not accompanied by any noise, Mikal briefly imagined a beeping tone traveling into the vast empty space above them. It would land on the ears of those within the Domain, and the Dalian refugees would soon be at their mercy.

The gray light soon proved itself to be a dawn, giving way to bright blue light that seeped into the windows of the ship, leaking into corners and making the fair skin of the Dalians on board seem even lighter. Over the next cycle, the people who had known only a dark moon, which hid in the shadow of a giant gas planet, huddled near any window they could find. They basked in the new natural light that suffused the ship. The crew members of the Domain were a study in opposing behavior. They stuck to the shadows and were out of sight of the outside world. The people who knew better were afraid.

"Keep my daughter from finding a way off this ship," Mikal had quietly instructed Five that morning on the bridge after Lu had left.

The crawler had looked askance at him, and Mikal had got the distinct impression that he had just told a harvester how to cut palia grain. He knew the crawlers were trying to keep Lu safe always, and they didn't need him to tell them how to do their job. Still, it made him feel better to say it out loud. That night he found his daughter quietly arguing with Charli in the cargo bay. The two girls were ringed by crawlers, and he could only catch snippets of their conversation as he approached them.

"You have no idea what you're talking about," Charli said anxiously.

"We may not be from the Capitol, but you shouldn't underestimate us," Lu said, her back straight and head held high.

Lu saw him then, and she stepped back from Charli slightly, forcing a smile for her father. First moved aside, and Mikal looked down at his daughter, studying her. Charli looked chagrined and lowered her head to study her own feet.

"Stap wanted me to tell you that dinner is almost ready," he said.

Lu's smile relaxed into something far more natural. "I wouldn't want to disappoint the chef."

Stap had become adept in the kitchen in the short time since their departure, and he had quickly become Gordo's right hand before mealtimes. Dalians and Domain crew members alike lined up outside the kitchen to receive their rations. Food had become common ground for those on the overcrowded ship. Deciding to let his daughter's argument with Charli go, he offered his arm to her so that they could walk together.

"Lu," he started after the others had fallen a little behind, "I know what it's like to feel powerful but helpless at the same time." When his daughter didn't say anything, he continued, "I think it's best if we lie low with these people. In many ways, we are at their mercy."

"They would have let us burn on Dalia," she said, shrugging her arm away from him. "Who knows what those people out there are facing."

"They are not our concern." He stopped and faced her in the hall. "These people are," he said and waved his arm around him to emphasize the Dalians giving them space even as they tried to make their way to the kitchens. "You could jeopardize their lives if you act too soon."

"You don't care about them," she said. "You were an assassin for the Sanctuary."

Mikal nodded, knowing he was about to say something he would regret. "You're right," he said. "I care about you."

His daughter clenched her jaw in an imitation of his own frustration, and the two stood locked in an emotional stalemate until Sen found them.

"We shouldn't keep Stap waiting," he said cautiously as though he could feel the air crackling.

"Fine," Lu said and walked ahead of both Mikal and Sen toward the kitchens.

"She won't listen to me," Mikal said.

"You raised her not to listen to anyone," Sen said seriously.

Mikal's daughter ignored them both.

37

Lulu stood with her hands on her hips, glaring up at First. The crawler looked nonplussed by her demand, and she sensed he wouldn't give in.

"I just need one night," she whispered harshly up at him.

"*One night is all it takes to be killed, little sister,*" he answered in her head.

"You don't have to listen to him," she said, knowing she didn't have to say Mikal's name.

"*You said I don't have to listen to anybody. We can do what we want.*"

"Then let me do what I want," she said with a sly smile.

The crawler shrugged, unable to argue her logic. When she tried to move, his enormous hand gently grabbed her arm, forcing her to look in his black eyes. Having spent so much time with the crawlers and their stoic features, Lulu could detect the fine lines of concern crinkling at the corners of his eyes.

"I will turn around the minute there is danger," she said.

First looked torn, but his grip loosened. Lulu crept off in the night. The entire ship was dark, and the Dalians, now just experiencing night and day for the first time, had passed out into a deep sleep. It was the type of sleep that Lulu imagined only people who felt safe experienced. Her father had been sleeping by himself since they fought the day before. It was all the better for her. That man never missed a thing.

As she stepped over another sleeping form in the hallway, Lulu heard a shifting noise behind her. She turned and in the darkness, she could see an even blacker shadow loom to block most of the hall.

"You can't stop me," she whispered.

"You said I can do what I want. I want to go with you," First replied.

Lulu sighed at the frustrating crawler and said, "Just be quiet."

He crossed his arms over his chest and narrowed his eyes at her. Lulu shook her head and turned to continue navigating her way down the main corridor. As they approached the door, the number of people lessened. They had sensed the fear of the crew members and instinctively stayed away from the only possible entrance to the ship. The only sign of life outside had been the wind rustling the tops of the trees, and Lulu had a burning need to see what the people who had been selected for this particular planet were like.

Charli's words resonated in her bones. The Domani chose people to endure harsh environments for the purpose of making more like her. That meant that OR-32562 had people just like the Dalians on it. They were placed there against their will, and they must be as terrified of this place as the crew members were. What could have been so terrifying about the peaceful green planet, Lulu couldn't venture to guess. OR-32562 had all appearances of a paradise compared to the barren moon she was born on.

Standing in front of the door in the now empty hallway, Lulu took a few quick steadying breaths and tried to slow her heart rate. First stood off to the side, looking as stoic and bored as always. She smiled, secretly grateful for his presence, and her hand hit the large glass button built into the wall. The door flipped opened silently to her relief, and the top edge landed in the soft dirt, kicking up a small cloud of dust. Lulu didn't hesitate to step out into the crisp night air. Once First was out of the ship, she turned and pressed an identical button on the outside of the ship, and the door closed with a satisfying click.

Walking away from the ship, she felt exposed, and her pace quickened to a jog. There was no noise or wind to be heard or felt. The whole planet had the feeling of being wrapped in plastic. If there was no

CAROLYN GROSS

wind, she thought, what had been moving the treetops? Lulu looked up and almost tripped over her
own feet.

With no planet to block the view and no lights
coming from below, the entire universe seemed visible.
Surely any life out there could see her walking like an
insect across the only large patch of dirt, like a wound
on a planet otherwise carpeted in green. Surely, the
Domani could see her from their seat of power. Her
irrational fear caused her to quicken her pace toward
the tree line. First was close on her heels, his lumber-
ing footfalls steady and slow compared to her own.

She reached the tree line, and quiet isolation no
longer penetrated her bones. Catching her breath,
she looked up at the giant next to her, who no longer appeared uninterested. Something had her
crawler on edge. Lulu straightened and listened, but
she couldn't hear or see anything. They were alone
among the trees.

She shrugged and decided that they couldn't
stand there forever. Lulu started walking forward,
but she hadn't taken two steps before she heard footfalls behind them. Groaning inwardly and expecting
to see Mikal, she turned and saw a leaner form running after them. As the man came closer, he slowed
until he was standing before her. From the tension
behind Sen's eyes, visible even in the darkness, Lulu
could tell he was not happy with her.

"I won't go back," she said.

"I know."

"I need to see these people," she continued.

"I know."

"Then why did you come if you can't talk me out of it?" she asked. "I'll be fine. I have a crawler you know. No need to put yourself at risk."

He looked down at his feet, seemingly unsure of what to say next. "If anything happened to you…" he started. "Look," he said, after a moment, "if you're here, then I'm here. End of story."

Lulu stared up at him, not knowing what to say. He shook his head slightly at her as if he couldn't understand her and then moved on into the trees. She stood watching his back before trotting to catch up to him. First stayed behind them as she joined Sen. The ground was littered with dry and brittle leaves that had fallen from above. Sen barely made any noise as he walked over the ground, but her feet crunched the debris like the dried-out bones of insects, sounding too loud to her own ears.

She looked back at First to see that the usually stoic crawler was tense and uneasy. She could feel it coming off him in waves. She never would have admitted it, but Lulu was glad to have Sen by her side. He was calm and assuring as they walked deeper into the thick darkness—where the trees blocked out all light, even the stars of the Domain.

She hadn't realized that she was spinning the bracelet her father had given her until Sen's long fingers closed about her wrist. The warmth and steadiness of his grip on her reminded Lulu to breathe and focus. Using him as an anchor, she slowed her heart rate, and her footsteps felt lighter. The noise of the brush below quieted, and the three walked as if in a vacuum.

"Stop" came the command from First, like a booming in Lulu's head.

Her feet froze, and Sen, quick to respond, tightened his grip on her. His other hand produced an energy weapon that looked very much like one of Mikal's. The gun made a familiar charging sound that seemed to echo through the trees. First stood like a giant statue beside them as though waiting for something. His fists were clenched at his sides, and his gaze shifted in all directions at once.

"What is it?" Lulu whispered, her voice sounding too loud.

The crawler put his hand up for patience, and she waited. After a moment, she heard it. It was a clicking sound that bounced around the forest until it was impossible to tell the origin. The noise was quiet at first, but with each rhythmic click, it grew louder. Releasing his grip on Lu, Sen walked slowly in a circle around her.

"Where's it coming from?" Lulu asked uselessly, knowing that neither of her companions had an answer for her.

The noise filled the air around her, like bones breaking against the trees. There was no movement to be seen in the darkness, and Lulu suddenly worried that, surrounded by the enormous trees and disoriented by the sound, they would have no idea how to get back to the ship. The clicking grew so loud that it caused pain in her ears, and that's when the frequency picked up. Faster and faster, it hammered between the trees with an urgency that reverberated through Lulu's blood vessels.

Then, just as quickly as it had come, the clicking stopped.

Once again in a vacuum of silence the three stood with their backs to each other, waiting. A soft touch on her head caused Lulu to look up and see the black shadows of green leaves falling from above like ash. They slowly floated down, spinning as they landed in her hair and all around them. Sen and First stayed tense, but Lulu extended her arms out and let the tiny leaves tickle her skin as they landed. She had never experienced so much life from a planet, and she let it surround her.

Her fingertips grazed the wrinkled edge of a tree. She stopped and caressed the carapaces that interlocked like a puzzle on the outside of the trunk. Then a piece moved under her fingers. Lulu jumped back.

"What is it?" Sen's hands were on her shoulders, and his quiet voice was concerned in her ear.

Lulu stared at the trunk, barely making out the shapes in the darkness. She walked forward slowly, hesitating.

"Don't!" First's gravelly voice rang out, and Sen heard it, pulling back on her shoulder.

Then, the pieces of the trunk, no larger than her hand, lifted at once and came alive.

38

For a brief moment in time, Mikal felt like he was standing back in the home that he had shared with his daughter on Dalia. Charli stood awkwardly in front of him just as a boy had once done after Lu had been taken into the Sanctuary.

"Stupid girl," Mikal murmured, just as he had then.

Charli's eyes widened in surprise at the insult, and she whispered, "She's a Domani."

"She's a stupid girl," Mikal spat back as he turned to put on his long jacket.

His fingers found and checked each weapon kept in the inside pockets. Everything was there except for the gun he carried in his belt. That one was missing. Of course, she had taken his favorite gun.

He glanced up at Five, who was standing silently by the door. The crawler looked ashamed, if that emotion could even be attributed to the passive giant.

"Have you seen Sen?" Mikal asked, turning back to Charli.

"The young man who was tortured by Tek?" she asked.

"Yes." Mikal sighed, realizing that this girl must have witnessed everything while working on board the ship after it landed on Dalia.

She shook her head, and Mikal started to get a sinking feeling that he knew where the former doyen had gone. He turned to walk down to main hall of the ship; dawning light from outside starting to flood the rooms spilled out into the corridor, intermittently lighting his way. He stalked the hall and found himself pounding on the captain's door.

Several crew members and Dalians peeked their heads out of their own rooms and stared unabashedly, but Mikal disregarded the audience. Lana, who had been in a room down the hall, was also now standing in the hall, watching the spectacle.

"Caden!" Mikal yelled into the door.

The bleary-eyed captain opened the door, flinching slightly as Mikal raised his fist to continue pounding on the suddenly open door.

"Yes?" he asked warily.

"Tell me what you're afraid of out there," Mikal demanded.

"Why?" Caden asked.

"My daughter left the ship," Mikal said.

"She what?" he asked incredulously.

Caden's eyes widened, and he paced back from the door. Mikal followed him into his room and noted the opulent decorations and the too-wide bed that had once supported Tek's girth. The padding on the floor beneath his feet seemed softer than the rest of the ship, and he briefly wondered that Caden hadn't offered to share his room with other crew members on the crowded ship. Lana followed behind Mikal, her slippered feet quiet on the floor behind him.

"How could she have left this ship?" Caden asked. "She was surrounded by tampered men."

It took Mikal a moment to recognize the Domain term for the crawlers. The way Caden had said it made the term disrespectful in his mind.

"She's resourceful," Lana said.

"No one asked you, Lesser," Caden snapped.

Lana took a step back as if she had received a physical blow. Mikal didn't have time to ask what the word "Lesser" meant.

"It doesn't matter how she escaped," he said. "She's out there now. We have to go get her. In order to do that, I need to know what I'm facing."

Caden looked up at him and laughed without humor. "We don't know what's out there. Every Domain citizen who has been sent out to explore the planet hasn't returned. Based on our surveys though, we know that there are some people alive out there."

"That's it?" Mikal asked incredulously. "That's all you can tell me? You landed us on a random outer ring planet with no knowledge of the danger except that no one from the Domain has survived on it? Why not pick a different one?"

Caden had backed up and was now leaning with the back of his knees against the bed.

"The other planets were not as safe to land on and wait for help," he whined. "No one has been killed on a ship. There's only danger when someone is stupid enough to go out there."

"I'll go out there with you to look for her," Charli said from the hall.

"So will I." Kelvin's voice rose from behind her.

Other Dalians murmured in agreement, and Mikal noted that Lana was conspicuously silent.

"Kelvin," he called out to the former harvester. "Gather the men who fought in the square. This is a voluntary mission. No one will be compelled to risk their lives on this planet unless they want to. Have them gather rations, weapons, and supplies. Meet me at the main door."

Kelvin nodded and trotted off.

Mikal turned back toward Caden, who was now sitting on the bed. "I'm leaving several crawlers on the ship to look after the Dalians on board. If I'm not back in three cycles, they will know why. Until your precious rescue arrives, we are still in charge."

Caden's eyes narrowed, and he said, "If you leave this ship, we will leave you to die on this planet. Lulu is as good as dead already."

Mikal glanced at Lana and her cropped hair that was starting to grow back. He noted Caden's hair was longer than the hair of other crew members and made a quick decision. Without another word, Mikal pulled a blade out of his sleeve and strode over the bed that Caden was sitting on. He lifted his boot to rest on the acting-captain's thigh, digging his heel into the meat of his leg painfully. Caden wrapped his hands around Mikal's ankle, trying to lift the foot off his leg.

Mikal wasted no time and quickly gathered Caden's hair in one hand and deftly sliced it clean off with the blade in his other hand. Then, with one hand against Caden's throat, he pinned him down on the bed, ignoring the fingernails clawing at his wrist. Mikal shoved Caden's own hair into his open mouth and made sure the other made eye contact with him.

"You are only alive because I allow it," Mikal growled. "I don't know what's out there, but my people and I have survived on a moon that was never meant to support life. Keep that in mind when you walk out of this room later, flanked by our 'tampered' crawlers."

He released him then, and Caden gasped for air, pulling tangled knots of his own hair out of his mouth. Tears had sprung to his eyes, and Mikal smiled at the fear that couldn't be hidden in the other's face. There was hatred too, but also fear.

He noted that Lana was also smiling as he walked past her out into the hall. Lana may have been a selfish dictator on Dalia who had only been out for her own interest, but she was still a Dalian. Some retribution for Caden's passive participation in her torture at the hands of Tek was well deserved. The Domain crew members who had been watching from a distance quickly averted their eyes as Mikal walked past. Many were anxiously ringing their hair in their hands.

Mikal didn't care about them. He could only think of Lu and Sen as he made his way to meet Kelvin and the other Dalians who had fought for him once before in front of the Sanctuary. A large hand reached out and urgently grabbed his arm from behind, and he spun to face Five, who had been close on his heels.

The crawler had the glazed appearance to his eyes that meant that someone else was communicating through him.

There was panic suffused in the crawler's voice as he said, "Avoid the trees!"

Mikal knew that his daughter had just delivered a warning and grabbed the crawler's head, searching his eyes.

"Where are you?" he asked urgently. Even as he spoke, the glazed look disappeared, and the normal expressionless black eyes of the crawler returned.

Mikal let Five go and led him and ten other crawlers toward the exit, leaving the rest behind to watch over the Dalians he was leaving behind on the ship. He turned the last corner toward the main door to find the hall crowded with all the men who had fought on Dalia. They parted respectfully before him. At the door he found Kelvin and Stap.

With them was Charli and one other unexpected crew member. Mikal nodded in thanks to Gordo, and the big chef nodded back with an expression that spoke volumes of equal parts fear and resolution.

"Where do we go first?" Kelvin asked, slinging a pack of supplies over his shoulder.

Mikal slammed his palm into the large glass button next to the door.

"We go into the trees."

39

As a child, Lulu had nightmares. They largely centered around the crawlers surrounding the ominous Sanctuary on Dalia. Crawlers, like the one now trying to save her life, had once chased her down dark corridors on a giant piece of rock shrouded in the shadow of a gas planet. When she would awake from those dreams, her child-self would experience a sick feeling of dread that was impossible to shake. It would stick to her bones and live in her stomach for almost half a cycle afterward.

As an adult, she was finding that her nightmares were benign, but that sick and familiar feeling of dread washed over her in an instant as the statuesque trees around her shed their outer covering. They released millions of malevolent creatures that took flight, surrounding her in a cloud of clicking wings and spiny legs. The leaves that had showered her before were now replaced by a cloud of insectoid monsters that hummed menacingly in her ears and filled her vision with darkness.

Then the stinging started. Any exposed skin was targeted, and Lulu soon felt like her arms, legs, and neck were on fire. She instinctively covered her face even as she ran blindly through the trees. She had the wind knocked from her chest when she was abruptly brought to the ground from behind and covered by a dark cloak. Her face pressed against the dried leaves carpeting the ground, and she felt the weight of Sen on top of her. In a moment of forethought, she reached out to Five, knowing he would be with her father.

Her vision doubled, and she suddenly saw Mikal walking with purpose down the corridor. In an instant, she took in the set of his shoulders and recognized anger. He was going to come find her, but to enter the forest meant death.

"Avoid the trees!" she screamed into the dirt beneath her, hoping Mikal would hear her.

Then suddenly the weight on her shoulders lifted, and she broke the connection with her father. Sen stood slowly and carefully above her; his hand was dripping tiny rivulets of blood even as he reached down to help her stand. His arms had taken most of the stings, and pieces of his cloak were ripped into shreds by the flying insects. His hair was disheveled, and his eyes briefly scanned Lu to make sure she was in one piece.

First was standing in the clearing before them, covered in tiny wounds and panting. He held a large stick in front of him and let its point dip to settle in the ground. He was surrounded by a ring of dead insectoids.

The creatures that had surrounded them were now concentrated in a giant ball. They consumed half the forest in their numbers and hovered quietly in a dark cloud. The loud clicking and buzzing that had once filled the forest air was now a quiet hum. Lulu ignored her own stings and took a step toward them, but Sen stopped her with a protective arm.

"Wait," he whispered. "We don't know if they'll attack again."

"Something made them stop," she said quietly.

"*We need to leave this place and those tiny flying death machines,*" First declared loudly in her mind.

Between the millions of insects watching them quietly and the canopy of leaves above them, the darkness felt like being back home on Dalia. Lulu squinted, allowing her eyes to adjust. After a moment, she thought she saw movement in the trees next to them. With no need to stay hidden—their presence had been announced—she called light to herself.

"Don't," Sen started, but he was too late.

The forest around them was suddenly filled with green light that seemed to appear from nowhere. It filled Lulu and saturated the trees. Long shadows were cast in sharp relief, like long tentacles reaching out around them. The flying cloud in front of them shrank away from the light as if it was one giant animal that had been poked with a stick. Lulu smiled.

"I should have done that earlier," she said.

"It could have enraged them further," Sen mumbled under his breath.

"How are you doing that?" a rough voice asked in front of them.

Sen put his arm in front of Lulu and stepped in front of her. First stood straight and raised his new-found wooden weapon in front of him. Their protection seemed hardly necessary against the man emerging from the swarm. On Dalia, people did not live to be as old as the ancient man squinting at Lulu in the light. His white hair grew long around his shoulders, and his back was hunched over a stick similar to the one First had found on the forest floor.

He shuffled more than walked, and his brown cloak dragged in the leaf litter on the ground. As he drew closer, Lulu could see his eyes were slanted and half-buried in piles of wrinkles at the corners. His too-long, gnarled fingers curled around the wood he held like they were cemented to the grooves of it. He walked within feet of her and Sen and peered up at them, ignoring the crawler who watched him warily off to the side.

"Which one of you calls the light?" he asked.

Lulu stepped out from behind Sen, and the man opened his mouth in a parody of a salmee.

"Ah," he said. "The gats are all worked up over you."

"That's what those things are called?" Sen asked. "They almost killed us!"

The man glanced at Sen and looked him up and down appraisingly. "Of course they did. It's their job." He shrugged as if that would explain everything.

"Who are you?" Lulu asked, stepping closer to him.

"I am one chosen such as yourself I expect," he said. "This is my home. What are you doing here, is a better question I would dare say. Domani belong in the Capitol."

"I am not one of them," Lulu shot back with some force, causing the man to take a step back. She felt her neck flush and amended herself. "I mean to say that I'm not from the Capitol."

"Oh, that I can tell," the man said with a wry smile. "And neither is that tampered one standing behind you."

"Papa!" a girl's voice called from the trees.

The man in front of them turned his head toward the sound for a moment before turning back to Sen and Lulu. The easy demeanor he held before was now replaced with an obvious strength Lulu wouldn't have felt possible in such an elderly man. "I need to know what your intentions are with that energy you're harnessing, and I need to know it now."

The implied menace in his voice caused the gats behind him to condense and rise an inch higher than they were. First raised the stick he was holding, scraping the tip on the ground. Sen spread his feet casually, and the air seemed to crackle around them.

"We need help," Lulu pleaded. "Our home is now a burning rock, and we commandeered a Domain ship, which brought us here."

The man hissed slightly between his teeth. "You brought the Domain here?"

"We don't mean any harm," Sen said.

"You need to leave," the man said. "You don't know anything about the power you possess, and there are those here that would see it used for a greater purpose, including myself."

Lulu was about to speak when a brown creature on four legs leaped out from the tree line into the cloud of gats. It was half the size of a human, but it jumped to a height that was well above Lulu's head. The gats moved away from the creature in one fluid motion, just barely evading the outstretched blades that seemed to grow from its hands. Lulu felt herself shoved back by First, who had moved swiftly to block her from the creature's line of vision.

The three Dalians walked backward away from the thing in front of them, and Lulu peered from behind First's arm to see the creature. It was on the ground now, snapping large teeth in frustration at the congregation of gats above it. It had a long tail that flicked back and forth in annoyance, and it paced back and forth underneath the flying creatures.

The man they had been speaking with laughed at the creature. Lulu watched as it looked at him and snorted in the dirt before setting its eyes on the strangers he had been speaking with. Noticing their presence, its lips peeled back in a horrifying rictus, exposing pearly teeth that tapered into sharp points.

It slowly padded to stand next to the man, and to Lulu's amazement, he placed a hand on top of its head between two tall narrow ear points. The thing sat down calmly and gazed at the three of them expectantly. It was covered in sleek short hair that seemed gray and brown at the same time, changing colors in the light.

Lulu stepped out from behind First, who still held a stick in front of them protectively. "What is it?" she whispered.

"It's not an it!" a girl's voice answered, and Lulu looked to her right to see a child half her age emerge from the trees. She was short and thin, but she held herself like someone twice her height would. Her long hair hung in disorganized strands about her shoulders. "She's a lady, and her name is Sunshine," the girl said forcefully.

"Sunshine?" Sen asked incredulously.

The girl gave him a look that could have burned a hole in the tree next to them, and Lulu smiled.

The man sighed and said, "These people were just going back to where they came from, Mina."

"Where is the light coming from?" the girl asked.

"From me," Lulu said and looked at the man pointedly. "I'm from a place where there was no light, and I can call it to me if I want." She looked at the way the man protected the girl next to him and recognized the same look from her own father. "If we go back to where we came from, some bad people may hurt me and my friends."

The girl tilted her head slightly as though she was listening to something. Sen shifted his feet uncomfortably, and Lulu looked at him and shrugged her shoulders. Finally, the girl was the one to break the silence.

"Sunshine wants her to stay."

The man sighed loudly and brought his hand to his forehead. The animal at his feet relaxed and lay down with its giant arms crossed regally in front of it. The gats behind him seemed to relax, and at once they spread apart to sedately attach themselves to the nearest bare spots on the trees. Lulu spun and watched as the forest changed color, and in mere moments, the trunks of the trees were rough with the statue-still gats that linked together like armor plating.

When the humming ceased and the forest was still, Lulu looked at the man who was studying her with a dangerous expression. She knew in that moment that she had crossed a line by getting the girl involved.

"You two and your tampered will follow me," he said.

He turned and the girl and animal followed at a leisurely pace.

"Well," Sen said, "let's follow Sunshine."

40

The girl named Mina moved with a grace that mimicked the large animal at her side. Sunshine walked sedately, but the animal's muscles moved like liquid solidified. Mina picked up a stick and swung it about her as they walked, occasionally swiping the side of a tree, stirring up a swarm of gats in the process. The tiny creatures seemed unharmed by the encounters, but they settled back with an obvious agitation and collective annoyance.

"Mina!" the old man in front of them admonished.

The girl dropped the stick she had been carrying in an instant. Her posture was sulking after that, but she walked quietly with Sunshine at her side. The sleek animal rubbed her chin against Mina's arm, causing her to stumble to the side, and she obliged the creature by resting her arm over her shoulders. Sunshine stood almost as tall as her.

"What do you think she eats?" Sen whispered in Lulu's ear.

"*Foreigners,*" First answered in her head before she could reply.

Lulu stifled a laugh, and the beast twitched an ear so that the tip was pointed at them. She put her hand over her mouth, suppressing her own mirth, and the beast snorted.

Lulu looked up and tried to determine the direction of the starlight streaking through the canopy overhead. The encounter with the gats had caused her to lose all sense of direction, and even though she had let her own light dissipate, the light above was insufficient. After a moment, she ventured a question at the man leading their mismatched party through the uniform trees.

"Where are you taking us?" she asked.

"To a place the Domain can never know about," he answered.

"That was helpful," Sen murmured.

Mina turned to look back at them with her arm still casually draped over the big animal at her side. Her intelligent eyes studied Sen for a moment before she stuck her tongue out at him. Lulu laughed at the display, and the normally serious former doyen stuck his own tongue out at the girl. Mina flashed a quick smile before turning back around.

Eventually they arrived at a clearing, and Lulu could see the blue star that lit the planet setting just beyond the edge of the tree cover. She took a moment to show Five where they were, allowing the double vision to take over. When she looked back down, she saw the old man scrutinizing her, and she felt a flash of fear. He looked away as though nothing had passed between them, but Lulu was left shaken.

He walked over to a tree just like any other lining the clearing and placed his hand on the trunk. The gats covering the outside of it moved away to outline his hand, and a ripple effect moved up the trunk with a wave. Lulu watched in amazement as all the trees in the clearing seemed to move their "skins" of gats in synchrony until the ripples disappeared into the treetops. The old man moved away to stand next to Lulu and Sen. He looked up and smiled at First, who was passively watching him.

"Watch this, tampered one," he said.

The treetops above them started to quiver all at once, and Lulu craned her neck to watch as a giant wooden platform was lowered by ropes, blocking out the blue starlight above. It made a creaking sound above, but it descended smoothly to land with a soft thud in the leaf litter at their feet. Sunshine leaped gracefully onto the platform, landing on all four feet at once. Mina skipped behind the animal and sat comfortably, leaning against her shoulder.

The man smiled at Lulu and Sen and said, "The way forward is up."

Sen lightly held Lulu's hand and led her toward the platform. First stood at her back and followed them as they stepped up. Then in an uncharacteristic display, the crawler turned and picked up the old man under his arms, lifting him up and setting him down gently before stepping up himself.

"That was nice," Lulu said in his head.

"I don't know what came over me," the giant replied.

Then the platform jerked to lift off the ground, and Lulu grabbed Sen's arm to stay upright. The ascent was almost as fast as the descent, and the creaking above grew louder as they climbed higher. Lulu looked down once as they rose and instantly regretted it. It reminded her of the cliff edge on Dalia as the ground seemed to sway beneath them.

When she looked up, she could almost make out the wheels the ropes were attached to, but they were shadows against the blue starlight behind, and she couldn't make out details until they were close. Lulu was so focused on the mechanism behind the ropes attached to the platform that she almost missed the treetops surrounding them until she heard Sen gasp beside her.

The platform clicked in place seamlessly with a walkway that wound over the tree branches and split off into hundreds of other man-made paths. Lulu spun slowly and saw that the branches and tops of the trees held countless walkways that sloped gently up and down with the natural height of the trees around them. Humans and beasts like the one beside them moved about the walkways with agile grace, most not caring to look at Lulu and Sen as they gawked.

"It's a city," Sen whispered. "There must be more people living in the trees here than the whole of Dalia."

There was just enough leaf cover over them to hide the entire metropolis from sight above. It was easy to see how they could remain hidden from the Domain.

"I don't know where Dalia is, but this is just the edge of our home," the old man grunted. "Come. We have to convene a council to decide what to do with you."

With that he stepped onto the walkway, not looking to see if they obeyed. Lulu didn't need to look down again to know that they had no choice but to follow him. Mina was staring at her with an unreadable expression, and the girl waited with her animal guardian for the three Dalians to step off the platform before following suit.

41

Mikal had no idea in which direction his daughter had gone, but Five seemed to know exactly where to go. The crawler was like a homing beacon, and the Dalians followed, trusting the former soldier of the Sanctuary to lead them through the quiet, windless, uniform forest. While on the ship, Mikal had noted a breeze moving the treetops like ripples in water. Now, walking in between the massive trunks, everything seemed still. It caused the hair on his arms to stand on end.

He was not the only one on edge, and he nearly pulled a weapon when Five suddenly stopped beside him to intercept Gordo. The ship's cook was reaching toward the tree trunks and his fingertips and had almost made contact with the rough tree-skin when Five's hand clamped down on his chubby wrist.

"Hey!" Gordo's exclamation echoed through the forest around them.

Most in the party stopped to watch the exchange. Gordo struggled against Five's iron grip, but none of the Dalians made a move to assist him. They watched cautiously and silently.

Mikal made his way over to the two of them and nodded to Five for him to release the crew member.

"What is the meaning of this, brute?" Gordo asked indignantly, rubbing his wrist where the crawler had detained him.

Ignoring the question, Mikal studied the tree next to him where Gordo had been about to touch it. In the blink of an eye a piece vibrated as though adjusting itself under his gaze. The movement happened so quickly that Mikal almost missed it. His arm moved out in front of Gordo's chest, and he stepped backward, forcing the cook to come with him.

"Don't touch the trees," he said quietly.

"Why?" Gordo asked.

"They're alive," Charli answered for Mikal.

He hadn't even noticed the girl standing beside him. He looked at her eyes and saw that she was afraid, staring at the trees. With her answer, all of the Dalians moved away from the trees to stand closer together. Their feet crunched debris underneath, and Charli bent down to pick up a dead leaf in between her fingers. She spun the thin, cackling thing in her hand and stood straight. She turned it over and saw thin, pointed legs protruding from a desiccated underbelly.

Charli looked up at Mikal with an unreadable expression. He didn't need to touch the dead creature to know that it was no leaf. It was the same thing he had seen move against the tree. His eyes scanned the trunks beside him, and the multitudinous creatures that covered the trees threatened to overwhelm his senses.

Charli looked up into the sky and said, "The light is going away."

"On Dalia," Kelvin said, "we don't fear the darkness."

"That's right!" Stap chimed in.

"In the Domain," Charli answered without wavering, "darkness brings death. This place brings death. Can't you feel them surrounding us? We have been trapped here to die."

"We're not dead yet," Mikal cut in. "Those who want to leave may head back to the ship."

All the people in the group looked at their feet, none willing to speak.

Gordo looked Mikal in the eyes and said, "We are committed to finding your headstrong daughter." After a moment he said, "If this boy insists on staying, then so do I."

He placed his hand on Stap's shoulder, and the boy beamed back up at the ship's cook. It was clear that the orphan had found someone to take him under his wing, and Mikal felt a brief flash of fear for the brave souls with him. The former assassin found

himself caring for those under his charge and quickly decided that the feeling was uncomfortable.

Then a distant clicking arose in the dusk.

"*We need to run!*" Five's voice rang clear in his
head.

Mikal allowed the crawler to lead them at a dead
run through the darkening forest. The giant crawler's legs gave him a short lead at the head of the pack
while the other crawlers fell into step surrounding
the group. Mikal glanced back and saw a crawler
flanking the last man.

The clicking grew louder.

The rhythmic tempo of the sound bounced off
the trees they passed, and Mikal tried to keep his
head on Five's back as he ran. Their group became
longer as those with shorter legs and those less conditioned started to lag. One of the crawlers moved
behind Mikal, and he saw that he had bodily picked
up Charli and Stap—one in each arm. Not for the
first time, he was amazed at his daughter's influence
on the crawlers.

Then Mikal felt a stinging sensation and heard a
loud collective humming as the creatures covering
the trees released their linked armor plating to take
to the air. The sky above them darkened, but not with
the setting star. The rescue party was soon enveloped
by a menacing and vicious cloud. Mikal instinctively
brought his arms in front of his face and felt the flesh

on his forearms pierced hundreds of times at once even as he continued his headlong run forward.

The crawlers swung with fists, impotent against creatures so small. Mikal drew an energy gun from under his jacket and shot blindly into the sky. The weapon lit up the night with a bright flash of light, and the creatures uniformly shied away from it. Seeing this, he started to empty the reserves in all directions even as they continued running behind Five.

It wasn't until they reached a clearing that his gun was empty and the creatures surrounded them again. Mikal nearly collided with Five's back when the crawler suddenly stopped and looked up. He expected the flying creatures to dive at their group, but they stayed at the perimeter of the clearing like a fog that clung to the trees.

"Why won't they attack?" Kelvin asked, moving to stand at the edge of their group huddled in the center of the clearing.

"We're too far away from the trees," Stap said confidently even as the crawler gently deposited him to stand on the ground next to a shaken Charli. "You chitlings aren't so brave now, are you!" the boy yelled at the hovering creatures, referencing the vile vermin on Dalia.

"What now?" Gordo asked.

"*We are prisoners being held in this clearing,*" Five said in Mikal's head.

"We wait," Mikal said aloud.

He moved to the edge of their group as close to the line of flying creatures as he dared. Then, in a show of patience he hoped would resonate with the group behind him, he sat cross-legged in the dirt. Mikal meditated, focusing on his heart rate and ignoring the soft clicks interspersed in the ominous humming that surrounded them.

"Sen is with her," he said quietly to himself.

42

Darkness settled in the trees, but the natives to OR-32562 walked the narrow walkways in the trees with sure footing. No railings existed to protect them from falling, and Lulu looked down through the web of branches crisscrossing below.

"That would not be a pleasant way to die," Sen whispered next to her.

Almost without thought, she called the green energy to her and let the familiar warmth suffuse her bones and vision. Children playing with round stones in a circle on a nearby platform gasped when she passed, and Lulu playfully released a tiny ball of light to bounce and dance in their circle before fizzing out into the wood below. Laughter pealed out into the night, and she smiled. The old man ahead of her looked back, and his face was passive while he waited for them to catch up to him.

Adults were less amused by her light, and she noted the frightened faces of those they passed. They were dressed in clothing that looked patchwork in various shades of brown and green, like giant leaves stitched together. They whispered to each other and watched with open distrust for the group flanked by a giant crawler.

Lulu caught snippets of words as they walked the winding pathways.

"Tampered…"

"Domain…"

"Domani whore…"

Sen stiffened beside her at that, and Lulu grabbed his hand.

"They're like us," she said quietly. "These people have been outcast by the Domain to live in a hostile world without any control."

"Oh, I think they've achieved some measure of control," Sen growled. "You needed to see these people, Lu. Now they hold us prisoner as surely as anyone from the Domain ever did."

Lulu didn't respond. She focused on the winding walkway before her. Sunshine's tail swayed in agitation at the edge of the light, and her tufted ears twitched back toward them with every other step of her silent pads. Occasionally, they passed by another creature like Sunshine, and Lulu noted the flick of tails and low growls they exchanged in greeting. It was not hostile.

Eventually they were brought to a tree unlike any other. It was the largest in sight and rose well above the others. It was not the size that made it special though. The tree had been carved into and built upon to make a colosseum that dwarfed the Wards' chamber on Dalia. Much like that room, there was a balcony that spread out from either side of the trunk of the tree to surround the hollowed-out base. Tiered benches led up to the highest row of observers, and Lulu could see that seats were filling quickly.

Lulu, Sen, and First were led into the central area, and once they were standing in the center on the polished wood floor, old man left them.

"You will wait here," he said gruffly.

Mina and Sunshine nimbly climbed up to the second row, where the large animal curled up next to the girl. They politely watched the central arena and waited patiently. The man who had led them there slowly climbed the rows to sit at the highest point at in the center of the tree trunk. Any hint of friendliness that had lived behind his eyes was gone as he looked down on the three intruders.

Lulu felt exposed as people of all ages filled the rows to look down on them.

"*This feels familiar, little sister,*" First said in her head, and she felt, more than saw, an image from Dalia.

It was of Lulu standing in the center of an open room surrounded by a balcony of Wards and the spinning planet of Laima overhead. Her vision doubled for a moment, and she stumbled slightly, losing her balance. The image of the girl Lulu once was, standing defiant with a bruised nose, burned behind her eyes.

"I didn't know you could do that," she said aloud to the crawler.

"Do what?" Sen asked.

"He showed me a memory," Lulu said quietly.

Before Sen could respond, a loud bang on the wood of the trunk sounded and reverberated to vibrate under their feet. Lulu looked up sharply and saw a large man holding a mallet and standing next to the hollowed tree trunk in front of them. He had hit an eroded circle in the wood, which looked like it had been chipped over cycles of abuse from that mallet. The gats, having been disturbed by the mallet, agitatedly circled the tree trunk before finally settling back down against the wood.

Lulu squinted into the shadows of the tree trunk, studying the wood, and saw another familiar sight. She saw rows of runes extending upward and down the center of the base. The symbols had been burned black into the wood and had been scrawled to wrap around the outside. She recognized the patterns for just an instant before it was once again covered in gats. Her heart pounded in her chest, and she took an involuntary step back from the tree.

"Whoa," Sen said, gently placing his hand on her shoulder before she could turn to run. "What's wrong?"

"Another memory," First said aloud in a voice gravelly from lack of use.

"Fellow dissidents," the old man proclaimed above them, stopping any further discussion. "We have a situation."

"I'll say, Seamus," another voice yelled from below. "Why have you brought these creatures of the Domain into our midst?"

Murmurs of agreement spread.

"Should have let the gats kill them!" a woman yelled, and the murmuring grew louder.

The old man, now known as Seamus, watched and waited patiently for silence to return. To Lulu's eye there was no question of who oversaw these people.

"I was going to let the gats finish their job," he said simply. "Then this one sent out a call." He pointed at Lulu, and she felt Sen's hand tense on her shoulder. "Her voice called not for help for herself. She used her one last communication to stop others from following her into danger. She used such force and power through the tampered connection that even I heard her loud and clear."

The spectators turned toward Lulu with renewed interest in their eyes.

"She is a Domani. She may be able to activate the runes," he said finally, and the entire circle erupted in a mix of protest and support all at once.

"You have always voted against activating the runes!" someone shouted.

"Ay, I have," Seamus said, looking down at Mina. "I have been reconsidering my position. No longer can we ignore the other outer planets and let the Domain control them. We have been isolated for too long. Now may be the time to reenter the universe."

First moved to stand in front of Lulu, and Sen stayed at her back. Lulu thought furiously about the runes on the tree. She recoiled from the thought of touching them. To activate them was to bring the Domain to this place. On Dalia, they had lived in dark squalor, never knowing of the existence of the Domain. They would have burned into extinction, believing that was the end of humanity. In their naïveté they thought that if there had been others out there, surely the Dalians would have known about them.

Tek had said that Dalians were prisoners, abandoned on a moon that was like a ticking time bomb. In a flash of insight, Lulu knew that it was the Wards who had saved them by making her. They had worked tirelessly to breed their salvation into existence under the guise of doyens devoted to Laima.

These people though, these dissidents of OR-32562, they knew. They knew of a better life and had been made involuntary pioneers on this outer planet. They knew why they had been exiled. They had been sent there to breed.

"I won't go back to that corrupt opulence," a wizened woman said, her voice clear above the others squabbling.

"I don't mean to take us back to the Capitol," Seamus said, looking across the arena at her. "I mean to bring them here. I mean to kill them here."

Lulu felt bile rise in her throat, and she turned to run back down the path they had come. Several men moved to block her way, and she unconsciously brought the light to her. She felt the power reaching down to her fingertips even as she ran at them. Fear and confusion warred when her hands met their outstretched arms, and she released a fraction of the energy she had used to obliterate Tek. Still, it was enough. The men stumbled back and fell. Their heads hit the planks of wood, already unconscious. The others, feeling the static of unspent energy around her, gave her space. Lulu took the opening and ran.

43

Lulu ran without direction. Her feet pounded on the wooden boards and seemed to match the blood surging through her ears. Her vision blurred with tears, and her foot slipped off the edge of the walkway and she fell forward, catching herself painfully with hyperextended wrists. She scrambled back onto the narrow boards and rolled onto her back. For a moment, she lay there nursing scraped palms and testing her wrists as her breathing slowed. She hadn't heard anyone pursuing her, and she had taken so many turns that she was sure it would take a crawler to find her.

She looked through the tiny holes in the leaves of the canopy above her and saw pinpoints of distant stars glittering beyond. The Domain. It was quiet. Lulu imagined the Domani like the Wards, only more powerful and opulent. Unlike the Wards, they were surely softer, like Tek had been. She knew she would never be one of them.

Lost in her thoughts, she didn't hear the silent steps approaching her until it was too late. In an instant she felt an enormous weight crushing her chest, and she scrambled to free herself, clawing at something soft and sleek. Unable to wriggle free, she lay pinned, and the thing on her chest laid its enormous blockhead down next to her and groaned.

"Sunshine!" Mina hissed next to her. "You're scaring her. Bad chattle!"

"Sunshine?"

Lulu felt herself starting to panic under the weight of the big animal. She imagined the beautiful white teeth that were the almost as thick as her forearm biting into her side and almost lost all composure. She slapped at the beast with her arms and wriggled fiercely to sit up. Sunshine seemed inconvenienced enough to roll onto her side, and Lulu sat panting from exertion with her legs still trapped under the heavy animal.

"You promise not to run?" Mina asked.

The girl was squatting next to Lulu, her face calm and intent. Lulu nodded, not trusting herself to speak so close to Sunshine's waiting teeth. The girl seemed to consider her for a moment, and Lulu suddenly feared she didn't believe her, but in an instant, she smiled, and Sunshine lazily rolled off Lulu's legs.

Lulu pulled her knees to her chest as soon as they were free. She scooted back to the edge of the walkway and watched Mina and Sunshine warily with her back to the open night-air.

"It's all right," Mina said, still smiling. "I was only able to find you because of Sunshine. Those gabos on the council won't know where we are for a while."

"Gabos?"

Lulu couldn't think of anything else to ask. Her head was spinning.

"Yeah, gabos!" Mina said, shaking her head. "You don't know what a gabo is?"

Lulu shook her head.

"You really aren't from the Capitol, are you?" She didn't wait for Lulu to answer. "Seamus says that we mustn't breed talent to talent. He says it would risk making someone dangerous." She tilted her head slightly. "Someone like you."

"I am dangerous," Lulu murmured.

"Why have you come here then?" she asked. "We were just fine without you. I have never seen Seamus like this."

"I should have never come here," Lulu said to herself. Then she looked up at Mina. "I am sorry. Can you take me back to the ship?"

Mina stood considering. She was a child, but her countenance suggested a wisdom beyond her years. "I am not the only one who can talk to the chattle and the gats," she said. "I could try to take you, but the others would find us."

"Can you hide me?" Lulu asked, hearing the desperation in her own voice. "My ship sent out a distress signal, and the Domain will come for them soon. I need to hide until I can get back to that ship. Then we will leave this place like we found it."

"Promise?" Mina asked. "Just like you found us?"

"Yes," Lulu said, feeling the force behind her own words. She wanted nothing more than to leave this place and its people alone.

Mina nodded and spit in the palm of her hand before reaching out to take Lulu's hand to help her up. She held out her spit-covered palm expectantly, and Lulu awkwardly spit in her own palm before they clasped hands. Mina released her, seeming satisfied with the procedure that just took place, much to Lulu's relief.

"Are Sen and my crawler safe?" Lulu asked her.

"The tampered one?" Mina asked.

"Yes."

"They are safe with the council," she said thoughtfully. "Besides, as long as you are missing and considered dangerous, they would not wish to anger you."

Lulu nodded thoughtfully. The girl turned down the pathway, surefooted in the darkness; her bare feet slapped the wooden slats confidently. Sunshine waited behind Lulu for her to follow, and she did, aware of the chattle behind her back.

"How many, uh, chattle do you have here?" Lulu called ahead.

"Oh, there used to be more of them than us!" she cheerfully answered. "Now most of them live on the ground. Only a couple hundred stay with us who are gifted, in the trees."

Unable to help herself, she asked the question that had been burning in her mind since she first saw Sunshine. "What do they eat?"

Mina stopped and smiled back at Lulu. "Foreigners," she said smoothly.

"No, really," Lulu said forcefully, feeling involuntary laughter bubble to the surface.

"They eat gabos mostly," the girl said matter-of-factly. "Though Sunshine here once caught a live gat. Can't get her to think of anything else since then!"

Lulu refrained from asking what a gabo was again. She instead asked another question, keeping her eyes on her feet in the darkness. Her vision was adjusting back to the shadowed Dalia, and she found herself becoming more accustomed as they walked further down the paths.

"Is Seamus your father?" she asked.

The girl scoffed. "He wishes!" After a moment she said, "He took me in after my parents died."

"I'm sorry," Lulu said. She didn't know why she apologized. It was still something that seemed universal.

"That's why Seamus wants to leave," the girl said. "More and more of us are getting sick. He says we don't live as long as those on the Capitol. It's the blue star."

283

Lulu nodded, understanding. Many people on Dalia were getting sick from the dust, and she imagined that no planet was perfect for people to thrive on. She said as much to Mina, and the girl shook her head, blond hair swaying in the darkness.

"The Capitol is perfect for people. It is where we were born. That's what Seamus says. He says people on the Capitol have so much health that they focus on power instead of survival. They worry about riches instead of things like star-sickness."

Star-sickness. The light here was dangerous. Lulu felt a cold chill creep up her arms. She found herself preferring the darkness of her home. The gats made soft chirping and rustling noises as Mina passed. It was almost as if the girl was talking to them. Every thirty feet or so, Sunshine would snap at one on the edge of a tree branch, and the small creatures would shift so suddenly they were like a blur. The big chattle never caught one.

Lulu found herself so lost in thought and the rhythm of the trees that she forgot to count her steps. She had no idea where she was or how to get back. Her father would be so disappointed in her, she thought, even as she nearly collided with Mina's back. The girl had stopped and was rooting around in a hidden pocket in her tunic for something.

When she produced what she had been searching for, Lulu wondered how it could be useful at all. It looked like a bent stick in her hand, like any other you could find on the ground here. Then she approached a large tree and waved her hand at the gats covering the surface. As they dispersed and settled on other trees, Lulu saw that they had been covering a door.

"Seamus doesn't know about this one," Mina said as she maneuvered the stick through a tiny hole in the door. "It's just me, the gats, Sunshine, and now you."

"Not even your friends know?" Lulu asked.

"Pff. I don't have any friends I would want to bring here. Even Gideon doesn't know about this place," Mina said.

"Gideon?" Lulu asked.

"Yeah, he's my partner in the game," she said as if that explained everything.

The door opened with a creek that seemed to wake all the gats within earshot. Mina disappeared inside, and Lulu shrugged, following her in the darkness, still flanked by Sunshine. Once inside, she was assaulted by the smell of damp wood. The hollowed tree extended all the way to the sky so that stars could be seen through a small hole at the top. Lulu stepped forward and was stopped by Mina's hand on her pant leg. It was a good thing because the ledge they had been standing on ended abruptly. The hollow in the tree wound all the way down to the ground. The ledge they were standing on wrapped around the outside, but it didn't fill the middle of the tree. Dirt Lulu had kicked off inadvertently rained down, making soft ticks on the dirt and leaves stories below.

"You have to be careful not to step off the ledge," Mina said needlessly.

Before she could respond, the door closed behind them and the gats settled around the tree, causing the blackness to settle inside except for the stars shining through the small opening above.

44

Mikal opened his eyes. The blue star above had long been set beyond the rim of the planet, and he found himself in a familiar setting. Blackness had settled on his shoulders like a blanket, and he could see tiny motes of dust swirl in the faint light of the stars above their clearing. It reminded him of the dust and ash that pervaded the atmosphere on Dalia. The violent bugs that coated the trees around them had gone quiet except for an intermittent click that sounded almost restive, if those creatures could be said to have such emotion.

Mikal turned and studied the dark mounds behind him—Dalians who had chosen to risk their lives for the sake of his headstrong daughter. He had brought them here to this strange planet that was so unlike their home. He was responsible for their safety. The large mound closest to him moved, and the crawler turned his emotionless face toward Mikal.

He had opened his eyes, mostly occupied by black pupils, and was studying Mikal in turn.

"*She is safe,*" Five said in his head.

Mikal knew that the crawlers communicated with each other, but he had no way of knowing when or how often. He didn't question him. Five was a creature of his daughter's design just as much as he had been made by the Wards. She had changed them without thought, and they belonged to her just as much as she now belonged to them. It was not long ago that Mikal would have been worried about their safety in such close proximity to a crawler. Now, he never felt safer than he did with a crawler at his back.

A rustling from above caused both of them to look up, and Mikal rose in one fluid motion, pulling a small blade from his sleeve at the same time. He held it, concealed under the cuff of his cloak, and he and Five waited for more movement. The night was silent above them. His arms stung with the superficial wounds in his skin from the flying bugs on the trees, and he watched the still trunks around them. His eyes strained in the darkness, waiting for the skin cloaking the pillars to peel away into the air and attack. It never happened though.

Instead, they were greeted with a new type of predator.

Slanted eyes at the height of Mikal's waist slowly revealed themselves at the edge of the tree line. The creature slowly and smoothly advanced into their clearing. Mikal took an unconscious step backward. The crawler beside him stiffened, and he spoke in a rough whisper.

"Brother."

The creature's tufted ears pointed forward at that, and it sat back on its haunches. Mikal felt his grip tighten on the blade in his hand. The creature turned its attention toward him, opening its mouth in a seemingly indifferent yawn. The gaping maw revealed glistening teeth that could penetrate through a man's torso, and Mikal knew that this yawn was not a sign of boredom or relaxation. It was a sure sign of restrained aggression.

"This is a brother to you?" he whispered to the crawler standing beside him.

"Both have been tampered with," said a voice concealed in darkness not far behind the smooth-coated creature still relaxed on its haunches. "Unlike your creature though," the voice said, "our chattle are not in violation of Capitol laws." The man stepped out into the clearing, and Mikal could see his wizened face held proud in contrast to the bent and arthritic body beneath it.

"What do we care for Capitol laws?" Mikal said.

The man smiled and said, "Surely some laws are meant to protect humanity against itself. Even if those laws come from an inhumane juggernaut of excess." He placed his hand gently on the head of the creature next to him, and the chattle relaxed its ears slightly, leaning in to the touch. "Animals respond to tampering with acceptance. To them it is accelerated evolution. Humans do not. They fight against their own makers, ever searching to get back to themselves or for one that appeals to them. I suspect you know something of the one that appeals to them."

Mikal had never heard someone speak so frankly about the crawlers, and he stood still, fearing to break the spell of information.

The old man tilted his head studying him and finally said, "She is like you."

At the mention of his daughter, Mikal did not hesitate. He pulled the blade from his sleeve and released it. It spun quickly and quietly through the night air under the old man's left ear, shearing pieces of his long white hair in its passage. The blade landed with a dull thud, buried in the wood of a tree. The bugs reacted quickly and scattered off the trunks, surrounding them in a thick swarm at the periphery of their clearing. They still did not enter, and the man put his hand in the air, signaling for stillness.

The creature he had called a chattle was standing now, crouched with hackles raised and teeth bared. A low growl emitted from its throat, and Mikal smiled. He welcomed the challenge of fresh violence in the face of his recent frustrations. He and the beast seemed to share a language.

"Peace," the old man said. "You are surrounded."

Mikal looked around and saw the now familiar gleam of dull light amplified by the golden eyes of chattle around the clearing. Just as he had done near the Sanctuary when outnumbered by the Domain soldiers, he surrendered the energy gun from his waist. It clattered to the ground at his feet, and the man's eyes widened slightly at the sight of it. Mikal caught the surprise and made a mental note of it.

"Where is she?" he asked. He did not need to elaborate.

"Sen told me you would be direct," the old man said.

Mikal relaxed slightly at that and relaxed his tone. "Take me to them."

The old man nodded and lifted his right arm. A creaking sound from above rang through the forest, and the slumbering Dalians in the clearing stirred. Mikal kept his hands at his sides and looked down when he felt Charli brush his arm. The girl's face was stiff with suppressed panic at the sight of the chattle surrounding them, and she grabbed Mikal's wrist.

He purposefully softened his face and said, "He is taking us to Lu and Sen."

"These animals are tampered," she said, her voice shaky. "They are dangerous."

"So are we," Mikal said.

They stood in the circle while the others quietly awoke and joined them. The creaking had been from the release of a large platform that would only fit ten of them. Two of the chattle gracefully jumped up onto the wood after it settled in the dirt.

"We will send food and supplies down to the others," the old man said. "Choose who will go up into the trees."

Mikal didn't have to choose. Charli, Stap, Kelvin, Five, and surprisingly Gordo stepped up beside Mikal. They were not exactly the strongest warriors in the group, but Mikal sensed they were tactically outnumbered up there anyway. It would take knowledge and diplomacy of a different sort to survive. He stepped up without hesitation, and the chattle closest to him stretched in a gesture of indifference. Charli still clung to his wrist, but she moved her feet to stand behind him at the furthest corner from the sleek beasts.

Oddly enough, Five chose to stand as close as possible to the chattle without touching them. The normally stoic crawler was transfixed with the creatures. For their part, the chattle sniffed the air beside him and lifted their front lips. Their faces reminded Mikal of tasting something tangy or bitter.

"*Careful, father, they will follow this man to the death,*" Five said in Mikal's head.

Mikal tried not to start at the use of the word "father." It was the first time the crawler had called him anything directly. "*That may be their fate,*" he grimly thought back.

The platform creaked slowly upward in fits and starts to bring them into the treetops just as the giant blue star that lit OR-32562 started to make a grand reentrance on the opposite horizon.

45

Lulu woke to the sound of muffled growls. Her body ached in protest to movement, and she found herself curled in a fetal position, her head and arm uncomfortable against rough and splintered wood. Muted blue light shone in a beam of light on a section of the platform next to her head. Dust swam in the star-beam, and for a moment she watched it and listened.

The growling sound she had heard outside was interspersed with light laughter. The two sounds were in such sharp contrast with each other that Lulu wondered if the scene was one of mad chaos. It hurt to sit up, but she pushed the pain aside while she carefully took in her surroundings. She was sitting inside an enormous hollow tree trunk, and the smell of musty wood heavily permeated her lungs.

She thought back to the last thing she remembered before falling asleep. The girl Mina had brought her here with Sunshine. Lulu had closed her eyes—her nerves on edge while the giant chattle watched over her and the girl, not expecting to fall asleep. Looking about her now, she realized she had not only fallen asleep, but she had let her guard down so much as to let Mina and her chattle slip out unnoticed.

Lulu crawled forward painfully with her knees scraping the uneven wood to peer down into the dark abyss that was the center of the hollowed tree she had been left in. Her fingers gripped the edge of the landing, and for a moment her stomach lurched, threatening her empty stomach with a wave of nausea. She sat back and realized she hadn't eaten a decent meal since leaving the relative safety of the ship. She rose on unsteady feet and, clinging to the wall behind her, walked toward the doorway Mina had shown her the night before.

The door was outlined with a sliver of blue light, and her fingers found the edge before her feet collided with a heavy canvas bag.

"Ah!" She inhaled with the pain as her toes collided with too much force.

Sitting down, she gripped her toes with her fingers and waited for the throbbing to subside. She looked over at the offending bag and dragged it in front of her to inspect its contents. It was as if Mina could read her mind. From inside the bag she pulled out bits of dried meat that reminded her of a chewy, smoky version of salmee. Lulu took no time to wonder at the generosity and continued to rummage with her mouth full of the stuff. It gripped against her teeth but made her salivate like nothing she had ever eaten on Dalia. Swallowing past the large mouthful, she popped in a handful of small juicy berries that were haphazardly thrown in the bag.

Lulu wiped her mouth with her sleeve and realized that the bracelet her father had given her was no longer on her wrist. She searched herself and patted down her clothes, eyes squinting in the darkness, searching for some sign of the twisted delicate metal. There was nothing. It was gone. Fighting against the pit of emotion in her stomach, she continued to remove the contents of the bag in front of her. She could still hear the laughter and growling outside, falling and rising in a fever pitch.

Lulu laid out a blanket, rope, and a wooden flask. The biggest object she removed last and placed it in front of her with a heavy metal clank. Her fingers inspected the edges, and she found a depressible button and pushed. The inside lit up with a hiss and a golden flame. Lulu stared at the small torch and saw that the longer it was on, the brighter it became until its light reached the opposite end of the hollow tree.

"If only we had something like this on Dalia," she murmured, thinking of the darkness and sparsity of lights provided by the Sanctuary.

She stood gracefully and pried her fingertips in the crack of the doorway, looking for a latch or release mechanism. There was none to be found, and the door wouldn't budge. She threw herself against it and punched against the unforgiving wood, bruising and scraping open her knuckles in the process.

"Why hold me captive, Mina?" she asked the door as if it would answer her.

She looked over at the small window and noted a depression next to it that she hadn't seen before she lit the torch. She walked over to stand beneath it and felt along the wall. She smiled as her fingers found tiny handholds and ledges to climb and place her feet. Of course, Mina would want to have a way to climb up to the window. This was her hideout after all.

She grabbed the rope and slung it around her shoulder. Lulu tried not to think about what falling inside the giant of a tree would mean as she carefully made the climb up to the window. Once she reached the ledge, she found that it was just wide enough to perch on and that there was no barrier between her and the dizzying fall below. Her eyes squinted as they adjusted to the light outside, and once they did, she almost fell at the pandemonium before her.

Chattle were launching themselves off perches and branches to leap over the clearing next to her tree. There were at least ten of them, and they growled with each leap and landed with precision, claws digging into the wood of nearby ledges and branches. Their powerful displays looked like a dance, and Lulu was mesmerized by the near misses as they passed by each other in midair. The seemingly impossible acrobatics were not even the most impressive part about the display. It was the children who rode on top of the chattle that made her gasp in fear.

Among them, Mina stood out with her radiant blond hair. She sat astride Sunshine's back with both hands wrapped around a long wooden pole. Mina used no hands to steady herself on the enormous chattle as Sunshine lifted her haunches in the air and propelled herself using powerful hind legs across the open clearing. When Mina reached the center, another child, a boy riding a slightly larger chattle, met her head on. The two clashed their poles together with a loud clack, and Mina deftly slipped the end of her pole underneath the other's defenses to jab him painfully in the ribs. The boy doubled over but managed to stay on the animal as it scrabbled onto the opposite ledge.

Cheers and laughter erupted around her, and Lulu registered the people scattered on the crisscrossed walkways and branches of the surrounding trees. Adults and children alike were taking pleasure in the violent struggle below. Mina proudly held her head high as Sunshine paced in tight rings on their small ledge opposite from where Lulu sat.

The boy who had been bested shouted, "Lucky shot, Mina!"

"You know luck had nothing to do with it," Mina replied indignantly.

Sunshine growled, and the others around the clearing laughed.

"We'll see about that," he said and launched himself toward her again.

Sunshine didn't hesitate and leaped midstride to meet the boy and the other chattle head on. From her angle, Lulu had a hard time seeing the boy's face, but she registered the last-minute shock on Mina's face as the boy pulled a shorter stick from his pocket with a sharpened end on it. Mina ducked, but the new weapon grazed her back and tore down the back of her shirt. When Mina landed below Lulu on the ledge below her window, she could see a large red welt on her back with red droplets accumulating on the edges.

Lulu expected the girl to cry foul play, but she kept her mouth shut. The boy grinned on the other landing and blew her a kiss from his own landing.

"In your dreams," Mina shouted.

"Maybe one day, daughter of Seamus," he called and leaped off his chattle to descend on a set of winding stairs around the tree.

Sunshine roared in the universal tone of frustrated rage, and Mina reached down to rub the beast's ear affectionately. Mina glanced up and smiled when she saw Lulu perched in the window but looked quickly away before somebody noticed her. Several other children and their chattle joined her on the ledge, and the children put their heads together, talking animatedly about the game they had just played. Lulu realized it had been just that, a game. The spectators calmly gathered their belongings and left to go about their day.

Lulu saw that a hole had been made through the wood on the side of the window that would allow her to attach the rope Mina had left for her. Eventually, the chattle and their charges left, still talking excitedly in pairs. The world was quiet except for the occasional click of a gat across the clearing. Lulu sat perched in the opening of the towering tree and waited before she threaded the thick rope and swung it around her waist, knotting it carefully. She tugged on it tentatively and placed her feet on the window ledge, slowly leaning back on the rope to test it. When she didn't fall, she carefully started walking down the wall of the tree.

46

ikal tried not to gawk at the network of pathways and scrawling civilization before him. He kept his face schooled and impassive and was rewarded with a grunt of dissatisfaction from the old man, who guided them off the platform. His companions were clearly impressed though.

"Bale would have loved this," Stap whispered.

Mikal nodded. The self-proclaimed orphan leader would have reveled in the network of bridges and pathways. It was an organized chaos that reminded Mikal of the twisting alleyways of the shanties back on Dalia.

"Your brother would be proud you are here in his stead," Gordo said from behind them.

Mikal almost started at the Domain cook's insight into Stap's life, but he reminded himself that the two of them had spent much of their journey from Dalia cloistered in the ship's kitchen. Stap beamed back at Gordo, and Mikal tried to not smile at the interaction.

"These animals are unnatural," Kelvin murmured from behind Mikal, referencing the chattle that walked casually in front of and behind their group.

"So am I," Five said aloud in a gravelly voice.

"Point taken," the big harvester said, spreading his hands in defeat.

After what seemed like half a cycle, the old man had brought them away from the populated parts of the metropolis and to a single boardwalk that led to a modest building nestled in thick branches and nearly hidden from sight. During their short journey, he had amiably schooled them on the treetop city and the gats that coated the trees in a fine armor. They walked up to it and heard a struggle from inside that shook the walls from within. As they approached, Mikal's hand instantly went to a blade handle he had hidden on his waist. A man's voice could be heard roaring in defiance, and the ears of the chattle next to them pinned back in agitation.

"I see he refused the food and drink offered to him," the old man said ruefully.

"Seamus!" a frantic voice called from the doorway, and a man dressed in white strips of cloth ran out toward them, slamming the door behind him. "He got loose," he said breathlessly, slowing in front of them.

"Loose?" the old man Mikal now knew as Seamus said. "You let that tampered one get away?"

Seamus's annoyance and disappointment was plain in his voice, and the man in white cringed but made no move to run back to the house. "Not the tampered one," the man said. "That one has been calm, like he is waiting for something."

"Well, perhaps you can help us," Seamus said, looking at Mikal.

Just then, the door burst open to reveal a disheveled Sen standing on the threshold. Mikal had never seen the former doyen lose the cool exterior that normally dominated his features before. Even after he was tortured by the Domain captain, Tek, once he had recovered, Sen remained calm. Now, the man's face was affected by a rage and frustration that made even Mikal take a step back.

"Where is she?" Sen asked darkly as he descended the steps down to the pathway.

Of course, this would have to do with his daughter.

"I have told you," Seamus said, spreading his hands out and stepping backward, "we don't know."

"You have control over the creatures that attach themselves to the trees," Sen said, clenching his fists. "You have clawed, furry assassins patrolling the walkways. You have single-handedly ensured that no Domain soldier has survived the journey into this damned forest. Yet, you expect me to believe that you can't find a girl who practically radiates with power?"

Mikal started laughing. He knew the others were staring at him, but he couldn't control himself. The relief that she had escaped on her own had washed over him, and the tension he had felt budding in his gut that she was at the mercy of this treetop society and their tampered creatures dissipated. Lu could take care of herself.

After catching his breath, he said as much to Sen.

"They tried to get Lu to activate their runes," Sen said, anger lacing his voice.

"They what?" Mikal asked.

He hadn't even thought about the possibility that every outer planet was a prison like Dalia. There was one key to escape, and it involved calling the Domain down on them through ancient runes—runes that were only activated by one powerful enough to draw energy from the cosmos. That one was his daughter. She was the one they had been trying to breed into existence. Lu should have been born on a planet like this, not on a moon destined to be destroyed.

Seamus, for his part, looked almost sheepish. "I am an old man. My time to protect my people is ending, and I mean to destroy as much of the Domain as possible before I die. Her power calls her to activate them. She won't be able to resist it for long."

"And yet you lost her?" Mikal asked, not waiting for an answer.

Five had disappeared into the house, and no one had made a move to stop him. Mikal followed the crawler, leaving Sen to stand outside with Seamus and the others. Five didn't hesitate to walk to a back room, his heavy footfalls causing the old wood to creak uncomfortably. Mikal followed him to find First shackled to a wall. The chains seemed too small to hold him, but Mikal suspected there was more to them when Five tried to break them and could not.

Mikal slipped out a small energy gun from his inner coat pocket and pointed the gun dead center on the chain and blasted it. The thin metal melted away, and First stood, dropping the shackles to the floor.

"Where is she?" Mikal asked.

"Safe, father," First said in his head. *"She is being kept hidden by the old one's granddaughter. The chattle are watching over her. They are drawn to her, like we are drawn to her."*

Mikal didn't want to think about what that meant. He nodded, satisfied that for now she was somewhere the Domain and the people of OR-32562 couldn't use her. Still, he needed to know more about the Domain and the Capitol. Soon, they would send a rescue for the ship stranded outside of the trees, and Mikal had to decide what to do for his people. He looked around and briefly entertained the thought of making a home here for his daughter and the other Dalians.

Eventually, Caden would make his move against them. The man had been cordial to the Dalians thus far, but in the end, he was still an animal of the Domain. Caden had shown his colors before Mikal had left him. Still, Mikal had left his people in that ship. It felt like time was running out for them.

He and the crawlers emerged from the house to find Seamus and Sen had apparently reached an uneasy truce with each other. Sen had snapped a branch off a tree and had the jagged point of the wood pressed against Seamus's throat. The old man was pinned on the ground beneath Sen's foot. Kelvin, Gordo, Charli, and Stap had retreated to the far corners of the wide walkway and were wisely staying silent.

The chattle surrounded Sen and Seamus with teeth bared and growls that reverberated through the wood beneath Mikal's feet. They circled the two, walking sideways with ears pinned flat against their heads. Sen appeared not to notice them. The former doyen seemed to have found his calm again.

Mikal sighed.

47

As soon as her feet landed on the ledge below, Lulu turned and found herself nose-to-nose with Sunshine. She had been watching for the chattle but hadn't noticed her return. Lulu's hands were shaking from the burning of the rope and the adrenaline of belaying down the side of a tree taller than the Sanctuary. She dropped the rope and put her hands in the air in the universal signal for surrender. The chattle chuffed at her shirt and surprisingly rubbed her giant head up against her waist.

The force of the affectionate rub was enough to almost knock Lulu off her feet, but she steadied herself and dropped one hand to tentatively rub one of the beast's ears as she had seen Mina do. It was softer and warmer than she expected, and Sunshine leaned into her hand, demanding more. Lulu felt herself helplessly grinning.

"She likes you," Mina said, dropping down from the branch above the ledge. "Chattle only like those born with the gift."

"I don't know that I would call anything I can do a gift," Lulu said thoughtfully, still rubbing Sunshine's ear. "I only bring violence and ruin."

"The chattle disagree," Mina said as if that settled the matter. "You should try riding one!" she exclaimed after a minute of thought.

"Oh, I don't think that would be a good idea," Lulu said, laughing.

"Sure, it would," Mina said, beaming. "Sunshine thinks so. Don't you, Sunshine?"

The chattle leaned further into Lulu's touch as if in answer, and Mina grabbed her other hand to pull her further toward the giant animal. Lulu's heart was racing, and she didn't know why she was allowing this little girl to talk her into something so crazy. Sunshine crouched low, and Lulu found herself swinging one leg over and…

The chattle moved with such blinding speed and grace that it stole the breath from Lulu's lungs, and she scrambled to hold on to Sunshine's shoulders. They bounded up toward the top branches of the trees effortlessly. Lulu resisted the urge to grab onto the fur, thinking that would hurt just as much as getting her hair pulled. Instead, she tried to do what she had seen the children do and gripped with her legs. Sunshine seemed to respond and leaped into the sky.

Lulu's stomach lurched, and she found herself releasing the chattle as they dove, her arms extended out like she was flying. The landing was jarring but not as much as she had expected, and Lulu found she was disappointed that they were back with Mina. Her short ride was over already. Her hair was disheveled, and she felt her face flush as she stumbled off Sunshine. Lulu walked to sit on the edge of the landing with her feet dangling over the edge to comb out her braid with her fingers.

Mina sat on her right, and Sunshine flopped down on her left.

"How's your back?" Lulu asked after a moment.

"Oh, that?" Mina asked twisting to get a look at her torn shirt. "That's nothing. I was mad at myself. I should have seen that coming."

"He cheated," Lulu said.

"No, he didn't." Mina smiled. "It's called battle, and Gideon is my partner. He is supposed to be tough on me. That's what Seamus says. There are no rules. Seamus says there aren't rules in real life, so we shouldn't show weakness by playing with them."

Lulu shuddered. She thought back to the fights she had seen orphan boys get into in the shanties. They had been preparing themselves and each other for a life of servitude to the Wards. They didn't hold back on each other either.

"Seamus says the Domain doesn't fight fair. Why should we?" Mina asked, echoing her thoughts.

"How long has Seamus been talking about fighting the Domain?" Lulu asked.

"Ever since I was born," Mina said. "He talks to the gats better than anyone, and he's the one who set them up to kill intruders. He's the reason we're all safe and no one bothers us." She eyed Lulu up and down and then amended, "Till now."

Lulu shuddered. She wondered what kind of death the gats could deliver. The tiny pinprick wounds they inflicted would have taken a while to add up. It would not have been a pleasant end.

"The Domain is evil," Mina said.

"How do you know?"

"They breed humans," she said without hesitation. "They dropped us here, weak. Many died and were laid to rest beneath that tree. We remember them at every council." Mina pointed back at the hollow tree she had left Lulu in. "The Domain left us here knowing that the blue star was poison."

Lulu had once thought she had known why her people had lived in darkness. Deep down she felt they had deserved it. Mina, on the other hand, had been raised to know better.

"We don't want to fight anybody," Lulu said, knowing it was true. "Dalians are just looking for a home."

"This place isn't our home," Mina said gravely. "Seamus always reminds us. Our home is the Capitol."

They sat in silence and listened to the stirring of the gats. Lulu had come to learn that it wasn't the wind that moved the forest on this planet. There was no wind. It was just the gats shifting, causing the tree-tops to sway. She thought of Sen. Mina had told her he was safe, but she reached out to First to make sure.

The double vision almost caused her to lose her balance, and she felt Mina's hand on her arm. The scene before her was unexpected and alarming. Sen was standing over Seamus, threatening to impale his jugular vein with a stick while two chattle nervously paced around him. Even more alarming, her father was with them.

"We have to go," she said, shaking off her connection with the crawler and swallowing past the pain blossoming in her head.

"Aren't you going to keep hiding?" Mina asked.

Lulu shook her head. "Can Sunshine carry us both?" She found herself secretly wanting to ride again.

"She can, but there are others that want to take you," Mina said. "The chattle are attracted to you like gats to a light."

As if on cue, the tree branches rustled around them, and several of the beasts in varying shades of sleek brown appeared to shove Sunshine and Mina out of their way. They descended on Lulu, and she stiffened as they sniffed at her, chuffing in her hair and clothes.

Mina giggled in the background. "They like you."

"They could eat me in a second," Lulu said nervously.

"Yup!"

"That doesn't make me feel better, Mina."

Then she registered the thoughts invading her head. It felt like the crawlers, only less coherent. She understood the meaning of the noises, but not the language. They were all "talking" to her at once, and she was reminded of the time she first saw the crawlers follow her father to reach her on the street in Dalia. It was overwhelming. She put her hands over her ears, knowing it wouldn't help.

Then one of them lashed out at the others, driving them back with sharp claws and guttural cries. Once they were far enough away, that one rubbed up against Lulu, filling her head with only one voice. It conveyed acceptance and a need to be with her. Lulu found herself reaching out with a similar emotion, and she hugged the chattle around the neck. She hadn't realized she was crying or that she had fallen to her knees until the chattle sat back on its haunches to look at her with a feral grin.

"I've never actually seen that happen to someone else before!" Mina exclaimed excitedly.

"Seen what?"

"You were chosen to be bonded, just like Sunshine chose me." The girl was practically beaming at Lulu. "Oh, now you have to name him and learn everything about him. There is so much you need to know."

Lulu felt like her head was spinning. She was not only connected to the contingent of crawlers from

Dalia, but also had inadvertently bonded with a chattle now. She still wasn't sure what they ate. Was it a gabo? She thought back to Sen and her father. How was she ever going to explain this to them?

Sen and her father.

"We have to go," she said, standing up abruptly.

The chattle moved to stand against her as if to steady her, and she rested her hand on his shoulders.

"All right," Mina said, already astride Sunshine. "Where are we going?"

"Where can we find Seamus?" Lulu asked.

"Oh, that's easy," Mina said. "He'll be at his house."

She looked at Lulu and must have seen her hesitate to get on the big chattle. This one was even bigger than Sunshine.

"You should trust him," Mina said.

"I do," Lulu said, knowing it to be true.

She delicately sat on top of the animal, and he straightened once she was on, leaving her feet dangling off the ground. Once he was at his height, Lulu realized he was a full head taller than Sunshine. When he leaped from the platform, she never lost her balance. It felt like the chattle was making minute adjustments to keep her upright. She lifted her arms in the air, feeling the leaves whoosh past her fingertips. He was hers, and he wouldn't let her fall. They flew through the blue-dappled light like her chattle had wings.

48

Mikal needed to diffuse the situation. He had never seen Sen provoke violence, and, Mikal had to admit, it was justified. Still, this was unlike him.

"Sen," he said, carefully taking a step forward.

Sen didn't acknowledge him. The chattle didn't look at Mikal either, their eyes trained on the former doyen, teeth bared. Mikal watched the people around him. Kelvin looked surprised, the big man's eyes wide. He would have watched Sen calmly give sermons on the steps of the Sanctuary. Now, he was seeing another side to the religious figurehead. Stap had a small smile on his face. The boy, growing up in the shanties, had a taste for violence that he had been taught by his brother. Gordo didn't know Sen very well, but he was cautiously eyeing the situation all the same. It was Charli who caught Mikal's attention.

The beautiful girl had befriended his daughter and volunteered to join them. She was a daughter of the Capitol but had expressed disdain for their ways. She had shown Lulu respect and awe while on board the Domain ship. Mikal would have expected her to be trembling at the scene laid before her, but she showed no fear as she studied the chattle and Sen.

Her eyes glanced up, and she saw Mikal studying her. She shrugged her shoulders at him, as if to say she had no idea how they had gotten there. Her face had relaxed, and Mikal judged that he had miscalculated her strength earlier. He pushed the girl to the back of his mind. He had more pressing things in front of him.

"Listen, son," he said, using the title he used when Sen had been just a boy Mikal had plucked off the streets.

At that Sen glanced over at him, but only for a moment before he turned back and pressed the shredded wood further against Seamus's throat.

"This man may be able to help us against the Domain," Mikal said, trying a different tactic. "He may be able to help us with the Dalians still left on that ship."

Sen's shoulders dropped imperceptibly, and Mikal knew he had him. He was about to press further when the trees above them erupted in a shower of leaves and agitated gats.

Not much could break Mikal's composure. He had watched men die by his hand and had moved on within seconds to kill another. He hadn't even been shocked when Laima lit the dark Dalia skies in eerie, swirling green light. Mikal was a mask of self-possession. The sight of his daughter bursting through the trees while sitting astride a chattle, however, broke through his composure.

"Lu?" he asked, hearing his own voice echoed by Sen's, as the beast landed with protracted claws finding purchase on the wooden walkway.

His daughter looked exuberant. In that moment, she was a replica of her mother Tess, and Mikal had to blink to focus his vision. She seemed reluctant to get off the beast. Once her feet were planted, her chattle strode over to the other beasts threatening Sen. It let out a roar that sent a shock wave through the gats on the trees. The beast was clearly bigger than the others, and he seemed to radiate a confidence that declared him to be in charge. The other chattle seemed to sense it too, backing off with their ears still pinned flat. They lowered their heads so that their big chins almost brushed the floor.

"Sen, are you all right?" Lu asked.

Sen dropped the stick he had been ferociously brandishing until a moment ago and ran to Lu. They collided, and Sen's arms wrapped her in a tight embrace. Mikal let the moment linger as Seamus struggled awkwardly to his feet. Mikal stepped forward and steadied the man, finding that a small girl who had ridden in on the other chattle was bolstering Seamus's other side.

"Mina, when did you find her?" Seamus asked sternly.

The girl looked at her feet sheepishly and quailed. "She needed time!"

"Time?" Seamus asked. "You know we don't have much time. The Domani are coming for that ship. We need something to draw them into the trees."

Mikal looked at his daughter just as she was being released by Sen. The former doyen had fiercely kissed the top of her head before releasing her. Mikal loudly cleared his throat; Lu ran over to her father, and he wrapped her up in a bear hug.

"I told you to stay away from the trees," she said, her voice muffled against his arm.

"Did you think I would listen?" he asked. "I told you to stay on the ship."

"Did you think I would listen?" she asked, releasing him with a grin.

"Lulu," Seamus interrupted the exchange, "will you at least listen to the council and consider how your power could be used to help my people?"

"Little sister's power is her own," said First in a raspy voice behind him. "No one else's."

Lu ran over to embrace the crawler while he awkwardly patted the back of her head. The chattle who had attached himself to his daughter startled Mikal with a loud sniff on his pant leg. Lu laughed and walked over to rest her hand on the chattle's wide forehead. The creature leaned into her hand and sat down next to her as she faced Seamus. Lu seemed to stand taller with the chattle by her side. All of the "tampered" beings seemed to orbit their attention around Mikal's daughter like she was Laima itself.

"Her power will soon belong to the Capitol," Seamus said fiercely. "They will come for her once they know she's here. You left others back there on that ship. Even if you don't know what you have, those people surely do. It is better to draw the fight in here and draw them in on our own terms."

Mikal had to admit that the old man's words made sense. Caden had seemed angry he had lost Lu, even though he considered her dead already. They could just remain hidden and hope that the Domain assumed they had been lost for good. Not if Seamus got his way.

"They won't come out here unless they know she's alive," Mikal said, and Sen nodded in silent agreement.

"You would leave the rest of the people from your planet on that ship to be distributed as they will?" Seamus asked.

"They are still better off than they were on Dalia," Mikal said.

"You know nothing of the Domain," Seamus said. "They would have been better left to burn."

Kelvin sprang forward, reaching for the old man's throat with a primal roar of rage. One of the chattle intercepted and tackled him to the ground before he could reach the old man. The two slid in an intertwined mess of man and fur across the platform until they stopped at the edge. The chattle placed both paws on the harvester's chest and bared his teeth, mere inches from his face.

"It was the fate of some Dalians to stay with the planet," Mikal said quietly, briefly envisioning Kelvin's mother overtaken by smoke and flames.

The old man seemed taken aback by Kelvin's sudden attack, but at Mikal's words he let out a sharp whistle. The chattle responded by stepping off Kelvin's chest. The big animal paced next to him, warily watching his prey as Kelvin found his feet. He held his hands in the air, signaling a truce.

Seamus cleared his throat and said, "I merely meant that the Domani would make your people into slaves. They have no skills to be soldiers in their fleets. They would be laborers in the Capitol or breeders on an outer planet. Only the Domani and the Lessers have power in that place."

"Our people don't want power," Lu said.

Seamus looked at her thoughtfully. "You came from a dark planet, yes? Just a moon really if my history serves. You weren't the only ones sent to live in the dark ring. There is no sun nearby. You only existed thanks to the radiation belt that heats the system."

"How do you know all of this?" Lu asked shrewdly. Mikal had been wondering the same thing himself.

"I worked in the Capitol. I was educated in the Capitol. Everyone there knew you were destined to burn eventually. They teach it to their children. You were just one of many experiments in the dark ring. Unlike where you are from, the outer planet ring is rich with toxic suns. It was the hope that we would breed stronger because of it—just as it was the hope with you in the darkness."

Mikal thought of the surprise in the faces of the Domain soldiers when they first saw a crawler. They had not expected the Wards, or Lessers, to "tamper" other human beings. They hadn't even expected Dalia to still exist. The Wards had encouraged worship of Laima, and the people looked to it for strength. It had been ingenious. For the first time, Mikal wondered if he had been used just to create Lu. He thought of Tess's dying face as she stared blankly at the green-lit planet circling above.

"They left beacons across the galaxy for one such as you to activate," Seamus said. "You are very special to them, Lulu. Only eleven others had activated the beacons in the decade before I had left the Capitol. These Domani now serve in the highest order."

"What am I?" she asked, and Mikal ached at the anguish he heard in his daughter's voice.

"You are immune to the radiation of the cosmos. You can use it and call to it, just as it calls to you," Seamus said. "Help us fight the ones that made you. Don't become one of them. They will brainwash you into believing in the beauty and power of the Capitol. They will tell you that being close to the Capitol is to be close to God."

"So, I should become one of you?" Lu asked sharply. "I should want to destroy others and throw my own people into danger to fight against the Capitol? I should want to fight against a power that I've never seen because you tell me it's evil?"

Seamus swallowed what he had been about to say next. "Yes," he replied simply instead.

"No," Lu said and walked away. Her enormous chattle and two crawlers followed readily until they rounded the corner and were lost in the trees.

49

harli could hear her own heart beating in her ears. Her breath came raggedly as she ran, and her feet pounding the ground sounded loud in the still night air. Her hands burned from sliding down the thick rope that held the platform leading up into the trees. Her ankle had rolled painfully when she dropped the last ten feet or so to the ground, and she felt it swell against the inside of her boot as she ran. She had swung wide so as not to disturb the sleeping Dalians who had been left in the clearing. As she ran through the trees now, Charli felt the sleeping gats stir at her passing.

With every step, the hairs on the back of her neck tingled in anticipation of being stung and covered with the deadly creatures. She knew that the torment they felt while being corralled into the clearing had been child's play to the gats. Charli knew that the gats were responsible for the deaths of Domain soldiers who had come before. She knew that they could eat the flesh of a man off his bones. With each passing step in the darkness, she felt her heart rate accelerate with adrenaline. She knew she could die returning to the ship, but Charli had to try.

Charli had grown up as the child of a Lesser on the Capitol; Charli had listened to Seamus's words and knew the truth of them, from his perspective. Her father had taught her the way of the Domain from a young age, and she had grown up knowing that he served a higher purpose. He served to advance humanity. It was a shame that her pretty mother soiled their genes. If not for her, Charli might have been born gifted.

Still, Charli could see the strain of power in Lulu's features. She did not envy that type of power, but she knew it had been wasted on the one from Dalia. Lulu hadn't even known what the Capitol was. That moon was like an uneducated orphan, lost to time and space in the dark ring. The people it had spawned were savages. Even the Lessers were defiant, creating tampered abominations out of their own people. It made Charli nauseated to think about it. They should have never landed on Dalia. They should have let it burn with that beacon. Lulu was not worthy of the Domani.

Her breath was shorter as she ran, but the stirrings of gats caused her to spur on against the pain blooming in her chest from the exertion. Charli had one motivation for survival. She needed to get to Caden. She needed to warn him.

Standing among the beasts on OR-32562 and that radicalized old man, Charli had felt her pulse quicken. The uneducated Dalians had not seemed a threat until that moment. They were docile as long as they weren't threatened. It reminded Charli of the animals in the menageries on the Capitol. As long as their young were not mistreated and they were fed, the animals would let themselves be held captive. Her father had taken her there, and they often strolled the paths between exhibits, discussing the breeding programs that made the colors of the offspring so much brighter than their parentages'.

Except the darkness has leached these ones of color, she thought, running through the silent trees. Charli felt the trees watching her and knew that the old man saw her. Why did he let her live?

When she finally reached the tree line, Charli's steps were no longer fast. She was uncoordinated with fatigue, and her feet stumbled in the grass. She reached the door, and her numb fingers finally hit the button to open the hatch after a few tries. Once inside, Charli collapsed. Even with the door closing behind her, she felt like her skin was being stung by gats chasing her. She cried into the soft, padded floor in wracking sobs until one of the Dalians found her there.

The Dalian wrapped her in one of their dirty cloaks and helped her walk to the ship's bridge, where she saw Caden. His long blond hair, once a marker for his high station in the Capitol, had been severed. No longer was it tied at the nape of his neck, but it was tucked awkwardly behind his ears in the style of a boy just released from his parents. His face bore the countenance of a man though, and his eyes widened in surprise at the sight of Charli standing in the doorway.

At the sight of Caden looking at her, she squared her shoulders and shook off the help of the Dalian helping her. Her shoulders felt dirty after being touched by those pale hands.

"Charli?" Caden asked. "I thought you went to find Lulu."

"I barely managed to escape with my life," she said breathlessly.

Charli found her pulse quickening again as Caden approached her. The entire crew was watching them, but she had eyes only for him. His hands grabbed her arms roughly as he moved her to a chair. She sat, her eyes avoiding the charred spot of melted metal that had once been the captain's chair.

"Tell me everything," he said, kneeling in front of her so that his face was in line with hers.

Charli was lost in his eyes. "I went to see if I could get more information about the planet and to keep an eye on the Dalians for you."

Caden's eyes softened as he realized her devotion to him. "Of course, you should be commended for doing something so selfless and brave."

"Oh, Caden," Charli said, tears spilling down her cheeks.

Caden brushed her face with the back of his hand. Charli noticed the crew looking away and pretending they were not in the room. Charli had met Caden when they were training for the fleet. They had always been friendly, but Caden had never known her silent devotion to him. He would never know what she had to do to make sure they were assigned to the same ship together. He would never know the lengths to which she would go to be with him.

"Sh," he soothed her. "You're safe now."

"No," she said. "We're not safe. Those people out there will kill us. They mean to attack the Domain and fight us."

Caden laughed. It was instantly clear to Charli that he had no idea of the danger of these people. She had to get him off this planet. She had to make sure he was safe.

"Lulu is dead," she said quickly. "We have no reason to stay here. We need to leave the Dalians here and use the remaining fuel to return to the Capitol."

Caden frowned. "Are you sure? You've seen her body?"

"Yes," Charli said. "I barely escaped with my life."

Caden seemed disappointed and thoughtful. "What of her father?"

"He's dead too," Charli said, looking him in the eye. "We need to leave now, or these savages with kill us too."

"We just got signal from the rescue ship," he said. "They'll be here in less than a cycle. It's going to be all right, Charli. We're going home."

Charli sagged against his chest, feeling the warm embrace of his arms. Caden was safe, and they would leave Lulu and her pale ilk to rot on OR-32562.

50

Lulu watched the bustle of people below. She sat perched on a branch that hung over the main thoroughfare. She hadn't been able to sleep on the wide branch, even nestled against the warm back of her chattle. Now, in the morning light, the people of OR-32562 walked in the shade. Their bare feet hit the wooden boards, naturally and casually avoiding the rays of pale blue starlight that shone between the leaves. Lu recalled Mina telling her of the blue-star-sickness, and she wondered if merely touching the light caused them to be ill.

The chattle who lay next to her shifted his weight and yawned, exposing pearly white teeth as long as her forearm. Lulu felt enough trust for this new-found creature in her life that she would have placed her arm in his mouth without fear. She studied the chattle, and her eyes followed the way the blue light dappled against his soft coat. Brown in some areas,

when the light hit it, his coat turned silver. He reminded Lu of the ash that permeated the atmosphere on Dalia.

"Ash," she said to the chattle. "That is your name."

The beast squinted his eyes briefly at her, and
his tail flicked in acknowledgement. Lulu felt his approval in her mind, and she smiled. She looked down
to see if the crawlers were still standing guard in the
shadows on the walkway. She had needed to clear
her head up in the trees, and her wayward crawlers
were not about to make the climb behind her.

"*You go,*" First had said in her head, looking up. "*I
am not about to disturb the tiny, sharp flying things.*"

Lulu had barely noticed the gats since being up
in the trees. They seemed so passive to the people
who lived here. It was a wonder that they could be
so dangerous. On an impulse, Lulu hopped off the
branch, sending a simultaneous signal to the giants
waiting below. Her stomach lurched with the fall,
and she felt weightless for a moment before landing
safely in First's arms.

"*A little more warning next time, little sister,*" the
crawler thought.

"I need to keep you on your toes," Lulu said
aloud, patting his broad chest as he set her down.

If Lulu hadn't known better, she would have said
that Five rolled his eyes. That one has been spending too much time with her father, she thought. Ash
dropped down gracefully to land next to the three

of them, and First acknowledged the chattle with a nod of his head.

"Well, I suppose we should go back to Sen and my father," Lu said.

They walked down the winding pathways, and Lulu intentionally let the blue light hit her shoulders and head as they made their way. It felt good, and she closed her eyes at the peace of the trees and the light.

"Excuse me!" An older woman bristled when Lulu nearly collided with her.

"I'm sorry," she said, sidestepping.

The woman stopped and stared at Lu for a moment as if deciding something. Finally, after interminable scrutiny, she asked, "Are you going to call the Domain here?"

Lulu was taken aback by the woman's directness. The woman's eyes bored into her, and Lulu felt acutely uncomfortable.

"Should I?" she asked.

"It doesn't matter what you do," the woman said. "The Domain will find you." She glanced at the crawlers. "You bleed the power they seek, like a walking sun."

With that, the woman gathered her skirts and brushed past her. Lulu stood in the pathway dumbfounded by the interaction. Ash rubbed against her side—causing her to stumble sideways—and she shook her head, smiling at the chattle.

"You're right," she said. "Let's go."

They kept walking until they rounded the corner to Seamus's house. Lulu half expected to find them still standing outside in front of it, arguing among themselves, but they seemed to have moved inside. Two chattle paced in front, and they both dipped their heads at Ash as they walked by.

"You in charge here?" she asked the chattle.

Ash huffed in response.

Lulu quietly snuck in through the front door to find Mina arguing with Seamus in the main room of the house. Sen and Mikal were standing awkwardly side by side against the back wall. Her father had a careful mask of indifference, and Sen looked calm as they watched. The others who had been with them weren't in the room.

"She'll come back," Mina said defiantly. "We should just stay here."

"We need to find her before it's too late," Seamus said. "You just don't know what you're speaking of, Mina girl."

"I know because Sunshine knows," Mina said. "She'll be back."

"The council meets midday, and we need to have an answer," Seamus said. "Ask that blasted chattle of yours where she is now!"

"Right there," Mina said, pointing at Lulu standing in the doorway.

When Seamus turned to look where she was pointing, Mina stuck her tongue out at the back of his head. Lulu almost laughed, but she registered the serious expression on Seamus's face and wisely schooled her face. Lu gave a sheepish wave to Sen and her father. The former had a grin on his face, but Mikal looked wary. His expression told her he thought she should not have returned.

"Ah!" Seamus exclaimed. "We were just discussing you."

"I heard," Lu said simply and Mina giggled.

"Well," he said with his hands resting on his hips as though he was about to roll up his sleeves and get to business. "The council will be pleased you could join us." He put up his hand before she could say anything in protest. "Now my girl, I know you are a guest here and we asked quite a bit of you last time, but I assure you, this will be a discussion. Nothing more."

Lulu thought back to her first encounter with Seamus. His eyes, buried in wrinkles, were sharp and shrewd underneath. Those same eyes implored her to follow him now. No longer did he command her to do things as he had once done when they first arrived. Lulu sensed a shift in her status and wondered if it had anything to do with her display at the last council meeting. Sensing her agitation, Ash stood in front of her, casually placing his body between her and Seamus.

"I will go," she said, and her father sighed.

"It's settled then," he said, clapping his hands together with wrists resting on top of the curved wooden stick he leaned on. "The council meets when the star sets. In the meantime, you must be starving. Mina girl, don't just stand there being useless. Find our guest and her, eh, companions"—he gestured at the crawlers and Ash—"something to eat and a place to wash up and sleep."

Mina looked flabbergasted at the change in tone from Seamus, but she walked up to Lulu and took her hand to lead her toward the back of the house. Sunshine gracefully rose from where she had been lying next to Mina to walk next to Ash, rubbing against the bigger chattle affectionately. Lulu could feel the warmth coming from him in her mind.

"You like her a bit, Ash?" she whispered.

Ash shook his head, letting his pointed ears flop with the motion. Lulu knew that if he were human, he would have been blushing.

"Ash?" Sen asked, joining her as she followed Mina.

The big chattle's ears perked up, and he watched Sen with a side eye as they walked.

Lulu stepped closer to Sen so that they were almost touching. "It's his name," she said. "He's like the floating pieces of burned rock on Dalia."

Ash inserted himself between them, nosing Sen aside. Sen looked down at him with a small crooked smile. "It seems he doesn't share well."

Lulu dipped her head, not knowing what to say to that. Sen seemed to smile more lately. She found that she liked it.

"Ahem." Mina cleared her throat at an alcove with a washbasin and a small pallet in the corner.

It wasn't much, but to Lulu it looked like heaven.

"I'll come back with some food," she said.

Mina left, but before Lulu could collapse on the soft bedding piled in the corner, her father rounded the corner. She sighed, sensing a lecture. Sen backed up a step to defer to Mikal.

"What were you thinking coming back here?" he asked.

"Well, I thought you might be worried," she said, hearing her voice sound weak to her own ears. She knew that wasn't the real reason.

"You know what they want you to do," he said.

Lulu nodded. She knew.

"We could just stay here and make a life, Lu," he said. "It's what Tess would have wanted for you. There is light here. There are no Wards, and there is no Sanctuary. We could hide from the Domain."

Lulu closed her eyes. She thought of the warm blue light hitting her shoulders and the docile gats that somehow made her feel safe. She thought of riding Ash through the leaves and the feeling of flying. All those images shattered in her mind like so much glass. The older woman was left standing on the wood in front of her mind's eye.

"You bleed the power they seek, like a walking sun."

"We can't hide," Lulu said.

Mikal nodded. It was clear he had come to the same conclusion, but he had been hoping she hadn't. Mina returned with a plate of foods that carried unfamiliar scents. It made Lulu's mouth water. She reached for the plate and started eating without hesitation. By the time she looked up, half the plate was clean. She licked her fingers once before attacking the second half of the dish.

"Well, we know somebody could poison her food without her noticing," Sen remarked dryly.

Lulu stuck her tongue out as she had seen Mina do, and she moved to sit on the fluffy pallet tucked back in the alcove. Any plans to rest in peace were dashed by the presence of a chattle. Ash's legs and tails spilled over the edge of the pallet in an uncomfortable-looking fashion, but the big animal was already asleep.

Lu shoved the big creature over, and he didn't stir as she nestled against his warm body. Ash moved a giant paw to gently drape it over her, and she settled in. As Lu fell asleep, she heard the muffled voices of Sen and her father discussing the council of OR-32562.

51

On Dalia, Finn had just been a harvester. He had always been considered a careful and quiet man. He worked under Kelvin in the back fields with only the soft sound and sight of palia grain. When Finn closed his eyes, he could still see the faint phosphorescent glow in the darkness. The ash would settle on his back as he worked, but he would gladly breathe that in than spend one more minute on the Domain ship.

Finn had never been a family man, but now he found himself a steward of tens of orphan boys. They looked to him for leadership, and he tried to keep them busy with team exercises and menial tasks, knowing from his own childhood that this was what all boys needed. He had made it his new life mission to cultivate these boys of Dalia, just as he had cultivated palia grain.

Now, he stood in front of Caden, the unofficial captain of the ship, as he surveyed the cargo bay where the boys had made their home. Many of the boxes had been appropriated into shanty-like homes that now wound in organized mazes. It was a mini-replica of the shanties that sat in the shadow of the Sanctuary. The boys were proud of their work, and Finn did not discourage the activity. "What harm could it possibly do?" he had asked himself.

"The Domain rescue ship will be here any minute, and we are to empty the cargo bay of anything valuable so as to load it onto their ship," Caden said, pacing in front of the impressive architecture. "How are we supposed to get through any of this with this mess?"

The boys were hiding in their makeshift shanties, and Finn could see a wisp of hair sticking out here and there. He thought he even heard giggling from some of the younger ones.

"The boys were homesick is all," Finn said.

"Homesick?" Caden asked. "For what? The dark hole you people called a home?"

Finn could see the pretty girl who had made friends with Lulu standing behind Caden. Charli was her name, he thought, proud of remembering. Her smile had once seemed friendly, but now it held only disdain. He wondered how she had come back, but there had still been no sign of Mikal, Kelvin, Sen, or the others.

CAROLYN GROSS

"Yes, sir," Finn said. "Dalia was the only home we knew."

"Well, now you will know better," Caden said. "The Domain will enlighten you. The Domain will make all of you savages human again."

"If being human means being like you, we don't want it!" a child's voice called from within one of the cargo crates.

Caden stopped pacing and walked toward where he heard the voice.

"Come out, little one," he said. "Don't be frightened."

"We're not scared of you!" another voice called.

"Oh, is that so?" Caden asked.

He kicked over one of the leaning towers of crates, exposing several boys. They tried to scatter, but Caden caught one by the neck and lifted him bodily off the ground.

"Your hair looks stupid," the boy spat, his feet futilely kicking at the air.

It was just the type of silly thing a boy would say, but Finn winced. Caden squeezed and the boy squealed in pain, clawing at Caden's fingers. Finn even heard the pretty Charli inhale sharply at the sound. The harvester didn't think. He picked up one of the boards that had come loose from the cargo crates and threw it at Caden with all the force he could muster.

The wood clanked off Caden's head, and the captain lost his grip on the boy, who ran away as soon as his feet hit the ground. Caden turned his ire toward Finn, but before he could make his way toward the harvester, a crawler stood in his way. The boys nearby gathered behind the legs of the giant crawler, and Finn listened in astonishment as the black-eyed crawler spoke.

"You will not touch these people," the crawler said in a voice that was raspy from disuse.

Caden had seemed intimidated at first, but then a slow, sick smile spread across his face. It was as though he remembered something only he found funny. It made Finn feel the acid in his stomach. Caden snapped his fingers, and several soldiers seemed to materialize from where they had been lining the walls. They unwound thin metal chains from their sleeves and, without a word, started whipping and restraining the crawler with them.

The giant of Dalia, a creature of Laima in Finn's eyes, didn't go down without a fight. He roared and swung his arms, but eventually he toppled beneath the weight of the tiny metal chains.

"The Domain has ways of subduing creatures made by the gifted," Caden said with a smile. "Even if those creatures happen to be abominations against the laws of man. Carp metal has a nasty way of binding even the biggest tampered."

Finn wondered at the vicious metal links and thought that surely the abomination must be them. The people of Dalia had long been afraid of the crawlers, but since the fall of the Sanctuary, the giants had done nothing but protect them. Looking at the crawler panting beneath the overwhelming weight of the thin carp metal chains, Finn felt his own rage and frustration grow. He was no longer afraid of the Domain. He was certainly no longer afraid of the so-called captain standing in front of him.

The once-harvester, who hailed from a planet shrouded in darkness from the scorching light of a too-bright sun, felt his own time slow down. He looked at the faces of the orphaned boys watching and cowering behind storage crates. Many had tears streaking down their faces, no longer covered in soot but pale all the same.

Finn had always been considered a careful and quiet man.

He picked up a heavy beam of wood that had broken free from a large crate and, without hesitation, swung with all his not-inconsiderable might. The end of the board connected with the back of the head of a nearby soldier with a sickening thwack. Before the others could register what was happening, he crouched and took the same board, now with its end covered in hair and blood, and swung it wide and low. It connected with the next soldier's shin bones, causing him to pitch forward onto his face.

By now, the element of surprise was gone, and the soldiers all turned their attention to Finn. With no fear for his personal safety, he leaped forward into the fray like a berserker. Every foot gained toward the prone crawler was a victory for Dalia. He barely felt the slice of a blade or tissue-damaging punch of an energy wand as he drove through the Domain soldiers. Bloody and battered, Finn reached the crawler and found himself disoriented and on his belly. He reached forward and grabbed a handful of the thin chains weighing him down. They had tiny spikes that drove into his skin as he closed his fist around them and pulled.

Finn had always been considered a careful and quiet man. So, it was that he surprised even himself with the last roar of defiance as he pulled on the chains that bound the crawler who would protect the orphans. His boys of Dalia would see what a true Dalian spirit fought like. His last thought was of Bale, standing on top of the shanty roof, screaming in defiance at the Domain soldiers. The young leader had defended the only home he knew. He had defended a maze of cheap shanties that nestled on top of the layers of ash that had piled up in the shadow of the Sanctuary. Finn died knowing that he had done the same.

52

Lu walked above the trees. Her feet moved, but she could only feel air beneath her. She heard no sound and felt no wind on her face. She walked toward the bright blue star in front of her and spread her arms wide as if to embrace the roiling waves of radiation and light that emanated from it. She looked down at her outstretched hands and saw that they also emitted light, but it was green. Lulu wanted nothing more than to combine herself with the star in front of her, and she yearned to touch it.

The star moved inexorably away from her, and no matter how much she struggled in the air, she couldn't get any closer. Her feet pinwheeled, and she looked down to see that she was falling and fast.

"Little sister!" The voice shattered her dream as her body hit the ground beneath the trees.

Lulu sat up trying to catch her breath. Sweat beaded down the back of her neck, and she gulped back the sickening feeling of dread that had washed over her. Ash, her chattle, wrapped his paw around her midsection and pulled her closer to him, carefully keeping his claws concealed. Lu allowed herself to feel his presence at her back, and she rested her head in her hands.

She realized that she had not really fallen but was sitting in a house built from the trees that dominated OR-32562. Sen knelt in front of her, and she slowly lifted her head. She had known it was him by the way he moved on silent and careful feet.

"Charli is gone," he said simply.

"She is?" Lu asked numbly.

She had been so preoccupied with her own dilemma that she had failed to pay attention to her new friend who had risked life and limb to help find her. A wave of guilt washed over her.

"Do you think she's lost?" she asked.

Sen shook his head.

"Mikal thinks she may have headed back to the ship," he said.

"Why would she do that?" Lu asked.

"We can't do anything about that now," he said. "It's time to go to the council these people have prepared."

Lu allowed Sen to bring her a towel drenched in cool water, and she buried her face in it. She hastily ran her fingers through her knotted hair and pulled it back in a fresh braid. Ash busied himself by brushing his own fine fur with a roughened tongue. Lu had never seen anything like it, but it seemed like a natural thing for such a creature to do.

As they emerged from the house, they were joined on the walkway by Lu's father, the two crawlers, Stap, Kelvin, and Gordo. Seamus and Mina led the way, but Sunshine chose to walk slightly behind Ash instead of in the lead as she had done before. They walked to the council in a sedate procession. Lu was lost in her own head, still reeling from the dream and the voice she had heard on waking up.

She tried to focus on her feet in front of her, and her mind wandered to what Sen had told her. Lu couldn't understand why Charli would have gone back. After all the conversations they had about the Domain and Dalia, Lu would have thought the girl a stalwart ally.

"This looks familiar." Stap's voice broke through her thoughts.

The inside of the great tree that opened up into the widened wooden arena, surrounded on all sides by a balcony of observers, revealed the scrawling and scorched runes inside. Lu looked at Stap and smiled wryly at the echo to her own thoughts when she first saw it. She had almost forgotten Stap's presence in the chamber when she had lit the runes back on Dalia.

"Don't worry," she whispered. "This won't be the same as Dalia."

Lu hoped she wasn't lying, but she could feel a familiar tug in her hands as her eyes followed the pattern on the wall.

Sen's hand reached out to hold her wrist, and he looked down with a small frown on his face.

"Where's your bracelet?" he asked.

Lu shrugged. She had noticed its absence in the tree that Mina had hidden her in and assumed it had been lost when she fell running from the council the previous night. She had tried not to think about how much the thin band of metal, given to her by her father, had meant to her.

The group of Dalians, Ash, and Gordo waited in the center of the floor as Seamus slowly and carefully made his way up to the balcony.

"Fellow dissidents," he greeted, once he was settled at the center of the arena. "Once again, we are presented with an opportunity. We can continue to hide here from the Domain and live in fear of our own sun while we wait for one of our own to be gifted enough to ignite the signal. Or"—he paused for dramatic effect—"we can take the opportunity that has been granted us. These people come from a dark ring moon. They come from a place forgotten by the Domain. They bring one among them who has the power to call the Domain back to us."

"And what do you propose we do when they get here, Seamus?" one of the older men sitting across from him called.

The group of Dalians shifted their stance to look at him and then back to Seamus.

"We fight," Seamus said. "As I have said many times before."

"We're not ready!" a woman wailed.

"We will all die here," another man said.

Lu wondered how her own people would have faced the choice. As it was, she hadn't given them one, and they were forced to fight. Of course, her home had been about to burn. She had never seen a civilization where people felt they could participate in such discourse. Dalians had only ever done what the Sanctuary told them to do. They had been blindly led by Wards—Lessers, she amended herself—under the guise of a god planet.

"At least it would be your choice!" she called up to the bickering leaders.

They became silent and looked down at her as they would at a stray gat, dying on the ground in the clearing. She almost shrank within herself; Sen's hand on her wrist squeezed, and she released him to step forward.

"Our enemy was shrouded in mystery from us," she said. "On Dalia, we thought we were the only ones in existence. We didn't know there were more. Had we known..." She trailed off.

"What would you have done?" Seamus asked quietly, his voice projecting anyway.

"We would have called the Domain sooner," Mikal said.

Lu looked back at her father and knew the truth of his words. Dalians would have fought sooner.

"We would have fought," Kelvin said, echoing her thoughts.

"Little sister!" The voice cut through every other thought, and Lu grabbed her head in both hands as she was ripped away from the council and made to see what the crawler back on the ship saw.

53

Charli watched the display of violence in horror. Her beautiful Caden seemed to relish the moment that the Dalian went down. The big man was prone on the floor, broken and bleeding. Only then did Caden leave the protection of his soldiers and step over an injured comrade to kneel next to the man. Charli didn't know what he said to him, but astonishingly, the big man lifted his head and spit blood-tinged saliva in Caden's face. It spattered in stark contrast across his blond hair, and Caden fell back as if hit. The big man pulled back with a defiant roar and ripped the carp metal free of the crawler it had been detaining.

Charli had seen carp metal lining the cages of the menageries on the Capitol. It leached the very essence of creatures that had been tampered. She had never seen one touch something though. As the crawler stood after having had the carp metal ripped off him, Charli saw that his skin was torn in thin ribbons running down his arms. His eyes took on a dull gleam for a moment, and he stood as if in a trance.

Caden used the moment of distraction to pull an energy gun from his belt, and he pressed the cold barrel against the back of the Dalian man's neck. He fired, and it was over in a second. Charli squeaked in shock at the sound it made in the enclosed cargo bay. Her ears confused the high-pitched echo of the shot with the scream of one of the boys who were hiding in the disgusting crates so that she couldn't tell the two sounds apart.

Caden stood and casually pinned his once-beautiful blond hair behind his ears. He brushed the red-tinged spittle from his cheeks and turned to Charli. She was surprised to find herself crouched by the doorway, hugging her knees to her chest. Her father would have been disappointed in the display of weakness, especially in front of a man like Caden. Charli stood and smoothed her skirts, simultaneously wiping the moisture from her palms.

Caden casually turned his back on the tampered one, trusting his soldiers to rally behind him and subdue the creature once more. As Caden drew closer, Charli started to shake. He reached a hand toward her, and she tentatively took it in both of hers. It was a moment she had waited for since meeting Caden. She pushed down the background noise of children sniffling and injured soldiers moaning.

Charli wouldn't let that ruin the beautiful love that she and Caden obviously shared.

He looked her in the eyes, and Charli caught a glimpse of the tampered beast behind him, watching them. Caden turned, following her gaze.

"He is nothing more than a tool," Caden said, turning back to her.

He left her and roughly grabbed one of the crying children by the arm, lifting him bodily off the ground in one motion. Caden held the child in front of the crawler and said, "You understand, don't you?" He shook the child in front of the tampered monster.

The crawler nodded once. There was indeed understanding behind the black depths of his eyes.

"You will submit, or these children will be the first to die for the Domain," Caden said.

The crawler tilted his head, studying Caden. He seemed docile, but Charli felt a cold, icy tingle crawl up her spine.

"Caden, leave him be," she pleaded.

Caden turned back toward her, releasing the pale-skinned urchin at the same time. The child scampered back into the crates like an insect, and Charli shuddered. As Caden made his way back to her, another sound started to build beneath their feet. The rumbling permeated the walls, and Charli steadied herself with one hand on the wall behind her. The crates rattled against each other, and a few fell from their leaning towers, scattering boards across the floor.

Caden looked at Charli, and a slow smile started to spread across his face. "The rescue ship."

Charli felt herself smiling back. Finally, they would leave this place and the Dalians behind.

Caden brushed past her to get to the door. "Find the other crawlers and restrain them," he ordered as he left.

Charli followed him and saw that he was trying to smooth back his cropped hair in vain. It was no use. He couldn't hide the length and settled on leaving it smoothed behind his ears as they approached the main door of the ship.

Caden hit the button, and they emerged into the sunlight, followed by several crew members who had joined them from the bridge. The ship that was rescuing them dwarfed their own. Having been so far removed from Domain's magnificent fleet for so long, Charli felt breathless in the ship's shadow.

"Our distress beacon must have drawn down a blessed destroyer," Caden crooned.

Charli gulped past a knot of dread in her throat. Destroyers carried the top echelon of command. They wouldn't be happy to hear of the debacle on Dalia, nor how they lost the prize they had obtained. Gifted ones were too rare to lose.

"Caden, we can't tell them about Lulu," she said, allowing panic to suffuse her silent plea as she tugged his shirt sleeve.

"Well, she's dead now," he said. "We can't help that the girl went and got herself killed on an outer planet. Calm down, Charli. It's going to be all right."

Charli couldn't help but glance into the tree line. It was as if her lie could walk out any minute and rain death on her and Caden with a thought.

"Please," she said once more into Caden's ear.

He ignored her and busied himself with straightening his uniform as the stairs descended from the massive destroyer. Their own ship fit nicely in its shadow, and Charli was reminded of the awesome power of the Domain. Armored plates that reflected burnished gold slid against each other as the ship continued to settle on the ground. It gave the effect of water reflecting the yellow sun of the Capitol. Charli was so entranced in the moving armor that she missed the first officer and his retinue descending to the ground. Ten men and women followed the officer in perfect, practiced precision. They made the crew of the *Raider* look like children playing in the sandbox.

"Tell me who you are and how this happened, soldier," the first officer said before they even reached each other.

He was a tall man with slightly hunched shoulders. His face was slightly gaunt with hollow cheeks, not from poor nutrition like the Dalians, but more like a man with chronic illness, Charli thought. He carried himself with an air of annoyance and was not amused by the short-haired Caden, puffed up in front of him.

"Caden Larsen, sir. I am the acting captain of the *Raider*. Our ship responded to a beacon from Dalia."

The man's eyes widened and lit up with sudden interest. Charli felt the knot in her throat move to her stomach.

"A beacon? From that piece of black rock in the dark ring?" he asked incredulously. He turned back to one of his officers asked, "Had we even left runes on that one?"

The man behind him said, "I don't know, First Officer. Part of the dark ring was colonized after the development of the beacons. So, it is possible."

"It was a true beacon," Caden said, his voice a little defensive. "Our former captain, Tek, was murdered by the Domani that activated it."

"Yet you managed to contain him?" the first officer asked, doubt lacing his tone.

"Her," Caden corrected him. "We allowed her and the people of Dalia to think they subdued us and brought them as far as we could with what resources we had left. That is how we ended up stranded here."

"Where is she now?" he asked with interest, scanning the faces standing outside of the *Raider*.

"She ventured off the ship despite our warnings, sir," Caden said. "The forest has taken her."

"You let her go?" the first officer asked. "On this barbaric OR planet?" His voice was suddenly quiet.

"I had no choice," Caden said, his tone now verging on a whine. "They had tampered humans with them, and the girl was powerful."

"Tampered humans?" the first officer asked, and Charli could see the mirth that was spreading through the destroyer's crew behind him.

Clearly, Caden's story was too incredible to believe. Charli had to help him.

"It's true," she said. "We have one bound with carp metal in our possession. The others are also being subdued."

"You have more than one in your possession?" he asked.

Charli nodded.

The man pressed a finger to his ear, and his eyes glazed over for a moment. He was communicating with someone inside the destroyer. Charli had heard of ear implants on the Capitol before but had never seen one used so close to her. This destroyer was not just any destroyer. Ear implants required wiring the brain itself to act as a communications device. It was not something seen with run-of-the-mill officers. They might even have Lessers on board the ship. This was not good.

She looked over at Caden, who seemed not to notice the use of the technology. Two of the officers behind the first officer moved in synchrony to a silent command only they could hear. Within moments they had apprehended Caden and were binding his arms behind his back.

"What is the meaning of this?" Caden quailed.

"You understand this is only a temporary measure until we can verify if there is any truth to your story," the first officer said. Then he moved close to Caden so that only Charli could overhear his next words. "If you did let a Domani die on your watch, then you may be sentenced to death yourself."

Caden's eyes widened, and Charli gasped. She had never been part of a beacon mission. The *Raider* was supposed to be patrol ship. She had no idea that there were laws protecting the Domani before they even reached the Capitol. She didn't know that Caden's life could be forfeit.

Then, as if by command, Charli's vision turned green.

54

Lulu felt the pain in the crawler's arms as the vile metals chains were wrapped around him once more, and then the connection was lost to her. She stumbled back, and her vision went dark with the pain blossoming in her head from staying connected for so long.

Sen's steady arms caught her, and his strong voice murmured in her ear, "I have you now."

It wasn't just the familiar pain in her head that overwhelmed her; it was what she had seen back on the ship from the eyes the crawler.

Finn. He was a Dalian. Finn fought the Domain, and it took his life.

The Domain was Charli, watching the destruction of people and yet taking no part in it. It was a pretty smile and a promise of prosperity. It was the Wards, hiding behind mysticism in their tower. It was power, unrelenting and unchecked. Lulu felt hatred for it.

She found her footing, but Sen kept his hands on her arms to steady her. Lu looked up to see her father standing nearby, his face a mask of concern. She smiled briefly at him, knowing that he understood the anger she was about to display. She looked up at the council and their silent faces studying her. A wave of acceptance and trust washed through her, and she knew it was Ash. The chattle was bolstering her.

Lu wasted no more time.

She walked toward the runes feeling heady power grow within her with every step closer to the giant tree. She stepped into the cool hollow shadow and saw that it was stone. This tree was not wooden like the others. The gats clicked and settled in her presence. Lu walked up to the stone face of the runes, and without preamble, she rested her hand flat against the runes. Rivers of green light raced from her fingertips and traced up the runes to illuminate the hollow stone tree with a spider web of light. The clicking of gats reverberated off the walls, and the hollow space filled with the overwhelming sound.

Lu felt her vision go black again, and she almost fell back, but Ash leaned against the back of her legs. She found herself grounded in him and rested her hand on his shoulder. The chattle was rumbling beneath her touch, and she allowed him to lead her, stumbling, out of the tree. The scene outside was chaotic, and as her vision adjusted, Lu saw the council evacuating from the platform even as it started to crack and shift beneath her feet.

Lu remembered the cavern and how it had collapsed the seemingly indestructible Sanctuary, and she felt her pulse quicken. Gordo had already grabbed Stap, and Kelvin was helping some of the council members descend the steps of the balconies. Sen grabbed Lu's arm and yelled, "Let's go."

Lu allowed herself to be led, flanked by her crawlers, even as she watched her father bound up the steps to bodily pick up Seamus. Lu saw a pale-brown streak fly by and knew that it was Mina on top of Sunshine, ascending into the safety of the other trees. She and the others made it to the walkway moments before Mikal and Seamus did. The rest of the council was well ahead of them.

Lu looked back and saw the collapse of the platform and watched it break apart on the branches of the trees as it fell toward the unforgiving ground below. The tree itself looked like it was bursting at the seams. Gats were flying away from it now in all directions like tiny projectiles.

The green light that Lu had ignited finally spilled out into the sky and set the pale-blue star on fire. In an instant, the entire planet was now bathed in her familiar green light. The branches of the trees cast stark shadows over everything in the now bright sky.

Lu turned to see a civilization in chaos. People, who had been taught to avoid the blue star's light, were now exposed in a far more dangerous light meant for the Domain.

"What have I done?" she asked herself.

"What you were born to do," Seamus answered her as Mikal set him on his feet beside them.

"The rescue ship is here," she said, looking at her father.

His eyes widened slightly in understanding. "You saw."

Lu nodded. "Caden killed Finn and is subduing crawlers with a cruel metal. I can't get to them anymore. I think all of them have been restrained with it."

She couldn't feel them anymore. Lu felt tears come to her eyes, and the fire of hatred that had fueled her to bathe another planet in light was dissipating. Now it was being replaced with an overwhelming sense of responsibility and guilt.

"Finn?" Kelvin asked.

Lu nodded. "He died fighting."

"Like a true Dalian," Kelvin said.

The others were silent. They stood in the blunt relief of the green light in an unspoken moment of respect for Finn and the other Dalians who had died since the collapse of the Sanctuary. They may be without a home, but Dalia was at war all the same.

"Where can we gather those willing to fight?" Mikal asked Seamus.

The old man seemed thoughtful. "Mina will lead the way."

Mina dropped down from the branches overhead on Sunshine to land lightly in front of their group.

"The game platforms," she said.

"Yes," Seamus agreed. "Tell the others with chattle to gather as many as they can," he said.

"Gideon!" Mina called even as she and Sunshine turned away from them.

"Wait!" Seamus called before she got too far, and the girl turned to listen. "When you're done with that, get the other Dalians up here on the platform."

Mina nodded and leaped off the walkway on Sunshine.

Lu could tell Ash wanted to run after them, but the big chattle stayed with her as they followed Seamus. The dark wood now seemed pale beneath her feet. The well-worn paths of the people from OR-32562 were exposed in the new light. Every so often, Seamus stopped to knock on a door that they passed to gather more people. Their group slowly multiplied and grew as the call to finally fight the Domain was answered. Lu was amazed at the tenacity of these people. She couldn't help but feel she was leading them to their deaths.

Mikal, however, seemed in his element. Just like he had back on Dalia, Lu's father fell into the role of organized violence as if he had been born to it. He huddled with Sen and Kelvin at the front of the crowd, and Seamus listened from behind, only interjecting occasionally with information about the terrain and resources. By the time they reached the enormous tree where Mina had kept Lu hidden, Mikal had an air of confidence and clear purpose about him. He exuded anticipation.

The group of Dalians who had been left in the clearing, corralled by gats, seemed no worse for the wear as they joined them. They looked about the maze of platforms and walkways with a mixture of awe and respect. People lined the walkways and large platforms meant for chattle to launch back and forth across. Soon, there were so many faces facing each other across the circle that they looked like gats.

"Fellow dissidents," Seamus started, and the murmuring of the crowd quieted down. "We have been debating whether to call the Domain to us. Now, we no longer have a choice. The enemy is here. Our oppressor is here for us. We can choose to bend to their will, just as we had when we were 'selected' back at the Capitol. Or"—he paused—"we can fight."

The clearing was filled with anger and confusion. Some voices cried out in agreement, but Lu could see others shake their head in fear and reluctance. There was surely too much division to take on the Domain. Then her father stood. On Dalia, she had watched Mikal stand on the roof of a shanty and rally a group of harvesters and orphan boys to the call.

Now, she watched Mikal walk to the edge of a ledge to address thousands gathered on all sides.

"Fellow dissidents," he started, using the title Seamus had used. "This planet could burn, and the Domain wouldn't bat an eyelash. Dalia was left to perish and burn in the dark ring. We had no history. We had forgotten the Domain just as it had forgotten us. We had a religion that kept us cowed in its absence. We lived in darkness."

Mikal waited until he was certain he had the attention of every person gathered.

"The Domain left you here to survive or die. They only stand to gain from your survival and evolution, but they lose nothing from your death. A power that cares nothing for its own body parts is destined to fail. It will encounter a moment where it is destroyed by its own flesh. Now is that moment. Now is the time that we rise in the light as the flesh of the Domain. We show them that they have something to lose in our survival."

He had them now. Lulu could feel him exert his power just as surely as she had lit the beacon floating above their heads. It crackled in the air and caused the hairs on her arms to stand.

"Fellow dissidents," Mikal continued, his voice rising louder, "you have evolved past the Domain. Your children command the life around them with their minds. You have survived the radiation of your own sun to be stronger. The Domain is soft. The Domain is weak. They are no longer the hand that feeds you. You are the hand that feeds them."

Lulu felt the power of his words. She saw the fervent light in the eyes of those listening.

"Will you now stand with Dalia in the light?" Mikal asked.

The trees erupted in a thundering chorus of humanity. Gats lifted into the air and filled the clearing before them in a beautiful clicking twister. Chattle roared across from them, and Ash bellowed next to Lu, the sound filling her rib cage. Flooded by the green beacon's light, OR-32562 was awake.

55

Charli blinked in dawning horror as her lie came to spectacular life. The pale-blue star above their heads was now overflowing in green string-like flames that seemed to threaten the treetops over the horizon. The gold-plated armor of the magnificent destroyer reflected the radiating light of the beacon and nearly blinded those standing on the ground. Caden, his arms bound behind him, looked at Charli with betrayal written on his face.

She had just wanted to protect him. A wave of nausea threatened to overtake her as Caden was dragged away from her to board the destroyer. Charli barely felt the hand roughly grab her shoulder and force her to turn away from Caden. She allowed herself to be led back into the *Raider*, numb to the chaos and the barking of orders around her. A muffled voice broke through her daze.

"Where are they?" the soldier who had grabbed her asked.

"What?" she asked dumbly.

The look on his face told her he had been trying to ask her the same question for some time. "The tampered humans," he said, exasperated.

"Oh," she said, coming back to her senses. "There is one in the cargo bay, and the others are scattered among the Dalians."

The soldier with her looked at the pale refugees with disgust as Charli led him past them to the cargo bay. She spied the short red hair of the Lesser who had called herself the leader of the Wards—Lana.

"That one is a Lesser from Dalia," she said, pointing at the woman.

Charli wanted all Dalians to suffer for what they had done to Caden. So, it was with no remorse that she watched the woman apprehended by the Domain soldiers. They were not gentle, but the woman still held her nearly bald head high with pride as she was led off the ship. Charli gave her no more thought.

She led the soldier into the cargo bay. He still held her with fingertips digging into the soft flesh beneath the front of her shoulder bones, but Charli barely felt it. She deserved the pain. The tampered one was still miraculously standing in the center of the cargo bay. The carp metal should have weighed him down to his knees, but he stood in the center of the room, surrounded by pale urchins.

To Charli's disgust, the boys stood around the crawler and the dead Dalian man, brandishing broken wood slats that had been pulled apart from the crates. The *Raider* soldiers were standing off to one side, having obviously deemed the situation under control.

"Holy Domani!" the destroyer soldier said, releasing Charli's shoulder. "Look at him."

Charli had been unimpressed with the self-titled crawlers. They were enormous to be sure, standing twice as tall as a normal man, but their mental faculties seemed to be lacking. They could barely speak unless prodded to.

"He is magnificent," the soldier said and walked up to the group of Dalian urchins to get a closer look.

The boys raised their makeshift weapons threateningly, but the soldier ignored them and turned back to Charli, a huge grin on his face.

"He is a tool," she said, repeating Caden's words from earlier. "Nothing more."

"He is a magnificent tool then," the soldier said, still in awe, inspecting the crawler from every angle.

"Can you help us get the metal off him?" one of the boys asked, standing at the edge of their circle.

"Why would I do that?" the soldier asked, his hands on his hips and an amused smile spreading across his face.

"It hurts him," the boy said.

"He will be fine," the soldier said.

"Can I tell you a secret?" the boy asked, glancing at Charli as though she was intruding on the game he was playing.

The soldier, still amused, leaned in closer. The boy whispered something in his ear, and the soldier's eyes widened in surprise right before the boy inserted a blade in between his ribs. In that instant, the carp metal dropped away from the crawler, having been cut earlier. The soldier fell forward, and the crawler lunged, carefully avoiding stepping on the boys who had surrounded him. He reached the distracted *Raider* crew before they could pull their energy wands and cracked skulls of two of them together. The boys followed him, screaming battle cries as they helped the massive tampered man dispatch the rest of the crew who had been left to watch them.

Charli ran.

She ran out into the corridor and leaped over an injured crew member almost as soon as she rounded the corner. Chaos and fighting was breaking out all over the ship as the Dalians, once docile, now fought alongside the godless creatures they had created. They fought with reckless abandon and total disregard for the sanctity of the Domain soldiers. Charli's stomach lurched at the violence, and she leaned against the wall for support.

She managed to make her way to the door and ran out into the green light, across the grass, to the safety of the destroyer. The door was extended and open, and she almost made it into the magnificent ship before a soldier caught her around the waist with one arm. Her legs kicked and her arms flailed in his grip, blind panic taking over.

"They're free! The crawlers are free and killing everyone!" she yelled.

"Crawlers?" the soldier said, trying to soothe her. "You're speaking nonsense, little miss."

Having grown up as the daughter of a Lesser in the Capitol, Charli had never been spoken to like that. The soldier set her feet down and held her against one of the gold panels with one forearm across her chest. With his other hand, he touched his ear, and his eyes glazed over. Did everyone on this ship have an implant? Charli wondered.

He looked back at her then, his eyes coming back into focus. "I've been instructed to take you to the bridge."

Charli thanked the gods. She nearly sagged in relief. The ship behind her, sitting in the shadow of the destroyer, seemed completely silent from the outside, but she knew the death and destruction that raged inside. Charli allowed herself to be led into the relatively quiet and opulent destroyer.

The floor was padded, just as the *Raider*'s was, but the air smelled cleaner somehow. She and Caden had dreamed to serve the Domain on such a ship. Now, with Caden having been detained and their own ship commandeered by godless heathens, she knew that those dreams were gone. Charli allowed herself to be led down the maze of corridors to the ship's bridge and tried not to gape at the beauty of Domain engineering laid before her. The massive star screen dwarfed anything she had ever seen. Ten times as many chairs filled the bridge as the *Raider*'s, and the clean technology of the bridge filled every one of her senses.

"What is your position on the *Raider*?"

The tall first officer she had met outside walked up to stand in front of her and the soldier who had detained her. Charli studied his name badge—Officer Nunaz.

"I am, or was, a technical officer, sir," she said, proud that her voice didn't quaver.

"One of my soldiers made it off your ship and appraised me of the situation before you escaped," he said. "You should know that the Domain considers your ship a loss. We are prepared to destroy it once we leave this planet. The 'crawlers,' as you call them, can have that husk of useless scrap metal."

Charli tried not to get defensive of the ship she and Caden had called home for several rotations. The *Raider* had certainly seemed impressive when they first left enlistment camp for their assignments. Now, standing in a destroyer, she could see why Officer Nunaz felt that way.

"We might have use for you though," Nunaz said. "Your former captain said that you went out into the trees to find the Domani."

"Yes, sir," she said. "I wanted to see if we could retrieve her."

That was a lie.

"Very valiant behavior for a technical officer," Nunaz said, scrutinizing her.

Charli tried to seem impassive. His gaze made her insides squirm. He circled around her, letting his eyes linger over her. Charli focused on keeping her back straight, but she flinched slightly when Nunaz bent down and sniffed her hair. The other crew members on the bridge seemed to take no notice, and the soldier who had brought her to Nunaz stared straight ahead.

"Your former captain," he whispered, "seems to think very little of you."

Charli swallowed back the bile that rose in her throat. She was the daughter of a Lesser on the council in the Capitol. She was better than this.

"He swears to the gods that you told him the Domani was dead. And yet"—Nunaz swept his hand out in front of him, simultaneously changing the view screen to show the star that the planet orbited, now lit from the inside with roiling green fire—"it seems that she is not only alive, but she is screaming for my attention."

Charli shuddered.

"You will come with me to my chamber and tell me everything you know about this planet and the Domani that currently hides on it."

His hand was light and gentle on the small of her back as he led Charli away from the bridge.

56

It was three cycles since Lu had lit the beacon. It was ample time for Mikal to devise a plan for defense of the forest. Now, he sat on a branch of one of the trees lining the clearing where they had initially landed. The *Raider* was dwarfed and almost completely hidden from view by a massive gold-plated ship. The gods-blighted thing occupied half the clearing.

The large chattle shifted behind him and groaned at the inactivity.

"I know, Ash," Mikal said absent-mindedly.

His daughter's chattle had convinced one of the females to allow him to ride her if Lu was with them. It made for faster travel beyond the city's walkways. The other chattle, a more petite but still impressive animal, was settled on a different branch. Her intelligent eyes were trained on the clearing.

"You don't even know what Ash is thinking," Lu said from one branch over.

Mikal smiled at his daughter. "I don't need to be gifted to know what someone is thinking."

"I think you are gifted," Lu said. "The Wards chose you for a reason, right?"

Mikal dipped his head slightly. He had always believed that Tess had loved him, and that was the only reason she chose him. He would continue to believe that long after she was gone.

"That is not the reason you were born," he said.

Lu nodded, dropping the subject. It was not the first time during the past three cycles that she tried to insinuate that he was gifted. She was convinced he had done something to influence the people of OR-32562. All Mikal had done was understand human nature. He had studied it enough while under the employ of the Sanctuary.

Suddenly, something within the massive ship shifted, and a wide ramp was lowered from its belly to rest softly on the grass. Soldiers started to emerge in perfect rows of ten. This was it.

Lu looked at him and closed her eyes. Ash leaped from his branch to steady her while she communicated with the crawlers back in the center of the forest. Once Lu opened her eyes again, she and Mikal mounted the two chattle, and Mikal took one more look back at the clearing.

The soldiers poured out of the ship's mouth like a river. He had known they would fight on foot but gained little satisfaction from knowing he had been right. From what Mikal understood, Lu was too valuable a prize to risk destroying by attacking blindly from the air.

The chattle under him leaped off the branch, and Mikal crouched low over her shoulders to steady himself as she used her claws to propel from branch to branch. His daughter, with her eerie connection to Ash, sat perfectly balanced on his back with her arms held out. Even though they were about to start a battle they would more than likely lose, Mikal couldn't help but smile at the joy on her face. They had come so far from the ash-covered darkness of their home.

By the time they reached the others, Lu's crawlers had started to prepare everyone for the impending invasion. The chattle brought them to the "game arena," and he dismounted in front of a familiar scene. Stap had his hands on his hips and was arguing with Gordo. The big cook had been embroiled in the same discussion with the Dalian orphan since they decided to fight. Mikal was beginning to feel sorry for the Domain man. Gordo and Stap had single-handedly led the organization of the food supplies they would need. Even with all the work that needed to be done, Stap still found time to argue.

"I have fought in battle before," the boy raged.

"You were an orphan before." Gordo hammered back.

"What do ya think I am now?" Stap countered.

The big chef was getting red in the face, and he switched tactics. "Not everyone in the Domain is bad."

"So?" Stap asked. "We are still at war with them."

"You are a young one," Gordo said. "You are still innocent. You shouldn't be killing people."

"I have killed before," Stap mumbled, turning away from the big man.

"Listen to your mentor," Mikal said as he walked by him to confer with Sen and Seamus.

"Yes, that's right!" Gordo exclaimed. "I am your mentor, and you should listen to me."

Lu laughed and went to grab a bite to eat from the massive stockpile Stap and Gordo had organized. Both stopped their bickering to shoo her away from the food, but only after she had pilfered two rations. As Mikal approached the enormous oak table that had been assembled on one of the game platforms, Sen rose from his seat to greet him. Lu joined them moments later, mouth full of food.

"Seamus has assured us that Mina has just as much control over the gats as him. Lu and I will take her to this point"—Sen jabbed his finger down into the crude model of the forest Seamus had made— "and wait until they are all within the trees."

"And if they split up their forces?" Mikal asked.

"Lu connects with Five, who will stay hidden with Seamus. She will let him know where the others approach."

"Good," Mikal said, pleased that they knew their roles.

It was only the first plan of attack that had been organized for the Domain troops. Still, for all their advantages, Mikal worried that these soldiers seemed far more organized and skilled than the ones they had faced on Dalia.

"Are you ready, little girl?" Seamus asked, looking up into the trees.

Mikal looked up and caught the tips of Sunshine's ears pointed out from behind the leaves of the trees. Maybe they had some advantages of their own. Mina nimbly hopped down and ran to hug Seamus in an uncharacteristic display of affection. She had tears in her eyes when she released the old man, and Mikal saw that Seamus was emotional as well.

Mina then did something unexpected. She sheepishly walked over to Lu and fished something small out of her pocket. Mikal was shocked when he saw that it was the twisted metal bracelet he had given Lu when she was a child. It had been a present from Tess for him to give to her.

"You had this?" Lu asked.

"I took it from you when you were sleeping," Mina said.

"Why?" Lu asked.

"I thought it was pretty," she said. "It was wrong."

"It *was* wrong to take it," Seamus said.

"No, I mean the metal was wrong," Mina said. "I couldn't talk to the gats as easily when I was wearing it. Sunshine said it made her feel sick."

Mikal walked over to the bracelet and inspected it. The gold was intertwined with a silvery metal, but it was otherwise an ordinary bracelet. Lu looked thoughtful.

"I thought it was the blue star," she said.

"What was the blue star?" Sen asked.

"I have felt more powerful," she said. "It feels like I'm bursting at the seams here."

"Give it here," Seamus said, taking the bracelet and inspecting it. "Carp metal," he said, handing it back to Lu. "There's not much of it there, but it's enough to keep your gift muted I would wager."

"Tess," Mikal said. He looked at Lu, who still seemed confused. "She gave it to me to give to you. She must have known what it was. She wanted to keep you hidden from the Wards."

Lu studied the bracelet and thoughtfully put it in a pocket lining her jacket. Mikal thought back to when his daughter had been wearing it. If she had destroyed Tek while wearing that bracelet, what could she do when she was unfettered? Sen must have been wondering the same thing because he whistled low through his teeth.

"Thank you," Lu said to Mina.

Before they left, Mikal's daughter embraced him. In one hug, Lu managed to convey love, forgiveness, and acceptance for everything that Mikal was and had done. Lu was better than the sum of he and Tess, and Mikal was prepared to fight the entire Domain for his daughter if he had to.

57

Charli stood on the beautiful bridge of the destroyer. She watched the massive screen spread before her in anticipation. First Officer Nunaz stood to her left with his hands casually folded behind his back. When the two of them had entered the bridge together, she noted the way the rest of the crew failed to meet her eyes when she looked at them.

Nunaz shifted his feet, and Charli tried not to flinch away from him. She focused her attention on the magnificent display in front of her. The soldiers who had been deployed on the ground wore body cameras that synchronized the visual information they processed with each other. The result was the accumulation of video feed that produced a nearly panoramic view of the action from the soldiers' perspective.

Even though she was standing on the clean and quiet bridge of the destroyer, the visual feed on the screen before her caused Charli's heart rate to accelerate in anticipation. She had told Nunaz about the gats and the giant beasts that occupied the trees, but the first officer still insisted on starting his approach from the ground. It was almost as if he was using the lives of his soldiers as bait to get the Domani to show her hand.

"Here we go," Nunaz said as the first line of soldiers entered the shadow of the leafy canopy above.

Charli's eyes searched the tree trunks for movement. She desperately wanted the gats to show themselves early on so that some of the soldiers could still escape.

"Everything's quiet, sir." The leader of the ground squad radioed into the bridge.

Indeed, nothing moved around them. It was just as Charli had remembered. The only difference was the color of the light that shone down intermittently in thin shafts. The green hue lent an otherworldly feel. The gentle swaying of the leaves that could be seen from a distance seemed to stop once they set foot on the forest floor. Charli knew that it was like stepping into a vacuum. She glanced sideways and saw a cocky smile on Nunaz's face. He hadn't believed her.

"Try touching the tree trunk," he said.

One of the soldiers split from the group after a hand signal from the squad leader. Charli thought she saw a slight tremor to the man's hand as his fingers grazed the rough armor plating of the tree trunk. "Pieces" of the covering fell away at his touch and fell to the ground as dried husks. He looked down, and Charli almost fell forward as the visual feed focused on what he was seeing. It was just the thin outer shells of the gats she had seen. The pieces didn't even have legs. Charli felt her neck burn bright red as she could feel the first officer's gloating gaze rest on her.

The soldier rejoined the others, and they continued their slow march into the forest. Despite Nunaz's distrust of the information Charli had given him, he still chose to trust her direction toward the center of the city hidden in the treetops. With no one else from the Domain ever having left the forest on OR-32562, he had no other choice but to listen to her.

The soldiers walked forward into the peaceful quiet of the forest. Everyone on the bridge seemed to breathe quietly so that the only sound that could be heard anywhere was the gentle crunch beneath their feet. They made it further in than Mikal and his Dalians had when they had first entered the forest, and Charli started to feel hope blossom in her gut. Maybe the beacon had somehow killed the gats. Maybe the people had chosen to hide or flee rather than fight.

Then the clicking started.

It was not the slow, warning tempo that Charli remembered. It was fast and loud and quickly filled the forest around the soldiers. The noise reverberated around them, multiplying in intensity, and filled the bridge. Charli saw crewmen cover their ears and wondered if the implants made it worse. She looked over at Nunaz and saw that his confidence had been replaced with a look of consternation. Charli took little satisfaction in it. She turned back to the screen just as the black cloud of gats descended on the screaming Domain soldiers.

The light had left the forest, and it was now shrouded by stinging death as the now naked trees around them stood to watch.

"Keep the men together!" Nunaz shouted.

"Retreat!" called the squad leader to his men.

The video feed broke up in the chaos so that the squad leader's camera dominated the screen. The well-trained soldier ran, abandoning the others. He passed by men covered from head to toe in the gats—so that they looked like mutated trees themselves—falling to their knees and reaching toward the sky for mercy. Some, already on their bellies, scrabbled at the dirt or clawed at themselves to find some relief from the consumption.

Then the squad leader himself went down; his screams rang through the bridge of the destroyer until they were finally muffled by gats filling the man's mouth and throat. Then everything was quiet except for the occasional click that persisted. The man had fallen with his video feed up to the sky, and the gats could be seen sedately returning to the trees, where they settled down against each other once more. Green light from the beacon above once again shone through the gaps in the leaves.

Charli didn't remember dropping to her knees, but in the sudden quiet she realized her hands were splayed on the padded floor in front of her. Her fingers had curled into the forgiving material until her knuckles were white. In her wildest imagination, she had not imagined the swift death that had been dispatched from the trees. She belatedly realized that the harassment the gats had given her and Mikal in the forest was just that. They had been gently herded to go where Seamus had wanted them to go.

Charli let out a gasp of surprise as Nunaz roughly grabbed her under her arm, dragging her to her feet. He pulled her, stumbling, off the bridge. Charli tried to bring herself back to reality. Surely, the Domani on the Capitol would have wanted Nunaz to retreat at this point. He just lost an entire squadron of men in the blink of an eye. It was time to cut losses and run. Charli knew that.

"We have to leave this planet," she said, realizing she was sobbing.

Nunaz did not answer her. He continued to drag her down winding corridors until her feet started to echo on smooth flooring. They started to pass more and more soldiers, armed with energy weapons, lining the walls. Suddenly, a door slid open before them, and Charli gaped as Nunaz dragged her into a large hangar.

"You will not be able to get her," Charli said, realizing he was taking her to one of the fighter craft being prepared to take off.

Nunaz rounded on her and raised his hand, causing Charli to flinch. "I do not intend to retrieve her," he said. "I intend to cause as much damage as possible to the ones she loves."

He dragged her to the relatively small craft, and Charli saw that, even as they approached, an away team of soldiers was being loaded into the back. She looked around and saw that four other ships were being loaded the same way. Nunaz had apparently been readying the ships using the implant in his ear since they had left the bridge.

He pulled her, stumbling, up the ramp to get into the cockpit of the craft. Her feet echoed thinly on the metal planks until he dropped her unceremoniously into the chair next to his. The first officer placed himself in the pilot's chair and started to deftly manipulate the switches on the control panel. Another soldier sat in the chair next to Charli. He smiled briefly at her as he strapped her in before adjusting his own straps. In seconds, the doors closed. Charli glanced behind her to see rows of armed soldiers filling the back of the craft.

When she turned back to the front, the hatch on the destroyer was already halfway open, and the hangar was filled with bright green light that leaked into the fighter craft. It turned Charli's golden-hued skin a sickly color. As soon as the hatch rested in the open position with a clunk, Nunaz shifted and the craft shot forward, propelling Charli into the back of her seat.

"Show me where they are," Nunaz demanded, turning back to her.

The Dalians had ruined everything that had existed between her and Caden. They had caused Nunaz to come into her life. It was because of them that she would never be the same. Caden could never love her now. Charli remembered every step from her headlong run out of the forest. She was able to easily guide Nunaz back to Lu and Mikal.

58

Lu kept a steadying hand on Ash's warm fur while she watched the destruction below. Mina was stone-faced as she focused on the black cloud of death that peeled away from the trees around them. These soldiers were coming for her and her people. The girl had been trained to fight since she was born under the harsh radiation of a blue star. Mina did not hesitate to command the gats to defend her people now.

During the worst of it, Lu looked away. She saw Sen standing behind Mina on the wide tree branch they shared with Sunshine and the other chattle that had carried him. He had his hand on the girl's shoulder, sharing her burden of violence. He looked calm and resolute. Sen did not take his eyes off the death they rained down below.

Once it was over, the quiet that returned to the forest was disturbing. The shapes on the ground, permanently frozen in the positions of their demise, were still. Sen finally looked away and met Lu's eyes. She saw that it had been just as hard for him to watch as it was for her. They had certainly sent the Domain a message if nothing else.

Ash leaned against her, and she climbed onto his back. Mina seemed to still seethe with the anger of the gats as she climbed onto Sunshine with a growl. Sunshine responded with a roar of her own as the three chattle launched from their perches. Their next rendezvous point was back with Mikal, who was preparing for the inevitable air attack that Lu's father was certain would come next.

Ash's movements were certain beneath her as he led the way. Lu focused on his movements as he carried her to the next position, and she allowed herself to get lost in the rhythm of his stride.

By the time they reached their destination, Lu lamented the end of the journey. They arrived at the clearing with the platforms, designed to lift people and resources from the forest floor. The three chattle used their claws in the wood to slow their momentum, and Sen dismounted before his had even fully stopped. Mina hopped off Sunshine and went to go brood at the edge of the platform. Lu almost went to comfort her but thought better of it and left the girl alone.

The former doyen ran to the lever that Mikal had left for him to pull, and he used all his body weight to lower it. The pulley system that had raised the platforms before had been repurposed to lift a flag suspended from dead branches hastily tied together. It was a signal Mikal felt the Domain could not ignore. The giant cloth flag had been painted with a depiction of Laima. The swirling gas planet that had shielded Dalia for generations was painted with the orange and black juices of the fruits that grew on the trees.

Lu had gotten the idea from the mural in the house that she and the orphans had hidden in back on Dalia. She looked up at the flag that had been raised and felt its shadow fall over her face as it swayed and blocked the green light of her beacon.

"Once again, we stand in Laima's shadow," Sen murmured next to her.

Lu looked at him and was reminded of the doyen who once stood on the steps of the Sanctuary to preach to a people shrouded in darkness. She shook her head to clear the image and climbed back on Ash. In the tree branches above them, her father waited with the people of OR-32562 to spring the trap that had been set.

59

Charli gritted her teeth with the speed of the fighter craft. Nunaz flew erratically, but he followed her direction. That was until they saw a giant flag flying on the horizon. Charli squinted, unable to make out the image on its billowing folds. Nunaz saw it too and shifted the craft toward the flag. As they got closer, she saw that it was a crude painting of the giant gas planet that had caught Dalia in its slow orbit. Charli tried to wrack her brain to remember the name of it but could not.

"What does that mean?" Nunaz asked her.

"It's the planet next to Dalia," she said. "It was not there before."

At her words, Nunaz slowed their fighter craft. After a moment's pause for Nunaz to communicate through his ear implant, two of the craft that had been flanking them advanced toward the flag. They dipped low over the trees as they approached to investigate from both sides. Charli watched with her heart in her throat as the ships closed in on the flag. She was trying to remember where they were and realized it was the same place the platform had lifted them into the walkways. They were very close to the center of the city.

The two craft hovered silently; the air they used to propel themselves caused the branches and leaves to flatten on the treetops.

"The area is silent, sir," one of the pilots spoke into the intercom.

"Is there a place to land?" Nunaz asked aloud.

"Yes, there is a clearing below," the pilot said.

Charli could hear the trepidation in his voice. Those who had not been on the bridge had surely heard of the gats. Word traveled fast when people had implants connecting their ears and brains to other people. He must be dreading the command that was about to come.

"Land it," Nunaz said.

"Sir," the pilot started, but he didn't get to finish his sentence.

The familiar flash of an energy gun ignited from the treetop just below the fighter craft. The blast only had to travel a short distance before it impacted with the belly of the craft. Whoever had made the shot had known what they were doing. The energy pulse met with the hot air being expelled from the exhaust of the fighter craft and exploded. Metal shards were blasted in all directions, and the shrapnel slammed into the nearby craft, causing it to spin out of control. Both were down in an instant, swallowed by the forest below.

Nunaz didn't bother to investigate the crashes for survivors. He turned back in the direction Charli had been taking him. His face was set in stone, and Charli watched his jawline harden as he propelled them forward. The other two fighter craft followed obediently.

Charli leaned over to look down at the treetops but could not see the maze of walkways she knew was hidden just below the surface.

After a certain distance from the clearing she said, "Stop."

Nunaz obeyed and turned to her. "You are certain they are hidden here?"

"It is where the leader lives," she said, thinking of Seamus holed up in his house.

He turned back to his controls and casually sent a volley of energy three times as powerful as the one shot from a blaster into the trees below. The branches cracked and folded under the heat, and a giant hole was exposed through the leaf cover. Charli hid a smirk of satisfaction as she saw small figures running away from the blast site to take cover. The wooden walkway snapped in half, and several people fell to their ends on the ground below.

Seamus's house was not quite in that exact location, but the blast had revealed the path leading up to it. Nunaz deftly landed the craft on the walkway, and the other two followed through the defect in the leaf cover that the blast had uncovered.

"Those things won't come after us here, will they?" Nunaz asked Charli once the craft had settled.

"They didn't attack us here," Charli said, shrinking back in her chair under his gaze.

Nunaz continued to look at her while he pulled the switch to open the doors. Soldiers, having been silent in the back of the fighter craft, now filed out in well-disciplined rows. Nunaz grabbed Charli and dragged her out into the open. Despite her assurances, she still looked at the gat-covered tree trunks in terror.

"Where is it?" Nunaz asked.

"The leader's house is hidden in that leaf cover over there," Charli said, pointing up the winding walkway that had been left intact from the blast.

Nunaz dragged her up the walkway with soldiers surrounding them on all sides. Charli breathed an audible sigh of relief when the house appeared out of nowhere, still safely nestled in the trees. As they approached the front door, Nunaz pulled an energy blaster and shot at the wood, causing it to erupt in a shower of splinters and smoke. His soldiers walked through it without hesitation.

They spread out through the front rooms, and Nunaz waited patiently in the front doorway, holding the back of Charli's neck. His long fingers reached around the front of her throat and compressed the blood flow on one side until her head felt heavy from the pressure of it.

"This place seems like an unlikely location for the leader of a planet to live in," Nunaz whispered in her ear, "even one as unofficial as you claim him to be."

Charli heard the implied threat, and her knees felt weak. So far, nothing had been found, and she knew that she would be blamed for the house being empty. Just as his fingers grew tighter around her throat, they heard a scuffle from the back of the house. Having been there, Charli knew that it was the room that Seamus had contained one of the crawlers in. She had been about to say as much when shouting caused Nunaz to tense behind her, and a soldier's body was thrown past them to land awkwardly against the wall beside them. The man slumped, unconscious, with his leg bent backward, and Charli shied away from him.

Nunaz started to back them out as more of his soldiers poured into the back room. A defiant roar could be heard, and the activation of energy blasters filled the front of the house with pinging whines and smoke. Nunaz stumbled back, still holding Charli in front him like a shield.

Then there was silence. Nunaz held his finger to his ear, and Charli waited. Then he started laughing. The sound was bubbled up from his barrel chest against Charli's back. A soldier emerged from the house, holding his shoulder, his arm hanging at an odd angle.

"We lost twelve men, sir," the soldier said.

"A small price to pay," Nunaz said, smiling.

Then three men emerged, dragging the corpse of a crawler out of the house by his arms. His black eyes had turned into a sightless gray, and his head hung back as he was dropped in front of the house. Nunaz walked over to inspect the body as though it was an experiment he was keenly interested in. Charli covered her mouth and looked away.

Then one more soldier emerged from the house with Seamus in tow, hobbling with his cane. The old man scanned the faces outside, his eyes resting briefly on the crawler. If Charli didn't know any better, she would have said that he was heartbroken at the death of the creature.

"Is this him?" Nunaz asked, pointing at Seamus.

Charli nodded.

Seamus looked at her and smiled without humor. His wizened face seemed to say that he knew her and found her to be lacking. She hated him.

Then the clicking started.

"It's him!" Charli cried shrilly. "He is calling the gats down upon us!"

Nunaz looked at her, alarm now plain on his face. He walked up to Seamus and casually pulled a knife from his belt. The blade slit across the old man's throat with ease, and as Seamus fell to his knees, the clicking stopped. Charli thought he wanted to say something, but the words would never come. Seamus fell on his face to lie next to the crawler. The clicking stopped.

60

"No!" Lu cried, clutching her head.

Mikal looked up to see Sen was with her on the tree branch with the chattle. Lu was wracked with silent sobs that broke through each breath.

"What is it?" Mikal asked.

Sen, kneeling to hold Lu against his chest, looked back and called down. "I don't know. She won't tell me."

Mikal had been wading through the wreckage of the small ships that they had managed to crash at the landing. The group of people from OR-32562 were scattered and organizing the pieces of scrap metal and technology to see if they could be useful. One of the ships was mostly intact, and Mikal hoped they could make it fly again. He, Kelvin, and First had made quick work of the survivors. There had been no need to leave any of them alive. The Domain soldiers were useless left alive.

Now, he looked for a way up into the tree to get to his daughter and noticed First standing as still as a statue amid the wreckage. The crawler had a dull gleam to his eyes, and his shoulders sagged. It was a posture of sadness. Mikal looked back up at Sen, who was trying to soothe Lu.

The female chattle walked over to him, and he assumed it was Ash who had sent her. Mikal climbed on her and allowed her to scale the tree next to him with her sharp claws digging into the wood between the columns of gats. She deposited him next to Sen and Lu and saw that she was calming down.

"Not Five," she whispered. "Not Five, not Five, not Five."

"Five was with Seamus," Mina said quietly behind Mikal.

He hadn't even noticed the girl walk up behind him. He wished he could tell her that Seamus was all right, but Mikal had never been a fan of lying to children. Sparing them only hurt them in the long run. A look of understanding passed between Mina and Mikal, and she moved to get on Sunshine.

"Stay here," he told her. "Once we have a plan, we will go find out together."

Mina seemed reluctant but kept her feet on the wood.

"What happened?" he asked Sen.

"She said that the Domain was in the house. Then she's like this," Sen said.

Mikal looked at his daughter. For all that she had influenced the crawlers, they had clearly left their mark on her.

"It's okay, Lu," he said. "The others need you. I need you to help First."

Lu stopped rocking back and forth and tried to catch her breath. She opened her eyes and registered her father and Sen.

"First is in trouble?" she croaked.

"He's down in the clearing, but he's not right," Mikal said, lifting her to her feet and helping her onto Ash.

The big chattle was making a soothing rumbling sound from his chest, and Lu leaned down to hug his shoulders. Mikal watched Ash carry her down before joining her with Sen and Mina. Once in the clearing, he found that Lu had already made her way through the wreckage and into First's arms. The big crawler had come awake and had lifted Lu off the ground. By the time Mikal reached them, he had set Lu down and the two seemed to have come back to their senses.

"I felt him die," Lu said, looking at Mikal and Sen.

Neither said anything. There was nothing to say. Mikal called the people scattered around the clearing around them. Once he had their attention and they gathered in front of the small craft, he told them that Seamus had been attacked.

"I am going to investigate," he said. "I want you all to proceed to the game arena as planned."

Most of them would have to go on foot, but Sen, Mina, and Lu would be there first on the chattle. Mikal would depend on First to watch over the group as they made their way through the forest.

"I am going with you," Mina said.

"You will go with the others. It will be better if I go alone," Mikal said.

"I can stay hidden," Mina said. "Besides, Sunshine and I will follow you whether you like it or not."

Mikal was reminded of Lu when they were about to fight the Domain soldiers on Dalia. Mina was so much like her that it was scary.

"Fine," Mikal agreed reluctantly.

He kissed Lu on top of her head and got on the chattle that had allowed him to ride her. Mina followed suit with Sunshine, and they left toward Seamus's house. The big animals lunged with a sense of urgency, and Mikal held on as he was propelled upward at a ninety-degree angle, grabbing a handful of fur and skin for balance.

It wasn't long until they reached the walkway to the house hidden in the trees. The chattle stopped above the charred remains of the main walkway, and Mikal tried not to examine the shapes on the ground, visible in the now gaping hole, too closely.

"Stay here," he told Mina.

It was not a request, and the girl seemed to understand. Mikal dismounted and dropped down to land softly on the wooden beams. There was no sign of the other ships, but they had surely been there. Scorch marks were visible on the widest part of the walkway, but Mikal did not stop to inspect them. He reached the house to find a scene of chaos. The place had been ransacked, and the bodies of Five and Seamus were left exposed outside the front door.

Mikal grabbed a cloak from inside and covered Seamus with it before Mina could see. He searched the house to find that the crawler had taken down his fair share of Domain soldiers before going down.

"You didn't go down without a fight, my friend," he said, gently closing the now-gray eyes that stared up at the green, backlit sky.

"He was my only father," Mina said from behind Mikal.

She was staring at Seamus. Mikal stood and allowed Mina to embrace him. He wrapped his arms around the girl and picked her up to carry her away from there. Sunshine was waiting, and he placed her on the back of the chattle. Mina sniffled and wiped her face with the back of her forearm.

"We have work to do," she said seriously.

So much like his Lu.

61

Lana didn't have much to work with. She unconsciously tried to smooth back her red hair that was no longer there. Instead, she ended up absent-mindedly scratching her scalp and the new fuzz that was growing in. So much of Domain culture was tied into hair that she understood the symbolism behind Tek's action. Still, when the fat man had shaved her head, she had wanted nothing more than to see him suffer. The end that Lulu had brought to him was too painless for Lana's taste.

Now, she found herself standing in front of twenty-four crawlers, a group of worked-up orphans, and any other able-bodied Dalian refugee that she could find. They looked to her for guidance, and, as a Lesser, she was still responsible for them.

Lana had been raised in the Sanctuary and taught to revere the Domain and welcome its salvation through dutiful and thoughtful breeding.

She had, however, realized at an early age that the Domain had long forgotten its devoted followers. It seemed that they would never come for her. Then, Lulu lit the beacon. It was as if her prayers to the gods had been answered.

The glorious return to the light she had envisioned was never to be. Instead, the Domain sent soft-bodied corruption into their midst. It had been easy for Lana to fall into step behind her former assassin. The man was charismatic after all. Now, she stood on the *Raider*, looking at the tools left to her with a critical eye.

Lana had felt a brief absence of the power she had once enjoyed from Laima. Now, with the blue star radiating overhead and Lulu off the ship, no longer calling all the power to herself, Lana could feel some of her gift returning to her. She was just a Lesser, just a Ward, but a powerful one who had almost lit the beacon herself at a young age when she was tested. Lana had been the closest before Lulu. All their hopes had rested on Sen, but that boy was like a sink. If anything, he absorbed the power around him. She should have known he was not Tess and Mikal's.

She was trying to devise a plan when the crawlers suddenly changed.

Through a tenuous connection she still shared with them, she could feel the anguish and rage that suddenly coursed through the room. One of their own had been killed out in that forest. Initially taken aback by the sudden onslaught of emotion, Lana stopped and reassessed the situation.

"This could be useful," she said aloud, looking at the seething crawlers standing before her.

"I found it," said an orphan standing in the doorway, panting.

She had sent several of the boys out into the ship to split up and find the weapons cache that she knew must be somewhere. Lana smiled at the boy standing in the door of the cargo bay.

"Good job," she said. "Show me."

The boy led her to Caden's room. They went inside, and he pushed a button hidden between the bed and the wall. This caused the wall to slide back and reveal a massive supply of energy weapons and ammunition.

"How did you know to look there?" she asked.

"If I was the captain, it's where I would have hidden 'em." The boy shrugged.

"Of course," Lana murmured. "Go get the others so that they can arm themselves."

The boy ran off to gather the other orphans, crawlers, and Dalians. Lana stepped into the cold cache of weapons and grabbed a curved blade for herself. She slipped it in her waistband before grabbing a more traditional gun. It felt awkward and heavy in her hand, but it would do.

The others arrived and armed themselves in a quiet, organized, single-file line. Her Dalians had had enough. Now was the time to fight back. Lana waited for them to finish and gathered them so that they filled the wide corridor outside of Caden's room. She couldn't see past the tall shoulders of the crawlers, but she knew they filled the space to reach all the way back toward the kitchens.

Lana would make no fancy speeches today. Dalians didn't need them. They had seen Finn's body in the cargo bay. They had fought the Domain soldiers unlucky enough to be left behind on the *Raider*. Now, they would bring the fight closer to the Domain itself.

"Let's go," she said, letting power lace her voice as she had once done back in the Sanctuary.

She turned and led her makeshift army down the corridor and smacked the red button, releasing the door and letting green light flood the interior of the exit. Lana let the crawlers leave first, knowing they would make a fierce vanguard. Then, the former Ward led her people onto the grass to cross the divide between their little ship and the massive destroyer.

"Well, at least they will be surprised," Lana said to herself as the crawlers converged on the ten soldiers left standing to guard the entrance.

62

Lu tried to shake off the feeling of death as she clung to Ash. The animal shifted his weight under her and seemed to sense her need to escape. He pulled ahead of Sen and the female he rode so that Lulu could convince herself she was alone in the forest. They soared between the branches, and she tried to center herself in the feeling of weightlessness. Lu had grown so close to Ash that she hardly knew if she was embracing her own feeling of flying or his.

When he abruptly stopped, Lu was nearly pitched forward to fly off his back, but Ash raised his head to stop her momentum at the last second. Still, she nearly lost her balance and found herself clinging to his neck.

"What are you—" she started to ask but stopped herself at the scene below.

Ash had made it to the game arena in record time. It seemed that the small away ships had beaten them there. Domain soldiers were ransacking the food supplies. At least a hundred people, Dalians and OR people alike, had been corralled onto the platforms while the soldiers went about their business. Lulu looked down, between the trees, and saw shapes on the leaf litter grown below that looked like people. She swallowed back her hatred and rage and started taking inventory like her father had taught her.

Approximately ten soldiers were by the main food supplies. They were laughing and stuffing their faces while Stap and Gordo were on their knees with their backs against a large tree trunk. Another fourteen were collecting jewelry from the women corralled on the platforms. Still, and what Lu suspected was the most important, another ten surrounded a tall, lanky man with gaunt features. That man stood with his hand rested casually on the shoulder of a girl Lu had once considered a friend—Charli.

She watched as he walked her around, giving orders and overseeing the chaos around him. Something was different about Charli. Her ready smile was certainly no longer with her. It had been replaced by fragileness, a jittery fear that was palpable from the tree branch where Lu was perched on Ash.

"I will ask one more time," the gaunt man said, his voice booming into the trees. "Where is the Domani?"

No one answered. Lu felt a surge of anger rise in her gut. These people did not know her, yet they protected her. She wouldn't let the Domain hurt any of them anymore. Before she could act, the tall man nodded imperceptibly, and one of the soldiers who had been harassing the women on the platform casually grabbed an older woman and pushed her to the edge. The woman wailed and was thrown over the edge in an instant.

Lu's heart lurched with the woman, and Ash growled low in his throat. She felt a scream rising in her throat, but she swallowed it when a chattle seemed to appear out of nowhere to catch the woman as she fell. The beast had propelled itself from one of the platforms and now clung to the side of the tree trunk.

The gaunt man giving orders raised his eyebrows and said, "Now that was an interesting trick." He paced to the edge of the platform, holding Charli out in front of him as though she was a shield. He gazed down at the chattle, and the beast, with the woman gripping his neck, roared up at him. The man stepped back and seemed to consider things for a moment. "Let's see if you can repeat it."

With that, another soldier grabbed Stap and held the boy under his arms. Stap kicked with all his might, and Gordo lunged at the soldier, only to be kicked in the face. Blood sprayed from the big man's nose and he fell backward, unconscious. Lu screamed, and the tall man looked up in her direction. The soldier froze after some unseen command, and he stood still, holding the kicking, writhing Stap out in front of him.

"Is that you, little Domani?" the tall officer asked. He stepped forward once more, this time leaving Charli behind so that he was out in the open. "All you have to do is come out, and I can leave these people in peace." He smiled, his hands out in supplication. "They were much better off before you arrived here. You know that. Your power is dangerous, and it needs to be contained. Back on the Capitol, we can help you. We can teach you. There are others like you."

Lu stepped off Ash and walked forward. She wanted nothing more than for the fighting to end. She needed to protect these people. She needed to protect Stap. Lu would give herself to this man and end it. Her feet reached the edge of the tree branch, and she could feel the light drawing to her from the beacon above. She lifted the branches to reveal herself to the Domain soldiers below.

"I am here," she called down, projecting her voice.

The tall man looked up at her, and their eyes met. He smiled, and the soldier holding Stap threw the orphan Dalian off the ledge. Something had twinged in her mind just before the soldier obeyed. It was like a prick of power that she could feel like static electricity.

This time, it was Ash who jumped for Stap. The big chattle flew by Lu, causing her hair to fly in her face in his wake. Ash grabbed Stap's shirt with his teeth and swung the boy up onto a tree branch with his momentum. The big chattle grappled with the small branches on the way down and managed to propel himself to the smooth tree trunk of the dead tree Lu had stayed in while she was hiding. His claws scrambled for purchase, and he slid all the way down to the ground. Lu could feel the painful landing but knew his injuries were minor.

Something niggled at her, and she focused on the tall officer, whose eyes had never left her.

"Come down, little Domani," he said. "No one else will get hurt, I promise."

Lu turned to hop down on the next branch that had curved stairs leading down to the game platforms. She could see that there were already soldiers making their way up to meet her, slowly and cautiously. Just as her foot left the branch, she was pulled back, and the wind was sucked out of her chest with the force of it. Sen had wrapped his arm around her waist and pulled her against his chest.

"You will never belong to them," he said gruffly into her ear.

Lu tried to wrestle away from him, but Sen wouldn't release her. For all the power that she felt at her fingertips, she would never use it against him. He was stronger than her. The soldiers on the stairs were approaching them, and the voice of the tall officer called form below.

"Where did you go, little Domani?"

Then the clicking started, and everyone stopped.

Sen released her and said, "The gats?"

"You killed Seamus!" Mina screamed.

Lu whipped around to see the little girl with blond hair standing on a branch above the soldiers on the opposite side. Her bare feet were almost directly above the tall officer. "I have command now, and you will leave us!" She lifted her arms, and the gats on the trees around them lifted into the air at once. They didn't consume the soldiers as they had done on the ground, but they harassed and stung, driving the soldiers mad with fear. Several soldiers, having seen what the gats could do, threw themselves off the ledge to die a less painful death on the ground below.

Lu watched as the tall officer grabbed Charli and tried to escape with her.

He was stopped by a quiet Dalian assassin. Mikal came quickly from the side—seemingly materialized from the tree next to them. He grabbed Charli and tossed the girl aside to land with her back against the tree where Gordo lay. In the same motion, he used his less dominant hand to grab the front of the tunic of the tall first officer and slam him down onto his back.

The officer was not slow. He reached for the energy gun at his waist with blinding speed, but Mikal was quicker. Mikal drew a blade and sliced it across the officer's throat. The officer's gun fell from limp fingers, and Mikal stood back to watch the man die. Lu had seen him kill before, but never had she seen her father watch someone die with such satisfaction. He looked up at Mina, who was still standing above him and something significant passed between them.

Sen left Lu to stand on the relative safety of the branch while he helped restrain the remaining soldiers on the ledges who had surrendered. The people of OR-32562 were more than happy to beat the soldiers until they could be properly taken as prisoners. The gats, calm without Mina's anger driving them, returned to the trees to click occasionally in agitation.

Charli crouched against the tree trunk, trying to make herself invisible, but Sen had not forgotten her. The former doyen reached down to help her stand and then promptly handed her off to one of the women of OR-32562 when she tried to talk. Those women did not look friendly. Lu smiled despite herself and turned to see that Ash had made his way back up the tree. The big chattle was conveying a sense of self-congratulation, and he clearly wanted praise.

"You are the biggest hero of the day!" Lu said, hugging Ash's neck and relishing the warmth he gave her in return. "What a daring rescue."

The moment was short-lived. Lu found herself bombarded by the distress of crawlers reaching out to her from the ship.

63

"I have to go to the ship," Lu shouted from the tree branch across from him.

Of course, she did, Mikal thought. It seemed they didn't have time to pause. He watched as his daughter, riding Ash, made her way down the trees to sprint on the ground toward the clearing where they had landed the *Raider*. She would meet First along the way. He turned to tell Sen to follow her, but the former doyen had already sprinted past him on the female chattle he had been riding.

Mikal almost followed them, but he had to gather a bigger force to fight if they were to stand any chance against the force left on that oversized ship. Stap climbed up the ledges to run to Gordo's side. He knelt next to him and looked up at Mikal, pleading.

"He's gonna be all right, right?" the boy asked.

Stap was so hardened, it was easy to forget that he was still a child. Mikal knelt next to Gordo. He felt a strong pulse, and his breathing was slow and steady.

"He'll wake up with a sore face and a fierce headache, but I think he will be all right," Mikal said.

"I will stay with him until he's awake," Stap said, rubbing the snot away from his nose with his sleeve.

"He'd like that," Mikal said.

He stood and saw that the people of OR-32562 and Dalians who had been at the game arena had already taken all the weapons away from the Domain soldiers and had them tied and subdued. One by one they stopped and looked to him, waiting for the next move.

"Those still willing to fight," Mikal said, "will march with me to the ships."

Every able-bodied person in the clearing stepped forward, and Mikal was overwhelmed by their resolve. A few of the children whistled, and chattle started to drop from the trees to join them on silent, padded feet. Mikal counted about twenty and wondered who should ride and who should lag.

"This girl from the Domain," said one of the women from the murmuring crowd, "she can help us."

Mikal craned his neck to see an older woman, thin and frail-looking, with her clawed fingers around Charli's arm.

She walked Charli up to Mikal, and he said, "This one cannot help us. She can only betray us."

"She will help us all right," the lady said. "She is a coward. She will do as we say because she cares about being alive. She knows how to fly one of those."

The woman pointed back to an intact fighter craft, partially hidden by the trees.

"I don't know how to fly that," Charli pleaded. "I only know what I saw Nunaz do."

"Nunaz was that man's name?" Mikal asked, pointing to the tall officer near his feet.

Charli nodded. "You did me a favor by killing him, I swear it. I would help you if I could." Her eyes darted as though there might be others listening. "They have Caden prisoner. He's going to be blamed for all of this."

Mikal laughed loudly. Charli flinched. It could not have been better. He didn't believe her about not being able to fly.

"It's not his fault!" she cried. "You would let Caden live, wouldn't you?"

Mikal leaned down so that his nose was inches away from Charli's. There was deception behind her intelligent eyes. He should have seen it sooner.

"You will help us," he said, coming to a decision.

"But I don't know anything," she said.

"Tell us what you do know," Mikal said, grabbing her by the sleeve to pull her toward the sleek fighter craft.

Charli reached up and grabbed a handle on the side that released the doors. Both the side door and a hatch in the back flipped open with the sound of smooth hydraulics. They walked in with several women and men following to watch. Charli sat in the front left seat, and her fingers lightly touched the buttons on the screen.

"Keep in mind," Mikal said quietly in her ear, "you will fly in this thing with me. So, if I crash it, you will die with me."

Charli looked up with her eyes pleading. "Please, don't make me go back to the destroyer with you."

"Is that what that monstrosity of a ship was called?" It seemed like an appropriate name to Mikal.

"You are coming with us, willingly, or if I have to tie you to one of these chairs."

Charli flipped the final switch, not taking her eyes off Mikal, and the craft rumbled awake. Mikal knew from his conversations with the crew on the Domain that she, like every other soldier of the Domain, knew the basic operations of the small ships. They never knew when such information could save their lives. In Charli's case, it would bring her back to the fray. Mikal sat next to her, and Charli wordlessly showed him the toggle that controlled the direction of their flight.

Brave souls of OR-32562 and Dalia boarded the craft and filled it to the brim. With pride, Mikal noted that many of them carried weapons they had pilfered from the Domain soldiers being held prisoner in the game arena. Mina poked her head in, and her eyes widened at the controls.

"We will follow you on the chattle," the blond girl said and darted off, calling after someone named Gideon.

"Everybody in?" Mikal asked.

He was met with nervous laughter and nods from the people jammed in the back. Charli hit the switch for the doors, and Mikal pulled back on the toggle. The fighter craft responded to the motion with more sensitivity than Mikal was prepared for. They lurched forward, shoving Mikal back in his seat and sending some of their passengers flying to plaster against the back window in awkward positions.

It seemed like they hit every tree branch on the way out, leaving a shower of leaves and agitated gats in their wake. Once out in the open air, Mikal eased up on the toggle, causing the nose of the fighter craft to dip down and drop. Charli grabbed the toggle and steadied it before they took a nosedive back into the forest.

Mikal, a man of precision and deadly capabilities, felt entirely uncomfortable with this process. Once he saw the subtle adjustments she was making, he took the control back from her. He flew more slowly than he suspected the craft was capable of, but the top of the destroyer was soon visible beyond the treetops on the horizon. As the trees thinned below them, leading on to the clearing, Charli grabbed the toggle and pushed forward, slightly causing them to smoothly slow down.

Mikal looked down, assessing the clearing for a place to land, and he saw a herd of chattle carrying their people burst free of the tree line. They moved in synchrony and at a ground-eating pace. Mikal shifted the toggle so that they were to the side of the chattle and at a distance from the destroyer.

Charli made him set the toggle in neutral, and her finger pressed a single red button on the left of the screen. The fighter craft made a perfect landing straight down to rest softly on the grass. Mikal heard a collective sigh of relief from the people in the back.

"I'd like to see them try it," he muttered, rising from his chair.

Charli sat motionless, glued to her seat. He reached over her to pull the switch that he had seen her use to close the doors. They opened with a satisfying hiss of the hydraulics. Mikal was not about to let Charli escape, and he pulled her up from her chair gently under her arm. The girl flinched as if he had hit her, and he wondered what had caused such fear since he had last seen her.

"I'm not going to hurt you if you don't try to run again," he said, annoyed by her reaction.

He left the fighter craft to stand in the grass before the group haphazardly gathering before him. They were not the organized soldiers that the

Domain employed, but they were certainly more motivated. He looked them over clumsily adjusting the Domain weapons and nodded his head in respect.

"I don't know what we face on the inside of that destroyer, but if we can overtake it, we stand a chance against anyone else who would come and try to control us," he said.

Mikal knew that the Domain's control over these people's lives dictated their existence on this undeveloped outer planet. They had been placed here against their will and wanted nothing more than the ability to decide where they go next. He saw Seamus tap into this whenever he spoke about the fight to anyone who would listen. Mikal would pick up where the old man had left off.

"Let's go," he said and turned with Charli to trot toward the looming destroyer.

The chattle had beaten him to it and had somehow disappeared inside the ship. Mikal tried to imagine what the big animals would do to anyone they encountered in the corridors and shuddered. He wouldn't have to wait long to find out.

64

Lu hadn't even thought twice about letting Ash run headlong into the open maw of the destroyer. She knew Sen was not far behind her, but the chattle he was on was not as fast as Ash, and Lu did not wait for him to catch up. It was amazing luck that no one had closed the opening to the ship, and she wondered at the overconfidence of the Domain. Ash's claws dug into the padded corridor floor, and she could see injured soldiers and blood on the walls at the entrance.

Ash stopped at the first intersection, uncertain which direction to take. The beast was breathing hard under her, and she tried to gather her wits. Then the bright-white lights switched off. They were replaced by a dark red strobe that cast shadows down the halls. Lu smiled. This was more like it.

She tried to sense where her crawlers were, but they were scattered throughout the ship. Several of them had winked out of her brain, but she had not felt them die. Two were badly injured, and one was dying as she searched. Lu allowed the emotion and rage of his death to overtake her, and she turned Ash left toward where the crawler had been fighting.

Ash's large body took up half the corridor as they ran, and he used his claws to shred the flooring when they rounded the next corner. The hallway opened up to a large galley that was multiple stories high around the perimeter with a central depression, where most of the food was prepared and stored. Lu could hear fighting and screaming echo off the walls around her from all levels.

"Are you ready?" she asked the chattle.

Ash responded with a roar that caused some of those fighting to stop and stare at the enormous animal standing on the threshold to the galley. Lu could feel Ash's anticipation, and she released him. She drew a short blade from her waist and brandished it with her right hand while her left held Ash's scruff for balance. Ash pierced the metal walls with his claws, and they climbed vertically to the second story, where her crawler had just perished. Four Domain soldiers were standing in front of his prone body, and one raised an energy weapon to shoot at her and Ash.

Lu drank in the scene as Ash advanced. The beast didn't slow down and drove her into the soldiers with claws and teeth bared. The soldier didn't have time to fire. Lu's knife slid across his midsection with the force of Ash's momentum. Ash had disposed of one of the other soldiers, and they pivoted to face the other two. They were running away. Lu smiled, and Ash rose to the chase. He overtook them in four strides, and Lu drove the point of her blade down into the chest of one of the soldiers who had fallen on his back. She leaped off Ash and grabbed the dying man's energy gun. When she straightened, Ash had returned to her, and she stepped back on him seamlessly. He roared in delight and was answered by three other chattle that had entered the galley.

Children, brandishing long poles, jumped the chattle from wall to wall, from second story to first story and back. The game that they had played in the trees was now being played out against Domain soldiers. The men shot wildly at the chattle, but the beasts were too fast. Lu thought she saw Gideon with a blade attached to his pole, and he swung it and twisted it about his forearm in an impressive display right before landing the point of it into the midsection of a Domain soldier. Others were knocking men off the second or third stories to land painfully on the cooking utensils below.

Mina directed them with a keen eye and the command of a girl accustomed to being the captain of the game they played back in the forest. Her blond hair streaked across the galley on Sunshine, and the nimble chattle seemed to have a feral grin on her face as she swiped at the soldiers each time she landed.

Lu winced as one chattle lost its footing and took an energy blast to the chest. The young person attached to the beast flew off its back to land gracefully on his feet. Lu lamented the animal's loss and felt Ash's distress as if it was her own. She knew she had to focus, and they turned back to the fight. The skirmish in the galley seemed to last an eternity, but she knew it had only been minutes before all Domain soldiers in that area had been taken care of.

One of her crawlers walked up to her, bloody and limping.

"The Ward is in the bridge," he communicated.

"The Ward? Take me," she said.

Ash and the other chattle followed the crawler who trotted down the labyrinth of corridors, focused on his destination. Lu looked back, glad to see the fierce Mina and Sunshine on their heels.

They passed several areas where fighting was breaking out. Lu saw her own kinsmen, armed with Domain weapons, fight with ferocity. She knew she had to keep going, but she wanted to stop and personally fight every battle they passed. The chattle followed Ash as they had done in the forest. Ash held his head high, his fur splattered with blood as they made their way through the destroyer.

The crawler suddenly stopped.

"The doyen," he said, looking back at Lu with bottomless black eyes.

"Sen?" she asked aloud.

They rounded the corner and saw two wide doors that had been blown off their attachments. The metal was bent, and they hung open. Through the doors was an enormous screen and rows of cascading chairs that Lu could only assume was the bridge. In it, a lone figure was fighting with three injured crawlers at his back and a prone chattle at his feet. Sen.

Static electricity flew at Lu from the bridge, and she was reminded of the sensation she got from the first officer back in the forest. Something about the room felt off, and she felt sick as Ash walked into it. She pushed the feeling aside and focused on Sen. Taught to fight by her father from a young age, she could see that he had taken down a fair number of the soldiers on the bridge. He used a pole seemingly pulled from the wreckage. It whirled in front of him in a blur, causing shots to ricochet off into the group of soldiers surrounding him.

Many lay motionless around his feet, and yet they kept coming. They used long blades, changing their tactic. His back was to the screen behind him. Oddly enough, it showed a beautiful image of green sky interlaced with branches as though it was from a perspective of lying on one's back in the forest. It was a peaceful counterpoint to the violence playing out in front of it.

Ash roared to get the soldier's attention; some turned to the group of chattle, but others continued to come at Sen with a mad intensity. He remained calm amid the storm of soldiers flying at him, but Lu watched him falter for a moment, and one of the soldiers got through. She vaulted off the chattle underneath her and ducked under the blast from an energy gun as she ran.

The sound of claws clashing metal and men screaming filled the doorway behind her as she made her way to the front of the bridge. Lu deftly maneuvered around overturned chairs and smoking consoles while Sen continued to fight. Blood now ran down his side, but he continued to use that arm as though nothing had hit him.

Lu was close to the back of the group of soldiers when something grabbed her ankle. She looked down to see the shorn red hair of Lana. The woman was crouched down amid the wreckage of the bridge, and she pulled Lu down to her level.

"I have to get to him!" Lu yelled over the chaos.

"You have to put an end to this, Domani," Lana said. She looked at Lu's bloodstained blade still held in her hand and laughed. "You don't have to fight like them. They are filled with the technology you control. Can't you feel it around you? Gods, girl, even I can feel it."

Lu tried to focus on Lana's words but kept her eyes on Sen. He was tiring.

"It hurts," she said, recognizing that it did, in fact, hurt.

It felt like static filled the room. It was an intrusion into her brain.

"Then make it go away!" Lana cried.

"I don't know how," Lu said.

"When has that ever stopped you?" Lana asked, annoyance lacing her voice.

Lulu tried to feel the power as she had done when she melted Tek or when she attacked the men trying to keep her at the council with the runes. She started to feel power build so that it vibrated her fingertips. She needed to make the noise and the pain and the electricity go away. She breathed it in and stood. Once she stood she saw Sen go down. Soldiers crowded over him, and she could no longer see his black hair or pale skin beneath the bodies.

Fear and rage warred within her until she released everything she had.

65

Mikal found the chattle bottlenecked in the door to what he could only assume was the bridge of the ship. He had encountered less resistance and more evidence of fighting than he expected getting there. The noise and ferocity of the chattle fighting caused him and the people behind him to pause. He advanced behind them to look in the room in time to see Sen at the front of the bridge. Mikal's eyes searched for his daughter, but he could not see her.

He edged in between the chattle that were clawing their way through soldiers at the front, wary of the energy blasts flying in front of him. He found Ash at the front of the pack, but Lu was not with him. Mikal threw a blade into the chest of a soldier who was taking aim for Ash, and he fell into a crouch to advance further into the room.

That's when he saw Sen go down and his daughter stand up. Something about her appearance caused the hairs on the back of his neck to stand on end. She looked like Tess standing above him with Laima floating overhead. Only she was more dangerous than any Ward he had ever seen. Power radiated about her, causing the objects in her vicinity to lift off the ground. Chairs creaked and consoles groaned against the bolts that held them to the floor.

He spied Lana backing away from Lu on her hands and feet, her face frightened.

Mikal tried calling Lu's name, but his voice sounded muffled in his own ears. Then she released everything that had been building within her. It came out in a shock wave that physically propelled him backward. The chattle held their ground and roared at the release of power.

Everything stopped.

Mikal registered screaming and looked at the soldier next to him writhing on the ground. He was covering his ears with his hands, and blood was seeping through his fingers. Mikal stood and saw that almost every soldier there was in the same condition. They were moaning and whimpering in pain with blood seeping out of their ears. He touched his own ear and was relieved when his fingers had no blood on them. He looked back and saw that none of the OR people or Dalians seemed to be affected either.

Charli stared at the soldiers with a horrified expression on her face. Something told Mikal that she knew what was happening to them. He would remember to ask her.

Mikal ran toward the screen, unable to see Lu or Sen from where he was standing. He vaulted over chairs and slid down the incline toward the screen. He found his daughter, having crawled on her knees to where Sen lay. She was on the ground with tears in her eyes and her outstretched hand holding Sen's. The former doyen's arm was exposed under the injured and now incapacitated soldiers, but Mikal couldn't see the rest of him. He moved the moaning and bleeding men off Sen with little care for their well-being. Mikal almost collapsed in relief when Sen opened his eyes and looked up at him.

"You never taught me to fight so many at once." Sen let out a raspy laugh. "This is your fault, assassin."

Mikal could see that he was bleeding from several stab wounds, but a cursory glance told him none of them would be fatal. He looked back at Lu, who was still holding Sen's hand, but she had closed her eyes. She had the deep, even breathing of someone unconscious. Mikal had seen her like this before, after she had expended so much power against Tek. The crawler next to him confirmed his suspicion.

"She will be fine, father," he said to Mikal.

Mikal looked back and saw that Charli had disappeared amid the aftermath of chaos. The door was occupied with chattle licking their wounds and the soft moaning of Domain soldiers bleeding from their ears.

He looked back at Lu and said, "It's almost like she just doesn't want to help clean this mess up."

The crawler did not seem amused, but Mikal thought it was funny. He knelt and helped Sen stand and sit up in a chair. He applied pressure with a rolled-up tunic taken from a Domain soldier to the worst of his stab wounds. One of the Dalian women who had been left on the ship came over to him and took over for him, seemingly more than happy to tend to the wounded doyen.

Mikal turned to pick up Lu, but he was beaten to it by First, who had made it into bridge after running all the way there on foot. The big crawler pushed aside anyone who stood in his way, and he knelt next to Lu, picking her up with surprising gentleness.

"I'm taking her back to the *Raider*, where it's safe," the crawler said.

His tone was almost scolding to Mikal, and the assassin looked around him at all the bleeding-eared men and said, "You're right, First. She can't take care of herself."

The crawler ignored him, and Mikal finally sat down on the floor, letting the relief that they had survived wash over him. Lana sat next to him, and Mikal didn't have the energy to tell her to leave.

"You make a much better leader than you did an assassin," Lana said. "I can see what Tess saw in you."

Mikal looked at her, astonishment plain on his face. His mouth gaped open like a salmee. He didn't know how to respond.

"Just don't let it go to your head," the former Ward said.

She stood and left him dumbfounded. He watched her proud back as she walked away. The woman who had once had complete control and power in her hands was now just a Lesser in the eyes of the Domain. He watched her leave the bridge before putting his head in his hands.

"Listen to me when I'm talking to you!" Mina yelled.

A boy's voice broke in. "I don't think they can hear you anymore."

Mikal looked up to see Mina with her hands on her hips, staring down at a prone soldier. The soldier pointed at his ears, and Mikal could tell that the boy was right.

"Oh, I think he knows what I'm saying, Gideon," Mina yelled. Then she turned back to the soldier and said, "I said get up. We have to clean this place."

The soldier, still dazed and concussed, shook his head as if to clear it. Mikal could only imagine what it would be like to have your ears blown out and then be yelled at by a little girl as you were recovering. He stood to take control of the situation, cognizant that he still had Charli to find and deal with.

66

Charli had never been on a destroyer before, but she knew the general direction of where she needed to go. She was the daughter of a Lesser and knew what the loss of a destroyer would mean to the Domain. Any peace the disgusting Dalians and the savages of OR-32562 could hope for would be short-lived. The Domani would not leave them alone for long. Right now, she only had one thing on her mind.

Her path took her past the hangar and toward the center of the ship. The area she sought would be as far away from the bridge as possible, by design. She passed many soldiers, shaken and disoriented by the destruction of the ear implants that had been wired into their brains. Their hearing was likely destroyed, along with a piece of their brains. Charli couldn't imagine what it felt like. She stepped past them, irritated when they tried to delay her with their silent pleas.

By the time she reached the back of the destroyer, Charli knew she was on the right path. The hospital wing was on her left, and she turned right and there it was. There he was.

Caden sat slumped in the holding cell, once separated from her by a shield that had been short-circuited by Lulu's temper tantrum. Now he was free, and yet he didn't run. Her Caden sat against the wall with his head between his knees.

"Caden?" Charli approached tentatively.

Oh, how she wanted to run to him and throw her arms around him. Caden looked up, and recognition dawned on his handsome face. Instead of the relief she had hoped to see, his eyes were hard as they looked at her. He stood and she backed away from him, her breath coming faster.

"You did this to me," Caden said. "They sent the missive with my sentencing right after they threw me in this cell. First Officer Nunaz told me what you told him. I am to be exiled to a dark ring planet as soon as we get back to the Domain."

Caden was advancing on her, his posture stiff.

"Caden, I didn't tell him anything about you," she said. "The destroyer has been commandeered. We have to get out of here."

"You would do anything to get ahead, Charli," Caden said. "You've always been a whore for power."

He spat in her face, and Charli turned her head. He had her backed against the wall, and she started to hear herself whimper.

"You slept with him," Caden said. It was not a question. "He told me everything you did together."

"Caden, I would never want to hurt you. I only wanted to help you," she started, but the words died in her mouth as his hand wrapped around her throat, pinning her against the wall.

He squeezed and stars danced in her vision. A part of Charli accepted and welcomed death by Caden's hand. She felt that she surely deserved it. She relaxed under his grip, and he squeezed harder. Her vision went dark; suddenly the grip on her throat was gone, and air rushed into her windpipe.

Charli staggered, thankful that Caden had decided to let her live. She looked at his face, but something was wrong. He looked confused. Charli reached for him, but he fell to his knees in front of her with a loud crack of bone on the hard floor of the holding cell.

A crawler stood behind him, blood dripping from the blade in his hands. Charli's frantic eyes registered the wounds on the crawler's arms from the carp metal that had bound it in the cargo bay. The abomination stood in front of her, staring at her with his cold black eyes.

A sob wrenched free of Charli's chest as she knelt before her fallen love.

Caden fell into her arms, and she lowered him to the ground. She barely noticed the crawler close the solid door to the outside of the holding cell. She lay next to Caden, kissing his face and professing her love to him long after his eyes no longer saw her.

67

Lu watched her father speak. Mikal sat at the head of a long table in what was now known as the state's room. Above his head was a painted rendition of the Capitol planet. Lu glanced up at it and saw the swirling white clouds blanketing green lands and blue waters. She knew that for all its beauty, it bred corruption.

The table was large enough to seat a hundred men, and the room sat adjacent to the bridge on the destroyer so that decisions could be made and discussed next to the control center of the ship. Lu looked down the long length of the table and saw that Dalians were intermingled with OR people and the occasional Domain defector.

Lu could never have imagined that they would survive to take the ship. When she awoke after the fight for the destroyer, she felt like she had died a hundred times over. Despite all her muscles screaming in protest, she shot out of bed with anxiety blossoming in her gut.

Sen.

He had been there, sitting next to her bed, waiting for her.

The man who she had grown watching on the steps of the Sanctuary was still shrouded in mystery to Lulu. He now sat next to her at the table, his eyes watching her, even as she studied the rest of the room. His black hair, once perfectly groomed as the doyen of her people, was now scruffy and unkempt. He had allowed it to grow over his face, and Lu had to admit, it was not a disagreeable look for him. Lu took an unsteady breath under his gaze and returned her attention to the room.

Crawlers and chattle lined the walls as if they were murals of creatures from a dream. First and Ash stood behind her, flanking her on both sides.

"The soldiers may be deaf, but they can still communicate with each other," Lana said, breaking into Lu's thoughts, her red hair growing back smooth and perfectly spiked on her head.

"We need them to get this thing off the ground," Mikal said. "We have no choice but to take that chance."

"I still think we should stay here," a woman from OR-32562 spoke up from the opposite end of the table.

"I would never force anyone to leave," Mikal said. "You may stay if that is your wish."

"We had some," Kelvin broke in, "who stayed on Dalia to burn in the fire that consumed it. I believe"—the big harvester paused—"that a fire of a different sort will consume this place too."

"Our best chance is to take the destroyer and whatever resources we can and find another OR planet to hide on and align ourselves with," Mikal reiterated. "We have been forged in a fire separate from the comfort of the Capitol. How do we know what resources are out there? There are others like us."

The room was silent. No one said aloud what everyone was thinking. How could they bring their fight to another innocent planet, and how could they know if they would be welcome? The Dalians had only recently discovered that they were not alone on their burning rock. Now they were faced with a decision between hundreds of other planets in a ring that surrounded a central Capitol. The beautiful state's room itself radiated Domain power and control, but the group that inhabited it now were desperate to get out from under the yolk of the Domain.

They were the start of a resistance.